BLADEN COLE:
BOUNTY HUNTER

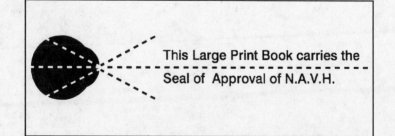

This Large Print Book carries the
Seal of Approval of N.A.V.H.

BLADEN COLE: BOUNTY HUNTER

BILL YENNE

THORNDIKE PRESS
A part of Gale, Cengage Learning

GALE
CENGAGE Learning·

Detroit • New York • San Francisco • New Haven, Conn • Waterville, Maine • London

Thorndike Press® Large Print Western.
The text of this Large Print edition is unabridged.
Other aspects of the book may vary from the original edition.
Set in 16 pt. Plantin.

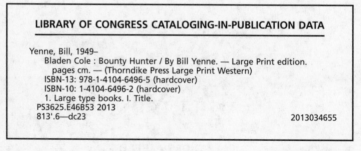

LIBRARY OF CONGRESS CATALOGING-IN-PUBLICATION DATA

Yenne, Bill, 1949–
   Bladen Cole : Bounty Hunter / By Bill Yenne. — Large Print edition.
      pages cm. — (Thorndike Press Large Print Western)
   ISBN-13: 978-1-4104-6496-5 (hardcover)
   ISBN-10: 1-4104-6496-2 (hardcover)
   1. Large type books. I. Title.
PS3625.E46B53 2013
813'.6—dc23   2013034655

Published in 2013 by arrangement with The Berkley Publishing Group,
a member of Penguin Group (USA) LLC, a Penguin Random House
Company.

Printed in the United States of America
1 2 3 4 5 6 7 17 16 15 14 13

BLADEN COLE: BOUNTY HUNTER

"Who called me that?"

The big man who had been leaning on the bar at the Palmer House Saloon for the past hour, gregariously telling tall tales, turned suddenly, jerking his head so hard that you'd have thought somebody had slugged the side of his chin.

"*Who* called me that?" Stewart Webb repeated.

All eyes were now on the man at the end of the bar. He had spoken to Webb, calling him by another name.

"That you?" Bladen Cole said, holding up a yellowish sheet of paper and tossing it on the bar. "Is that you . . . Alonzo Sims?"

Stewart Webb glanced at the stranger, at the gun on his hip, and finally at the paper. The only words that he could read at this distance were the one at the top — WANTED — and the ones beneath — ALONZO SIMS. Stewart Webb recognized the picture as one that had been taken of himself some years back, when he still *was* Alonzo Sims and when he led a different life.

Alonzo Sims had disappeared, and Stewart Webb had been leading his new life in Green River, Wyoming, for eight years. It had been long enough for Stewart Webb to believe that Alonzo Sims had gotten away clean and disappeared forever.

Stewart Webb led his new life under a purloined name, borrowed audaciously from another.

Stewart Webb was no more Stewart Webb than the Palmer House was *the* Palmer House. Just as the saloon's founder had poached its name from the legendary Chicago hostelry to lend his place undeserved prominence, so too had the man taken the last and middle names of Alexander S. Webb, a Union general who earned a Medal of Honor at Gettysburg. It gave this man leading a new life an aura of importance. Alonzo Sims had been at Gettysburg as well, but as far down in the enlisted ranks as Webb was high in officer rank.

Stewart Webb had lulled himself into the belief that this day would never come.

Now it had.

"That you?" Bladen Cole repeated.

"Don't recognize that name," Webb lied,

swallowing hard. He gritted his teeth, wishing that he could, by force of will, banish from his bloodstream all the alcohol he had consumed over the past hour.

"That's not me," Webb insisted. "My name's Stewart Webb. I'm a prominent member of this community. Ask anybody."

Even as he nodded toward the other patrons in the bar to vouch for his prominence, they were scuttling discreetly toward the door. Only the bartender remained, and he had moved as far as he could from where Stewart Webb was standing.

"Tell the man, John," Webb demanded of the bartender.

Nervous silence.

Barely out of his twenties, John did not want to die. He imagined that he had a life of some promise ahead of him and had no interest in seeing it cut short in the sort of cross fire that often followed the sort of fighting words that were being tossed about in his bar this afternoon.

"Tell him, *John,*" Webb repeated.

The bartender nervously edged toward the wanted poster, stopping when the words were visible and Webb's portrait was clearly identifiable.

It surprised him not in the least that Stewart Webb was not *really* Stewart Webb. Lots of men who came west — and not a few women — changed their names to avoid a past and get a new start.

John had pegged Webb as a scoundrel the first time that he had seen him, and that pegging had been borne out over the months that he had watched Webb cheat people at cards, run his petty scams, and become modestly rich from it.

However, not every scoundrel and card-sharp with a sketchy past who haunted the taverns of transient railroad towns like Green River was wanted for *multiple* homicides in Cheyenne like the man on the poster who had Stewart Webb's face.

"Don't know anybody by that name," John said truthfully, not going so far as to say that it was not Webb's likeness in the picture.

"No?" Bladen Cole asked, even though he could read the opposite answer on John's face.

"Never heard of this man," John said in a confirmed tone.

"You sure?"

"Yep."

"Then I'd say that this is very good news," Cole said with a broad smile. "Then Mr. Webb has nary a worry in the world."

"Huh?" Webb said, now confused.

"I hate to see a man wrongfully accused," Cole said seriously. "It puts him in all manner of danger."

"Huh?" Webb repeated.

"We just have us a case of mistaken identity," Cole grinned. "You and I'll just take the train back over to Cheyenne, and you can state your innocence. You can show the law over there that it's all a misunderstanding. We can get things all straightened out, and you can be back standing at this bar in two days' time."

"I don't think that's really necessary," Webb said, relaxing — just a little. "*You* could go . . . you could go'an tell 'em . . . explain to 'em."

"I think you and I both know that *you're* the one who's got to do the explaining," Cole said. "Till then, I think you had better relieve yourself of that gun you're carrying. If you would not mind, sir, I'd like to ask you to take it out of the holster and just lay it there on the bar."

Stewart Webb had always known that his life might come to this moment, but over time he had gradually deluded himself into believing that the odds were gradually growing less and less.

"I surely want no trouble," Webb said, reaching slowly for his gun.

11

His eyes locked on Bladen Cole as he lightly grasped the butt of the Colt with his thumb and forefinger.

Watching the stranger's eyes for any flicker of a blink, Webb rammed his hand into his holster, grabbed the gun full, and jerked it free.

He heard the shot at the very instant that he felt his wrist being shattered.

The wave of excruciating pain came over him a moment later in a blinding flash.

He now felt himself falling backward.

The gun was still in his hand, but in that hand, all feeling and all control had been severed by the impact of the bullet to his wrist.

Swimming out of the blinding flash, Webb could see the stranger coming toward him, his gun held at his side.

As his right hand dangled uselessly, there was still one card left to be played in Webb's metaphorical hand.

Being a gambling man, he had an ace up his sleeve, though it was not among those in his marked deck.

As Bladen Cole reached the fallen man, he suddenly found himself staring into the delicate double muzzle of a little twin-barreled, over-and-under Remington derringer.

■ ■ ■ ■

Green River, Wyoming, being a railroad town, was one of those places where you could get just about anything. For ten years, since they drove the Golden Spike at Promontory, linking the West to the East with steel rails, Green River's Palmer House had had reasonable access to the same finery and sophistication as the original Palmer House in Chicago.

In Green River, you could find a glass of whiskey on just about any corner. If you paid the right price, you could find a glass of whiskey that tasted more like *whiskey* than it did like the Green River.

In Green River, you could find a lady with lips the color of the juicy red apples on your grandmother's tree. If you paid the right price, you could find such a lady who would tell you that you were the wittiest and most handsome man in creation.

In Green River, you could also find a carpenter. If you paid the right price, you could find a carpenter who could craft you an heirloom-quality rocker that your grandmother, the one with the apple tree, would envy. For a more reasonable price, you could take your pick of many carpenters

13

who were well practiced in the construction of six-foot boxes.

With the reward money having been wired to Bladen Cole, Stewart Webb left Green River for Cheyenne on his last train ride. Cole kept the derringer. It was still loaded when he'd slipped it into his vest pocket.

Cole was like a lot of young men who had come west after the War Between the States. They came west to seek their fortune or to answer the irresistible call of the horizon of the sunset. Many young men from his part of the country went west because there was literally nothing left for them at home.

Born in Caroline County, Virginia, Bladen Cole and his older brother, William, grew up on a prosperous horse farm and were educated in the best of schools. Bladen turned thirteen in the first year of the war and was seventeen when he rode with his brother against the Yankees in the war's final months. When he was growing up, Caroline County was known as the birthplace of the great explorer William Clark. When Bladen and his brother left in 1865, to follow William Clark's footsteps into the West, the county had become better known as the place where they had killed John Wilkes Booth.

With skills as horsemen that had been

second nature throughout their young lives, Bladen and William Cole were able to find work herding cattle in Texas and later hunting buffalo for railroad work crews in Kansas. Gradually, they worked their way farther west, following the promising trail toward the gold and silver strikes out in New Mexico Territory.

Tragedy struck the brothers in Silver City one night when William was gunned down by two lowlife drifters. Bladen shot and killed one and spent the better part of the next year hunting the other — to no avail. He had deliberately honed his skills with a gun to an unprecedented degree simply because, if he *ever* met that rat-faced man again, it would not be a repeat of the man's escape on that night in Silver City.

More than a decade later, that night continued to haunt Bladen Cole.

About a year or so after Will's death, Bladen had found himself in a small mining town not far from the bustling metropolis of Cripple Creek, Colorado. Through a series of auspicious events, he played a role in foiling a bank robbery and was asked by the city fathers to consider becoming their sheriff. By this time, he was starting to think that he should be thinking about his future, so he accepted, and decided to settle down.

He even met a young woman, named Sally Lovelace, with whom there was a mutual attraction, and a seriousness that had led *almost* to a wedding.

However, before that could happen, Sally took a fancy to a high roller who swept her off her feet. J. R. Hubbard was one of those men who attracted the attention of good women like a magnet attracts iron filings. Sally swooned to his charms and allowed herself to be seduced by the honey of his sweet talk and by starry promises that could never have been fulfilled by a man on a sheriff's salary.

At about the same time that Hubbard swept Sally away to San Francisco, Bladen uncovered a rodent's nest of corruption in city government but was thwarted politically in his attempts to bring the perpetrators in high places to justice.

Cole realized, as he had on that day when he and Will first followed the setting sun out of Caroline County, that he was not the sort of man destined to be too long in one place — and that he had been in *this one* too long. Having angrily tossed his badge on the mayor's desk, he climbed on his horse and rode away.

A week or so later, in a mining town up in Wyoming Territory, he began seeing wanted posters of a particular bank-robbing duo, and he decided that the reward money looked good. It also looked like his future.

Several wanted posters, and several successful pursuits, later, his remarkable skill with a Colt .45 had found Bladen Cole with a new career — and one which allowed him not to be too long in one place.

CHAPTER 1

"When the railroad reaches Gallatin City, we shall all be rich men," John Blaine said with effusive enthusiasm as Virgil Stocker unrolled the map with a dramatic flourish.

Dawson Phillips, their partner, lifted his considerable bulk from the chair and made his way to the head of a large oak dining table still set with the dinner dishes, rumpled napkins, and Mrs. Blaine's fine Bohemian crystal — imported into Montana Territory from Chicago at great expense.

The wives of the three men had excused themselves to the parlor when Blaine had brought out the cigars and offered the first round of brandy. The ladies were discussing matters more to their interest, gladly leaving the men to their heavily odoriferous tobacco and their "man talk."

These gentlemen, who now talked their man talk in the atmosphere scented by brandy and cigars, were entrepreneur merchants turned land speculators who had become Gallatin City's leading citizens. They had arrived in Montana Territory by various paths and had settled down to become the biggest fish in a small pond, and to do so by successfully betting that their small pond would become an increasingly larger pond. Blaine was a dry goods merchant, while Phillips was the proprietor of Gallatin City's best hotel and restaurant. Stocker was an attorney, and their fourth associate, not present this evening, was Isham Ransdell, who owned the city's only bank.

"Hmmm," Blaine said, studying the area that had been outlined in pencil. "Are you certain the Northern Pacific will lay its tracks through Gallatin City by this route?"

"I have it on good authority from a man in the very office of Fred Billings, the president of the road," Stocker assured his fellow businessman.

Having gone into bankruptcy in 1875 with its intended transcontinental line barely started, the railroad had been recently reorganized under the wily financier Frederick H. Billings, whose golden touch was about to revive the foundering project.

"Are you sure that there is going to *be* a

Northern Pacific?" Phillips said skeptically. "I know that there's been a great deal of positive excitement that he'll bring the road out of its three years of bankruptcy, but . . ."

"Billings is the man," Stocker insisted. "He has raised a great deal of money and has resumed construction."

"Hmmm," Phillips said thoughtfully.

"He's laid rails a hundred miles east of Tacoma on one side, and on the other his crews have crossed Minnesota, most of Dakota Territory, and within a year and a half, Billings will build the tracks straight into Gallatin City . . . straight into this wedge of land that we *own,*" Stocker exclaimed, pointing at the areas on the map north and east of Gallatin City.

The arrival of the Northern Pacific, upon which these entrepreneurs had set their hopes and dreams, would transform Gallatin City, as the arrival of railroads was transforming so many towns-turned-cities across the West. New settlers would arrive with more money and a need for the goods and services which these businessmen would provide.

More even than this was the fact that land values would increase, so with this in mind, the gentlemen had pooled their resources to acquire tracts of land that were of marginal value in a region not served by a rail link to the outside world, but which would be radically transformed when the rails at last reached Gallatin City.

"We have done very well for ourselves controlling the land between here and the diggings at Confederate Gulch," Blaine chortled.

Discovered more than a decade earlier by some expatriate Southern Civil War vets, the "Gulch" had been the richest gold find in Montana history. Though much of the easy pickings had been picked, a railroad would invite further investment.

"At the moment, most of the gold is going out on Missouri River steamers," Stocker continued, thumping his tobacco-stained finger on the map. "When the railroad reaches Gallatin City, *all* of the gold will go though *here* . . . through the land which we own. The railroad will *need* our land."

"If you are correct, sir," Phillips said, lowering his heft into a chair near the unrolled map. "We *shall indeed* be very rich men. I'd say that at the very least, this calls for another shot of your fine brandy, sir."

"Gladly," Blaine said, topping off the three glasses. "We shall drink to the four musketeers."

"To the four musketeers, then," Stocker said, touching his crystal goblet to those of his partners. "If California can have its 'Big Four,' its Huntington, Hopkins, Crocker, and Stanford, then Montana Territory shall have its own Big Four . . . Blaine, Phillips, Stocker, and Ransdell."

The men chuckled that their toasts were being made not just to the richest men in the city, but to the future richest men in Montana Territory.

"Pity that Ransdell couldn't join us at this table tonight," the portly Phillips said, patting his ample belly. "That was a fine roast that Mrs. Blaine placed before us."

"It's his loss," Blaine said with a smile. He was pleased that his wife's cooking had received a compliment from a man so evidently fond of eating.

As the toasts were echoing around the dinner table, the doorbell chimed.

"I wonder who that could be," Blaine said, setting down his glass without taking a sip.

His wife was already at the front door.

"May I help you?" Leticia Blaine asked as she opened the door.

"Looking for Blaine," a large man announced, stepping across the threshold without being invited to do so.

"*Gideon Porter*," she exclaimed, recognizing the man as he stomped into her parlor ahead of three companions. "What do you want?"

"Where's Blaine?" Porter demanded.

"You are a very rude young man," Mrs. Blaine said sternly, her hands on her hips. "You always were."

"I insist that you leave my home at once," John Blaine said angrily as he entered the parlor. "You are unwelcome in this house. Take your brother Enoch and these other hooligans and get out of here immediately."

By this time, Phillips and Stocker had entered the room as well.

"My husband has ordered you to go and . . ."

Crack!

The sound of the man's having backhanded Leticia Blaine across the face reverberated through the room.

For a moment, there was no sound but that of her crumpling to the floor. Everyone halted as though in shock. The sight of a man striking a woman so hard as to draw blood with a single blow startled everyone.

There was a pitiful, gurgling sob as Mrs. Blaine put her hand over her bleeding face, and a red-faced John Blaine slugged Gideon Porter with such force that his hat went flying.

All eyes were on Gideon as he staggered backward a step. Though Blaine was an older man, well past his prime, his punch still packed a wallop.

But Blaine's fists were no match for what came next.

K'poom . . . K'poom . . . mmm.

The thunder of two .44-caliber cartridges exploding in the confines of a moderate-sized parlor were as deafening as they were unexpected. Gideon Porter had drawn his gun.

The room filled with a bluish, choking cloud of gunsmoke as John Blaine dropped to his knees with a flabbergasted expression on his face and dark red stains spreading across his starched white shirt.

"Murderer!" Dawson Phillips screamed as he fumbled in his vest for the derringer he kept there.

As Enoch Porter leveled his Model 1860 revolver at Phillips, Mrs. Phillips leaped to her feet and let fly a stream of verbal vitriol unbecoming of a lady.

Enoch shifted his gaze and the direction of his gun to Mary Phillips and squeezed the trigger.

Her husband, who now had his derringer firmly in the grip of his fleshy hand, paused for a split second, watching aghast as his wife was struck down.

His split-second pause was all that it took for the revolver to be redirected at him.

A fourth shot was fired in the once-genteel parlor and then a fifth.

Dawson Phillips's body fell with a crash.

Virgil Stocker stepped forward to aid his fallen partner, but felt the impact of Gideon Porter's gun butt across his face, first once and then again and again.

As Gideon whipped the attorney with the pistol, Enoch turned his gun toward Sarah Stocker, who remained seated on the sofa, frozen in terror at the sight of her husband being beaten.

Seeing this, Gideon deserted Stocker and grabbed his brother's arm.

"Not the women, dammit!" Porter shouted. "We weren't supposed to hurt the *women*."

"You slugged *that one,* Gideon," Enoch whined, nodding toward Mrs. Blaine, who was now crouched over her husband's body, blood still streaming from her own wound.

"Let's get the hell out of here," Gideon ordered, picking up his hat.

CHAPTER 2

"That could have been *you,*" Hannah Ransdell told her father in a tone that was a mix of horror and relief.

"I know," Isham Ransdell said somberly as he and his daughter watched people urgently coming and going from the two-story, Victorian-style home where John Blaine and his wife lived — and the home where Isham Ransdell had been invited to dine this very night. Had it not been necessary for him to meet with a client on an urgent matter, he *would* have been there.

He stared at the house feeling the shock of knowing this. So too did his daughter.

Only twenty minutes or so had passed since Sarah Stocker had been found running down Elm Street screaming that people had been shot. By now, it seemed as though every one of Gallatin City's two thousand citizens knew of the shootings, and half of them had come out to gawk.

Sheriff John Hollin walked from the house shaking his head.

"What do you know?" Ransdell asked.

"Three dead," he replied. "Blaine and Phillips . . . Mrs. Phillips, too. Stocker and Mrs. Blaine are both hurt real bad. The doc's in there with them now."

"That's terrible . . ." Hannah said, putting her hand over her mouth.

"Do you have any idea who did this?" her father asked.

"Mrs. Blaine said the one who hit her was Gideon Porter."

"He's a cruel man, that Gideon Porter," Hannah interjected. "Him and his no-account brother, Enoch. Having Biblical names didn't prevent those boys from siding with the devil all their lives."

"It was them," the sheriff nodded. "Was Enoch who killed Dawson Phillips and his wife. The women said there were two more. Somebody saw four riders heading out of town in a hurry . . . heading north."

"So what are you waiting for?" Hannah demanded. "You should being going out after them!"

"Gotta wait for first light," Hollin explained patiently. "No good tryin' to track 'em in the dark."

■ ■ ■ ■

It was a few hours after first light and a few hours after the sheriff's departure, when a lone rider appeared on Gallatin City's main street. He was riding a strawberry roan and had the look of a man who'd been on the trail for all of those hours and more.

He dismounted, looped his reins around a hitch rail near a watering trough, and loosened the cinch on his saddle so that the roan would be more comfortable. As his horse drank thirstily from the trough, the man strolled into the Big Horn Saloon and ordered a beer to satiate his own thirst.

"Seems like a lot of excitement in town today," Bladen Cole said, making conversation with the bartender.

" 'Twas a shooting last night," the man behind the bar replied.

"Hmmm," Cole said, taking another welcome sip from his mug. His tone expressed the sentiment that shootings were not sufficiently uncommon to warrant the kind of excitement that was swirling around on the streets of Gallatin City.

"One of the town's leading citizens was gunned down in his parlor," the bartender added, sensing the need to elaborate. "In

29

fact, there was *two* prominent men killed . . . a third one in bad shape."

"Hmmm," Bladen Cole replied. The tone this time said that he now understood why the fuss on Gallatin City's streets was at a heightened level.

"One of 'em's wife was killed too," the bartender added when Cole's latest "Hmmm" also needed to be underscored, to stress that something *really* serious was going on. It was almost a matter of civic pride to emphasize the seriousness of Gallatin City's excitement.

"That so?" Cole replied.

"Yep," the bartender replied, happy to have gotten some actual words out of the stranger.

" 'Nother beer," Cole said.

His thirst satisfied by his first, Cole savored his second beer as the bartender went about his work, sorting glassware and topping off the whiskey bottles on the back bar from one of the big oak barrels that had been shipped out here all the way from Kentucky.

The big clock on the wall, flanked by a pair of angry-looking wolf heads, was striking four o'clock when someone rushed into the Big Horn.

"Deputy Johnson just rode back in," the

30

man shouted to the handful of patrons who were in the saloon. "They done got shot up. Sheriff Hollin got himself *killed.*"

The bartender stopped what he was doing and just stared at the swinging doors as the man ran down the street repeating the bad news.

"What's that all about?" Cole asked, eliciting the sort of elaboration that the bartender seemed to like to provide.

"Sheriff went out this morning," the bartender explained. "Tracking the Porter boys."

"Who's the Porter boys?"

"Ones they figure did the killings last night."

Tossing a couple of coins on the bar, Bladen Cole turned and stepped onto the street.

A crowd was gathered around a man on horseback who was slumped in his saddle, a pained expression on his face. People were shouting for someone to fetch the doctor.

As Cole watched, they carefully removed the man from his horse and carried him into the Big Horn, where they placed him on a table. Judging by his badge, it didn't take long for Cole to ascertain that he was the deputy who had survived the ambush. Judging by the placement of his bullet wounds, it didn't take long for Cole to figure that he would survive. He had applied a tourniquet himself, and although he was in shock, he was able to speak.

The doctor arrived, concurred with Cole's unspoken diagnosis, and prescribed a stiff drink from behind the bar.

Within fifteen minutes, the color had flooded back into Johnson's cheeks, and he was relating the tale of what had happened.

"We trailed 'em up and across the mountains toward Sixteen Mile Creek," he explained, his narrative punctuated by coughs. "Sheriff was the first hit. Head wound it was. Couldn't really see 'em. Hiding up in the rocks . . . up high. Ben Neff . . . he was riding with us. Got his gun out and got off a couple of shots. Both of us was returning fire. Couldn't really see 'em except for the smoke from the rifles, but the wind was blowing and it was hard to see. Ben got hit too. Then me. Didn't want to run, but I figured I'd have to get back . . . tell what happened."

"Did you hit any of *them*?" someone asked.

"The sheriff definitely hit one . . . in the arm," Johnson said with a nod. "Saw him get hit. His gun went flyin'."

"I've already got a wire off to the county

sheriff in Bozeman," a self-important man announced. "He'll get out a posse and catch 'em."

That seemed to satisfy the crowd, who began drifting away from the deputy and toward the bar.

CHAPTER 3

Bladen Cole awoke to the yammering of birds outside the window and to the unfamiliarity of waking up on a mattress and between sheets for the first time in weeks. He had treated himself to a hotel room, spending part of his reward money on unaccustomed luxury. If he continued with his plan for an extended hunting trip up into the Beartooth Mountains, he wouldn't be within a hundred miles of a mattress for the next month.

Snapping open his pocket watch, the sturdy brass mechanism which he still thought of as *his father's* pocket watch, he was stunned to realize how badly he had overslept. It was not that he was on any kind of schedule, but being asleep when it was almost seven o'clock in the morning struck him as an egregious waste of daylight hours.

Having allowed himself the luxury of a hotel mattress, he allowed himself the luxury of a "store-bought" breakfast in the hotel dining room. He was just marveling at the extravagance of drinking coffee from a porcelain cup when a well-dressed man came into the dining room and started staring at him. Cole straightened his right leg a little, so that his .45 would be easy to reach, and returned the stare. At last, the well-dressed man approached.

"You Bladen Cole?"

"Who's asking?"

"My name's Olson . . . Edward J. Olson. I work for Mr. Ransdell."

The man's tone made it sound like everyone knew who "Mr. Ransdell" was, and those who did not *should.*

"Who's Mr. Ransdell?" Cole replied, in a tone intended to make it clear that he didn't know and really didn't care.

"He owns the Gallatin City Bank and Trust yonder," Olson said, nodding in the general direction of across the street.

"Hmmm."

"So, *are you* Bladen Cole?"

"I am."

"Bladen Cole . . . the *bounty hunter?*"

"I am."

"Mr. Ransdell would like a word with you."

"I won't ask why, because the way y'all

35

said 'bounty hunter' makes it sound more like business than pleasure. If you'd excuse me while I finish this cup of coffee, I'd be pleased to make the acquaintance of Mr. Ransdell."

Ten minutes later, Olson was rapping on the front window of the bank with Bladen Cole in tow. It may have seemed to Cole like the day was half-gone, but by banker's hours, it was not even opening time.

Isham Ransdell heard the tapping and hurried to get the door himself.

Stepping inside, Cole scoured the room with his eyes. Ransdell was a wiry man with a narrow string tie and white sideburns that looked like they hadn't decided whether to get really bushy like Burnside's or allow themselves to be trimmed away entirely.

What caught Cole's eye, and would not let go, was the sight of a young woman in a gingham dress. It was conservatively high in the collar, but cut right in all the right places, and the places were very right, indeed. Her long, chestnut-colored hair was tied up, though loosely, in a blue ribbon which matched the color of her dress. Her eyes were big and gray, and she wore a confident, assured expression.

"Mr. Ransdell, this is Mr. Cole," Olson said. "Mr. Cole, Mr. Ransdell."

36

"Pleased to make your acquaintance," Cole said, gripping the man's hand and forcing his eyes away from the young woman.

"The pleasure is mine, Mr. Cole," Ransdell said, in the smooth voice of a banker. "May I introduce my daughter, Hannah."

"Ma'am," Cole said respectfully, touching the brim of his hat.

"Mr. Cole," she replied with an almost smile.

Ransdell invited the two men to sit down at a table in the lobby which Cole guessed was normally used for signing financial paperwork. He guessed that financial talk would be taking place there now.

Hannah, who apparently worked at the bank, sat down at a desk apart from the men, though clearly within earshot of the "men's business" that was about to be discussed.

"Mr. Cole, I'm sure that you are aware of the shooting that took place here in Gallatin City two nights past?" Ransdell began.

"I am."

"You may not be aware that the three men who were present at the shooting . . . including two who died in cold blood . . . were business associates of mine . . . partners in some important business ventures."

"I'm sorry for your loss, sir," Cole nodded politely.

"I know that you are also aware that Sheriff John Hollin and another man were murdered by the same men who did this . . . and that Deputy Marcus Johnson was injured."

"I watched him taken from his horse yesterday," Cole said, nodding toward the place where the sheriff's last ride into town had come so dramatically to its end.

"I know," Olson interjected. "I saw you there. Thought I recognized you from the papers. We heard about what you did down in Green River."

"Your reputation precedes you, Mr. Cole," Ransdell said, smiling.

"Well . . . that's a good thing or a bad thing, depending," Cole said thoughtfully. He knew that they were getting around to the place where the business talk was about to start. "What can I do for you?"

"There are four men at large who must be brought to justice," Ransdell said.

"I know," Cole agreed, "but from what I heard yesterday, the Gallatin County sheriff from down in Bozeman was being sent for. It would seem to be his job."

"Well, there's a little bit of a problem in that," Olson responded.

"Is?"

"Yeah. The Porter boys are headed up north. They'd be clear into Meagher County by now. That would put them out of Gallatin County jurisdiction."

"Why doncha send a wire to the Meagher County sheriff?" Cole said, asking a question that seemed to him an obvious one.

"Well, that would be up in Diamond City," Olson said, referring to the boomtown which had grown up in the heart of the Confederate Gulch diggings.

"So?"

"Let me put it this way," Ransdell interjected. "The law hasn't really taken root in Diamond City. Meagher County isn't quite as lawless, literally, as Choteau County, but it's not exactly as refined in its ways as places like Bozeman or Denver."

"I understand," Cole nodded. Nineteenth-century civilization had reached the West, but it had done so in narrow swaths.

"You sure it was the Porter boys?" Cole asked.

"Three witnesses recognized them."

"There were four . . . Did the witnesses know the other two?"

"Milton Waller and Jimmy Goode. They are known to ride with the Porters . . . do whatever Gideon Porter tells 'em to do. He has a way of mesmerizing others less long on mental acuity . . . of manipulating them."

"Hmmm," Cole said thoughtfully, in his typical manner, intentionally evoking a sense of thoughtfulness.

"Soon as the state judge down in Bozeman wires through a warrant, I'd like to employ you to go get the Porter boys and bring them in to face the music," Ransdell said emphatically, getting down to business.

"What sort of money are we talking?" Cole asked, also getting down to business.

"We are prepared to offer you a sum of three thousand dollars," the banker said.

To Cole, this was a great deal of money. It was more than most laboring men could expect to earn in a year. However, the sum said a lot about Ransdell, and one of the things that it whispered in Cole's ear was how important this affair was to the man. The other thing it whispered was that there was more money on the banker's table.

"Well," Cole said reticently. "I had a number a little north of four in mind."

"I suppose we could split the difference at thirty-five hundred," the banker said after a long pause to scratch some numbers on a piece of paper.

Cole smiled to himself. The man was used to dickering and anxious to cut a deal.

"Well . . ." Cole drawled thoughtfully. "I did say that I was thinking of a number *north* of four. There *is* four of them and one of me."

"Okay, I'll make it *four,*" Ransdell said. "And I'll pick up your tab at the hotel, and for your horse last night at the livery stable . . . and stake you to whatever provisions you'll need for this manhunt."

This time, the voice in Cole's head told him that they had reached the end of the dickering phase and it was time to extend his hand.

As Ransdell was writing out an agreement for them to sign, the boy arrived from the telegraph office with the warrant from the judge in Bozeman.

"Well, that makes it official," Olson observed.

Ransdell read the paper and handed it Cole.

"Longest telegram I've seen," he observed.

"Written by lawyers," Ransdell said wryly.

"Hmmm . . ." Cole said, half reading the document out loud. "Hmmm . . . 'armed and dangerous,' it says. Would have thought that this goes without saying."

"That's a way of saying they're wanted 'dead or alive.' It's a way of saying they're to be brought back by any means necessary, and in any condition necessary for them to be brought back."

"Most folks here in Gallatin City would rather see them *dead* than alive," Olson interjected.

Ransdell just nodded his head to confirm the assertion.

When they had finished signing an agreement and shaking hands a second time, Cole explained that he would be starting out first thing in the morning.

"Don't you want to get started right away?" Ransdell asked urgently. "You've got your warrant and they've already got almost a two-day head start."

"That's right, Mr. Ransdell," Cole agreed. "And at this point there's no way that hard riding will ever catch up to them. The only way that they're gonna get caught is if they can see that there's nobody coming after them. If they think they got away, they'll relax. They'll slow down. They'll get themselves caught. In the meantime, I'd like to spend what's left of this day taking a look at where the shooting happened and talking to them who was there."

"That sounds reasonable, I suppose," Ransdell admitted. "I guess you need to know who you're dealing with . . . Hannah, could you take Mr. Cole over and see if

42

Mrs. Blaine is up to receiving a caller?"

"Yes, Father," Hannah said with a nod of agreement.

Bladen Cole smiled, but Hannah scowled slightly. She found the tall stranger easy on the eye and a bit captivating in a dangerous sort of way, but she didn't want him to know that such was the case.

"What do you know about these Porter boys, Miss Ransdell?" Cole asked as they walked.

"They're no good," she said emphatically. "I knew them in school. A lot of the boys had a bit of the nick to them, but those two were just plain cruel . . . cruel to animals . . . cruel to people. Enoch was the worst. He had a taste for blood . . . torturing and killing cats and dogs . . . in ways I'd rather not describe . . . or *recall.*"

"They ever kill any *people* before?"

"Not that I know of . . . Of course, I have never made it my place to know all of what the Porter boys were up to."

"Why do you suppose they did it this time?"

"I dunno . . . some kind of grudge, I reckon." Hannah shrugged. "Gideon used to work for Mr. Blaine but got himself fired."

43

"What about the others?"

"Like my father said, they'll do anything Gideon Porter says to do. Milton Waller is dumb as a post . . . quit school in the second grade . . . Jimmy Goode is known all over Gallatin County as 'good for nothing.' "

"What do they do for work, these boys?"

"They cowboy around. There's a lot of need for extra hands on the ranches at branding time . . . roundup time. Man who's good with a horse and rope, you don't care if he's dumb as a post or that he used to kick puppy dogs around."

As they turned the corner onto Elm Street, the wind shifted and Cole caught a whiff of her perfume. It was just a trace, just barely there, not like the dolls in Denver who liked to really slather it on. She was naturally, and almost perfectly, beautiful, but the little threesome of freckles on her nose added a humanizing touch, softening the classical perfection of that beauty. This and the easy way that she smiled — now that she had relaxed and stopped forcing her jaw into a perfunctory scowl — made her quite attractive.

The Blaine home was guarded by a man with a rifle whom Hannah knew. It was not so much that anyone expected the Porter gang to return to finish her off, rather he was there to give Mrs. Blaine the assurance of security. Hannah instructed Cole to wait outside while she went in to inquire as to whether Mrs. Blaine was up to a visit from the bounty hunter hired to avenge her husband's death.

While she went inside, Bladen made conversation with the man with the rifle. Asked about the four perpetrators, he echoed Hannah's opinion, though his description of Gideon Porter's evilness, and Enoch's atrocious way with small domestic animals, was a good deal more graphic.

Finally, Hannah called from the front door and Bladen climbed the steps. He made a point of removing his hat and wiping his feet, something that had become his second nature growing up in Virginia, where a man was measured by his politeness.

"I want you to *get* that Gideon Porter once and for all!" Leticia Blaine exclaimed without the formality of an introduction.

She was seated in a large, overstuffed chair in a small room opposite the parlor. He figured that she was avoiding the parlor, and understood that she had good reason. Another woman about her age, probably a friend, was hovering nearby. The side of Mrs. Blaine's face was deeply black-and-blue, and she had a long cut in her lower lip that had been stitched.

"Yes, ma'am," Cole said.

"I want that Gideon Porter six feet under."

"Yes, ma'am," Cole repeated. "He's the one who done this to you?"

"Darn tootin' he is," the spunky widow confirmed.

"And shot your husband?"

"Yes sir," she affirmed angrily. "He is a *madman.* John rose to my defense and lost his life for it!"

"Ma'am, if you don't mind me asking, do y'all have any idea *why* they did this? Why they came to your home to shoot people?"

"My husband fired that cur six months ago, and he had to have his revenge, of course."

"Why do you reckon that he waited so long?"

"How should I know?"

"He just came here asking after your husband?"

"That's right. I answered that door right there and . . . they barged through . . ."

"Into the parlor here?" Cole asked, stepping into the other room. The bloodstains on the rich oriental-style carpets, now turned dark and all the more deathly, painted a vivid picture of the place where each victim had stood. In the room beyond, the dinner dishes from that night still had not been cleared.

"That's right," she shouted, remaining in her chair as Cole left the room. "My husband was in the dining room with Virgil Stocker and Dawson Phillips. They all came into the parlor when they heard the commotion. Porter shot John, then his brother murdered Dawson and then Mary . . . it was *terrible!*"

On this note, Leticia Blaine dissolved into tearful sobbing, and her friend moved in to comfort her. Bladen Cole thanked her for her time and expressed his sympathies, as he and Hannah Ransdell retreated out the front door.

"Any chance I could go talk to this man, Virgil Stocker?" Cole asked as he put on his Stetson.

"I suppose we could do that," Hannah said. She was kind of interested in the bounty hunter's "investigating," and she certainly didn't mind being seen around town with a handsome stranger. Nor did she mind taking an occasional glance at the whiskers that studded his face. His were a bit on the shorter side for her tastes, but she did have a fondness for a younger man with a beard.

"You been long in the Territory, Mr. Cole?" she said as they walked.

"No, ma'am. I passed through a couple years back and was headed back up north to do a little hunting when your father's friend, Mr. Olson, approached me in the cafe."

"Hunting?" Hannah said with a knowing tone. "I'd speculate that in your line of work that has a little bit of a double meaning?"

"Yes, ma'am, it does," he nodded. "But in this case, it was mule deer I was after . . . some for trade . . . some to dry for winter."

"Heard the stories about you down on the Green River," she said.

"Justice required . . . justice done," he said, phrasing his few words in such a way that he hoped to close out the topic.

"How did you get into this . . . mmmmm . . . line of work, Mr. Cole?"

"I sorta fell into it, Miss Ransdell."

"How does one . . . ?" Hannah began.

"When one finds that he's good with a gun, he can find himself on one side of the law or the other."

"And you picked . . ."

"I don't mind sleeping with one eye open sometimes," he interrupted. "I just figured that I couldn't live with having to sleep with *both* of them open."

Leticia Blaine's anger was a mere trifle by comparison to the rage expressed by Virgil Stocker, and the expletives he used were considerably stronger than "cur."

Likewise, Stocker's facial injuries were of an order of magnitude greater than those endured by Mrs. Blaine. She had suffered under the fist of her attacker, while he had been struck by the butt of a gun. Even the jagged cuts that remained unbandaged would leave a permanent reminder of that night in the mirror of Virgil Stocker.

As to the question of *why* this happened, Stocker's opinion coincided with the conventional wisdom. Angry at being fired, Gideon Porter had come for retribution, and things got horribly out of control.

"And the women . . . the poor *women,*" Stocker's wife interjected. She had sat quietly through her husband's tirade but felt the need to insert her own perspective on that terrible night. "Gideon Porter said that the women were not *supposed* to be hurt, but . . . poor Mary . . . For a man to strike a woman . . . much less shoot her . . . poor Mary Phillips. To watch her . . . writhing . . . writhing on the carpet . . . that terrible expression . . ."

"What do you think he meant by saying the women were not *supposed* to be hurt?" Hannah asked.

By this time, Mrs. Stocker was sobbing uncontrollably, reliving the horror of the deaths of friends with the survivor's guilt of knowing that of the six, only she remained unscathed — physically.

"She's been through *hell,*" Virgil Stocker said, rising to his feet and moving toward his guests in a gesture signifying the end of their visit, with Hannah's query unanswered. "She's been through *enough.*"

"Mr. Cole," Stocker said from the doorway as Bladen and Hannah crossed the porch. "I understand that the warrant has language in it that says . . . or at least insinuates . . . 'dead or alive.' "

"It does," Cole nodded.

"I hope you make sure that *none* of that bunch ever again breathes the air of Gallatin County."

"There's another thing you should know," Hannah said as they walked back in the direction of Main Street.

"What's that?"

"You know how my father said those men were his associates?"

"Yeah."

"Well, they were all having dinner at the Blaine home . . . the associates and their wives. My father was supposed to have been there, but he had a meeting."

"So he nearly . . ."

"Yes, he nearly wound up in the line of fire. That's why this is sort of personal. The reward money is coming from him . . . personally."

"Guess he and your mother are counting their blessings," Cole said.

"Um . . . actually my mother passed away three years back. If he *had* gone to that dinner party . . . he would have taken *me*."

CHAPTER 4

"It's him. It's John Hollin," Edward J. Olson said, the color draining from his face as he was overcome by the stench. "I recognize his shirt."

The sun was just coming up as Bladen Cole and the three men from Gallatin City descended the trail toward the place where Sixteen Mile Creek emptied into the Missouri River. When he had told them that he planned to leave "first thing in the morning," he had meant it. To the three men who had asked to accompany him as far as the ambush site to recover the bodies, it had been the middle of the night.

Cole studied the bluffs above the place where the bodies lay as the men from the town began the grisly chore of wrapping the deceased in canvas. They would soon be loaded on mules for their last ride home.

"Reckon this is where we part company, gentlemen," Cole said, touching the brim of his hat.

"Good luck, Mr. Cole," Olson said, his tone of voice suggesting that he figured the bounty hunter would *need* it.

With that, Cole rode north.

The breeze was rustling in the changing leaves of the cottonwoods as he paused to let his roan drink before they forded the creek. The Porter boys had left no tracks, but they were easy to follow.

After killing men whose deaths were guaranteed to raise the ire — or at least the attention — of Montana's powers that be, the next leg of their trail after the ambush was obvious. To have crossed west of the Missouri River would have taken them on a heading toward the territorial capital at Helena, while staying to the east would have taken them through Diamond City, which all agreed was an outpost of lawlessness.

Cole reached Diamond City as the autumn sun was dipping toward the mountains in the west and stepped into the Diamond Bar Saloon on the main street of Meagher County's seat for a late afternoon beer.

"Hello, darlin,' buy a girl a drink?" the seductively attired woman asked with an enticing smile.

After observing that the floozies were out

53

early, and appreciating the attractiveness of Hannah Ransdell by comparison to this girl, Cole smiled broadly and did, indeed, buy the girl a drink.

He knew the end to which the proprietor who employed her intended the interaction to lead, and he knew where *he* intended it to lead.

She had a few years on Hannah, and she had led a much different life. Her name was Aggie, or so she said. She had come to the lawless West with her father, a preacher, or so she said. Bladen told her that he had come west in the wake of the war, because there was nothing for him in Virginia, which was more or less true.

He let her sit on his lap, and she let him touch her leg. It all felt good to Cole, and he was tempted to allow it to play out as the proprietor had intended.

Knowing that her drink contained little but cherry extract and soda water, he insisted that she chase it with a beer. He knew that she wanted to, and so she did, and it loosened her tongue.

When she was at last comfortable, and had shared her fictional life story with him, talk turned to his "old friend" Gideon, who Cole was hoping to catch up with on the trail.

"Yeah, I believe I reckon to recall a man by that name was in here," she reckoned to recall. "I remember the name because it's from the Bible . . . and my daddy was a preacher, y'know. But you missed him . . . not my daddy . . . your friend Gideon. Day before yesterday, I think."

"He buy you a drink?"

"No, not me . . . I think Crystal . . . no, Crystal, she was talkin' with the one with his hand all bandaged up. I was with their partner. Your friend was in here with a couple of partners."

"Three partners?"

"Yeah . . . I believe there was three . . . total of four with your friend, Gideon. I was with this squirrely little fellow who kept saying he was good."

"Goode?"

"Yeah, that's what I said . . . *good* . . . 'cept your friend Gideon kept callin' him 'good-for-nothin,' and that made him mad. As it turned out, he wasn't very good at all . . . if you know what I mean . . . and that made him *real* mad."

"Sure wish I'd not missed 'em," Cole said, trying not to laugh out loud at Aggie's previous remark. "They say where they were headed?"

"Up Smith's River way," she said thoughtfully. "They were talking about Fort Benton and Blackfeet country."

Having gotten the essential information he needed, Cole let the small talk spin off in another direction, allowing their discussion of the man named "good," who *wasn't* very good, to be buried in the blur of other topics touched upon.

When at last Aggie got around to telling him that it was time to seal the deal of their implied contract, Bladen told her that it was time for him to get his horse taken care of for the night.

"I'll be right back, darlin,' " he promised as he touched the brim of his hat.

He had lied.

Bladen Cole bedded down in the hills east of town.

Sleeping with your head on a saddle was not nearly as desirable as sleeping with your head on a pillow — and not *alone* on that pillow — but if that pillow was in Diamond City, these arrangements in the hills east of town went further toward guaranteeing that your saddle would still be around in the morning.

Aggie was beautiful in that striking way that comes in part from being skilled at the brushwork that transforms a woman's cheeks and eyelids — and she was shrewd in that resourceful way that comes in part from being skilled at identifying what you want and knowing how to get it.

Naturally, he had also found himself comparing Hannah Ransdell to Sally — or more to the point, Sally as he had first known her. When you spend five years with a woman, she becomes a benchmark of comparison when a man finds himself crossing the paths of other women, even though in his present frame of mind with regard to Sally, it was more a contrast than a comparison.

Hannah did remind him a little of the younger Sally, the Sally with whom he had fallen in love — if it really was *love*. After all, he was not sure he knew what "love" meant.

Hannah was easy on the eye in a way that was different from the beauty of a woman such as Aggie. The color in Hannah's cheeks was as natural as the blush of a Georgia peach. Her girlish grin and those freckles on her nose were enough to make a man smile back just by watching her.

Hannah reminded him a little of Sally, when he had first crossed her path. Each woman was as sharp as a tack, and like Sally had been, back then, Hannah had that streak of stubborn idealism that comes from being long on brains yet still short on the experiences that come with years. For Hannah, these would come over time. With Sally, the time and experiences *had* come, and would continue coming. Naturally, Cole chose not to allow his mind to wander down the road of speculation as to the *nature* of the experiences Sally had been sharing with J. R. Hubbard out in San Francisco.

Cole fell asleep dreaming that the three stars in the heavens directly above his head were the freckles on Hannah Ransdell's nose.

Cole was boiling his coffee when the new day was just a narrow, pinkish-purple sliver on the distant horizon.

It was growing noticeably colder as the man and his horse made their way through the Little Belt Range, heading ever northward. Cole had ridden this roan for more than a year without naming him. The closest he got was *"whoa, boy,"* *"hya, boy."* He figured the roan didn't mind going nameless. The naming of horses had always been a matter of pride to the planters back in Virginia. Maybe that was why Cole now shied away from the practice.

They camped a second night where the Little Belts give way to the Plains and where Cole could look out and see the lights of the scattered, distant settlements and farmsteads along the Missouri.

If the Porter boys had kept to the plan that Aggie had overheard, they would certainly have come this way. They were running from the law, so wintering in Blackfeet country was a logical thing to do.

They could have crossed the Missouri to head north at any number of places between the Great Falls and Fort Benton, but provisioning at Fort Benton made sense. As a river steamer port, it was both big enough and transient enough for them to get what they needed and not attract too much attention.

With this, Cole naturally wondered, aloud, whether boys who were as witless as the Porter boys were supposed to be would think so logically.

Riding alone for the past couple of days, Cole had been doing a great deal of wondering. He had been going over the Gallatin City shooting in his mind and had been wondering about a lot of unanswered questions.

The Porter boys were impulsive punks who he could easily picture drawing their guns in a barroom brawl, but he had a hard time getting his head around Gideon Porter harboring a grudge for half a year before drawing his gun.

Cole also wondered why Gideon Porter had barged into John Blaine's house, with his gang, in order to shoot his former employer in front of a room full of witnesses. From the universal impression of Gideon Porter, he seemed to be the type of lowlife who would be more at home shooting a man in the back in the dark of night.

Another question that nagged Cole was one Hannah Ransdell had asked of Mrs. Stocker. What indeed had Gideon Porter meant when he told the impetuous Enoch that the women were not *supposed* to be hurt?

He hadn't said "don't hurt the women," he had said the women were *not supposed to be* hurt.

To Cole, this implied that the men *were* supposed to be hurt, and by "supposing" anything, the statement implied that they had gone to Blaine's house with a *plan.* This explained why it took four men. It was not an angry madman settling a score, it was a deliberately conceived *plan.*

The conundrum that Bladen Cole pondered most particularly as his campfire turned to embers that night was *whose plan* it had been.

As much as he was taken with the memory of gazing upon the loveliness of Hannah Ransdell, Cole wondered about her father. Why had Isham Ransdell *not* been at the dinner party? Of course, he had a reasonable explanation that was certainly believable, but why had he not been there, *really*?

Why had he been so anxious to hire a bounty hunter — at great expense and with his own money? Of course, his stated reasons were both reasonable and understandable, but why had he been in such a hurry to hire Cole, *really*?

Whose plan, indeed?

CHAPTER 5

The town downstream from the Great Falls, where Bladen Cole reached the Missouri, was hardly a town at all. It was merely a little no-name collection of shacks that had grown up around a place on the river where cattle could be loaded aboard steamers or barges for shipment to buyers downstream. This time of year, when the river was low, it was barely that.

Naturally, as in any cow town in Montana, or in the West as a whole for that matter, civic life was centered on the watering hole. Cole limped into this place, a combination saloon and general store, noticeably favoring his left leg, and ordered a whiskey.

"None of my business, but it's a little early in the day for whiskey, ain't it," the proprietor said as he poured a generous shot and scooped up the coin that Cole tossed on the bar. As was often the case in very small towns where the saloon doubled as a general store, the owner was more used to selling salt pork or horseshoe nails when the sun was this high in the sky.

There was another man in the place, noticeable by his especially large hat, which was tall in the crown. He was examining the wares in the general store part of the place and seemed to pay Cole no mind.

"Medicinal," Cole said sheepishly, nodding to his leg. "Part of the problem with camping for the night where others have camped."

"How's that?"

"Cut my foot on a piece of broken glass when I was answering the call of nature."

"Ow-ee," the man said, commiserating.

"Yep, two nights ago. Ain't feeling much better. I fear it'll be infected."

"If you been stepping where your horse been answering the call of nature, it shore 'nuff *will be.*"

"Do you know where a man might find some doctoring around here?"

"Which way you headed?"

"North."

"Nearest place would be Fort Benton."

"Thank you greatly," Cole said, holding out his shot glass for a refill.

"Must be something goin' on," the man said as he took Cole's coin. "There was another fella by here yesterday who was stove up with an infection. Nasty goddamn thing on his wrist. Also headed up to Benton. Around here that counts as an epidemic."

"Not Benton," interjected the man with the large hat. "They was headed *east.*"

"Well, then I guess the doctor will have time for me when I get there," Cole said, finishing his drink and turning to leave. "Much obliged, good day to y'all."

When he had limped back out to his horse, and the second man had thought him sufficiently removed from earshot, he began berating the shopkeeper.

"Damn you, man. They told us not to tell nobody which way they went."

"That fellow was no lawman," the shopkeeper said, referring to Cole. "I could figure that out, and so could you. Besides, he wasn't askin', I was tellin'."

"They told us not to tell *nobody.*"

Hoping that the disagreement would not go beyond verbal, Cole mounted up and rode out of town.

His feigned limp had allowed him to open the door into talk of a man who was injured, and now he knew that he was gaining on the Porter boys. He had started out more than two days behind them and had halved their lead.

As the faint sound of the argument died away, the only sounds were the songs of the meadowlarks in the tall grass. Except for the trail Cole was riding, the vast landscape surrounding the Missouri River in the valley below was as devoid of the hand of humanity as it had been when Lewis and Clark had been the first white men to pass through these parts more than seven decades before.

Their journals of their westward trek on the river recorded no sign of another person for the weeks they took to cross most of the vast expanse of what became Montana Territory. The Piegan, Gros Ventre, and Blackfeet hunters, who no doubt noticed them from the high bluffs above the river, discreetly chose not to make their presence known. When the white men returned, traveling eastward, it had been a different story, but even after the passage of more than seven decades, this stretch of the Missouri, flanked by cottonwoods and aspen in their yellow autumn raiment, had not changed.

Downstream at Fort Benton, it was a different story. William Clark had been dead for less than a decade when this town was born as a bustling riverboat port serving the fur trade. Through the years since, it had grown in importance as gold was discovered and as cattle ranching proliferated. The most navigable inland port on the Missouri, it was served routinely by steamboats heading downstream to the Mississippi at St. Louis, the Gulf of Mexico at New Orleans, and thence to the whole outside world.

With hyperbole based lightly upon fact, its boosters called their port city "the Chicago of the West." With hyperbole more closely rooted in reality, Fort Benton's detractors, complaining of gunslingers and river pirates, called its main street "the bloodiest block in the West."

Fort Benton was a place where four men on the run could lose themselves, and where a man with a wrist infected by a bullet wound could seek medical attention without the embarrassment of intrusive queries. So too could a man with a limp, who feared an infection of his own.

As had been the case in Diamond City, and as in the recent no-name cow town, the window into the soul of Fort Benton was the pair of swinging doors that led to the saloon. The only question when there were so many was *which* saloon?

Cole bypassed the places on the main street — especially the one from which a fistfight had spilled across the boardwalk and into the street — and picked a smallish tavern on a side street that seemed more likely to cater to locals.

Once again, he affected a limp, and once again he explained his need for whiskey as "medicinal."

"You oughta get that looked at," the bartender offered in the way of advice.

"Reckon I oughta," Cole said in a tone that lacked conviction. There was no sense in his betraying *too* much eagerness to find a doctor who catered to strangers with suspicious injuries — especially not when he was tasting good whiskey. And the whiskey *was* good. The closer a man was to the port to which the whiskey had been shipped, the lower the percentage of native water that was likely to have been added to "extend" it.

"Looks like winter's comin' on," Cole said, changing the subject.

"Saw some snow in the air the other night," agreed the bartender, who drifted away to deal with some other patrons.

When he returned to Cole, the bounty hunter grimaced a little and asked for another shot.

"If I was to want to have this looked at," he said as his shot was poured, "where would I find a doc to do the lookin'?"

"Hear of Doc Ashby?"

"I'm not from around here."

"Second street over. He takes a lot of folks just passing through."

"Much obliged," Cole said, laying a couple of coins on the bar.

Doc Ashby's shingle hung above the door that led to the second floor of a red brick commercial building. The bartender hadn't actually said how many doctors practiced in Fort Benton, but Bladen Cole figured himself to be on the right track when the first one to come to the man's mind took patients who were "just passing through."

There was no sign saying *closed,* and the door was unlocked. Cole took this to be a good indication. A little bell tingled happily as the door opened, and he began climbing the steep and creaky staircase. At the top of the stairs, standing behind a desk, was an older man in wire-frame glasses wearing a vest over a white shirt that was a little dirty in the cuffs.

"I'm Dr. Ashby," he said, extending his hand. "Can I help you?"

"Well, Doc, I'm actually trying to catch up with some friends of mine."

"How . . . ?"

"Well, one of 'em had an injury on his

hand, and I figure he'd be looking for a doctor such as yourself to patch him up."

"That so?" Ashby said, his friendly demeanor enveloped by a tone of suspicion. "I believe that your friend is my patient . . . but he's not really your friend . . . is he?"

"Nope."

"You a lawman?"

"No."

"Bounty hunter?"

"I am."

"A man who collects rewards for collecting people," Ashby commented, sniping at Cole.

"A man who enforces legally executed warrants," Cole said with more impatience than defensiveness. "Two men were gunned down in cold blood in the parlor of one of their homes . . . and then the wife of one of the men . . . and then the sheriff of Gallatin City, and finally a fourth man. I'm on the trail of men who've left a string of at least five bodies across this territory . . . I'm out to bring killers back to answer for those crimes."

"I'm afraid you will not be taking this man anywhere," the doctor said.

"Why's that?"

"Because within the next hour or so, he'll be going home to the Lord."

"That bad?"

"That bad. If they'd gotten him to me a day or so earlier, I might have taken off an arm and saved a life, but it's too late. The infection's spread . . . all the way to his heart."

"Can I see him?" Cole asked.

"Nothing wrong with that . . . I suppose." The doctor shrugged, nodding to a door on the wall opposite the head of the stairs. "Go ahead."

Inside, a man lay on a bed, his head on a pillow soaked in sweat. His boots and shirt had been removed. There was a fresh bandage on his wrist, but his arm and shoulder were deeply inflamed.

His eyes flickered open and rolled to look in Cole's direction, but otherwise he remained motionless.

"Which one of the Porter boys are you?" Cole asked.

"Ain't no Porter," he whispered at last. "Name's Waller . . . Milton Waller. If you're here to arrest me, you're too late. Sheriff done killed me already. He's a good shot. Thought he just nicked me . . . but he done killed me."

"Why'd you kill those people?" Cole asked. "Why'd you go after Blaine?"

"Got paid . . . paid good."

70

An attempt at an ironic chuckle was interrupted by a cough, followed by a choking sound.

"The railroad . . . land deal," the man explained between sputters. "They have to die . . . four partners . . . only one can survive."

"Who paid you?" Cole asked.

"Got paid to kill 'em . . . half up front," Waller continued, skating to the edge of deathbed delirium. "Had to get out of town without the rest . . . damn that Enoch Porter . . . he shot that woman . . . then it all fell apart . . . running out of time . . . had to get out of town quick."

"Who paid you?" Cole repeated.

"All fell apart . . ." Waller said. "He shot the woman . . . we're all scared . . . have to run . . ."

With that, Milton Waller ran out of time. His eyes went blank, his body flinched and relaxed.

Cole looked at Ashby, who nodded. Waller had gone home.

CHAPTER 6

Bladen Cole had a strange apprehension that he was congratulating a killer when he scrawled out a message to Isham Ransdell at the Fort Benton post office. He enclosed a copy of the death certificate and confirmed the death in his accompanying note. He wrote nothing, however, about Waller's last words, nothing about "only one can survive," because it had been Ransdell, conveniently absent from the shooting, who was the *one* who had walked away *completely unscathed.*

Cole had long been pondering the words of Gideon Porter as related by Mrs. Stocker that the women were not *supposed* to be hurt. From this, he had concluded that the killings were not a matter of an angry madman settling a score, but part of a deliberately conceived *plan,* leaving only the question of *whose plan* it had been. In his deathbed declaration, Waller's words had filled in this missing piece.

For Bladen Cole, justice, when applied to the Porter boys, was no longer a matter of "dead or alive." Justice could only be served by bringing the remaining outlaws back *alive* to point their fingers at Isham Ransdell.

The bounty hunter had hoped to continue his pursuit the morning after the demise of Milton Waller, but the time expended in getting two copies of the death certificate — one for himself and one to mail to Isham Ransdell — had cost most of the day. It had taken all morning and several trips back and forth to the county clerk's office to get copies of Waller's death certificate and to get them signed by both Doc Ashby and the coroner. He then had to chase down a notary whose office hours began only when he had slept off his night before.

Cole decided to sleep one more night between sheets in the fleabag hotel and bought his dinner at a little shack of a cafe near the levee. He decided to buy his whiskey at the saloon nearest his hotel, a typical Fort Benton dive, where trappers from the distant corners of the Plains and boatmen from the Missouri were being united with their first whiskey in months. The piano player was banging out some familiar Virginia marches, and it made Cole a little nostalgic.

He met a woman who craved companionship in a commercial, rather than nostalgic, sort of way, and he talked with her until he discovered that she had no information about the Porter boys. She too lost interest and drifted on to another prospect when she discovered that the only thing he was buying that night was drinks.

She had told him her name, but he forgot it right away. She too reminded him of Sally Lovelace in that way that most painted ladies now reminded him of Sally Lovelace. This one also had Sally's habit of making intense eye contact and telling him that she knew what he was thinking.

This night in this saloon reminded him of another night long ago in that other bar down in Silver City, where prospectors came down out of the Mogollon Mountains with too much gold dust and not enough sense.

The Cole brothers, William and Bladen, had been drinking far too long for their own good that night — he would grant that as a fact — but young men barely into their twenties cannot be told such a thing at the time.

So too had been another pair of young men barely into their twenties. As often happens in circumstances such as prevailed that night, neither pair of young men walked away, as they should have, from a quarrel that had ensued.

Perhaps if Bladen had tugged at Will's sleeve and insisted that they let the two men go, it never would have happened, but he had not, and it did.

It happened so fast, and in such a fog, that Bladen never really knew which man drew his gun first, but Bladen knew he was the *last.* When the dust had settled, two men lay dead, and one was Will. The fourth man, the cowardly one with the narrow face of a rodent, had vanished into the night.

Through all the ensuing years, in saloons like this one in Fort Benton, Cole had found himself scanning the patrons who swirled in the kerosene glow, searching the room for the rat-faced man who took his brother's life.

Through all the ensuing years, he had yet to see that ugly face again.

Doc Ashby had confirmed what Aggie in Diamond City had said that she had overheard. The Porter boys were headed across the Marias River into Blackfeet country. In Montana around this time, you could more or less dance all around the law with impunity, but *only* more or less. The only place you could *really* outrun the law was where there was *no* law. It was commonly stated that there was "no law north of the Marias."

The cold wind blowing from the Arctic across the Canadian prairies stung his face as Cole rode the undulating landscape of apparently endless flatness alternated with broad gullies cut by streams and filled with golden aspen.

It was, in the eyes of an outsider, a trackless wilderness unpunctuated with landmarks, like the open ocean. To those who had been here for generations, each of the monotonous series of hills and gullies was as unique as a city street marked by a unique street sign.

The Blackfeet, called Siksikáwa in their own tongue, had inhabited this distant corner of the Plains for centuries. For the most part, the white man had yet to build up the momentum to exploit this place. Aside from a few distantly separated trading posts, there were no people living north of the Marias — in a vast region larger than Cole's native Virginia — whose grandparents had not been born here.

Late in the afternoon, Cole noticed a cluster of scavenging birds circling and squawking, and he detoured slightly to investigate. They were not the remains of three men ambushed by Blackfeet, but the bloody and scattered bits of something else that had recently been living. The pieces were so far dispersed that it took Cole a few minutes to ascertain that these remains were, or had been, a bull elk.

The big animal appeared to have been blown apart by a stick of dynamite, though in fact it had been attacked, killed, and partially consumed by a grizzly. A lump rose in Cole's throat as he realized that this slaughter had occurred within the past hour. The meat was fresh, the blood still runny.

The roan began acting nervously, jerking and snorting like a person who had come under the spell of an evil sorcerer. Cole had had barely a moment to understand why his horse was spooked, when he saw the reason in the corner of his eye.

The bear arose with a crash and a snort from a thicket of willows. From a crouching position, it unlimbered itself to a standing posture and bellowed ominously. The grizzly is an enormous creature, taller than a man standing in his stirrups while on his horse.

Cole felt the blood drain from his face as the roan reared.

The signature terror of the remote corners

of the West, the grizzly was a creature so fierce that all others avoided it — when they could. The Indians approached it with a mixture of reverence and trepidation. White men avoided it because it could not be killed. As many a man had learned the hard way, its skull was so thick and the muscle mass of its body so dense that only a lucky shot, a one-in-a-hundred shot, could bring one down.

For the first time in years, Cole found himself frozen in fear. The first reaction of a person to a grizzly, that being to run like hell, was often fatal. As clumsy as they seemed while lumbering about, grizzlies could outrun a man, even a man on a horse.

He pulled his Winchester from its scabbard and began backing his horse, figuring that his *best chance* was to get away slowly before the bear decided to drop back down to four legs and charge him.

The Winchester represented his *last chance.*

For a short while, it worked. The bear watched the mounted rider as though bewildered by the jerky backward motion.

At last, the grizzly decided that despite an apparent backward movement, this intruder represented an interloper at his supper table.

With an angry snarl, the beast charged.

The roan bucked, and Cole felt himself losing his balance.

In the process of trying not to lose his rifle, Cole lost his reins.

For a moment, he felt himself sliding sideways from a galloping horse.

In the next instant, he was colliding awkwardly with the ground.

The Winchester, on which he had lost his grip, dropped about six feet away.

The sound of the bear galloping toward him was like thunder.

He literally threw himself toward the gun.

Grabbing the rifle in mid-tumble, Cole fired without aiming.

The bullet struck the bear with little more annoyance than a horse fly caused attacking a person. Cole might as well have poked him in the shoulder with a stick.

However, the sound of the shot, something this bear had never heard, and the smell of the gunsmoke, something this bear had never smelled, provided a momentary pause.

It is curious to contemplate the sorts of things that go through a man's mind when he is about to die. They say that your whole life flashes before you, but what do "they" know?

Bladen Cole thought about that Sunday

in the Congregational Church in Bowling Green when he was about twelve, when he had thought about the effectiveness of prayer for the first time. The preacher's remarks had lost him in the bobbing sea of his own daydreams, and he had wondered whether prayers went answered. He guessed that most did not, but he wanted to believe that some *did.*

In that split second before the moment in which he expected his own violent and painful death, Bladen Cole prayed.

He also squeezed the trigger again, and saw the lead tear into the cheek of an angry bear whose rapid progress toward him was not slackened.

He could smell the disgusting stench of the grizzly's breath as he fired the *last shot possible* before ten angry, raging claws reached him and ripped him apart as they had the elk.

The slug impacted the bear's left eye, cleaving straight into his brain.

The inside surface of the back of the bear's skull, being too thick to be penetrated by the bullet, caused it to ricochet, then ricochet again. Each time that the bullet zigged or zagged in the soft tissue of the brain, it tore a separate path and ripped

away another swath of the bear's consciousness.

Cole rolled to the side as the bear reached
him.

He felt the pain of the bear's leg falling on
his, but he barely avoided having the full
weight of the animal's thousand pounds
crush him.

He imagined that he was being mauled,
and he struggled to get away, but the frightening gyrations were merely the bear's death
throes. By the time that he had at last gotten out from beneath the enormous mass,
the grizzly had twitched its last.

Cole gasped to catch breath, inhaling the
rankness of the sweaty monster, but was
overjoyed just to be breathing at all.

CHAPTER 7

Cole camped that night among the aspen, washing himself off and watering his roan in the trickle of a stream that ran there.

He awoke suddenly to the hot breath of an animal on his face, immediately imagining it to be another grizzly, but it was merely his horse. He now realized how his subconscious mind had shifted into wilderness mode. Would he have mistaken his horse for a grizzly two nights earlier when he went to sleep with the lights of Diamond City twinkling in the distance? He had not and probably would not have before the experience of the day just passed.

Waiting for his coffee to boil, he watched the stars wink out in the lightening sky of dawn. He thought of what he had read of seafaring people using the stars as navigational tools, and of how he had always used the North Star as a reference point in unfamiliar territory.

As he rode north with the gathering dawn and turned westward in the direction of the Rocky Mountains, he saw a small group of pronghorns at a great distance, but aside from that, the only sign of life was the usual companionship of the meadowlarks and a hawk circling in the distance.

Shortly after his lunch, which consisted of a scrap of hardtack eaten in the saddle as he rode, he saw them. Two riders had materialized out of nowhere, or so it seemed. One minute, the hill about a quarter mile ahead and to the right had been deserted, and now there were two men there. He could make out the golden hue of their buckskin shirts and the long black hair that framed their heads. The fact that he had seen them at all signified that they wanted to be seen.

Cole raised his hand to signify that he saw them and meant no hostility. The men returned the gesture and waited for him to reach them.

"Good morning, fellows," he said in English, more to establish that his intention was to greet them than in the belief that they could understand his words. "My name's Bladen Cole."

They responded with a gesture to the tongue, which signified their not being conversant in his language.

Cole knew a few Lakota words — as did most white men on the northern Plains, because the two groups had had much contact over the past three decades — but almost nothing of the totally unrelated Blackfeet language. What he did know pretty well, and what did unite the tribes on the Plains who could not communicate verbally, was the universal sign language.

Using this, Cole was able to explain that he was looking for three men, three *white* men, who had come into Blackfeet country in the previous couple of days.

Without saying whether or not they had seen the Porter boys, the two men replied that they had problems of their own. There was some sort of intertribal squabble going on, and they were on one side of it.

One of them pointed to the Winchester Model 1873 rifle that Cole had in the scabbard attached to his saddle. At first, he thought that they were proposing to trade. One of them carried an older model, U.S. Army–issue "Trapdoor" Springfield, and he could see the distinctive bronze-colored breech of the Winchester '66 carried by the other. Neither gun was desirable in a trade for a '73 Winchester, so he declined.

At this, the man who was doing all the

talking said that Cole was mistaken. They didn't want his Winchester, they wanted *him.* They indicated that their head man had sent them to "volunteer" his services as a rifleman.

Cole found it hard to stifle the laugh, which, when he suddenly guffawed, noticeably startled his new Siksikáwa friends. Bladen Cole, the hired gun, was being hired for a second job in parallel to that which had brought him north of the Marias.

The two men were looking at each other with bewildered expressions, when Cole let it be known that he *would* help them.

On one hand, allowing himself to become embroiled in a Blackfeet civil war was an unnecessary distraction from his purpose, but if he had any hope of completing a successful manhunt in this enormous land, he needed friends. And he was about to make some.

They had ridden together for about an hour when Cole started to see the blue haze of many campfires in the distance. At last, as the sweet smell of smoldering cottonwood reached his nostrils, they came over a rise and saw a village below. There were more than a dozen tipis clustered along a quarter-mile stretch of a stream. People were going about their daily chores, and horses grazed on the hillsides.

As they rode through the camp, Cole smiled broadly at the children who eyed him curiously. One group of preteen girls giggled and turned away as he caught their eyes.

They stopped before a large tipi which was decorated with a variety of pictograms painted in both red and black. By its location in the center of the camp, Cole concluded that this was the chief's house.

The three riders dismounted, and one of the Siksikáwa men approached the open flap of the lodge. He spoke to someone inside and gestured for Cole to come in. The bounty hunter grabbed a knot of smoking tobacco from a parcel that he carried in his saddlebag and approached the opening. He wasn't fully conversant in native customs, but he did know that among the people of the Plains, it was always good manners to present your host with a token gift of tobacco.

"Assa, nápikoan, oki," the man said cordially as Cole appeared in his doorway.

Though he claimed less than the barest understanding of the language, Cole did recognize the greeting "*oki*" and term for "white man," "*nápikoan.*" He had always appreciated that it was a more literal translation than the Lakota word for his race, which was the derogatory *"wasichu,"* meaning "the one who steals the bacon fat."

Cole handed the chief the tobacco, a gesture which the chief seemed to appreciate. With this, the old man shot a glance toward one of the younger men which needed no translation. It said pointedly that "this white man isn't as discourteous as you thought."

"Ke-a-e-es-tsa-kos-ach-kit-satope," the old man said to the young man, who immediately spread a buffalo robe for Cole to sit on.

The chief had a leathery, lined face that was deeply tanned in contrast to his long, snow white hair. His eyes were bright and sharp, and it was hard to judge his age. By those eyes, he could have been thirty. By the texture of his skin and the color of his hair, he could have been a hundred.

"Nitsinihka'sim O-mis-tai-po-kah," he said. introducing himself. *"Kiistawa, tsa kitanik-koowa?"* he continued, pointing at his guest.

The words made no more sense to Bladen than water gurgling over rocks in a stream bed, but by the gestures, he understood that the man had introduced himself and wanted to know his name.

"Bladen Cole," he replied, pointing to himself.

"Ahhh, Bladencool," the man said, leaning back on his buffalo robe.

With this, evidently believing now that "Bladencool" understood some of the rudiments of the *lingua franca,* the man began relating some sort of story. Though it was accompanied by gestures, Cole became completely lost. He recognized the sign for "horse," but beyond that, he couldn't follow the man's narrative at all.

Finally, this confusion became apparent, and the chief impatiently turned to one of the younger men, who got up and left, as though he had been sent to fetch something.

The chief continued, but with simpler and easier to understand sign language. The fellow was making what amounted to small talk. He asked how far Cole had come and nodded his understanding when Cole explained that he had been following the three men for four sleeps.

They were deep into their conversation when a shadow appeared in the doorway.

Cole looked up to see a young woman with dark, riveting eyes, who looked to be in her early twenties. Her features were as smooth and delicate as the old man's were hard-edged and textured. Her long hair, which she wore in braids, was as black as his was white. She was wearing a double-row necklace made of elk teeth and a buckskin dress, lightly decorated with porcupine quills.

She listened intently as the old man spoke to her, nodding periodically and glancing occasionally at the white man. Cole could not take his eyes off her and savored the grace of her movements as she was invited to sit on a buffalo robe near him.

"Mr. Bladencool," she said looking at him, appearing to work hard to choose her words. "My name is Natoya-I-nis'kim. My uncle . . . his name is O-mis-tai-po-kah . . . has requested me to translate his words to you."

She smiled bashfully and asked, "Do you understand my words? I have not spoken in English for many months."

"Yes, I understand you just fine," Cole replied, trying to enunciate clearly. "Actually my name is Bladen Cole . . . two words."

"I'm sorry . . . Mr. Cool. I understand. Two names . . . yes, I understand."

"You speak English very good," he said to compliment her. "Where did you learn . . . way out here?"

"I was taught at the mission school. I attended as a girl. I am happy I remember the words."

"Your uncle seems proud of you," Cole said.

"My uncle, who is named O-mis-tai-po-kah for the white medicine buffalo calf who was born at the same time as he, is *iikaatowa'pii,* very powerful with spirit power . . . great medicine."

"What is it that your uncle wants with me? I understood something about horses . . . but that was about it."

"There were Pikuni Siksikáwa renegades who stole many *ponokáómitaa* . . . many horses . . . from us," she said, gesturing elegantly. "They have become into one band with the Káínawa Siksikáwa who live in the red coats' country."

"So that I understand," Cole recapped, "some people from your own tribe stole some of your horses and they're running with some people from the Káínawa Black-feet up in Canada?"

"Yes."

"And your uncle wants *my* help in getting the horses back?"

"Yes . . . and also to punish the Pikuni for riding with our enemy."

As with many tribes, including the pale-skinned ones from Cole's world, people who seemed indistinguishable to outsiders were often rivals — or worse. The Pikuni Siksikáwa of Montana and the Káínawa in Canada shared a language and a culture, yet they had been openly hostile with one another forever. Of course, in Cole's own generation, the Civil War had consumed nearly a million lives of men, men just like him, men who were on two sides but who nevertheless spoke the same language.

"Where are they now, the renegades and the Káínawa?" Cole asked. "Did they go back into Canada?"

"No . . . they went to the *Mistákists Ikánatsiaw,* the mountains which go to the sun," she said, ". . . one or two sleeps toward the place of the setting sun . . . to the west from here."

"Why does he need an outsider for this?" Cole asked.

"Because most of our young men have gone away to hunt the *iiníí* . . . the buffalo . . . far to the east . . . many sleeps. They stole the horses because we were in a moment of weakness. We need help."

"How did you decide to pick me?"

"Ikutsikakatósi and Ómahkaatsistawa," she said, nodding to the two young men. "They spotted you this morning as the sun rose. They told my uncle about the white man riding where white men usually do not come. He said to get the white man to help."

91

"You don't see too many white men out here, then?"

"No, not this side of the trading posts, not in many moons."

"I was told there were three others who came this way a day or two ago."

"I haven't heard of them, they must have gone some other way," she said. Her expression agreed with her words.

"Must have," Cole said.

The old man said something, but Cole didn't hear it; his rapt attention had been on watching Natoya's graceful gesture as she pointed to the west.

She heard it though and quickly translated.

"You will go now . . . you will go *aami'toohski* . . . westward at once."

The chief said something to the men that caused them to grimace and Natoya to giggle slightly.

"I have one more question," Cole said, turning to Natoya. "Why me? Why did I get singled out for this escapade?"

"Because Ikutsikakatósi and Ómahkaatsistawa could see by your guns that you were a man who could fight . . . O-mis-tai-po-kah could see by your eyes that you are a fighter who does not like to lose."

"If I would *not* have come with them . . .

if I wouldn't have agreed to this . . . ?"

"They would kill you and take your guns," she replied, her expression very matter of fact.

The three men rode out of the camp together, but when they crested the hill at the far side of the river valley, the Blackfeet reined their horses ahead of Cole's, deliberately shunning him. It was obviously a matter of hurt pride that a *nápikoan* had to be hired to help them do their job. Being thusly ostracized did not bother Cole in the least. If it was him, he would have felt the same way.

Nor did it bother him to be riding alone. He had long preferred it that way, he thought to himself. But, thinking of Will, he recalled that he had not *always* felt that way.

As they rode westward toward the descending sun of mid-afternoon, he thought about the Porter boys and about their biblical names. From what he recalled about his own Bible learning, which was not that much, Gideon's biblical namesake was called "the Destroyer," but he did his destroying on orders from God. There were a couple of Enochs in the Bible, but Cole could remember only the one who was the son of Cain, who had committed the world's first homicide. He wondered whether the missionaries had taught the Blackfeet children about these men.

The Porter boys were his reason for being out here in the first place, and his thoughts turned to their whereabouts, and how long it would take to find them in this country. They were at least a day ahead of him, but having crossed north of the Marias, they had crossed north of their past, and they would no longer be running. Their pace would have slackened, and they would have relaxed and made their presence known to the locals.

If not Natoya's band, then some other Siksikáwa band or other out here would have seen them, and word would spread. That word would not spread to ears accustomed to English, but it would spread, and sooner or later, Cole would know.

As he had done since crossing the Marias, Cole was keeping his eyes on the horizon. Yesterday, he'd had *potential* enemies in anyone who might choose to distrust a stranger. Now that he had taken a side in a civil war, he had *real* enemies. He could count on the wary eyes of his two companions to see danger first, but still, he kept his eyes on the horizon.

The last place that he had expected to see

that horizon populated was in the direction straight behind him — yet there it was, a rider coming up from behind at a gallop.

The two Siksikáwa men reined up their horses and exchanged words which Cole did not understand, except that they were more of aversion than alarm.

Cole could see why. The rider was Natoya-I-nis'kim, loping toward them on a paint, her braids swirling about her head as she came.

"liksoka'pii kitsinohsi!" she said to the two men, laughing as she brought her horse to a stop. Even back home in Virginia, where women took to riding with great pride of accomplishment, Cole had never seen a woman who could handle a horse with such skill.

They spoke with her angrily, pointing their fingers back in the direction of their village. Cole chuckled as she told them off. At last, the argument reached an impasse. They turned their backs on her and resumed the westward trek, ignoring her as they had been ignoring the white man.

"What was that all about?" Cole asked.

"I told Ikutsikakatósi and Ómahkaatsis-tawa I am happy to see them," she said, smiling mischievously.

"They aren't happy to see *you*."

"I don't care," she said playfully.

"Why are you here?"

"Uncle told me to come," she explained. "There will be a need to translate. Ikutsikakatósi and Ómahkaatsistawa would not speak to you if they *could,* but they *cannot.*"

"They don't want to speak to *you* either . . . at least not to say a civil word."

"This is not a place for a woman, they said," Natoya explained with a smirk.

"It isn't," Cole agreed. "This will be dangerous."

"*I* will be dangerous," she said with a slight grin, pulling back the edge of her buffalo robe to show him that she had a holster strapped around her waist that contained an older model Colt Navy revolver.

"Where did you get that?"

"Trader."

"Have you used it?"

"Yes."

Bladen Cole held his tongue. It really *wasn't* a place for a woman, even if she could handle a horse and use a gun. Where there was the probability of a gunfight, it was a bad place for a woman, but it was, he decided, not his place to tell an Indian girl, especially one displaying such confidence, that she was in the wrong place.

On the other hand, the old man was right, an interpreter *could* prove useful — not only in accomplishing the old man's purpose, but in accomplishing Cole's as well. It was just a pity, he felt, that there were so few men in the camp that the chief had to send his young niece.

"When will the other men be back from their buffalo hunt?"

"Before the snow," she said, looking to the north and speaking without her previous assurance.

"Your uncle is named after the white buffalo?" Cole said, making conversation after a mile or so of riding in silence.

"Yes, a calf was born when he was born."

"You didn't tell be the meaning of *your* name," he said.

"*Inis'kim* is the 'Medicine Stone,'" she said. "'Medicine *Buffalo* Stone.'"

"That sounds important."

"My mother found one when I was in her belly," she explained. "It is the stone which sings. It is the stone bringing good luck. Long ago, in the winter that the *iiníí* . . . the buffalo went away, a woman found the first stone in a cottonwood tree when she went to a stream to get water for cooking. The *Inis'kim* sang to her and told her to take it home to her lodge. It said that buffalo will return and hearts will be glad."

"Did it work?"

"She taught the *Inis'kim* song to her husband and the elders. They knew that it was powerful. They sang. They prayed. The buffalo *came.*"

"Does your mother still have it?"

"My mother has gone . . . Absaroka raiders. My father too."

"I'm sorry to hear that," Cole said meekly, knowing that he had touched a nerve.

"That's when I went to the mission school," she said, wiping a tear from her cheek.

Cole made another innocuous comment about the weather and the approach of winter, and afterward, they rode on without talking.

CHAPTER 8

The wistful girl with the tear on her cheek reasserted herself at the camp that night. When the Siksikáwa men, each a head taller than she, insisted that water be fetched for cooking, an argument ensued. It ended with Ikutsikakatósi taking the basket to the stream.

Bladen Cole found this greatly amusing.

"We'd better build this fire good so we don't get a visit from a grizzly tonight," Cole said, shoving some cottonwood sticks into the fire.

"Yes . . . you are right," Natoya agreed. "It is a dangerous animal . . . and a powerful animal in many ways."

"That's for sure," Cole agreed.

"And he is a very powerful animal with *nátosini* . . . um . . . how to you say . . . medicine?"

"Supernatural power?"

"Yes . . . supernatural power, *nátosini*."

"So the grizzly is sacred to the Siksikáwa?" Cole asked.

"In the way that everything in the world is sacred," Natoya explained. "In the way that the black robes thought we 'worshipped' trees and badgers."

Poking a stick to turn a piece of cottonwood in the fire, she continued her recollections of the missionaries.

"There was *one* black robe who understood . . . but mostly they did not, and we laughed at them behind their backs. That is not very polite, I know . . . but we were children . . ."

"I think it's funny," Cole chuckled, imagining a bevy of Blackfeet girls giggling about the inability of the missionaries to understand the people they were teaching.

"Of all the *kiááyo,* all the bears, the *apóhkiááyo* . . . you call him 'grizzly,' is feared and respected above all," Natoya continued.

"So that makes him *sacred*?"

"I do not have the *Naapi'powahsin* . . . the English words to explain. It is not 'sacred' in the missionary way of being sacred, just as we do not 'worship' trees in the missionary way of worshipping. *Apóhkiááyo* is *important* to the Siksikáwa . . . not the same way as the buffalo . . . but . . . I don't have the words . . . *apóhkiááyo* is greatly feared

100

and greatly respected. I'm sorry that is the best I can explain."

Cole disagreed. "You have very good English words," he said. "I know a lot of white people who do less of a job explaining things."

"Don't let me be selfish," she said.

"How do you mean?"

"I am so happy to have someone . . . so I can speak my *Naapi'powahsin* . . . my English words."

"You're not selfish at all . . . I'm happy to have someone to speak English words with myself."

She smiled and turned away.

"But about the grizzly . . . and it being sacred in the way that it is . . . and I know that's the wrong English word . . . There's something that I gotta tell you . . . gotta admit to."

"What's that?"

"I killed one yesterday. I killed a grizzly."

Natoya-I-nis'kim looked at him with a mixture of shock and bewilderment.

"Yeah, I was coming across the plains and I came across a fresh elk kill," he said. "The thing reared up and charged before I knew what was happening. I got off three shots . . . the last one was a lucky shot. So I killed a sacred bear. I'm sorry to say that, knowing that they're important to your people . . . to the Siksikáwa . . . but it was him or me."

"It is a very great thing to overcome *apóhkiááyo* in a fight," Natoya said.

She seemed impressed, rather than upset, a fact that caused Cole to breathe a sigh of relief.

"Because of their strength, and their great *nátosini* . . . It is hard to kill him in a fight. Most men cannot. Most men die. A man who kills him in a fight inherits his power."

"How does that work?" Cole asked.

"Power . . . medicine . . . comes to all animals from *Natosiwa,* the sun. When *apóhkiááyo* is beaten in a fight, his power is then granted to the man. The man receives the character and spirit of *apóhkiááyo.* Of course he was powerful in the start . . . the man. He has to be to overcome *apóhkiááyo.* You are a powerful man, Mr. Cool."

"I didn't feel any different," Cole admitted, "except kind of dirty from having this sweaty bear dead on top of me."

Natoya laughed.

"By the way," he said. "Since you seem to appreciate the grizzly, I'd like you to have this."

He reached into his pocket and took out a sharp and frightening six-inch grizzly claw.

"I took this from that one yesterday," he

said, handing it to her. "I want you to have it."

She took the object as though it were a religious artifact, for to be given a grizzly claw by a man who had triumphed over *apóhkiááyo* in battle was an amazing gesture.

She looked at it with an expression of awe. It was, Cole thought, like having handed a white woman a fistful of diamonds.

Natoya then looked at him with an expression of speechless gratitude.

In the morning, only Natoya-I-nis'kim among the three Siksikáwa accepted the coffee that Cole offered, though she found it not to her liking.

By the middle of the day, the jagged peaks of the Rockies could be clearly seen, rising abruptly from the Plains.

"Mistákists Ikánatsiaw," Natoya said with a nod as Cole pointed toward the snowcapped peaks. The trail of the horse thieves led toward the mountains, just as O-mis-tai-po-kah had predicted. They had not been hard to follow. It is hard to move a herd of a couple dozen *ponokáómitaa* without leaving ample evidence of their passing.

Cole could tell by the fragrance of the "ample evidence" that it was more recent than it had been during the previous day. Thanks to Natoya's having insisted that they break camp very early, they were now only a matter of hours behind their quarry. The fact that the thieves' pace had slowed meant that the renegades were confident of not being followed. Just like the Porter boys, Cole hoped.

Gradually, they passed out of the rolling hills dotted mainly with aspen and came to a ridge whose western, windward slope was covered with gnarled and windblown spruce. As they crossed the ridge, they were greeted with a breeze which blew colder than what they had experienced thus far.

Natoya reined up her horse and pointed through the trees.

In the distance, they could see a long, slender lake hugging the base of the mountains. The winter, which all expected, had already come to the high country. The jagged peaks were heavily cloaked in snow.

Natoya identified the lake as Natoákio-mahksikimi, but she translated the names of the peaks they saw. There were Red Eagle and Little Chief, and occupying a prominent place above the lake was Going-to-the-Sun. To the left, she pointed out one named for a man called Imazí-imita, whose name, Natoya explained, meant "Almost-a-Dog."

A short distance down into the valley of the lake, the horse thieves had steered their purloined herd onto a broad trail. Natoya identified it as being a main thoroughfare for the Siksikáwa which led down into the valley of the lakes.

The "ample evidence" was now exceedingly fresh, and the Siksikáwa men pulled their rifles from the scabbards. Cole instinctively drew his Colt and spun the cylinder to count the cartridges. He knew it was loaded — this was just a ritual. As he undid the leather thong that secured his Winchester in its scabbard, he noticed that Natoya's hand was resting on her holstered weapon as well.

They rounded a bend near the base of the ridge, and the landscape of the valley revealed itself. There, not far below and swirling about in a meadow near a stream, was the stolen herd. Cole counted eight men.

As he and his companions watched, their number increased by two with the approach of a pair of *nápikoan* riders.

Cole squinted hard, determining that these white men were not the Porter boys. One might have been, but the other was much too fat.

"Buyers," Natoya whispered.

Cole nodded. It was obvious that the two white men had been invited here to purchase the stolen herd.

"I think something better happen before this transaction is completed," he said under his breath.

Natoya nodded and repeated this to the Ikutsikakatósi and Ómahkaatsistawa, who nodded their agreement.

"Cover me," Cole said as he spurred the roan forward.

A few minutes later, the ten riders in the valley turned their heads at his approach. Hands tensed and touched guns.

Cole raised his hand in greeting and rode toward the two white men.

"Good morning, sir," the heavyset man said cautiously. "To what do we owe the pleasure of seeing you here?"

"Good morning, sir," Cole said, extending his hand. "My name is Bladen Cole. If I'm not mistaken, you're here to buy some Indian ponies."

"Name's McGaugh," the man said, taking Cole's offered hand. "Benjamin McGaugh. You'd be correct in your supposition. We were informed at the Indian Agency that a herd would be available here this morning. I'm here to pick out four or five of the finest of these ponies."

"Would it make any difference to your plans if I was to tell you that these animals are a herd stolen from my friend White Buffalo Calf, whose lodge stands about two days' ride east of here?"

"If that were to be a fact, it would certainly make a difference. I am not in the business of accepting stolen property . . . certainly not Blackfeet property on Blackfeet land."

"I hoped that would be your position," Cole said.

"Mason," the big man said, turning to his companion. "Ask these boys about that. Is this a stolen herd?"

The other man, who looked to be part Blackfeet himself, queried the apparent leader of the horse thieves, who vehemently denied the assertion. However, the opposite message was conveyed by the nervous apprehension of the others when they heard the question asked.

"There we have it," the man said. "A denial from the man with whom I am about to consummate a transaction."

"And an admission from the expression of the others," Cole added.

"Were I to accept the discrepancy that you have pointed out," said the man, who was certainly not one to use one word when three would do. "Then I would say that we are at a bit of an impasse. For argument's sake, if I were to accept this discrepancy and agree with your opinion, then I would be faced with refusing the deal being offered and riding away without my friends getting the gold which they desire."

"That would probably be the case," Cole agreed.

"This would make my friends angry," McGaugh continued. "I would not want them angry, nor would *you*. May I remind you, sir, that we are several days' ride inside Blackfeet country and outnumbered. I suggest that our conversation never happened, and you may convey my heartfelt condolences to your friend, Mr. White Calf."

"If I had ridden all this way from Mr. White Buffalo Calf's camp alone," Cole began, "and if we really *were* outnumbered, I would be strongly inclined to agree with you . . . but that is not the case."

Turning toward the hillside, he raised his fist.

As the eyes of everyone in the valley turned to follow his gesture, Ómahkaatsistawa rode out onto a bluff, raised his rifle over his head and shouted the Siksikáwa greeting *"Oki!"*

Moments later, Ikutsikakatósi, in a far removed place, repeated the greeting. Cole was pleased that they had moved apart. This suggested that a much larger contingent was present.

Realizing that the deal was off and their position compromised, the horse thieves immediately moved to secure their assets and get out of their present predicament. The only way to do this was to stampede the herd and make a run for it.

There was a crackle of rifle fire to spook the horses, and the mass began to move.

Cole knew that the first volley was meant to stampede the horses, but any second volley would be designed to remove the inconvenient *nápikoan,* so he drew his Colt.

Almost immediately, he watched the leader of the thieves draw a bead on a startled Benjamin McGaugh.

Hoping that he had the range to make a difference, Cole aimed and fired.

He watched the man jerk sideways and tumble off his horse as his rifle flew through the air.

Mason had pulled a rifle from his scabbard and gotten off a couple of shots, but McGaugh was having too much trouble controlling his spooked horse to draw his gun.

Another of the renegades rode at Cole firing his rifle.

Keeping low, Cole ran at him rather than retreating, which seemed to surprise him a little.

In the split second that the man's hand was on the lever of his Winchester, Cole aimed and fired. The bullet caught him on the jaw and the lower part of his face exploded upward in a pink cloud.

It was not so much a running gun battle as a swirling gun battle. The horse herd had been grazing when it all started, with individual horses facing in every direction of the compass. Therefore, when the stampede began, it was a stampede that went nowhere but to turn like a cyclone, folding in upon itself and creating confusion and panic among the undisciplined herd.

Some of the renegades were in the midst of this, first trying to straighten the herd, then just trying not to be knocked off and trampled.

Other renegades were on the outside the cyclone. One fired at Cole. The miss was so close that Cole heard the lead hiss past his head like an angry hornet. When Cole's return shot struck the man's chest, he knew that it was a fatal hit.

Out of the corner of his eye, he saw three riders coming at full gallop from the woods, firing as they came. In the center was

Natoya-I-nis'kim. The Colt looked like a cannon in her small hand, yet she held it as steady as if it were bolted to her horse.

She had shed her buffalo robe, and it was obvious — at least to Cole — that her slender, bare arms were not those of a man. What would the renegades do when they saw that they were being attacked by a woman?

The answer was a split second of disbelief on the part of the nearest horse thief as she entered the fray, a split second that cost the man his life. Cole saw the big pistol buck in her hand and the man topple awkwardly from his horse.

Suddenly, Cole watched in unanticipated disbelief as she pointed the Colt directly at *him*! For a moment, he froze as he stared down the muzzle with her riding directly at him. She was scarcely fifteen feet away when he found himself staring down a muzzle flash.

Almost at the same moment, he heard a horrific shriek that seemed to come from his own shoulder.

He turned to see a man hovering in the air, almost on top of him. Blood was splattering everywhere, and the contorted expression on his face was that of the most frightening banshee imaginable.

As Natoya and her horse raced past him like a rocket, so close that Cole could feel the heat of her sweating mount, he realized what had happened. While he was distracted by the sight of her coming into the fight, one of the renegades had come within two feet of him for a certain kill.

Natoya-I-nis'kim had just saved his life.

The thunder of hooves — both panicked and purposeful, clamoring within an immense and growing cloud of dust — was punctuated by screams of anger and screams of pain — and by gunshots.

Bladen Cole looked around. His eyes probed the choking yellow dust. He had emptied his revolver, dropping three men. He had now drawn his Winchester from its scabbard, and his eyes searched for more targets. Suddenly, he saw them, two riders who had bolted, leaving the scene and riding north at top speed.

He raised the rifle to his shoulder, sighted, and squeezed the trigger.

One man tumbled off his horse.

He hated to shoot a man in the back, but there was a job to be done. Again he aimed, but this time, before he could fire, he heard the crack of another rifle.

The rider jumped slightly, but did not fall.

The dust from his horse faded and disappeared into the distance.

Cole looked down. Ikutsikakatósi was just lowering his Trapdoor Springfield.

As the dust settled, he saw Natoya, riding hard to round up the stragglers from the stampeded herd. Realizing that she was the one working while her companions merely gawked at the battlefield, Cole went into action, chasing some stragglers and getting them back to the group.

Benjamin McGaugh, who had started the day with a simple horse-buying trip, sat on the ground staring at the lifeless body of his hired man and gripping a blood-soaked sleeve.

He was uncharacteristically speechless when Bladen Cole knelt beside him, ripped off his shirt, and constructed a tourniquet.

"You seem to know what you're doing," he said weakly.

"Learned it in the war," Cole said succinctly.

"Oh yeah," said McGaugh with a nod. "The war."

The two men could tell by their respective accents that they had been on opposite sides. It had been a long time, but nobody who was there would ever forget the war.

Cole stood him up and walked him to the

nearby stream so that he could get a drink.

As McGaugh sat at the edge of the water, he began to shake, not from the cold, because the afternoon had proved to be fairly warm, but from the onset of shock.

Natoya, who had retrieved her buffalo robe, rode up, dismounted, and without a word, wrapped it around his shoulders.

With that, she lay down and submerged her face in the gurgling waters of the creek. After what seemed to Cole and McGaugh to have been about two minutes, she sat up abruptly, shook her wet braids vigorously and, obviously refreshed, smiled a smile which, had Cole been a poet — which he was not — he would have called angelic.

"Thank you," Cole said, looking at her, she who had been *his* guardian angel. "Thanks for saving my life out there."

She looked down and then off to the horizon, still smiling, and began to blush.

The only sounds were the gurgling of the stream and the background racket of Ikutsikakatósi and Ómahkaatsistawa searching for trophies among their fallen enemies.

CHAPTER 9

The sun was dropping into the storm clouds enveloping the peaks of the Rockies when four horses and three riders lumbered into the isolated trading post on the river which the Siksikáwa called "Two Medicine" because it flowed out of the mountain valley where the sundance lodges of rival Siksikáwa bands stood side by side in a celebration of tribal unity. It was ironic, Cole thought, after a day marked by such deadly tribal *disunity.*

Across the saddle of the riderless horse was tied the body of the half-breed named Mason, whose Yankee father had wed a Siksikáwa woman in this land many years ago.

Bladen Cole and young Natoya-I-nis'kim had accompanied the wounded Benjamin McGaugh to this place, having agreed to a proposal made by Ikutsikakatósi and Ómahkaatsistawa that they be allowed to return the herd of recovered *ponokáómitaa* to

O-mis-tai-po-kah. They had wished to do this because it would allow them to save face in light of the fact that the bloody work of actually killing the thieves and the mundane work of rounding up the heard had been done mainly by a *nápikoan* and a *woman.*

Cole was happy to go along with this. He had done his part and paid the dues that bought him the credentials and credibility among the Siksikáwa that he would need to move about in their land and continue his manhunt.

Natoya was happy to do this as well. She was tired of the jealous taunting of the young men and relished the respect that she had earned, and now enjoyed, from this stranger from a distant world.

Benjamin McGaugh had begun to regain his composure by the time that he was delivered into the capable hands of the trader at the Two Medicine trading post. The trader and his wife were decidedly more conversant than the Porter boys in how to doctor a bullet wound, and therefore, the would-be horse buyer was spared the anguished fate that had been that of poor Milton Waller.

When the bullet had been removed, the wound cauterized, and a whiskey-sated Mc-

Gaugh was left snoring in another room, Cole sat down with the trader to ask some questions.

"Three white men?" the man asked rhetorically in reply to the bounty hunter's query. "Yes, done heard tell . . . about three days ago . . . over around Heart Butte."

"Three *nápikoan* gunslingers show up out here, and people tend to notice," the man's wife interjected. "Talk is going around that these characters are hoping to winter out in these parts."

"Damn fool thing to contemplate," the trader added.

"Guess that makes you and me a coupla damned fools," his wife said with an ironic grin.

At this, the two of them laughed hysterically.

The bounty hunter merely smiled. The phrase "stir crazy" entered his mind but went unverbalized.

Natoya stared without expression. Either she didn't quite grasp the joke, or she felt it insulting that someone would consider it foolish to winter where her people had wintered since the beginning of time.

"Where *exactly* would they be wintering, if they *did* winter out here?" Cole asked.

"Oh probably over at Heart Butte," the

wife said.

"Yeah," said her husband. "That would be old Double Runner's band. He's been known to take in all manner of scalawags and fugitives from down south of the Marias. Law can't touch 'em up here, and he likes using them as hired guns."

"I've seen that happen in this country," Cole nodded, with a knowing look at Natoya.

Cole and Natoya-I-nis'kim accepted the hospitality of the trader, ate his food, and camped near the three-room building that constituted the trading post.

As Cole stoked the fire so that it would be with them through the entire night, Natoya reclined on the opposite side of the fire wrapped in her buffalo robe. She continued to relish the opportunity to use her English words with a willing listener.

"Do you know the story of A-koch-kit-ope . . . the one who the *nápikoan* call the 'Medicine Grizzly'?" she asked as the conversation turned to the powerful and magic creature of which they had spoken the night before.

"Nope, but I'd sure be happy to hear *you* tell it . . . and I like stories told around campfires . . ."

He was going to add the phrase "by beautiful girls with the firelight flickering in their deep, dark eyes," but he did not.

"If it was a *nápikoan* story it would start with 'once upon a time,' " she laughed.

Cole laughed too. He liked her sense of humor and her ability to make word jokes in a language not her own.

"Go ahead and tell it that way," he said with a smile.

"Okay, once upon a time, Stock-stchi, whose name means 'Bear Cub,' was telling stories about a war party he had led across the mountains to attack the Kotoksspi, the people who live over there to the west. You know, the people who the *nápikoan* calls the 'Flathead.' It was a warm summer night . . . not like this one . . . and he sent his wife to get water. She saw a stranger in the light of the moon."

Cole enjoyed the smoothness of her gestures as she signed the expression for getting water, then pointed to the moon.

"The stranger was part of a raiding party from the Piik-siik-sii-naa people, who call themselves A'aninin."

"What does Piik-siik-sii-naa mean?" Cole asked.

" 'Snakes,' " Natoya said.

" 'Snakes'?" Cole repeated with mock indignation.

"You white people call them by the name Gros Ventre, which means 'big bellies,' " she laughed.

Cole couldn't help shaking his head with an ironic half grin. Outsiders from all sides seemed to have unflattering nicknames for the poor A'aninin people. Of course, people everywhere seem to have derogatory names for *other* tribes. He recalled the names that his fellow Virginians had for the freed slaves, and how the Lakota had named white people "bacon thieves."

"The Siksikáwa attacked the A'aninin before they could attack," she continued, making a point of using the tribe's name for its own people. "And they killed the whole raiding party except one man, who was a *natoápina,* a medicine man. They shot many arrows at him, but he could not be killed."

"Reminds me of what my people say about the grizzly," Cole interjected, "that it can't be killed."

"Exactly," Natoya said. "You are understanding the story already. The man shouted that his name was A-koch-kit-ope, and he had powerful medicine . . . and the Siksikáwa believed he did. He said he would stay to guard his dead brothers so the Siksikáwa would not take trophies."

"Scalps?" Cole asked, more as a statement than a question.

Natoya nodded, then continued.

"The next day, they killed A-koch-kit-ope, but it took all of them to do it. They discovered that he had an *apóhkiááyo* claw . . . like the one you gave to me last night . . . tied into his hair. They realized that he had the spirit and power of the grizzly, and they were frightened. So they burned his body."

Natoya nodded toward their own fire and explained, gesturing as she did, how they captured all the embers that escaped so that they could destroy and contain his grizzly medicine.

"Did it work?" Cole asked, entranced by the motions of her hands as she told the story.

"No," she said with a graceful shrug that eloquently added, "They should have known better."

"A-koch-kit-ope reappeared as the Medicine Grizzly," she said, signing that it was a fait accompli. "This huge *apóhkiááyo* followed their trail and killed many of them the next time they made camp. When the Siksikáwa went back the next year to camp in the place where the story started, a large *apóhkiááyo* came into their camp the first night, scaring the horses and killing the dogs. The people were so scared when they saw it was A-koch-kit-ope. They did not dare to shoot at him. Even now, he is seen in the same place by a lake . . . deep inside the mountains. He is seen only by night, and he is never attacked because he is A-koch-kit-ope, the Medicine Grizzly."

Natoya-I-nis'kim smiled and reached to a narrow rawhide thong that she had around her neck. She pulled it from beneath the front of her buckskin dress and showed it to him. Woven to the end, in an elaborate and intricate pattern crafted by herself, was the grizzly claw that he had given her the night before.

"*Apóhkiááyo* gave you the power of his spirit," she said, the reflection of the fire twinkling in her eyes like stars. "And you gave that to me, and that was how you were saved from the Káínawa bullet today."

And that was the story told by the fireside that night.

Bladen Cole awoke to the feel of warm breath against his cheek. His first thought was naturally of the grizzly, but this was not a grizzly.

Had it been only two days since he had awakened to the hot breathing of the roan nuzzling him awake?

Then, it was a snorting, nudging, rude awakening. Today — or, more properly, tonight, as no sun warmed the world — the bounty hunter opened his eyes to the most divine of apparitions.

It was a phantom that drifted like sweet incense in the indistinct dimension between dream and dream-come-true.

Above him in the moonlight knelt Natoya-I-nis'kim. Her body, the most perfect of bodies, was clothed as it had been at the moment of her birth. Her long, jet-black hair, freed from the tightly wound braids, moved and flowed freely and most elegantly in the light breeze.

"Wake up," the Siksikáwa maiden whispered in a tone as rude to the dreamer as had been the prodding of the roan. "We must go . . . quickly."

It was, alas, a vision that quickly melded into reality, as she moved to clothe her most perfect of bodies as it had been clothed yesterday.

Their plan had been to start out at dawn, but Cole saw no dawn on any horizon, only the billion tiny campfires that dotted the heavens from edge to edge.

"It's the middle of the night," he pleaded weakly as he watched her put on her buckskin dress and gather up her robe. He did not bother to look at the watch in his pocket, but guessed it to be no later than four.

"We must go," she insisted. "We must be in Moisskitsipahpiistaki . . . Heart Butte . . . at dawn. I wakened with a thought in my mind. As the words of three men coming were being told across this country, words of *you* are spreading as well. You have heard of *them*. They will hear of *you*. We must go quickly."

As much as he would have rather spent the next hour — or the next lifetime — watching her in the moonlight, Cole knew that she was right.

They bade good-bye to the trader's wife, who was making her way to the outhouse as they mounted their horses, and rode away, guided by the stars.

"Kokumekis kokatosix kummokit spummokit!" Natoya said happily, looking up.

"Yeah, I agree . . . it's fun to look at the stars," Cole laughed, presuming that her words celebrated the heavenly spectacle of a clear night on the cusp of winter.

"That is a saying we have," she said, continuing to gaze skyward. "I guess it is sort of a prayer . . . asking the moon and stars to give me strength."

"I sort of guessed that," Cole said, putting the stress on the phrase "sort of."

"They *hated* this prayer at the mission school . . . they wouldn't let us say things like that. Finally an old padre came and asked about our prayers. At last, there was a black robe who understood . . . He thought it was splendid too."

"Me too," Cole agreed, looking at the stars.

"He was also one who understood about the *nátosini,* the power of Es-tonea-pesta," she laughed, pulling her buffalo robe tight about her.

"Who's *that?*"

"The maker of cold weather," she smiled.

"Yeah, he's sure working overtime to-night," Cole agreed.

In the predawn darkness, Es-tonea-pesta had the temperature near zero by the reckoning of the white man named Fahrenheit, but Bladen Cole felt sufficiently warmed merely by the presence of the girl named for the elusive Buffalo Stone.

"Tell me about Double Runner," he said after they had ridden for about another half hour.

"His name is Isokoyokinni in Siksikáwa," she said. "He is named for the footrace between the antelope and the deer. He lives *nápikoan*-style in a wooden house and takes in strangers. You can always find at least one *nápikoan* in his camp."

"The trader made him sound like as much of a scalawag as the scalawags he takes in," Cole said.

"I do not know this word."

"It means rascal . . . troublemaker."

"I do not think this of Isoko-yo-kinni," she said. "He is self-important, and he likes to have property and *nápikoan* things, but he is not *bad*. I think the trader sees him as a rival. Not every *nápikoan* who sleeps in Isoko-yo-kinni's camp . . . who rides in Siksikáwa land . . . comes to make trouble."

Cole nodded in agreement. *He* was a *nápikoan* who was riding in Siksikáwa land.

Just as it was stirring to life for the day, they arrived on a bluff near the heart-shaped butte from which the settlement took its name.

There were many tipis and a few clapboard buildings, making it a metropolis by comparison with the other places that Cole had visited in Blackfeet country. Around and among the tipis, a few women were stirring cooking fires to life while their men still slept. A couple of kids were running about, shouting and laughing.

"You should wait here," Natoya said. "I

will ride down and see what I can discover."

She was right. A white man with a Colt on his hip would attract a great deal of unwanted attention. A lone Indian woman appearing in an awakening settlement would blend in seamlessly — so long as her own Colt remained discreetly concealed beneath her robe.

Cole watched as she dismounted and led her horse through the fringes of the encampment. He could see her breath in the cold air as she spoke to the women who were cooking the morning meal. He could see her gestures and those of the women with whom she spoke.

Demonstrating no particular urgency, she worked her way through the camp toward the cluster of wooden buildings.

At last, he watched as her head turned directly, though very briefly, toward him. Her quick, though characteristically graceful hand gesture indicated that it was time for the *nápikoan* to ride into town.

Following her lead, he came slowly and casually, winding his way, rather than riding directly toward the building near which she stood. His heart skipped a beat, however, when he saw her go inside.

Gideon and Enoch Porter sat at a table eating a porridge of venison, while Jimmy Goode poured a cup of coffee — a distinct rarity in Blackfeet country — near a cookstove, which was another rarity in this country. Double Runner, wearing a white man's shirt and vest, sat at the table with the Porter boys.

Their conversation stopped when the door opened and a young woman stepped in.

"Oki, i'taamikskanaotonni," Double Runner said, greeting her and bidding her good morning.

"Tsa niita'piiwa, Isoko-yo-kinni?" she said politely and appropriately for a young person speaking to an elder, asking after his health.

"Tsiiksi'taami'tsihp nomohkootsiito'toohpa, Natoya-I-nis'kim," he said, recognizing her, and knowing that she was a relative of O-mis-tai-po-kah, whom he knew well, and saying that he was pleased to have her visit his home.

"Tsiikaahsi'tsihp nito'toohs," she said with a smile, replying that she was happy to be there.

The white men sat in stunned silence, reacting to Natoya's uncommon beauty as Bladen Cole had when he first met her.

"Who's this pretty little thing that's just walked in here?" Enoch Porter said, pushing the tin plate of porridge aside and rising to his feet.

"Sit down and finish your goddamn breakfast," Gideon snarled at his impulsively brazen younger brother.

"To hell with eatin' breakfast," Enoch said, taking a step toward Natoya. "I'd be wanting me a little taste of *squaw.*"

"*Tahkaa kiisto?*" she said angrily, demanding to know who he thought he was.

"Got a tongue on ya, doncha?" Enoch laughed. "Betcha this squaw knows how to buck."

"Sit down and leave her be!" Double Runner demanded, standing up and reaching for his rifle.

"Don't do it," Gideon said, firmly gripping the gun and pulling it away from its owner.

Turning to Enoch, he repeated his demand that his little brother sit back down.

Again, his brother ignored him.

"Gimme little kiss, *squaw,*" he said, grabbing her arm.

As his face neared hers, the disgusting odor of his breath nearly gagged her, but she managed to let fly and spit into his face with as much force as she could muster.

He staggered backward, momentarily stunned.

"Oh, you *are* a fighter, you little bitch," he said as he wiped his face with his sleeve. "If it's a fight you want, a fight you shall have!"

With a laugh, he seized and twisted her wrist, and her buffalo robe fell to the floor.

With her other hand, she drew her old Colt.

Without hesitation, as his eyes grew to the size of the plate from which he had been eating porridge, she squeezed the trigger.

Cli-ick.

The sound of the misfire echoed through the room, which was suddenly devoid of all other sound.

Enoch angrily snatched the gun from her small hand and threw it hard across the room.

Pushing her onto the floor, he grabbed roughly at her clothing and drew his knife.

"When I'm finished with this pretty little doe . . ." he said, licking his lips and touching her cheek with the steel blade. "I'm gonna mess up this pretty little face so's I'm the last one who ever lays eyes on —"

His words were swallowed by the thunder of an explosion, followed immediately by another.

The porridge of bone and flesh that had once been the back of Enoch Porter's head distributed itself randomly on the far wall of the room.

Jimmy Goode's quivering hand lost its grip on his coffee cup.

Gideon Porter's hand went for his own gun.

Bladen Cole's reproachful advice, supported by a gun aimed directly at Gideon's head, was that he should *not* do that.

CHAPTER 10

Relieved of his sidearm, a sullen Gideon Porter sat upon his horse, his wrists restrained by old army-issue prison manacles. The chain was looped through the gullet beneath his saddle horn, inextricably fastening him to the saddle. He bit his lip in reaction to the biting cold and to the bitter realization that he had been caught.

He watched as his little brother, now a rapidly cooling corpse wrapped in a cast-off scrap of canvas, was tied across the saddle on which he had ridden into Heart Butte the day before.

"Damn you, Enoch," his brother hissed quietly. Had it not been for Enoch's uncontrolled sadism, Mary Phillips would still be alive, and the cycle of events that had been neither anticipated nor desired by anyone would never have led to this humiliating moment.

They had gone to a house to kill three

men, but by Gideon's reasoning, Enoch's killing a woman with no good reason had ignited the fires of outrage that had put a bounty hunter on their trail — a bounty hunter who had apparently not feared following that trail into Blackfeet country.

Gideon had assumed they would be safe in this land of barbarians.

Gideon had been wrong.

"Damn you, Enoch," his brother hissed quietly. "Why the hell did you have to go after that damnable squaw?"

Had it not been for Enoch's impetuous, hotheaded lust, there would have been three guns to take on the bounty hunter. At least there would have been *two* — because, after all, Jimmy Goode was good for *nothing*.

Barely fifteen minutes ago, Jimmy had been enjoying a cup of coffee — poor coffee, but still coffee — but now both he and Gideon were manacled to their saddles in the icy arctic wind. Events had unfolded more quickly and with more complexity than the limited capabilities of Jimmy Goode's mind could process.

A squaw on the floor, and Enoch's brains on the wall.

A *very angry* squaw with Enoch's knife, and Enoch's manhood in Double Runner's potbellied heating stove.

Normally, Double Runner would have been displeased to have guests treated so harshly and blood spattered all around his parlor, but after what he had seen Enoch try to do to Natoya-I-nis'kim, he agreed entirely with the fate meted out to Enoch Porter by the bounty hunter.

After what Cole had told him about them, Double Runner was doubly pleased to be rid of the surviving strangers.

The Siksikáwa leader was also delighted that Cole had made the gesture of presenting him with Enoch's finely tooled leather boots, a pair which Cole had seen him admiring. Double Runner was pleased with this favor and called for his son and two other young men to ride with the bounty hunter and his prisoners as far as O-mis-tai-po-kah's camp.

As they rode out, all were silent.

There was nothing much to be said.

The two outlaws rode in the center, their horses roped together, flanked by the Blackfeet men, who were as eager to see them going away to justice as the bounty hunter. Cole rode behind, where he could watch his prisoners. He was flanked by Natoya, who rode parallel to him at a distance of about a dozen yards.

As Cole watched, over the first few miles,

the taut muscles in her face gradually relaxed. Rage had turned to anger. Anger had been slowly but surely consumed by the soothing mitigation of retribution having been exacted.

At last she shot him a glance, and he saw that for the first time, the frown had disappeared from her face. It was not exactly a smile, but it was an expression of thanks.

Cole nodded and touched the brim of his hat.

In the space of two days, they had each saved the other in dramatic fashion, thereby establishing a bond not unlike that of soldiers.

Cole had experienced this in those frenzied final days of the war, when the skirmishing seemed to run the length and breadth of Virginia's fields and farmsteads. He had saved a man's life, actually several lives on several occasions, and found his own preserved by the intervention of others more than once.

His mind wandered to those days, and to the lives preserved and the lives lost. Back then, momentous events involving tens of thousands of lives moved rapidly. In those days, there would have been no way to imagine long hours on these infinite, windswept plains where the mind could be allowed to sink into the monotonous reverie of contemplation.

"How many sleeps?" Natoya asked, pointing to the two prisoners and the distant horizon.

"Maybe four," Cole said.

His mind, having been allowed to sink into reverie, had just been contemplating the immense scale of the West in the abstract. Making conversation in an attempt to break the icy silence that had prevailed between them, Natoya had brought him back from the abstract to the real.

"Maybe more," Cole said with a lessened conviction that begged and received the addition of the phrase "maybe a week . . . or so."

She nodded.

Like him, she understood that it would take him longer to return with prisoners than it had for him to get here alone. A lone rider in pursuit of a quarry moves much more quickly than a man slowed by a pair of charges who would just as soon cut his throat as cast him a cutting glance.

Indeed, it might take a week. He would just have to see.

Montana Territory was a big place.

Around noon, as the glow of the autumn sun stood as high in the overcast sky as it would that day, he pulled a scrap of pemmican from his pocket and shared it with her.

For the first time since Heart Butte, she smiled.

So did he.

How could he not smile at the bashful way that she grinned and looked away with her face, but not her eyes. It was like when he had thanked her for saving his life.

After that, they made small talk. He asked about the missionary school. She asked about the place from which he came and wrinkled her forehead in bewilderment as he tried to explain how far away it was.

The West was a big place, and the East was still many, many sleeps beyond. He wondered what she would make of a place like Denver, or Kansas City, or Richmond.

The light was fading when they first saw the many smokes of O-mis-tai-po-kah's camp on the horizon, and nearly gone when they crested the ridge and saw the campfires.

The size of the camp had nearly doubled since Cole had seen it last, and the level of activity spread out before him between the tipis told him that the men who had traveled to the east to hunt buffalo had come home. By the looks of things, they had not returned empty-handed.

Riding through the edges of the camp, Cole noticed that Natoya-I-nis'kim was looking around intently.

Suddenly, she nudged the withers of her horse and galloped ahead a short distance, to where a group of hunters were unloading the fruits of their labors.

With one, graceful, fluid motion, she slid off her horse, shed her buffalo robe, and jumped on one of the men. Had he not been a tall, powerfully built man, she would have knocked him over. Instead, it was he who pulled her off her feet, raising her face to meet his. As they embraced, Cole understood in a moment who he was, and what he meant to her.

At last, as the hunter let her feet once again touch the ground, she turned and pointed to Cole. Pulling the man's hand, she practically dragged him to where the bounty hunter was dismounting.

Natoya introduced the tall man as Sinopaa, the man she loved and planned to marry.

As Cole signed a greeting, the man's expression said that her description of this *nápikoan* stranger with whom his fiancée had spent the last several days had painted him as one of the good guys.

"*Oki . . . napi,*" Sinopaa said, grabbing Cole's hand in a reasonable facsimile of a white man's handshake. The bounty hunter knew enough Blackfeet to know that the greeting was a formal one, meaning "hello, friend," and was reserved for use between men who truly respected each other. "*Tsiiksi'taami'tsihp nomohkootsiito'toohpa, Mr. Cool.*"

"He is happy to call you friend, and he is happy you are here," Natoya translated.

"Tell him that I am too," Cole replied.

O-mis-tai-po-kah rolled out a warm welcome for "Mr. Cool," inviting him to spend the night and to join in the celebration being held to welcome home the hunting party.

Even Ikutsikakatósi and Ómahkaatsistawa greeted Cole cordially. Though the two men had taken *most* of the credit for recovering the horses, they *had* acknowledged that the *nápikoan* gunman had participated bravely. Cole could tell by O-mis-tai-po-kah's wry grin that he understood the extent to which the two men had embellished the details. He was just glad to have his horses back.

The hunt having been successful, there were copious quantities of fresh meat, happily consumed by people who gathered around large fires near the center of the encampment. Being a guest, Cole was offered a hump steak, considered to be the prime cut, which he enjoyed. Porter and Goode, who spent the night chained to a pair of cottonwoods near the stream, were fed less desirable parts of the buffalo.

As the dinner party unfolded, Cole's eye was drawn, naturally, to his young friend, Natoya-I-nis'kim. He watched in the flickering firelight as she and Sinopaa sat beside each other on the periphery of the crowd, talking — and even giggling — like the young lovers they were.

He was happy for her, happy that she had a man who cared for her as much as he obviously did. At the same time, though, he could not help being jealous of Sinopaa. She was a beautiful woman for whom he had, himself, developed a great fondness.

Though Cole had imagined himself with her, he knew that such imaginings were unrealistic in the extreme. There was no place for her in the world of the *nápikoan,* or for him in her world. Sinopaa was a lucky man, and Cole knew that he knew it.

At one point, Cole glanced away to converse briefly with a man seated near him, and when he glanced back, Natoya and Sinopaa were no longer there. He smiled and reached to slice off another piece from the meat that hung over the fragrantly crackling cottonwood.

CHAPTER 11

The four white men — a bounty hunter, his two prisoners, and the remains of the late Enoch Porter — were on the trail even as the sun was a cold sliver on the eastern horizon.

Estoneapesta, whom the Blackfeet believed to be responsible for bringing the cold weather, had been plying his trade. It had not snowed overnight, but the frost was thick on the windblown prairie grass, and everyone's breath was visible, except Enoch's of course. At least the freezing temperatures made transporting a corpse more tolerable than it would have been in the heat of summer.

The two men from Double Runner's band who had ridden with them from Heart Butte had headed home, but as a friendly gesture, O-mis-tai-po-kah had assigned Ikutsikakatósi and Ómahkaatsistawa to ride with "Mr. Cool" as far as the Marias River.

He welcomed the company.

Though they were manacled to their saddles, the two felons still presented the potential for danger. So long as Porter and Goode were outnumbered three to two, they were unlikely to try anything, but once he was across the Marias, Cole knew that the tables would be turned.

As he had the previous day, Cole brought up the rear, positioning himself where he could watch without being watched. His helpers, meanwhile, functioned as outriders, ranging right and left of the manacled men. Because the country was so open, it was easy for four widely separated riders to travel abreast.

He had tied the horses ridden by Porter and Goode together with a forty-foot rope and ordered them to remain that far separated. Being tied together, and with Enoch Porter's horse tied to his brother's, they were unlikely to try to make an escape. This arrangement would also reduce, if not prevent, their talking to one another without him overhearing what they said.

It was not that either man was doing a great deal of talking. As yesterday, they sat silently and sullenly as the miles ticked slowly by.

Jimmy Goode, the young oaf who had, like

so many young oafs, gotten himself in over his head with bad company, displayed a jittery fear more than any other emotion. He feared being brought to justice and hanged, of course, but he also feared the wrath of Gideon Porter if they ever came within an arm's length of each other. Then too Gideon had told him that they were within a hair's breadth — as Gideon had sarcastically phrased it in an aside the day before — of having their hair lifted with a Blackfeet hunting knife.

Gideon Porter's expression betrayed anger, directed both at the world at large and, for their being caught, at the hapless Jimmy Goode, simply for being, as usual, good for nothing.

As Goode twitched and Porter stewed, Cole's mind wandered.

The only element absent from yesterday in his carefully arranged procession across the Plains was the company of Natoya-I-nis'kim. Though it was his preference to ride alone, he missed the pleasure of her shy smile and the pleasure of her company during long hours in the saddle in monotonous terrain.

"*Aakattsinootsiiyo'p* . . . we'll meet again" were the last words that Natoya had spoken as she waved good-bye that morning.

He was left to ponder whether she meant the phrase merely as a perfunctory "see you later" or as a more purposeful "we *will* see one another again." She probably meant him to ponder it — in a half-flirting, half "I hope you don't forget me" way. And so he pondered, all morning and into the afternoon.

She was perceptive beyond her years and no doubt knew how he felt. Like him, she recognized that they had developed a friendship that was and would remain, despite the unique bond of mutual life-saving, just and only that.

Soon she would be out of his mind — or so he insisted to himself.

They camped for the night overlooking the Marias. Of the four, five, or more sleeps to come, this would be the last one when Cole would not be alone with his captives. He had decided to avoid Fort Benton and stick to the open country as he headed south. The potential for complications associated with riding into an essentially lawless town with two criminals, two Indians, and a dead body was just too great.

Bladen Cole awoke with a start.

It was bitter cold, but quiet. Had the north wind not died down, he never would have heard it.

There it was again.

It was a crushing, snapping sound like a bear might make. He glanced quickly to where the horses were. They were standing calmly. Had there been a bear or a wolf in the vicinity, they would have been snorting and pawing the ground. They were not.

As he got his hand on his Colt and began to roll out of his bedroll, he saw something, or someone, moving. A moment later, he identified this something and squeezed his trigger.

In the cold, still air, the sound of a .45-caliber round being fired had the comparative effect of five pounds of dynamite going off.

In the muzzle flash, he caught a quick view of an angry face.

Gideon Porter, who had tried to sneak noiselessly to where the horses were tied, had been caught in the act and needed an alternate plan, immediately.

As Bladen Cole came toward him, he reached for the nearest weapon that he could see in the light of the quarter moon — Ikutsikakatósi's Trapdoor Springfield.

Meanwhile, Ikutsikakatósi had awakened suddenly at the sound of the pistol shot, and he reacted by grabbing his rifle back.

Cole's instinct told him to take an easy shot and send Gideon Porter to join his brother at the Devil's table, but instinct was outweighed by his commitment to justice. For that to be done back in Gallatin City, Gideon Porter would have to point his finger at the man who planned the crime that the Porter boys had carried out, and dead men can't point fingers.

He fired a second shot, aiming to miss the shadowy form of Gideon Porter, but to do so by as narrow a margin as possible.

Both Ikutsikakatósi and Porter paused, but only for the second that it took Cole to reach them.

In the split second that followed, Cole saw the flash of Ikutsikakatósi's knife coming out of its sheath like a bolt of lightning.

In the flash of a further second, split narrower than the sharp edge of Ikutsikakató-si's blade, Cole slugged Porter in the face with his gun hand.

The impact of a metal weapon striking his face with the tremendous force of Cole's blow, combined with poor footing on dark, uneven terrain, sent Porter sprawling backward.

Two men moved like pouncing cougars toward the fallen man.

One reached him by a margin of a split

second, sliced as thinly as a split second can be sliced.

Bladen Cole stomped his boot on Porter's neck, both because he knew it would immobilize him and because he knew that this neck was the destination of Ikutsikakatósi's eight-inch blade.

Cole fired a third shot into the ground eight inches above Porter's head. The feel of the gravel kicked up by such an impact was frighteningly indistinguishable from being hit.

As Cole had hoped, Ikutsikakatósi paused.

Cole dragged Porter to his feet in the moonlight, noticing that his face was sheeted by the dark shadows of blood, flowing both from his face and from his scalp.

Feeling Ikutsikakatósi nudging closer, with the probable intention of relieving Porter of that bloody scalp, Cole slugged the outlaw once again.

This time, Porter fell with a thud and made no effort to get up.

A half minute of gunsmoke and spattering blood was followed by nearly ten minutes of diplomacy as Cole tried, using sign language in the dim moonlight, to convince Ikutsikakatósi and Ómahkaatsistawa not to finish what Cole had left unfinished.

Finally, the negotiations reached a compromise.

Ikutsikakatósi agreed to forgo the taking of Porter's scalp in exchange for his boots, finely tooled like those of his brother, which were now on Double Runner's feet.

Cole also agreed to Ómahkaatsistawa's insistence that they throw in Enoch Porter's saddle, though not without some demonstrative complaining. Cole really didn't care. He argued only in the spirit of keeping up the bargaining, to add perceived value to the saddle. Enoch would certainly not be needing it.

With light already starting to appear in the east, the two Siksikáwa decided that it was time to get an early start on their trip home.

They said their farewells to "Mr. Cool," claiming, as he did to them, that they would be friends forever.

Nevertheless, Cole waited for about an hour before he made his way down to the river to get water to clean Gideon Porter's wounds. He was not fully convinced that these impetuous young men would not double back in the hope of catching Porter unattended.

In the gathering light of the promise of daytime, Cole could see what had happened. He had manacled Porter to a small aspen — mainly because there were no *large* aspen out here where the punishing winds blew — and the resourceful miscreant had actually climbed the tree to get the chain over the top. In so doing, he had bent the small tree over. The sound that awoke Cole had been that of the tree snapping back when Porter climbed off.

Just as Porter realized that he had dodged three bullets from Cole's gun in a literal way, Cole knew that he too had dodged a bullet of the figurative kind, whose potential was no less deadly.

If he had, as Natoya-I-nis'kim believed, inherited the medicine of the grizzly, such power had failed him.

Or had it?

CHAPTER 12

"Father, you have a letter here from your bounty hunter," Hannah Ransdell said. She had just returned to the bank from the post office and was sorting the mail, as she typically did each morning.

"I hope that he has some good news," Isham Ransdell said, approaching his daughter's desk. Hannah had started working at her father's bank when she was still in high school, but her duties had gradually increased and evolved and had long since warranted her maintaining a well-used desk not far from that of Mr. Duffy, the accountant who kept the ledgers. Duffy may have been the custodian of the numbers, but Hannah was the custodian of the customers. She knew them all by name and knew what sorts of accounts they all had at the bank.

"When was it mailed?" Isham Ransdell asked.

"A week ago from Fort Benton," she said, looking at the postmark.

"Never thought I'd see the day when you could get a letter all the way from Fort Benton to Gallatin City in just a week," Ransdell said, taking the letter.

"It'll be a lot faster than a steamer down the Missouri to Fort Union when the telegraph goes in," Hannah observed, handing her father a letter opener.

She watched curiously as he slit open the envelope and took out two pieces of paper, one a letter and the other an official-looking document. He handed the latter to Hannah out of force of habit. Through her experience at his bank, she had become so adept at grasping the legal wording of official documents that he often joked with her that he did not need the high-priced legal services of his associate, the attorney Virgil Stocker.

"Mr. Cole writes that Milton Waller is deceased," Isham said, scanning the handwritten note. "He goes on to say that he will be pursuing the Porter boys into Blackfeet country. What does that document have to tell us?"

"Much the same," Hannah said, handing it to her father. "It's a death certificate for Mr. Waller, signed by the Choteau County

152

sheriff and the coroner. The cause of death is 'complications due to a gunshot.' "

"Well, it seems as though Mr. Cole has earned part of his fee," Ransdell observed. "I wish him luck among the savages in Blackfeet country. I can recall the day when you had to worry about the Indians even in these parts."

"Yes, Father," Hannah said with a smile, humoring him as she always did when he reminisced about the "old days." Even though the "Custer Massacre" had taken place but three years before in the same territory where they were, the days of the epic struggle between two irreconcilably distinct civilizations seemed distant in time and place.

"In Blackfeet country, it's different," her father insisted. "General Miles may have run the Sioux and the Nez Perce to ground out here, but north of the Marias, it is an untamed world, untouched by civilization."

"Yes, Father," Hannah said with a serious face.

Hannah went back to sorting the mail, delivering three more letters to her father, and handing off a couple that required the attention of Mr. Duffy. She then set to work responding to the remaining queries and missives herself, as she typically did.

Most of the communications were as dry as the dust on Gallatin City's main street in August, but as she systematically worked her way through the pile, she came across one that she found particularly touching.

It was from Mr. Dawson Phillips, Jr., the son of the couple who had been murdered at the Blaine residence. In his letter to the bank, he expressed the great sadness of losing both parents to a violent criminal, and wrote that he would be coming to Gallatin City from Denver to settle the affairs of his late parents. He requested a meeting with Isham Ransdell, who was, of course, his father's banker.

Hannah checked the calendar that she kept of her father's appointments and noted that he would have time available in the week of Mr. Phillips's estimated arrival. She wrote back that a meeting could be arranged.

When she had finished the paperwork that required her immediate attention, she stamped the letters and put them into her bag.

"Father, may I get you anything?" Hannah said, sticking her head into her father's office. "I'm going to the post office with the outgoing and to Mr. Blaine's store for some ink and banker's pins."

"I find a lump in my throat at each mention of 'Blaine's store,' " he said sadly, looking up from his desk and wistfully removing his glasses. "It's hard to truly grasp the idea that he is gone."

"Yes, I understand," she said. "I feel that way myself."

The Gallatin City General Mercantile and Dry Goods, known locally as "Mr. Blaine's store," was still draped in black bunting. Leticia Blaine had insisted on it, and the store's general manager saw no reason to argue with his boss's widow.

The whole town was taking it hard. The hierarchy of society in any community will have its highs and its lows. It will have its center, and it will have its fringe. In the society of Gallatin City, the front and center had, until recently, been occupied by the Big Four of Blaine, Phillips, Ransdell, and Stocker. The loss of two men and Mrs. Phillips from among the most prominent figures in the community had left a tangible and powerful void.

For Hannah Ransdell, the black bunting prompted an eerie feeling. Since that night, she had been haunted by the notion that a bullet meant for her father had gone untriggered in that room. She had come within the minute thickness of a hair from losing her father and everything that mattered in her life.

Hannah loved her father, but she had *also* come to derive great satisfaction from her job. Her father knew, without having commented, that she had deliberately made herself indispensable to the running of the family business. Mr. Duffy knew it, and was happy with the situation. He was nervous around people, more comfortable beneath his green eyeshade working with his numbers, while Hannah's cheerful demeanor and intuitive personal skills had become the face of the Gallatin City Bank and Trust Company.

Edward J. Olson, on the other hand, was a man who believed that a woman's place was not in the affairs of a bank, or in business matters of any kind. Though he spent most of his time managing Isham Ransdell's other affairs and was rarely at the bank, Hannah's father often referred to him as his "right-hand man."

Despite the role that Hannah had carved out for herself, her father had never referred to her as his "right-hand woman." Hannah knew that if anything ever happened to her father, his right-hand man would ensure that there would be no woman of any hand at the Gallatin City Bank.

This would leave her having to start considering offers from eligible bachelors, which was something she had resisted, knowing that few men in Gallatin City and its environs would be pleased with a wife who spent her days at a job outside the home.

"Hello, Miss Ransdell, how *are* you today, dear?"

The voice greeted Hannah almost the moment that she entered the store. It was Sarah Stocker. She was much more composed than she had been that night when she was found running down the street screaming about having witnessed the murders.

"Good day, Mrs. Stocker," Hannah said formally, affecting a slight curtsey, as was expected of younger women greeting older women in polite company. "I'm well . . . and you?"

"Thank you for asking," she said with a flourish. "It has been hard. The terrible memories . . . the nightmares . . . and poor Virgil."

"How is *he* getting on?" Hannah inquired.

"As well as can be expected under the circumstances. The wounds are healing . . . the physical ones, of course . . . but the doctor says there will be scarring on his fore-head. The one on his chin . . . well . . . you know men and their beards."

"Yes, ma'am." Hannah smiled. She liked the look of a man with a beard.

"He is still haunted by the deaths of his colleagues, of course," Mrs. Stocker continued. "Your father must feel that way as well."

"Yes, ma'am, but of course he did not have to *witness* the horror of the attacks as Mr. Stocker did . . . and *yourself* as well."

"It is the worst terror of my life, *and* I can recall the war coming dreadfully close to our home in Pennsylvania."

"They say it was about revenge?" Hannah said, expressing her statement as a question. The killings had been, and continued to be, the talk of the town, and everyone had taken as fact the assumption that the motive had been revenge directed at John Blaine. Nevertheless, the wheels that turned in the back of Hannah's mind had left her wondering if there was more to it than that.

"Of course," Mrs. Stocker said, reacting to a skeptical tone which the younger woman had unsuccessfully disguised. "They burst in and started killing people."

"Right away?"

"What?"

"The first thing when they broke in, they started killing people?"

"Well," Sarah Stocker said thoughtfully. Though the events of that evening gave her nightmares, they had also given her an element of celebrity in the town. She had come to take a certain perverse pleasure in the attention and the sympathy she received from her victimhood.

"Well, the *first* thing was that they asked for Mr. Blaine . . . next, my husband was struck. Then Gideon shot John Blaine and that wicked Enoch Porter shot poor Mary."

"You mentioned when we spoke before about Gideon Porter having said that the women were not *supposed* to be hurt," Hannah reminded her. "What do you think he meant by that?"

"I don't know . . . maybe even Gideon Porter realized that his heinous brother had crossed the line into the sort of unbridled savagery that we normally associate with the Indians."

"I still wonder why, if they were after Mr. Blaine, they killed the others?" Hannah said, again phrasing her statement as a question.

"Because," Sarah Stocker said, raising her voice, "the Porter boys are baleful monsters . . . and if you will pardon me for being unladylike . . . they should all be hanged

from the highest yard arm in Gallatin City and left hanging there until their bones are picked clean by the buzzards."

"Yes, ma'am," Hannah nodded, imagining the sight of skeletons covered by buzzards dangling on Main Street.

Sarah Stocker quickly regained her composure, and the two women politely bade each other "good day."

As Hannah turned her attention to a display of writing ink, the whirring motion of the wheels that turned in the back of her mind had slowed not in the least.

CHAPTER 13

The bureaucrats in Washington, or in Chicago, or somewhere across the eastern horizon had decided for the Marias River to be the boundary between the ancient civilization of the Blackfeet and the encroaching civilization of the *nápikoan* — but none of them had ever been here.

They had ordered their cartographers to delineate one side as being as different as night and day from the other, but to a person riding the hills and swales of this limitless country, the landscape on the south side seemed identical to that on the north.

The cartographers pictured the Marias as a great and imposing boundary, but today, the river, flowing forlornly low as autumn waited for winter, looked to the three riders who splashed across it this morning — you couldn't really say they forded it — no more distinguished than any other stream.

"How long you reckon . . . Mr. Cole?"

Goode shouted, turning his head as they climbed the bank on the southern side.

"How long for what?"

"How long you reckon till we get there?"

"Get where?"

"Back to Gallatin City."

"Guess you'll know it when you get there," Cole promised. He didn't know himself, and he did not care to speculate for the satisfaction of Jimmy Goode.

Porter shot Goode an angry glance, and he said no more.

This was the first time that Goode had spoken in a conversational tone since they started on this enforced adventure. Cole took it as a sign, an indication, that Gideon Porter, the mastermind whom Goode had obviously once idolized, might be losing his charisma.

Goode perceived himself to have been captured in Heart Butte not as an individual, but as part of the entourage of Gideon Porter, an appendage to his power and presence, a mere addendum to the man himself. Goode had dared not engage in conversation because Porter did not, and he was merely an extension of the great man's identity. Now, as the great man had been taken down a peg, Goode was flirting with the notion that he was, himself, a person with an individual identity.

Jimmy Goode had, Cole intuited, probably spent a lifetime kowtowing to Gideon Porter, and living in a deeper, more shadowy corner of his shadow than even Gideon's little brother, Enoch. In the past two days, though, Goode had seen Gideon Porter captured, humiliated, and beaten bloody. No longer was he the kingpin of a gang; he was now a humbled man chained to his saddle in his stocking feet, being fed like a baby from his own canteen by the bounty hunter who refused to unchain him for lunch, or even to take a drink. Gradually, Goode was realizing that he and Gideon Porter were essentially the same — except that Goode still had his boots!

Nothing more was said, though. Porter's glare was still cruel and still frightening. An hour passed, then two. The hours melted into one another as the skies grew dark and the wind picked up.

It was one of those days when the wind demanded that you keep your head buried so low in your collar that you never notice the first snowflake. The first ones that landed on the roan's mane disappeared almost immediately. It was when they started to stick that Cole decided it was time to look for a place to camp.

One side of him yearned to press on, to try to get far enough so that they could reach the Missouri River early tomorrow. The other side knew that getting caught in a blinding blizzard in a deficient campsite was a potential disaster.

Two ridges farther on, they came into a broad gulch where the streambed was populated with a handful of tall cottonwoods. Unlike the small aspen of the previous night, there was no way that Gideon Porter could ever climb these.

"This is it," Cole declared. "Off your horses."

Porter and Goode each struggled off his mount as gracefully as he could while being chained to the saddle horn. Cole uncinched Goode's saddle and let it slide to the ground, where the snow was starting to stick. Leaving Goode for a moment, he went to deal with Porter. With Cole's back turned, Goode could start to run, but he wouldn't get very far in a blizzard while anchored to a saddle. Cole was sure that he would not even try — after all, he had been told all his life that he was good for nothing.

"This snow is damned cold on the feet," Porter complained as Cole uncinched his saddle. "And *damn you* for givin' my goddamn boots to that heathen brute."

"Damn *you,* Gideon," Cole said, as he worked. "I didn't *give* your goddamn boots to the savage."

"Whadya call it when he rides off with *my* boots, and I walk away barefoot?"

"Tradin'," Cole answered succinctly.

"Tradin'?" Porter spat angrily. "Didn't see nobody get no goddamn thing in trade from that redskin."

"I expect that even if you're too stupid to notice that the Indian traded your *life* for those damned boots . . . you aren't blind enough not to have seen that knife he wanted to drag across your neck from one ear to the other."

"I saw the knife all right," Porter admitted.

"What do you think he wanted to do with it?" Cole asked sarcastically. "Play mumblety-peg with it?"

"Lost my goddamn boots," Porter said, trying to redirect the trajectory of the conversation.

"You still got your scalp?" Cole asked rhetorically. "Looks like, by the fact that you can feel the cold on your feet, you're still alive . . . Now, pick up that saddle and head over to that cottonwood on the far right."

Once he had each man chained face-forward around a separate cottonwood trunk, Cole started a fire. Fortunately, there were plenty of broken cottonwood scraps in the gulch to use as firewood. Soon a big fire was blazing, the horses were secured, and Cole sat down to cook some of the buffalo meat that O-mis-tai-po-kah had given him as a parting gesture of hospitality.

"What's gonna happen to us in Gallatin City?" Goode asked cautiously, keeping his voice low so that Porter, who was forty feet away, couldn't hear what he was saying over the roar and crackle of the fire.

"Reckon there's gonna be a trial," Cole said.

"I didn't shoot nobody," Goode insisted. " 'Twas Gideon and Enoch who shot all those people in that house. Enoch shot a *woman* . . . an *old* woman. I seen him . . . I seen him do it."

"Hmmm." Cole nodded. After having seen Enoch Porter in action at Double Runner's shack, after watching him display the brand of uncontrollable rage that would make a man try to rape a woman in a room full of people, it took little stretch of the imagination to see him gunning down Mary Phillips.

"And you got him dead already," Goode

continued. "You done got Enoch layin' there wrapped in canvas. You could let *me* go right now 'cause you got them who did *all* the killin'."

"Doesn't work that way," Cole assured him.

"You can't charge nobody for murder that didn't do no murder," Goode asserted.

"Why'd you do it?" Cole asked.

"I *didn't* do it . . . I didn't do no murder."

"Why'd you go to the house that night?"

"Gideon said we had to kill three of 'em," Goode insisted.

"Which three?"

"Gideon didn't say. I 'spect that Enoch musta knowed, but nobody tells *me* nothin'."

"Who told you to go there?"

"Gideon."

"Who told *him* to go?" Cole asked, hoping finally to know the truth.

"I dunno," Goode shrugged as best he could in his awkward position. "Maybe nobody. Maybe it was *his* idea, thought up by hisself. Like I said . . . nobody tells me nothin'."

"What are you talkin 'bout over there?" Gideon Porter yelled from across the fire. "Goode, I told you to keep your damned mouth shut and not be talkin' to that

167

bounty hunter."

"Shut up, both of you," Cole shouted back. "Get some shut-eye. We got an early start tomorrow."

With that, he lay his head back onto his saddle, pulled his blanket up to his chin, and stared up into the skeletons of the big cottonwoods illuminated by the fire.

His first thoughts went to his conversation with Jimmy Goode and his description of the lunatic Enoch Porter. Next, he went back to the nagging question of *why* they went to the Blaine house. Cole had found just over $200 in Gideon Porter's saddlebags. Taking into consideration that they had only received half the payment due them, and that they had probably spent a fair sum in the saloons of Diamond City and Fort Benton — not to mention whatever Doc Ashby charged — the *total* payroll for the crime, not just a sum advanced to each of the perpetrators, still only came to around $500. Now Ransdell was paying eight times that sum to have them brought in. There was more to all this than met the eye.

The snowfall, which had been coming down pretty heavily as they made camp, had finally slacked off considerably.

As the few random flakes drifting out of

the sky caught the orange light of the fire, Cole thought about that night out of Diamond City when he had dozed off comparing the stars to the freckles on Hannah Ransdell's nose. It was a silly, romantic thought, but more pleasant to fall asleep to than the probable sins of Hannah's father.

Lately, of course, his thoughts of women had turned to Natoya-I-nis'kim, and now they turned to a comparison between her and Hannah Ransdell. They were both smart and intuitive. Natoya was the first woman he had met in these past years whom he had *not* compared to Sally Lovelace. Maybe this meant he was getting over Sally. He wondered too if this meant that his faith in the character and motivation of the female species in general, so severely defiled by Sally, was slowly being rebuilt.

His final thought before he dozed was that Natoya-I-nis'kim also had the distinction of being the only woman who had ever saved his life.

CHAPTER 14

Gideon Porter looked more dead than alive.

Bladen Cole did not mind the inconvenience that he was suffering, but he did not want him dead. In fact, he wanted — more than anything at the moment — to keep this man alive.

After their conversation the night before, and his having learned how little was known by "good-for-nothing" Jimmy Goode, Cole understood that Porter was the *only* man who could finger the mastermind of the murder conspiracy.

"Goddamn you, bounty hunter," Gideon snarled as he woke up, greeting Cole and welcoming the new day with his characteristic lack of cheerfulness. "Damn near froze last night."

"No, you didn't," Cole said. "A chinook blew in after midnight. Besides that, I kept the fire stoked so your little stocking feet wouldn't be cold."

The face that glared at Cole really *did* look more dead than alive. The wounds from his having been whipped with a pistol the day before were healing, but they'd left jagged scabs that were nearly black with dried blood and dust. Three or four days without a shave had made Gideon look like a beggar. At least he still had his scalp, and that was thanks to Bladen Cole.

"Goddamn it, bounty hunter," Gideon whined. "Gimme some goddamn coffee."

"No man needs coffee to stay alive," Cole said calmly as he sipped his boiled concoction. He didn't let on that, despite its inviting aroma, it was pretty bad-tasting swill.

He hand-fed the two prisoners before chaining them back to their saddles. He loaded Enoch's body on his horse, and the procession started out at first light, configured as it had been for the previous two days.

The chinook had changed the landscape, raised the temperatures, melted some of the snow, and swept the sky clear of much of yesterday's overcast. The sun was barely up, but there was a promise that the day might almost be warm.

At last, the monotonous plains dropped away, and they could see the long, narrow forest of cottonwoods that marked the Missouri River. Within half an hour, they could see it, like a blue-green snake hiding among the trees, some of which were still decked with clusters of yellow leaves.

With remembered landmarks to guide him, Bladen Cole steered his charges to turn right and head upriver. He knew they were not far from that little no-name collection of shacks where he had bought whiskey and learned of Milton Waller's impending demise. Cole knew that the shopkeeper at that place had met the Porter boys on their way north, and he really did *not* want to take the time to explain why their condition was so dramatically changed on their way south.

With the Missouri at its lowest level of the year, finding a ford almost anywhere would be easy.

Had it not been for the terrain along the way, and for the fact that the river flowed through the big centers of population between Helena and Diamond City, Cole might have followed the Missouri all the way to Gallatin City, but Cole wanted the latter to be the *only* population center he saw until the reward money was safely in his saddlebags.

As they were scrabbling up the far bank after fording, Cole saw something in the distance that gave him pause. A pair of mounted riders was coming toward them.

The thought of adopting an alternate course to avoid them was dismissed. There was little advantage that might be gained, and to do so abruptly would almost certainly invite pursuit. Cole knew that his chance of eluding these men while keeping his prisoners was a remote one.

Instead, he waved in friendly greeting.

"Howdy, stranger," one of the men shouted as soon as they were within earshot.

"Hello there," Cole shouted back.

So far, so good.

As they came closer, Cole recognized the man who had spoken. By his tall hat, Cole recalled him as the one who had been at the general store in the no-name town, the one who had berated the shopkeeper for telling Cole about the Porter boys.

This was going to be tricky.

"Whatcha got there, mister?" the man asked. "Couple Indians? They look like the mangiest coupla Indians I've seen."

"Nope, not Indians," Cole said with a shake of his head. "Couple horse-stealin' sons of bitches."

"Oh yeah, I can see now . . . white men."

The others were on top of them now, and the question that Cole feared most came quickly.

"Don't I know you from somewhere?"

"Don't think it likely," Cole lied.

"I'm sure we met . . . maybe I'm wrong . . . can't place you."

Cole still hoped for the best, though he could see that Porter and Goode recognized the man, and he figured that the man would soon notice this.

"Yeah, I remember now," the man with the big hat said. "It was down at Sumner's Landing about a week back. You were favoring a leg."

"Oh yeah, that was me," Cole admitted. "Didn't recall you. Got a bad memory for faces."

"How's your leg? You got it fixed up?"

"Yeah, it's better," Cole said, wincing so as to suggest that it was still somewhat of a bother.

After pausing for a moment, Cole resumed the conversation, hoping to conclude it. "Well it was good seein' y'all again. I guess it's time for me and my friends to get movin' on."

"What a minute," the man with the big hat said. "I recollect now that you were asking after four men who'd been through a day or so before, and now I'm seeing that you got yourself two of the four right here. Hardly recognized 'em. Look like Indians.

Look like they been through hell. Guess you found 'em."

"Like I said," Cole explained calmly. "Horse thieves."

"Wait a minute," the man said suspiciously. "I'm not the sharpest bull in the herd, but I'm startin' to figure out somethin'. This feller here, who looks like some savage tried to scalp his face, handed me a twenty-dollar bill . . . You remember that doncha, mister? You paid me to tell any lawman from down in Gallatin City that I saw that you was headed *east,* not north."

Gideon Porter just looked away.

"Well, I reckon that makes you twenty dollars richer," Cole said, trying to appear calmer than he felt.

"Well . . . yes . . . it does, and you don't see that kinda money out here much, so what I got figured is that these fellers are wanted for a lot more than horse thieving . . . and you ain't no lawman . . . are you?"

"I was sent to bring back horse thieves, and that is what I'm trying to do, and if you'd excuse us, that's what's got to get done."

"Whoa . . . wait a minute," the man in the big hat said, as his companion began to grin avariciously. "Like I said, twenty dollars

175

handed out in the form of a single greenback is a lot for one man to be tossing around on strangers. This tells me that there's a good deal of money involved here . . . and since you ain't no lawman . . . that would make you a bounty hunter."

Cole could see where things were headed.

"Now, I'd not want to be getting in the way of what no lawman would be doing," the man with the big hat said after a long pause. "But since you *ain't* no lawman, this would be a strictly business-type deal . . . and somebody's *paying* a whole bunch of money for these fellers to be brought in. I know that you were planning on that bounty, but I think I'd like to take over from you and go down to Gallatin City . . . get that bounty for myself . . . er . . . what I mean is that my partner and me want that bounty for *ourselves.*"

"You're aiming to *steal* my prisoners?" Cole asked rhetorically as he unsuccessfully attempted to stifle an ironic laugh.

"If you'd be so kind as to step aside," the man with the big hat said, his right hand going to his holster.

Cole had seen his gun clear leather before the first shot was fired.

The partner of the man in the big hat, who had not spoken and who would speak no more, had also drawn his gun before he died.

The man with the big hat toppled to the ground as his horse reared at the sound of Cole's two gunshots, but the other man remained seated as his mount sidestepped, whinnying, for about ten feet. His previous grin had been superseded by a dumbfounded expression. He eyes dropped to the growing, reddish-brown smear on his shirt. His revolver tumbled clumsily from his hand as he reached toward the blotch, then suddenly, he jerked, like a man awaking with a start, and tumbled lifelessly to the ground.

Cole holstered his sidearm. In a space of time barely longer than it takes for the tick of a second hand, Cole had erased a potentially deadly threat with deadly action of his own.

If he'd had reason, after the near escape of Gideon Porter, to doubt his having acquired the spirit power of the grizzly, he now could wonder whether he might not have come by it after all.

Two mounds of stones surmounted with saddles marked the resting places of the two men who had chanced to express a desire to steal from Bladen Cole. The single word marked on each cross adorning those graves succinctly expressed the reason for which they were now at rest: "Thief."

The wind had picked up considerably by the time that the three men resumed their ride. About a quarter mile into this journey, they noticed an object tumbling through the brush near their route. It was an especially large hat that was quite tall in the crown.

CHAPTER 15

"Shut up, damn you," Gideon Porter screamed at the top of his lungs.

As on the night before, Bladen Cole had chained Porter and Goode to widely separated trees so as to discourage them from communicating with each other, and as on that previous night, Jimmy Goode had taken the opportunity to engage Cole in conversation, hoping he was out of earshot of the man in whose shadow he had all his life been accustomed to cowering.

"I done told him that when this thing gets sorted, I'm gonna get let go," Goode shouted back to Porter.

"What gives you that crazy idea?" Porter shouted back.

" 'Cause 'twas not me who shot them folks . . . because it 'twas that sonuvabitch Enoch and *you* who pulled the triggers," Goode said as though in triumph over the reasoning of his onetime master.

"Didn't that worthless mama of yours teach you that it ain't no good manners to speak ill of the dead? If you'd have had a father, you'd have got taught."

"Don't go bringin' my mama into this," Goode whined, omitting reference to the mention of a father he never knew, and whom his mother knew for but a short time.

"Shut up, both of you," Cole said angrily.

It was growing colder again, though the wind had died down. They had reached the foothills of the Little Belt Mountains when the shadows grew long, and they followed a deer trail until darkness overtook them. Cole planned to cross the mountains into the Smith's River drainage and stay east of Diamond City for the same reason that he had bypassed Fort Benton. Traveling with two men in chains and a dead body tended to attract the kind of attention that brought questions and unwanted intrusion.

The dark clouds that had built up in time to blot out the sunset had promised snow, but it was a fickle promise. The temperature descended from manageable to uncomfortable, and there were still patches of snow beneath the trees, but no flakes had been seen in the air as they settled in for the night.

"You see why we call him 'good-for-nothing,' doncha, bounty hunter?" Porter shouted after giving Cole's demand for silence short consideration. "This fool don't know that there's a rope waitin' for *him* in Gallatin City . . . just the same as for me."

"I reckon there *will* be a trial," Cole said.

"Like you gave those strangers this day?" Porter said. "Didn't see them get a fair trial or anything of the sort. You were pretty fast with the executioner's sword . . . I hesitate to say 'sword of justice' because there ain't no justice in what you done to them."

"I guess you didn't see that both were in the motion of drawing their 'executioner's swords' on me at the time," Cole replied in a disparaging tone. "If that was me, not them, under those rocks back there, do you reckon you'd have ended up this day ridin' upright in your saddle . . . or sideways across it like your brother?"

Bladen Cole awoke to the sound of gravel kicked.

He sat up, trying to filter out the loud snoring of Gideon Porter and follow the direction of the sound. Something was obviously moving in the darkness not far from the circle of light from their fire.

Coyotes occasionally drifted near the fires of humans, especially in the desperate, hungry months when game was scarce and before the winter cold killed the weaker of the deer, antelope, and cattle, leaving them for the coyotes to scavenge. Being cowardly scroungers rather than serious predators, they were unlikely to attack an uninjured man or horse, but chasing them off was a formality necessary to prove that the humans were in charge.

Cole rolled quietly from his bedroll, grabbed his Winchester, and moved in the direction of the sound. As he did so, he glanced to the log where he had tethered Jimmy Goode. He was *gone.*

Cursing himself silently, Cole continued moving in the direction of the sound. He had expected Porter to repeat his escape attempt, and had taken special care to anchor him to a tree. He had meanwhile chained Goode to a log, incorrectly assuming that he would not dare to escape. Goode had allowed Cole to believe that he really *was* good for nothing.

There was a gully which led into the canyon to the south. Goode had evidently slipped in the dark as he stumbled down the slope.

Cole peered into the gloom, though it was impenetrable to the eye, and cocked his head for further sounds.

Hearing none, he pointed his Winchester down the line of the ravine — there was no such thing as *aiming* under the circumstances — and squeezed off a shot.

He heard the *t'zing* of the bullet ricocheting off a rock, and he heard the desperate scrabbling sounds of a frightened man moving as fast as he could through the darkness and the underbrush that choked the gully.

Cole fired again, this time at the sound. Again, he heard the *t'zing* of the bullet ricocheting off a rock, and the reckless crashing of a scared man.

Cursing himself not so silently, Cole returned to the campsite, where Gideon Porter had been awakened by the shots.

"What in holy hell you shootin' at, bounty hunter?" Porter demanded.

Ignoring him for the moment, Cole went to check on the horses. He was surprised to find all four still tied where he had left them. Why had Goode not taken a horse and scattered the others? Perhaps he had decided that getting away without being heard was worth getting away on foot.

The same question occurred to Porter as Cole began saddling his horse for the day's ride.

Porter groused. "Why'd that stupid Jimmy Goode leave the horses? What a stupid fool to walk when he could ride. Course he done got one over on *you,* bounty hunter!"

"Guess he's not good for *nothing,*" Cole replied, trying not to *sound* as chagrined as he *felt.*

Bladen Cole had made a significant error, and he cursed himself for it repeatedly, but Jimmy Goode had made several. He had proved himself not to be good for *nothing,* but his failure to take a horse was a serious mistake, putting him on foot in rugged terrain — with his wrists still in chains.

By panicking and starting to run when Cole had fired at him, he had confirmed the direction that he was headed. By chance, or by design, his choice of direction took him downhill, toward the Smith's River, and in the eventual direction of Gallatin City. These errors were duly and confidently related by Cole to Porter as they rode.

The fugitive had also failed to take any food or water, although, as Cole discovered — but did not tell Gideon Porter — Goode *had* taken the pistol that had been confiscated from the estate of the man with the large hat.

Goode also had a head start, a fact that Cole cursed, though silently in the presence of Porter. His head start, as short as it was, had been extended considerably by Cole's having not wanted to start out with the horses until there was sufficient daylight to see where they were going.

Because of the steepness, and the twists and turns required to follow the course of the dry streambed, while avoiding the periodic tangles of brush, the going was slow. Cole had planned to cross the mountains following the same deer trail that they'd been on when they had stopped for the night, but Goode had necessitated a change of plans. At least he was headed in the right direction.

Cole hoped that they would catch up with Goode, writhing in pain with an ankle twisted from a fall in the rocky gulch, but it was a wish that went unfulfilled.

Porter, who had been sullen and silent in the first days of captivity, had grown increasingly talkative. Having Goode out of the picture seemed to lift his self-imposed burden of perpetuating a facade of intransigence.

After spewing a tantrum of anger over Cole's having killed his brother over a "squaw," whom he considered somewhat less than human, he turned his attention to Jimmy Goode.

"That sonuvabitch coward could have

sprung me, but he just ran off" was a statement repeated often, which summarized Porter's indictment of the man whom he considered not just a buffoon but a traitor to his leader.

"Guess he got scared when you told him he was gonna hang," Cole replied.

"I don't plan to hang," Porter said defiantly.

"Why is that?"

"No way they're gonna *let* me hang."

"Who's *they*?"

"You'll see."

"Wasn't it *they* who put you up to this?" Cole asked, getting to the question that had been on his mind for days.

"Put me up to *what*?"

"Shooting those two men . . . and that *woman*," Cole said, putting emphasis on the fact that Mrs. Phillips had been among those murdered.

"I seen you shoot more people in the last four days than I shot in my whole life."

"I doubt it."

"Go ahead and doubt it," Porter said defiantly. "And you done murdered my *brother*."

"Murder's a strong word," Cole replied.

"What do you call shooting a man in the back?"

"Saving somebody."

"All's he was doing was tryin' to have a little fun with a squaw," Porter explained.

"Your brother seems to have had him a weakness for hurting women," Cole observed.

"Wasn't a woman," Porter insisted. "It was a *squaw.*"

Cole bit his tongue.

As the ravine widened into more of a valley, Cole found it necessary to take the lead in order to look for evidence of Goode's having come this way. The clumsy man made himself easy to track. He had kept to the path of least resistance, running downhill and following the streambed, while not making any effort to hide his tracks. Every fifteen feet or so, Cole could see the fresh footprint in the gravel of a man who was running hard.

If it had been flat, open country as in previous days, men on horseback would have caught up with Goode by now, but the present terrain favored a runner. Goode had remained ahead of them by running in a straight line, while they had to pick their trail carefully with the horses — *and* a frightened man running downhill can move very quickly.

As the ground grew more level, where

Goode no longer had the momentum of a steep slope, Cole's own progress was now slowed by the necessity of looking for his tracks. Where the streambed meandered into an oxbow, Goode had cut cross country, and it took time for his pursuer to find his tracks.

Each time Cole seemed to lose the trail, Gideon Porter was eager to point out the fact with a taunting phrase reminding him of his failings.

"Good-for-nothing Goode done got you there," he would laugh.

For Cole, it was no laughing matter. The narrower that they cut the distance, the more likely that Goode would hear the ranting Porter, and know they were closing in. If that happened, Goode would either quicken his pace or abandon the streambed. Cole hoped for the former, because a day of running would exhaust him, and he feared the latter, because tracking Goode on the hillsides, now covered with more and more ponderosa, would be much slower.

A third possibility troubled Cole even more.

What if Goode got tired of running and decided to ambush them with the purloined pistol? Cole guessed that Goode was not a good shot, but he did not *know* this. He did not want to ask Porter.

Gradually, the air grew colder, and the clouds became darker and more ominous. If it started to snow, the footprints in the gravel would be lost, but these would be replaced by footprints in the snow, which would be easier to follow. Even if he was a few hands short of a full deck, Goode would certainly be able to figure this out.

Coming to a place where it looked like Goode had stopped for a while and moved in circles, Cole dismounted. He let the roan graze, took Porter's reins away from him and led his horse.

About thirty feet farther on, they came to a place marked by the exposed roots of a large cottonwood that had been toppled a couple of years ago by a spring flood.

In among the tangle of roots, bleached white, and as thick and stiff as limbs, two roots had been broken to form some sort of tool. Cole could see that they were spattered with blood.

Goode had, with a frenzy born of desperation, tried and failed to use the roots to remove the manacles from his wrists. There was no way that steel would yield to cottonwood, but it looked as though the man had torn at least one of his wrists trying.

Cole reached out and touched the blood. It was fresh.

CHAPTER 16

Jeremiah Eaton turned his eyes from the morning sky to the dark ridgeline in the west. The contrast of the flakes against the heavily timbered hillside gave him a better take on how hard the snow was falling than to look upward into the uniformly gray sky.

"She's a-comin' down," he said to his wife, who stood a short distance away, in the doorway of their log home.

"Be comin' down *hard* before long, I reckon," Rebecca said as she glanced down to see whether six-year-old Thomas had bothered to put on a coat before he ran out to see the flakes. He hadn't. Early snowfalls were always a point of curiosity for youngsters, she thought to herself, before admonishing him to "Gitcher self inside and gitcher coat."

"Reckon I better ride on down the river and scare the cattle back up this way," Jeremiah said with resignation.

"Reckon," his wife nodded in agreement.

Early snowfalls were always a reminder of that moment in the cycle of months when it was time to button up their affairs, time for Rebecca to be glad that she had finished canning the vegetables and crabapples, and for Jeremiah to hope that he'd put up enough hay to get the milk cows through till spring.

Four years now separated this cold autumn day from a moment of blissful, romantic dreaming on an Ohio front porch.

Rebecca had first heard the glittering tales in her mother's dining room. She had sat there, an infant on her knee, as a gentleman who was a cousin to her mother's best friend, related tales of the open spaces of Montana Territory. He had been there, having gone west to the gold fields around Diamond City, and he had experienced the land for himself. He had seen its sights with his own eyes. There were opportunities to be had — if one was of a mind for homesteading.

Four years ago, Jeremiah Eaton had come home to his wife and toddler, dejected and complaining. It had taken him nearly a year to get on at the mill, and now there was talk that those hands who were newly hired might soon be let go. Two years on, and the nation was still digging out after the Panic of 1873.

Somehow, it seemed to the young married Eatons that a place like Montana Territory was across the line that delineated the limit of the part of the world that could be affected by panics such as that of 1873.

Thanks to vague directions given by the cousin, and a great deal more luck than they'd realized they had, the Eatons found the end of their rainbow in a mountain valley in Meagher County, Montana Territory.

Canvas from the wagon that brought them had become the tent that was their home until the house was built. The team which had drawn their wagon maneuvered the ponderosa logs felled by Jeremiah, and the house was ready by Christmas.

The first year was hard, but the fact that it was the *hardest* separated the Eatons from the majority of homesteaders who came west in the decades following the Civil War. For most, each successive year was worse than the one previous, and by the third or fourth, dreams faded like dust devils in a field gone dry.

Jeremiah Eaton rode down along the stream that differentiated his 160 acres from those of the majority of homesteaders. At a time when most western homesteads re-

193

quired the sinking of a deep well at great expense and great labor, the Eatons' land was blessed with a running stream. Unlike those in some of the adjacent valleys, it ran all year. The fact that it had run all year for many, many years meant that the soil was good — once you got at it. Like the soil in every corner of the territory, it had never been tilled, and that was back-breaking work. Though Rebecca had vigorously opposed his taking up most of their emigrant wagon with it, she finally admitted that the single best possession they brought west with them was the old, one-runner plow.

Little Thomas — his mother called him Tommy — had grown up not knowing the Ohio reality of streets and street-lights, but the pains and pleasures of a lonely mountain valley. Sometimes this pained his mother, but mostly it made her glad. What mostly pained her was the fact that Tommy's younger sister would never know these things, and that the complications from her birth meant that, for certain, Tommy would grow up an only child.

For this reason, Rebecca had developed a protective attachment to the child which Jeremiah dared not describe as "spoilin'." There was one time that he had, but his wife's tears and his wife's words had told him it would be the last.

Jeremiah could, and often did, count their blessings. They had each other, and they had a "place" which had stood the tests of the seasons.

When she counted her blessings, and like her husband she often did, Rebecca arrayed few things in the opposite column. The one thing that most often headed this list, though, was the loneliness. The needs of the place kept her here. Except for a rare trip down to the small town at Camp Baker, or their annual ride all the way to Diamond City, she rarely saw another soul.

It was for this reason that the rapping at her door caused her an alarm that nearly found her jumping out of her own skin.

It seemed only natural that she should open the door. It was not locked, as doors in Ohio homes would often be, and Rebecca had long since forgotten her Ohio instincts.

Nothing among her faded memory of Ohio instincts, or her recently acquired Montana instincts, however, had quite prepared her for the sight she faced on her doorstep.

"Mornin', ma'am," said the stranger.

The sight of him pronounced the definition of "stranger" on many levels. He was the very embodiment of dishevelment, with his scraggly beard, his dirty clothing, and his hair askew. However, that which struck Rebecca as most peculiar were his scabby wrists and those gray chains that bound them together.

"I'm starvin,' " he insisted in a hoarse voice. "Could I trouble ya for a bite to eat?"

While it was not exactly a neighborly thing to be impolite to a stranger, the extreme strangeness of *this* stranger invited pause.

"Well . . . I never," was the first phrase to fall from Rebecca Eaton's lips.

"You look a fright, sir" was the second.

"If I'm forgetting any niceties might be due a lady," the man said, "I am powerful sorry . . . but I'm powerful hungry."

"I reckon . . ." Rebecca said, regarding the flakes of snow nestling in his unkempt hair, and nodding for him to enter her home.

She shot Tommy a "stay away from this man" glance, then ladled a bowl of the same cornmeal and elk fat porridge that she had served her family for breakfast and set it on the table for the newcomer.

"My husband'll be back soon," she said, staking out the fact that she was not alone in this remote location and that the stranger would soon be dealing with the man of the house.

"That would be good," the man said between bites. "I reckon he's got tools what might get these irons from my wrists."

"Looks like you been tryin' at that yourself," she observed as she watched him eat. "Looks like you cut yourself bad doin' it too."

"Guess so, ma'am."

"Who put those things on you?" Rebecca asked. "Are you runnin' from the law?"

"No, ma'am. It is God's honest truth that these were not placed here by no lawman."

"Then . . ."

"I was *kidnapped,*" he explained nervously. "Me and my partner was. We was kidnapped by an angry stranger done have designs on sellin' us to the Indians up north."

"Well . . . I never," she began. She had been planning to add the phrase "heard of such a fool notion" to the usual expression, but she caught her tongue. "For what purpose?" Rebecca asked.

"Servitude . . . slavery . . . who knows what a savage would do to a God-fearing man."

"Who knows?" Rebecca nodded in mock agreement. "Where'd you get yourself caught?"

"Up north, up around Fort Benton."

"Guess you got away?"

"Yes, ma'am . . . been runnin' for days. He's after me."

"Who's that?"

"The slaver, ma'am. He's a mean one, he is. I fear he'll kill me."

"You must be an awful important slave to get yourself chased all the way from Fort Benton," she said sarcastically. She had heard of Indians *taking* slaves, but never of them *buying* slaves.

"Reckon I am," he said modestly, not catching the sarcasm in her tone.

Rebecca glanced out the cabin's one small glass window, anxious to see Jeremiah coming up the trail, but the trail that wound its way downstream to where the milk cows usually went to graze was empty.

"Reckon I could have some more?"

"Where are you from, sir?" Rebecca asked as she ladled another helping into the bowl.

"I'm from down toward Gallatin City. Headed home, I am."

"That's real nice," she nodded. "What did you say your name was?"

"Oh . . . I'm truly sorry . . . I reckon I failed to give my name. My name's Goode, James J. Goode."

"Good to meet you, Mr. Goode." She smiled. "You lived long down there?"

"My whole life," he said, as though a life

198

spent in Gallatin City was an accomplishment in which a man could take great pride.

"Your people been there long?" Rebecca asked. She was growing more and more anxious at the fact of having a strange man in her house and was hoping to prolong the conversation as a distraction until the image of Jeremiah appeared in the small window.

"Yes, ma'am. They been there since before the war. Don't recall exactly when . . . 'Twas before my time."

"I reckon," she nodded. "What do you do down yonder?"

"Mostly what comes up that needs doin'. Nothing regular."

The small talk continued thusly for a time, but at last the limits of Jimmy Goode's attention span were reached.

"You said your husband's comin' back soon?"

"Yes, I expect he'll be showin' up at any moment," she replied with a nervous lump in her throat.

"You reckon you could show me to your husband's tools so's I could take care of this iron on my wrists?" Goode said. "The itchin' is something fierce, and I'm longing to be loose of these."

"As much as I'd like to help you, Mr. Goode," she said. "My husband's tools are not something I handle . . . any more than I would have him thrashing around in my kitchen."

"If you'd just point me at 'em, I'd be much obliged," he said with a suggestion of irritation in his voice. "You would not need to touch nothin'."

Looking into his eyes, she could see that the sustenance provided to this disheveled man had revived him from trembling hunger to an almost cockiness.

As he traced his tongue across his lips, her imagination did not like the way those eyes now regarded her, not as a good samaritan sating the pain of his empty stomach, but as a female body that might satisfy other hungers.

Having rounded up his cattle, Jeremiah Eaton had paused at the southern extremity of his 160 acres to restore some lodgepoles to the top rungs of several sections of his fence. It was a chore that would be exponentially more difficult in deep winter snow, and hence it was better to address it when the snowfall was still measured as less than an inch or two.

The snow had stopped for a while but was picking up again as he made his way home. There were few chores awaiting him other than getting the cattle situated in the pasture nearer the house, so his ride home was not done with particular urgency.

As he neared the house, the column of smoke promised a fire before which he might warm himself, but as he rounded the bend and came within sight of his homestead, he was startled to see his wife walking toward the barn with a man.

He had to blink a couple of times to assure himself that his eyes were truly seeing this. Visitors were a rarity out here, and unexpected visitors unheard of.

Leaving the cattle to graze lazily in the yellow, foot-tall grass that rose above the thin dusting of snow, he galloped toward the barn.

His wife and the man turned to watch him approach.

"This would be Mr. Goode, Jeremiah," Rebecca explained as her husband dismounted. "He has a problem that he's anxious to have your help in getting out of."

"Would that be those irons that you got on your wrists, Mr. Goode?" Jeremiah asked.

"That would be right, sir," he answered, his tone reverting to its earlier politeness.

"You're a long way from anywhere, Mr. Goode. How'd you get way out here?"

"He's on the run from kidnappers," Rebecca said with a note of sarcasm that was not lost on her husband.

"Done escaped . . . but they're after me. Trailing me right now too," Goode explained.

"You sure it wasn't the law that put these on?" Jeremiah asked skeptically.

"Like I told your missus, I would swear on a stack of Bibles that it wasn't no lawman what chained me up."

"Kidnappers?"

"Yes, sir."

"But why . . . ?"

"They planned to sell me and my partner into slavery among the Indians," Goode insisted.

"Never heard of no Indians *buying* slaves from white men," Jeremiah said. "Heard of people . . . fair sum of people . . . gettin' theirselves taken by Indians, but I never heard of Indians *buying* slaves . . . but then there's lots of things I've never heard of. Lemme take a look."

Jeremiah's credulity concerning Goode's story held no more conviction than his wife's had, but he figured he would give him the benefit of the doubt — at least until he figured out what was really going on with this man.

"These are built to last," Jeremiah observed. "Lot heavier steel than handcuffs. I see by the markings that they are U.S. Army issue."

"I reckon he musta stole 'em," Goode said. "I seem to reckon the slaver told how he stole 'em from somebody over at Fort Ellis."

"I have no saw that will cut steel," Jeremiah told the man. "Breaking the locks with a hammer could not be done without breaking your wrists . . . somethin' it looks like you damned near done already."

As he spoke, Jeremiah's eyes began flicking toward the ridge opposite the cabin. Instinctively, Rebecca looked in that direction, and Goode noticed this.

"Whatcha lookin' at?" Goode demanded.

"Nothin,' " Jeremiah told him. "Just the snowflakes in the air."

"You was looking and she was looking," Goode said nervously, following their gazes. "You'd be lookin' at something."

After a moment of silence, Goode gasped.

"Christ almighty," he hissed. "That consarned slaver done caught up to me!"

As the three of them watched, a lone rider made his way down a hillside three-quarters of a mile away.

Suddenly, Goode reached beneath his

long coat and pulled out the Colt .45 that had once been carried by the man with the big hat. With his other hand, he grabbed Rebecca's wrist and pulled her close to himself.

"No way in hell I'm gonna let that man take me," Goode said, shoving the muzzle of the pistol painfully into the small of Rebecca's back and pulling her backward toward the cabin. "When he comes by here, tell him . . . I don't know what to tell you to tell him . . . Just get rid of him or this lady gets a hole blowed in her . . . *please.*"

Jeremiah saw fear on his face and tears in his eyes.

CHAPTER 17

Bladen Cole had not let on to Gideon Porter that he had lost the trail of Jimmy Goode in the fading light of yesterday. He had rousted the outlaw so as to be on the trail at dawn, hoping to see the smoke from Goode's campfire somewhere ahead — but he hadn't. Either Goode had known that a campfire would reveal his location, or he had not been able to get one started. Cole was hoping for the latter.

Cole had allowed Porter to believe that he was still following a trail, when the only thing he was following was a hunch. He figured that a man who was in desperation to the verge of recklessness — which he believed to be the case — and who was increasingly tired, cold, and hungry — which was sure to be the case — would follow the path of least resistance. Therefore, they continued south, down the southern slope of the Little Belts.

"How the hell can you see where he went?" Porter demanded.

"Practice," Cole lied.

"Reckon it's easy to trail somebody who ain't good for nothing except givin' the slip to a bounty hunter," Porter said to taunt him.

"Hmmm," Cole replied, thoughtfully staring at the ground, at an imaginary track that, obviously, Porter could not see.

About a half hour out, they came across a gently flowing stream, and Cole paused to water the horses. In a silent, thoughtful way designed to convey to Gideon Porter the illusion that he knew what he was doing, Cole figured that Jimmy Goode would probably have followed this stream.

By now, it had started to snow. Cole held out hope that he would soon be seeing the footprints of a cold and desperate man who had spent a night nearby in this wilderness without a fire.

After another hour or so on the trail, they could see a column of smoke rising into the windless skies in the distance.

When this turned out to be coming from a homesteader's cabin, Cole chained Gideon Porter to a ponderosa, tethered the horses, and circled around to approach the cabin from high ground so as to make himself visible — and coming from a direction away from the place where Porter was chained.

A man was standing alone near the barn as Cole rode toward him through the scattering of randomly floating snowflakes.

"Mornin,' " Cole said as he rode up.

"Mornin,' " the man said, returning the greeting. "You're a fair distance from anywhere."

"Yep," Cole agreed.

"Where ya headed?"

"South . . . Gallatin City."

"You got some ridin' to do."

"Yep," Cole agreed. "By the way, I'm looking for a man who'd be passing through this country yesterday or today."

"Haven't seen nobody," the man replied quickly.

"You sure? Skinny fellow with a long gray coat and no hat?"

"Can't say as I have. We don't see too many people out here."

"We?" Cole asked.

"Me and the missus."

"How long you been living out here?" Cole asked, making conversation and trying to get a read on the man. He wondered where the wife was. If they did not have many visitors, as the man said and as Cole believed to be the case, why had she not appeared at the cabin door, out of curiosity if nothing else?

"Four years last summer," the man replied. "Goin' on five."

"That's pretty good. Most homesteaders don't make it that long. By the way, my name's Bladen Cole."

"Jeremiah Eaton," the man said, reaching up to shake Cole's hand. The slight tremble in Jeremiah's hand told Cole that Jimmy Goode and the stolen pistol were not far away.

"Well . . . nice makin' your acquaintance," Cole said, reining his horse to ride away. "Reckon I'll get going."

"So long," Jeremiah said, watching him go. As the stranger rode away, he wondered whether he was a lawman or a slaver. He had showed no badge, but Jeremiah still doubted the latter. What other possibilities could there be? At the moment, it really did not matter.

"Don't make a goddamn sound," Jimmy Goode whispered nervously as he trained the pistol on Rebecca Eaton with a shaking hand.

"What would your mother say?" she asked in a low voice. "Cursing at a woman in that foul tone?"

Jimmy was in deep. He was in over his head. He cursed the day that he had met Gideon Porter. Had that never happened, the road of Goode's life would never have reached this place.

Everything about the way that his mother had raised him, everything in his being, told him that he was wrong to drag a woman into her home at gunpoint — but circumstances had forced this as the only course of events he could imagine. He was doing, in short, what one of the Porter boys would have done.

Tommy sat in the corner, trying not to be seen, and looking with great trepidation at the man's pistol and the way he pointed it recklessly at his mother.

Rebecca watched as Jeremiah waved half-heartedly, and the horseman rode away.

"Your mother would have a fit if she knew what you was doin'."

"Leave my poor, widowed mother out of this."

"Sorry to hear your papa died, but I reckon he spared the strap one too many times when you were growing up."

"Never knew him. He was with mama but a short time."

"How'd he die?"

"Nobody ever said."

"You ever ask?"

"Nope."

They both turned their heads as Jeremiah entered the room.

"Well, I done got rid of your slaver," Jeremiah said. "Told him I never saw you."

"Did he believe you?" Goode asked, his voice quavering.

"Didn't seem to disbelieve me."

"Now it's high time for you to be gettin' along, mister," Rebecca demanded angrily.

"I don't know . . ." Goode said, gritting his teeth. "I don't know what to do."

"Gettin' along would be a darned good start," Rebecca repeated.

"Shut the hell up," Goode shouted, raising his voice louder than either of them had heard him speak previously. "I'm tryin' to *think*!"

There was a long pause. Thinking was clearly something that came to him with considerable difficulty. His earlier tale of kidnapping and slavery *had* displayed ample imagination, though it had been short on believability.

The silence was broken by the crash of breaking glass.

Goode turned, pointing the muzzle of the Colt in the direction of the sound.

Had it not been for the saucer-shaped eyes of a terrified six-year-old boy, he would have pulled the trigger.

A faint trace of what Goode's mother *had* taught him grabbed his wrist and whispered in his ear that it was a very big mistake to shoot a little child for breaking a jar of crabapple preserves.

"Tommy," Rebecca said, standing up and moving quickly toward her child.

"I'm sorry," Tommy said, apologizing for breaking the jar.

"Oh . . . my baby," his mother said, embracing him. "It's all right, it's just preserves."

Both mother and son were crying, and this made Goode both nervous and agitated.

"All of you *sit down* where I can see you," he demanded in an almost pleading tone. "And shut your mouths while I'm trying to *think*!"

He could feel himself starting to sweat as he gritted his teeth and tried to decide what to do. Gideon Porter would know. He would have figured things out by now.

Or would he?

If Gideon Porter was so smart, why was *he* still a prisoner of the bounty hunter while Goode walked free? This thought gave him hope. He took a deep breath and tried to relax.

"Like the missus said, it's time for you to be movin' on and leave us be," Jeremiah said. "I done told the man that you were not here, and there's no way that we could tell anybody else that you'd *been* here. It's more than a day's ride to any town. Why would we even want to? You were the victim of a man who wanted to enslave you."

"Let me *think,*" Goode said, trying to be stern.

The man was right. He couldn't stay here. He really *did* have to get moving — and sooner, rather than later.

"I'll even saddle a horse for you," Jeremiah said. "It would be a neighborly thing to help a man who has been through what you been through . . . with the slaver and all. With a horse you could get down to a town where a blacksmith would have the tools to get the irons from your hands."

His wife gave him a glance that said "How dare you offer one of *our horses* to this evil man?"

Goode gritted his teeth. This sounded pretty good. He was being handed a free horse. It seemed too good to be true. Was it?

"That sounds mighty fine, mister, but how

do I know you ain't got a trick up your sleeve?"

"We got no bone to pick with you," Jeremiah said. "We didn't even *know* you until an hour ago. All's we want is to have you get on with your travels and leave us alone."

Goode anguished over the decision he had to make. He was not used to making decisions. What would Gideon Porter do?

At last he seized upon the course he would follow. He would take a *hostage.*

"As you say, it is mighty neighborly of you to offer a horse," Goode said with renewed confidence. "But I want you to saddle up *two* horses . . . and gimme all your guns."

"Don't got but that one," Jeremiah said, nodding at an early model Winchester repeater that hung above the doorway.

Jeremiah Eaton swallowed hard. The man obviously planned to take a hostage with him when he departed. He did not mind being a hostage to the crazy man if it meant leading him away from his home and family. The man had not yet pulled the trigger, and Jeremiah figured that he was not anxious to do so. Somewhere down the road, when the crazy man felt less boxed in, he would be able to trade both horses for his freedom and walk home.

The expression on Rebecca's face, however, was a mix of fear and anger.

The Eatons had just four horses, two riding mares and the aging draft horses who had pulled their wagon from Ohio and who now pulled the plow and did general work around the place. Jeremiah offered to scatter them so that Goode would not fear a double cross, and he did so.

With both horses saddled, Goode ordered a rope to be strung between them as he had seen Bladen Cole do with him and Porter.

Goode then lurched aboard one of the horses as gracefully as he could with his hands still in irons.

Jeremiah hugged his wife and started to mount the other mare.

"Not you," Goode said.

"What?"

"Not *you,*" Goode repeated. "Put the *boy* on the horse."

Jeremiah was dumbfounded, his wife apoplectic.

"You are *not* taking my boy hostage," she spat in a venomous rage. She impulsively grabbed Tommy by the hand and pushed him behind her.

"I have the guns," Goode asserted. "I have the guns and I'm in charge . . . you gotta *do what I say!*"

"Not my boy," Rebecca pleaded, tears

running down her cheeks.

"If I was to take his daddy, he might get tricky on me," Goode said. "This boy's gonna do what he's told . . . aren't ya, boy?"

"You can't do this!" Jeremiah insisted.

"Boy's a helluva lot better hostage than a man," Goode said with a smirk. "No way a lawman is gonna question a man ridin' with a boy."

"*Lawman?*" Rebecca screamed. "You said you was the victim of slavers and not an outlaw! Why are you worried about a *lawman* if you're a poor victim?"

"That's what I meant to say," Goode said, becoming jittery. "And you're tryin' to confuse me with your talk . . . Now, get that boy on the horse or I'm gonna start shootin' and I'm gonna start with *you.*"

Rebecca Eaton sat sobbing in the yard of their home, oblivious to the growing number of snowflakes floating down around her and oblivious to the cold.

The only thing of which she was aware was that her boy had been taken by a violent man with a gun.

She had been oblivious to what her husband had said about the mistakes that the kidnapper had made — such as not tying them up or searching the house for more guns, and thereby not finding Jeremiah's shotgun. She was oblivious to the fact that it might have taken hours for them to get themselves untied, meaning that the kidnapper might have had half a day's head start — instead of half an hour's — by the time that her husband had rounded up a draft horse and set out, riding bareback, in pursuit.

The only thing of which she was aware was that her boy — her *only* living child — had been taken by a violent man with a gun.

Jeremiah Eaton had been seething with anger and sick with guilt at not being able to protect his family, but unlike his wife, who sat powerless, unable to do anything, he had at least the small satisfaction that he was taking action.

Jeremiah took some solace in the fact that the boy had value to the man only if he was alive, and distress in the fact that he was an erratic and impulsive man who could not be relied on to make entirely rational choices.

The draft horse was slow, and the shotgun afforded but two shots between reloading, but at least he was doing *something* — though he had yet to decide exactly *what* he would do if he actually caught up with them.

The lightly falling snow allowed Jeremiah to follow their tracks, and to guess the timing of their progress by how much snow had collected *in* the tracks. He could see that the two-year-old mares were moving faster than the old draft horse and extending their lead. He hoped that they would stop at some point and that it would not start snowing hard enough to smother the tracks.

Young Thomas Eaton was afraid for himself and afraid for his family. In all his life, he had never been alone with a stranger, or indeed with anyone other than his parents.

He didn't know what he was supposed to think, but he *did* know he did not like this. He had stopped crying, but he was still afraid that the man would hurt him and nobody would be there to see it.

He was so preoccupied with his situation that he had forgotten for the longest time to worry about being cold. Except for the tips of his ears and his fingers, he wasn't, but he expected that later, he would be. He was glad that his mother had earlier demanded that he put on his coat, and he wished that he had picked up his gloves.

He had said nothing to the stranger, and the man had said nothing to him. He seemed to Thomas to be the kind of man who did not like to talk unless he had to.

As the miles went past, the snowfall slowed, stopped for a while, and then started up again, heavier than before. Thomas looked at the flakes settling on the horse's mane and remembered how his mother had told him that every snowflake had a design all to itself, and that no two snowflakes in all the world were exactly the same. He had enjoyed this special time with his mother — last winter, when he was five — and it made him cry to think of how much he was missing his parents.

The woods were thicker and darker now, and Thomas grew more frightened. He choked back his fear, wanting to be the kind of man of whom his father could be proud. He knew that his father was liable to say something about a man not being afraid in a dark forest.

He wondered whether his father would come for him, and whether he would see his mother again.

This made him cry.

The angry man growled when he saw the tears, and Thomas wiped his cheeks.

Soon, Thomas had another worry.

"Mister . . ." he said tentatively. "I gotta pee."

"Okay," Jimmy Goode said, after a moment's thought. "Make it quick."

The boy slid off the mare and began walking up a slight incline toward some trees.

"Where the hell you goin'?" Goode demanded.

"Ma says I should always go into the bushes," the boy replied.

"Okay," Goode said impatiently.

Deciding that he too could use a pit stop, Goode climbed off his horse, but he did not venture near the "bushes."

He paused to congratulate himself on his good fortune. He had made the transition from desperate fugitive to the man in control. He had gotten the bounty hunter off his trail, he had a horse, and he had a *hostage*. He was the man in control.

Nobody would call him "good-for-nothing Goode" today!

With his hostage, he could walk up to a blacksmith and say that he had rescued the kid from slavers. Nobody would question a man with a kid. They'd get to the next town, whatever it was likely to be, and go straight to the blacksmith, and then they'd get something to eat. Goode had no money — he wished now that he had taken some from the homesteading family — but who would deny a *kid*?

The kid. Where was the damned kid?

"Kid!" Goode shouted. *"Kid!* Get yourself back here and let's get goin'."

There was no hint of a reply from the "bushes" to which the boy had gone. Goode cursed himself for not keeping an eye on him.

Where was the damned kid?

He walked up the slope in the direction Thomas had been headed when Goode last laid eyes on him.

"Kid?" Goode shouted. "Get yourself out wherever you're hidin'. *Kid!* If you don't show yourself, I'm gonna have to get tough and tan your hide."

There was no reply.

Goode cursed himself again for not having kept an eye on him, but he dared not allow his mind to drift into thoughts that "good-for-nothing Jimmy Goode" may have been outsmarted by a six-year-old.

Where was the damned kid?

Goode decided to appeal to the boy's emotions.

"Whatcha gonna do when it gets dark out here . . . ? *Oooeee,"* he shouted, attempting to make a ghostly sound. "Whatcha gonna do when it gets *cold* out here? Whatcha gonna do when you get *hungry*?"

No reply.

"Whatcha gonna do when the *coyotes* get

hungry? They're gonna *eat* you . . . *eat you alive!*"

Still no reply.

"Okay, kid, that does it," Goode shouted. "I'm mad. I'm goin' hunting."

Lifting the muzzle of the Colt, he squeezed the trigger.

The sound of the gunshot in the deep pillowy quiet of the snow-blanketed woods was startling even to Jimmy Goode.

"No."

Jeremiah Eaton nearly jumped out of his saddle when he heard the gunshot.

"No," Jeremiah said to himself when he heard the thunderclap reverberate through the trees.

He prodded the big draft horse to run as fast as he could. In his prime, the big horse had had some pretty respectable speed in him, but age had tempered him. He moved as fast as he could, aware that his rider desperately needed him to do so.

"No!" Jeremiah repeated as he broke into a clearing and saw a man, *that* man, with a pistol.

He did not see his son. Was the boy lying injured on the ground somewhere? Was he lying . . . ? The anguished father could not finish the thought.

Jeremiah gripped the shotgun with his

right hand as the horse closed the distance between them and *that* man. He ached to use the shotgun *now,* but he knew that the range was too great.

Goode turned his attention from the bushes to the oncoming rider and took careful aim. He cursed himself for not tying up the homesteader and chasing the draft horses farther, but fate had given him a second chance. It is not hard to hit an object that is coming directly at you.

Suddenly, a withering pain tore through Goode's elbow.

He felt himself rendered helpless, knocked off balance, and thrown to the ground like a block of salt being kicked off the tailgate of a wagon.

Jeremiah watched this as he came on, clutching his unfired shotgun and wondering who had shot the man.

He arrived near Goode a moment later, slid off the horse, and looked around. The woods were silent but for the heavy, heaving breath of his horse and strange, animal-like sounds being uttered by Jimmy Goode.

As for most of the day he had imagined himself doing, he leveled the shotgun at the man who'd kidnapped his son.

"Where's my *boy*?" Jeremiah demanded angrily. "What did you do with my *boy*?"

"Don't shoot him."

Jeremiah looked up to see a man emerge from the trees carrying a lever-action Winchester and leading a group of horses. He recognized the man as the same one who had ridden into his homestead that morning. He did not recognize the second man seated on one of the horses, but he *did* recognize the government-issue manacles worn by this man.

"Don't shoot him," Bladen Cole repeated. "He's mine."

"Where's my *boy*?" Jeremiah demanded, pointing both barrels at Cole.

"Right there," Cole said with a nod.

Jeremiah turned to see Tommy running from the bushes at top speed.

"Papa . . . Papa . . . Papa . . ." he exclaimed as he hugged his father. Both of them had tears of joy streaming down their cheeks.

As Jeremiah turned to hug Tommy, he felt the shotgun being lifted from his grip.

"Who *are* you?" Jeremiah demanded of Cole. He made no attempt to retrieve his weapon, as both his arms were now wrapped tight around the sobbing boy. "What do you want?"

"My name's Cole, just as I said when we met back at your homestead."

He cracked open the shotgun, removed

the shells, and tucked them into the breast pocket of Jeremiah's jacket.

"Like I told you, I've been trailing this fellow for a time," Cole said, handing the shotgun back to the homesteader butt-first and picking up the revolver dropped by the outlaw. This too he emptied and handed to the homesteader.

"You a lawman? He said you were a slaver."

"A *slaver*?" Cole laughed as he applied a tourniquet to the injured man's arm. "That's a pretty fanciful yarn for somebody with the imagination of Jimmy Goode . . . No, I'm not a lawman, but I *am* the man that got sent to bring back a bunch of killers."

"Bounty hunter?"

"Yes," Cole replied. "Can you read?"

"Of course," Jeremiah said, slightly offended.

Cole took a scrap of paper from his pocket and pointed out the names and charges on the warrant.

"I knew from your manner that you were in trouble when I talked to you at your place this morning," Cole explained. "When I didn't see your wife, I figured that she was inside your house with a gun to her head, so I just backed off and trailed this man when he left with your boy. I knew that he wouldn't hurt him unless he was provoked, so I wanted not to provoke him . . . It was your boy who provoked him."

"What?" Jeremiah gasped.

"Gotta give you credit." Cole smiled at Tommy. "What's your name, son?"

"Thomas J. Eaton, sir."

"Yes . . . Thomas J. Eaton," Cole laughed. "Well, I watched where you were hiding. He was not even close to finding you. You were awful brave not to let out a sound even when he started yelling about coyotes eating you."

"I knew my papa would come to get me," Thomas said bravely, as the tears poured down his father's cheeks.

CHAPTER 18

"Father, Mr. Phillips is here," Hannah Ransdell said, putting her head in her father's office.

The banker looked up suddenly, startled by the sound of his daughter speaking those words. In his subconscious mind, "Mr. Phillips" was his violently murdered colleague, Dawson Phillips, and her use of that name was momentarily jarring. The person to whom his daughter referred was not, of course, the person to which his mind had leaped, but the son of that man.

"Send him in," Isham Ransdell said, quickly regaining his composure. "And get Duffy."

"Mr. Phillips," she smiled at the son and namesake of her father's late colleague, "my father will see you now."

She brought the younger man into the inner sanctum of the Gallatin City Bank and Trust Company. The proprietor rose to shake the visitor's hand as Duffy came in carrying his notes and ledger.

"Welcome, Mr. Phillips, it is a pleasure to meet you, though I deeply regret the circumstances that have brought us together," Isham Ransdell began. "This is Mr. Duffy, my accountant, and you've met my daughter, Hannah. She's my . . . uh . . ."

"Assistant," Hannah interrupted with a broad smile as her father grasped for words. He always did this. One of these days, she thought she might reply with a title that truly represented the work that she did for him. She could imagine his expression if she had said "general manager" or "vice president."

"First of all, let me say that I was personally acquainted with your late father. He was a fine man and a fine member of our community . . . as was your mother. I am very truly shocked and saddened by what happened to your parents."

"Thank you, sir," the younger Phillips said with an obvious lump in his throat. "Your words are much appreciated."

"The entire community of Gallatin City shares my sympathies. Your parents will be greatly missed."

Isham Ransdell then turned to the substance of his former colleague's affairs and spoke in generalities for a few moments. When the younger Dawson Phillips followed up with several specific questions, the elder Ransdell merely nodded to his daughter.

Hannah opened a folder and proceeded to explain, in minute detail, the nature and rates of all the many bank accounts and investments held by the elder Phillips. When it came to balances, she named them off the top of her head, each time asking Mr. Duffy whether the number was correct. Each time but once, he simply nodded that her numbers were accurate. The one time that she was wrong, he proudly corrected her to say that she was off by seven dollars and change, as her figure was that of the *fifteenth* of the month.

"I stand corrected," she said with a smile.

The younger Mr. Phillips began the meeting more impatient than amused that the banker was allowing his daughter to speak of financial matters, but soon he was just trying to keep up with her.

When Hannah had finished, she nodded to her father to name the total value of the elder Mr. Phillips's bank holdings, but he found it necessary to nod back to her for the balance with accrued interest at the end of the coming month.

"So there you have it," Isham Ransdell

said in summary. "Are there any further questions that we might answer for you?"

"Not at the moment," the younger Mr. Phillips replied. "But there may be after I've spoken with his attorney, Mr. Stocker, about the details of the will."

"Certainly," Isham Ransdell said. "We are ready and pleased to serve you, just as we were your late father . . . and once again, you have our fullest condolences . . . Hannah, could you get Mr. Phillips a cup of coffee?"

"Yes, Father."

"Where did you learn to do that, Miss Ransdell?" Phillips asked when Hannah handed him a cup of coffee and poured one for herself.

"Do what . . . ?"

"The accounts?"

"It's basic banking practice, Mr. Phillips," she said with a shrug. "I've worked here since I was a girl."

"Where did you go to school?"

"I went to school in Gallatin City. I was very good in arithmetic. The rest I've learned working here."

"You didn't go to college . . . or a secretarial school?"

"I doubt that numbers used in secretarial

school include any that had not yet been revealed to me by the time that I was in high school."

Phillips nodded. She had him there.

"If I might be so bold as to change the subject," he said, already changing the subject, "I was wondering . . . um . . . Miss Ransdell . . . if you would do me the honor of joining me for dinner at the hotel this evening?"

"I would be delighted, Mr. Phillips," Hannah said with a smile after a brief pause. It had been some time since she had been asked to dine with a gentleman, and his invitation pleased her as much as it startled her.

"Shall we say seven?" Phillips suggested, "I'll . . . I could . . ."

"I shall meet you there at that time," Hannah replied. She was delighted with the attention of a handsome young man.

"Thank you then, Miss Ransdell," he said, extending his hand. "Now, if you'll excuse me, I must go see Mr. Stocker about the will . . . Thank you for the coffee."

"My pleasure, Mr. Phillips," she said, shaking his extended hand.

Hannah Ransdell ascended the steps of the Gallatin House. The restaurant in the hotel

230

that had been owned by the late Mr. Phillips, Sr., was the fanciest and probably the finest between Bozeman and Helena. The high society of Gallatin City, to the degree that there *was* such a thing as a high society in Gallatin City, dined here. Her father occasionally took clients here, and Mr. Phillips had often entertained her father and his other associates in the bar.

She entered the front door as the hotel's big imported German clock was banging out the seven measured beats of the hour. Dawson Phillips, Jr., who was already present, rose from his chair to greet her. She smiled politely as he escorted her to the dining room.

Over appetizers, they made small talk. She asked, and he explained, about his life in Denver, and she told of life in this city, which he had visited only twice. He had spent his early years in Bozeman, when his parents lived there, but had been shipped off to boarding school in Denver when his parents moved to Gallatin City.

While she was just a tad closer to thirty than to twenty, she guessed him to be a little past thirty. This made him courting age, and had she lived in Denver, or he in Gallatin City, it might have been an opportunity worth encouraging. He was, indeed, a charming fellow, an entrepreneur like his father, *and* he did not seem to look down his nose at a woman working in a bank — at least *after* he had seen her in action.

For Hannah, more than for the man on the opposite side of the table, the subject of courtship was accompanied by the ticking of a clock no less real and tangible than the one in the lobby of the Gallatin House. In moments that alternated with her dismissive criticism of the eligible bachelors in Gallatin City she faced the reality that society had painted a narrow line between the age at which a young woman was suitable for courting and the age at which she was destined for eternal spinsterhood.

For the past few years, Hannah's life had taken its meaning from the pride of knowing she was good at her work. Young Mr. Phillips reminded her that there was more to life and gave her cause to believe that not all men were like the would-be suitors whom she had rejected thus far.

As Hannah had discovered, the typical young man in Gallatin City seemed to be quick to focus his attention on himself, before giving her an opportunity to develop a corresponding interest in him. She mentioned this to Mr. Phillips and learned that he had found much the same to be true of the young ladies whom he had courted in Denver.

"Your father has good cause to depend upon your expertise," Phillips commented when she explained her duties in the family business. "One does not often find a woman in such a role."

" 'One' will likely see more, rather than fewer, of us in responsible positions in the future," she smiled. "You may be aware that earlier this year President Hayes signed a law permitting women attorneys to argue cases before the Supreme Court of the United States. One day, we shall share the voting booth with men as well."

"Speaking of Mr. Hayes, do you believe that he will run for reelection in the new year?" Phillips asked, deciding that even politics would be safer ground for the continued conversation than women's suffrage.

"After his narrow election, or as some would say his *defeat* by Mr. Tilden in '76, I would expect that he will make good on his promise to let someone such as Mr. Garfield run for his party's nomination." Hannah smiled, impressing her companion with her knowledge of current affairs.

"This has been a very nice meal," she said, smiling again as they were beginning their desert. "Thank you again for inviting me."

"My pleasure." He smiled also. "And very nice company."

"Thank you, Mr. Phillips," she replied, still smiling. "*My* pleasure."

For both parties, it had indeed been a pleasurable evening. Both were happy to enjoy a dinner with a member of the opposite sex who was well versed in the matters of the day.

"Have you dined often here at the Gallatin House?" he asked.

"Sometimes, though not often," she replied. "I think of it as a 'special occasion' type of place. When I was growing up, my family came here for the occasional Sunday dinner. After my mother passed, I came here with my father a time or two."

"I'm sorry to hear about your mother, Miss Ransdell," he said.

"That was nearly seven years ago," she said. "And she died peacefully. I can barely conceive of the anguish you must feel about losing both of your parents so violently."

"It does cause nightmares . . . which I hope will subside with time . . . I understand that your own father was to have been present at the Blaine home that evening."

"Yes . . . and I was to have accompanied him," Hannah said. "I can only imagine the horror of having been present if a fatal shot had found him . . . but *my* nightmares of what *might* have been can only pale by comparison to *your* nightmares of what *did* happen."

"I will miss my father greatly," Phillips said, sadly.

"He was a well-respected man," Hannah said with sympathetic assurance. "He was justifiably proud of this establishment . . . it has a very excellent restaurant."

"I'm pleased to hear that," he said. "Um . . . I guess it's *my* restaurant now."

"I meant to ask how things went with the reading of the will," Hannah said, merely making conversation, under the presumption that it had been a perfunctory reading.

"Well . . . with my mother deceased," he said with a gulp, not resuming his train of thought without a sip of water. "The bulk of the estate went to me, except for the trust fund, which as you know, was set up at your father's . . . um . . . *your* . . . bank for my sister, who is married, and who lives in Cheyenne."

"That sounds reasonably straightforward." Hannah nodded.

"Well . . . it *was* . . . except for one thing," he said thoughtfully.

"What's that?"

"Are you aware of a tract of land . . . actually several parcels of land . . . that are located north and east of Gallatin City, and which were owned jointly by your father and mine, together with Mr. Blaine and Mr. Stocker?"

"Yes," Hannah nodded. "I am aware that they were buying land out there. It is not exactly prime real estate. It is in the direction of the Diamond City gold fields, but no gold has ever been found there. I know that they were buying it on the cheap."

"Were you also aware that their arrangement called for the partners to inherit the shares of their associates? With my father and Mr. Blaine gone, Mr. Stocker and your father are now the sole owners of that property."

"No . . ." Hannah said with genuine surprise. "I did not know this."

"How was your dinner with young Mr. Phillips last night?" Isham Ransdell asked as his daughter came into the bank.

He usually arose before she did and was frequently at his desk very early. She had arrived at the bank on time only once. When he made a comment about her keeping "banker's hours," she had made it a point thereafter to arrive at work no later than fifteen minutes before opening.

"It was very nice," she replied, hanging up her coat.

"I heard you come in," he said in an offhand manner. At one point in her life, he would have taken such a thing sternly. At this point, though, he was pleased with any attention that she might receive from any young man of courting age.

"I hope that I didn't wake you," she said as she situated herself at her own desk. She had come home well before ten and had nothing for which to apologize.

"No, not at all," he replied.

"Father, I was not aware of your arrangement with your partners about the land outside of town . . . that you and Mr. Stocker inherited the shares of the others."

"Oh yes, that's true . . . I had actually forgotten that we had drawn up the papers that way until Virgil reminded me this week. We acquired it as a partnership, and it is typical for partners to grant one another the rights of inheritance."

"I see," Hannah said, turning to her work. She had wondered why her father had made such an arrangement, but his explanation seemed reasonable. She had wondered why her father had not told her about it, but she realized she had probably been a teenager when the deal was done. Most daughters in their twenties knew nothing of their father's business dealings. The fact that Hannah knew *nearly* everything was highly unusual.

Thoughts of this deal about marginal pasture land faded as Hannah dealt with the opening rush of customers, helping them with their transactions and answering their questions. Finally, when there was a lull, she decided to pick up the mail at the post office. She called to her father to tell him where she was going. He just waved back. He was in a meeting with Edward J. Olson.

Her father's right-hand man came and went without a schedule. While she and Mr. Duffy put in more than mere "banker's hours," Olson kept no office hours whatsoever. He appeared unannounced from time to time, but he was always welcome in her father's office. To his credit, though, he seemed very competent in handling whatever task beyond the walls of the bank her father assigned.

Going to the post office reminded Hannah of that day a while back when the letter had arrived from the bounty hunter. There, she thought, was another handsome man. Unlike the clean-shaven Mr. Phillips, he had the beginnings of a beard, and she liked a young man with hair on his face. There was also a certain allure surrounding a man with danger in his life. The violence was both frightening and appealing. It gave her a thrill to think about the way he lived his life, but men like him were the ones you thought about, *not* the ones you thought about courting.

"Good morning, Miss Ransdell."

Hannah was so lost in thought that she was startled by the greeting from Dawson Phillips, Jr. He was tipping his hat as she glanced up from the mail.

"Oh . . . good day, Mr. Phillips. I was just picking up the mail."

"It's a lovely morning," he said with a smile.

"The snow seems to have stopped," she replied, also smiling. "And it looks like the sun wants to shine."

"I enjoyed our dinner last night," he said.

"And I did as well," she replied.

"I was wondering . . . um . . . if it wouldn't appear too forward of me . . . since you made a cup of coffee for me yesterday . . . whether I might return the favor today?"

"Well . . . do you mean right now?"

"Why not?"

"Well, I have to get back to the bank," she said in a tone that conveyed to him that there was no specific urgency.

"Of course," he said, sounding a bit disappointed.

"I suppose that my father and Mr. Duffy could hold down the fort for a *little* while," she said quickly. Though she had not yet decided whether the man from Denver was courting material, she certainly did not want to close the door — at least not as impulsively as she was in the habit of doing.

They sat in the same dining room at the Gallatin House as they had the night before, sipping coffee and sharing a croissant.

When the time came for Hannah to say that now it *really was* time for her to get back to the bank, she picked up her bag of mail and extended her hand.

"Thank you again, Mr. Phillips. Perhaps we'll run into one another again before you head back to Denver."

"That would be a pleasure, Miss Ransdell . . . Oh, one thing I've discovered since last night carries good news for your father and Mr. Stocker."

"What's that?" Hannah asked.

"The railroad . . . the Northern Pacific . . . Fred Billings has got the financing together to resume construction and will be building the tracks through Gallatin City."

"That will be wonderful news for us all,"

Hannah smiled.

"It will *certainly* be wonderful news your father, and my father's other surviving partner, to own land through which the rails will pass."

Hannah detected a trace of bitterness in his tone, but this was quickly washed away by his changing the subject. Talk of the railroad turned to talk of railroads in general, and thence to the general topic of the "progress" that railroads were bringing to the West. Dawson Phillips, Jr., smiled when he spoke of the changes he had seen in Denver in recent years, and Hannah found herself captivated by his charm.

She almost blushed when he politely, though nervously, asked whether he might enter into personal correspondence with her.

"Of course," she said with a smile.

CHAPTER 19

"Looks like the snow is piling up pretty good out there," Bladen Cole observed casually as he poured himself a cup of coffee.

"How's your friend doing?" Sheriff Joshua Morgan replied, ignoring Cole's observation, which was obvious to anyone who looked.

"He's gonna live," Cole answered, absentmindedly winding his father's watch.

"How soon, you reckon?"

"Few days. No more."

"That's good news," Morgan said, pouring a cup of coffee for himself and looking out the window.

"You expect to be needing that cell of yours in the next few days?"

"Never know," the white-haired sheriff said, still staring out the window at the falling snow.

If there was anyone in Copperopolis who

wanted Cole on the trail *out of* Copperopolis more than Cole himself, it was Sheriff Joshua Morgan. It was not that he particularly disliked Cole, it was just that he had an attachment to the status quo, and having to let a bounty hunter with a warrant use his jail cell was not part of the status quo. Cole had negotiated a deal for the use of Morgan's single cell for two dollars a day, plus another dollar for a place for him to sleep in the sheriff's office.

In the long years that he had been the sheriff of Copperopolis, Morgan had seen a lot of things come and go, and the gradual quieting down of the town suited the way that he imagined living out his later years.

Copperopolis was not much of a town, and as tedious as that was, Cole was pleased. For the same reason that he had been anxious to avoid towns entirely, he liked a small place with minimal comings and goings, which allowed him to keep the low profile that he desired. He did not want word of his whereabouts to get back to Gallatin City.

Copperopolis had not always been a one-horse town. In the years immediately after the Civil War, it had been a boomtown of sorts for the reasons suggested by its name. It never became the metropolis that its namers had imagined, and its fortunes began running in the opposite direction when the fires of avarice began burning brightly at Confederate Gulch. Why work your fingers to the bone for *copper* when you can work your fingers to the bone for *gold*?

Cole had not exactly come voluntarily to Copperopolis, but with a prisoner lying bleeding in the snow, he had but two choices — the obvious one, and finding medical attention to patch him up. Cole did not want a repeat of Milton Waller's final days, and he was determined not to abide the "dead" part of his prisoners being wanted "dead or alive."

Jeremiah Eaton had suggested Copperopolis as the nearest place that had a doctor, and thus Cole had come. Jimmy Goode was in a bad way when they had ridden into town the following day, but the doctor knew his way around a gunshot wound and lacerated wrists. That left only the wait for Goode to be well enough to travel. It seemed a terrible waste of energy, not to mention cash, to save a man for his own hanging, but Cole wanted to see the look on the faces in Gallatin City when he rode in with half of the Porter boys' gang still *alive.*

When he had recovered sufficiently to speak, Jimmy Goode claimed to be sorry, and he claimed to have learned his lesson. Whatever lessons he applied to whatever he had left of his misspent life, he would be applying them without the use of his right arm below his shattered elbow.

"Damn you to hell, bounty hunter," Gideon Porter barked in his usual manner of greeting, as Cole went back to check on him in Morgan's cell. "When are we gonna get out of this piss-hole?"

"You're awful anxious to get home for your own necktie party," Cole observed.

"I told you, bounty hunter," Porter said smugly, consistently insisting on calling Cole by his profession rather than by his name. "I told you my friends in high places won't let me hang."

"When are you gonna tell me the names of those friends in high places?"

"I done told you I *ain't* telling you."

"Suit yourself," Cole said, turning his back on his prisoner and slamming the outer door to the cell area.

Bladen Cole had been spending his days pacing back and forth in the snow between the jail and the doctor's office, where Goode's leg was manacled to an iron cot, and playing penny-ante poker with the middle-aged woman who owned the saloon that was conveniently located on the ground floor of the building where the doctor kept his office. To date, he had lost nearly seventeen dollars. Copperopolis was no metropolis.

"Slow this afternoon, Mary Margaret?" Cole asked as he walked into the saloon.

"Every afternoon's just peachy here in paradise," the proprietor said from behind the bar. Though her name suggested that she was a long-ago defrocked nun, it was clear that the things she had seen and done in her lifetime were beyond the imagination of most nuns. She had come with her husband in the boom years of Copperopolis and had stayed on after a mine explosion made her a widow.

"You here to lose another five dollars, Mr. Cole?" Mary Margaret asked as she turned to face him.

"Reckon," he said, pulling up a chair at the table that had become *his* table in the days he had been in Copperopolis.

Mary Margaret rolled a cigarette and sat down opposite him.

"When you gonna let me pour you a shot, Mr. Cole?"

"As I been tellin' you, Mary Margaret, I've gotta keep a clear head to keep an eye on my two rascals."

"The doc says the one upstairs there with his arm half-shot-off kidnapped a little boy off a homestead up in the Little Belts," she said, making conversation as he dealt the cards.

"That's about the size of it," Cole confirmed. He had been noticeably tight-lipped about his prisoners since he rode into town. Mary Margaret had described herself as being "not one to pry," but she was naturally curious.

"How does a feller get into a line of work like bounty huntin'?"

"Are you contemplating a career change?" Cole asked as he studied his cards and drew two.

"I figure *I'd* be the one on the lam," she said thoughtfully as she studied her cards.

"That so?"

"Yep. Figure I'm gonna have to shoot the dealer after gettin' a hand like this," she said disgustedly.

"You bluffin'?" Cole asked.

She just shook her head.

He threw a couple of extra coins on the table.

When Cole proudly displayed a full house, Mary Margaret tossed over all four jacks.

"You been at this long?" she asked.

"Not long enough to tell when a young lass like yourself is bluffin'."

"Not poker," she clarified. "Bounty huntin'."

"Few years," he said. "I had a town sheriff job down in Colorado for a while, but my feet started gettin' itchy."

"What was her name?" Mary Margaret asked as Cole shuffled and dealt.

"Whose name?"

"The woman down in Colorado that made you get itchy feet," she smiled.

"Didn't say it was a woman who made my feet itch."

"Oh, come on," she laughed. "I've been around the block enough times to know that there's only two things that'll get a man over the age of twenty-five to feel like he's gotta pull up stakes. By the fact that you've taken to deliverin' wanted men to lawmen, I can rule out the one that involves runnin' from the law."

"Sally," Cole said. He figured there to be no harm in talking about his almost wife. Mary Margaret was old enough to be his mother, and he figured her intentions to be more nosey than romantic.

"Who was the feller?"

"Cardsharp named Hubbard . . . heading out to San Francisco." He didn't ask how she knew there was a "feller."

"Were you married to her?"

"Nope . . . almost."

"Almost don't cut it for a lady," Mary Margaret said, shaking her head in a motherly way. "Did Sally marry the gambler?"

"Don't know. Reckon she has a lot more prospects out there if she didn't."

"Reckon."

"How about you, Mary Margaret?" Cole asked. "What made you decide to stay on in this town all these years?"

"In the time that I had with Mike in this place, it sort of became like home. I didn't have nothing anywhere else."

"No family?"

"We came over from County Tipperary when I was four. My parents died in the fifties, my two brothers joined up with the 74th Pennsylvania and got themselves shot at Chancellorsville . . . You weren't at Chancellorsville, were you, Mr. Cole?"

"No, ma'am," he said, knowing that she knew he would have been on the other side.

"So I stayed on here because there was no place else," she said with an affirmation flavored by a slight dash of wistfulness. "How about you? Now that you know all about me, what put you onto a life on the run?

"I can tell by your accent that you and I were not on the same side in the war, but I consider that water to be long past the bridge."

"No, ma'am, we were not. My family is still down around Caroline County, Virginia. I rode with the raiders for a couple of months in '65 . . . me and my brother, Will . . . then we came west. We were down in Texas . . . ended up in New Mexico."

"Where's Will now?"

"He never made it out of New Mexico," Cole said, trying to be matter-of-fact. "Got shot in a bar fight. I got one of them who did it. Other got away."

"You're still hunting him, aren't you?" Mary Margaret asked sagely.

"Still looking around . . . not exactly hunting."

"Guess that's why you didn't stay settled down there in Colorado when Sally ran off. Hope you find him. Hope you find somebody to fill that hole that Sally left."

"I never said anything about a hole," he replied defensively.

"Didn't have to," she laughed. "In all my years of standing behind yonder bar, I've heard it all . . . and I've heard it so many times that I don't have to hear it . . . I can read it in their eyes."

"Reckon I'm bothered by it to a degree," Cole admitted.

"I suspect that when you're ready for courtin,' you'll know it."

"I keep an eye open."

"I'll bet you do," Mary Margaret laughed.

"What about you, Mary Margaret?"

"Hmmm?"

"You keepin' an eye open?"

"Well . . . when Mike passed, it was not like he run off. He was taken . . . I sort of resigned myself to permanent widowhood. Once in a while there's somebody passing through."

"I suppose . . ." Cole nodded.

"I didn't mean *you*," Mary Margaret clarified. "I hope you won't take offense . . . or disappointment . . . but you're just a wee bit on the young side for me."

"My heart is broke," Cole said with a smile.

"If I was twenty years younger, it might not be," she laughed, rocking back in her chair.

"So you're keepin' an eye open yourself?" Cole asked.

"You never know what can happen," she said.

The way that her eyes flicked subconsciously in the direction of the jail, an idea

251

came into Cole's head.

"Joshua Morgan?"

"Let's play some cards," Mary Margaret said, beginning to shuffle the deck again.

Cole had just succeeded in winning his first hand of the four they had played when the doctor came in. He looked cold and had a dusting of snow on his shoulders.

"You got something warm behind the bar, Mary Margaret?" he said.

"I'll put on a pot of coffee on," she said.

"Not that kind of warm," he said. "I just got back from delivering a set of twins out at the Edredin place. One of 'em didn't make it.

"Sorry to hear that," Mary Margaret said sympathetically as she poured a shot of dark amber liquid from a bottle that she kept under the bar. This, Cole knew, was what she called "the good stuff."

"The missus took it real bad," the doctor confided as he sat down at the table and savored a sip of his whiskey. "So did her husband."

"How's the other one?" Mary Margaret asked in a motherly way.

"She'll be fine. Got a real set of lungs on her. Squealed herself pink in the first moments of life."

"That's a good sign," Mary Margaret said.

Cole wondered if she had ever had children.

She dealt the doctor into the game without asking, and he drew a flush that topped his companions.

"Lucky day after all," he said without smiling. He raked the coins to his side of the table and took another sip.

"How's our patient?" Cole asked the doctor as they studied their next hands.

"He's on the mend," the doctor replied. "I've been keeping him pretty doped up because he's been in a lot of pain. He did almost more damage himself to his wrists than you did to his elbow. People don't seem to understand that you gotta clean a wound out real good as soon as possible or it will go to hell real fast."

"When do you suppose he'll be good enough to ride?" Cole asked.

"As I told you before when you asked that, it's been hard to say," the doctor replied. "But I reckon he could tolerate ridin' in a saddle in a day or two."

"Good," Cole said.

"You gettin' tired of us, Mr. Cole?" Mary Margaret asked teasingly.

"Not at all. I'm just anxious to get these jokers to the courthouse and get on with things."

"Hope you'll come back and see us," she

said, smiling. Cole figured that she really would miss the company. With the onset of winter, there would be fewer people passing though.

"I don't know whether to think of you as a fool or a saint to pay good money to have me putting this character back together just to turn him over to the law," the doctor observed.

"In the first place, it's *his* money," Cole said, referring to the $200 that had been in Gideon Porter's saddlebags. "In the second place, there's a lot more to justice than getting these two into the dock."

The doctor just nodded.

CHAPTER 20

Hannah Ransdell had been back to the Gallatin House a time or two after young Mr. Dawson Phillips, Jr., had gone back to Denver. She had not gone there to dine, or to reminisce about a meal with a handsome city fellow, but to scrounge newspapers.

Out-of-towners of the sort who would tend to frequent Gallatin City's leading hostelry would be the type who would read newspapers. Being the out-of-towners they were, they would arrive with out-of-town newspapers, including big city newspapers, and said papers would be discarded once read. Hannah was bent on learning all she could about the railroading plans of Mr. Frederick H. Billings.

By cross-referencing the information in the news articles, she ascertained that after several years of the Northern Pacific being in bankruptcy, Billings was pouring money into it, tracks were being laid, and they were headed for Gallatin City.

Though it was not customary for a daughter to know the nuances of her father's business dealings, it bothered Hannah that the banker's "assistant" had not known about a business deal that had so much potential.

Hannah had discerned the trace of bitterness in the voice of Dawson Phillips, Jr., when he spoke of this deal among the four partners, and in recollection, she sensed a trace of accusation when he spoke of it in light of the coming of the railroad. She knew that she was the type to overthink things, but the more she overthought this one, the more it seemed to warrant overthinking. The wheels in the back of her mind were churning like the driving wheels of a Northern Pacific locomotive.

Her father and his colleagues were certainly aware that the railroad would be coming and that they owned land across which it would come. What did it mean that her father and Mr. Stocker had inherited the interests of two men who had died violently in a crime that she considered unexplained?

Was her father somehow involved? He had not been present on that terrible night. Had this been by accident or by design? As much as she tried, she found it impossible not to think, much less *overthink,* the unthinkable.

The only way to clear her father from culpability in the unthinkable within the court of her own suspicions was to learn as much about the situation as she could.

When her father went out to lunch, she went to the old records, hoping to find out what her father had paid for the parcels of land north and east of Gallatin City. She occasionally had to look at the "old records" for one thing or another as part of her job, but when it involved going behind her father's back, it made her nervous.

She insisted to herself that she was doing nothing out of the ordinary. The old records, which were exactly that, and were *called* exactly that, were rarely consulted in day-to-day business, but *rarely* did not mean *never.*

Her heart jumped slightly when she found the first payment issued by Isham Ransdell for property in the areas in question.

The next day, Hannah stopped by at the land office, where there were copies of recorded deeds. The clerk knew her father, but one of her school friends worked there, so Hannah waited for the man to leave before she went in.

"Hello, Phoebe," she said as she pushed open the door.

"Hannah . . . it's so good to see you . . .

How have you been?"

Niceties having been concluded, Hannah explained to Phoebe that she needed to look at some old land records.

"Most of the public records are down at the county seat," her friend explained. "But we do have copies that list owners, deed numbers, tract locations, and things like that."

"That will do," Hannah said. "Thank you so much."

"Everything is filed by location," Phoebe said. "Here's a map with all the grid numbers . . . Hey . . . we should get together for lunch sometime . . . since we're both a couple of working girls."

"I'd like that," Hannah said. It really *would* be nice.

Gradually, Hannah calculated the exact locations of the property acquired by the four men. By multiplying her father's payments by four, she also knew what they had paid for the property. What Hannah could not calculate was how much it might be worth.

"Good morning, Miss Ransdell, it's a pleasant surprise to see you here this morning," Richard Wells said as she came into his dry goods store.

In her unfolding plan, Hannah needed to talk to a businessman, and a businessman outside her father's circle of friends and associates. As a competitor of John Blaine in the retail world of Gallatin City, Wells fit the bill. The Ransdells traditionally shopped at the Blaine store because of the connection, so Hannah's coming in here was a surprise. Her smile on a cold winter day made it the *pleasant* surprise that Wells described.

"Haven't seen you here in a while, figured you to be one to shop over at Blaine's."

"I need some hat ribbon, Mr. Wells. I don't really care for what they have to offer."

"Let me see what I can do for you," Wells said, turning to a shelf. "Solid or floral?"

"Floral brightens up a winter day, doncha think?" Hannah asked rhetorically.

"Are you still working down at the bank?" Wells asked, making conversation.

"I sure am . . . Waiting for the right man to come along," she answered, telling it as she imagined he would expect to hear it.

"I'd think you'd not have trouble finding him," he smiled. "A man would be lucky."

"Thank you, Mr. Wells."

"And old Isham would be lucky too . . ." the shopkeeper continued, "lucky to have a son-in-law to take into the business."

Hannah bristled, but the retort she considered appropriate was neither polite nor in furtherance of her purpose.

She smiled, selected a nice length of ribbon, which really *would* look nice on a hat, and put a coin on the counter.

As she was putting the ribbon into her bag, she allowed a newspaper to tumble out.

"Clumsy me," she said. "Oh . . . did you see this? They're saying the railroad is coming."

"I believe it is," Wells said. "It has been long delayed, but old Fred Billings appears to be the man who will finally do the trick."

"What will that mean?"

"It'll mean that folks from right here in Gallatin City can be walking the streets of the Twin Cities in three days or so . . . or Chicago a day beyond that . . . and travel there in *style,*" Wells said effusively. "It means that a merchant in Gallatin City, such as myself . . . such as Wells Mercantile . . . will be able to offer the ladies of Gallatin City the fashions of Chicago or even New York City . . . in a matter of a week or so after they have them in those places."

"My goodness," Hannah said, pretending not to have previously grasped such a concept. "What would it mean to property owners . . . landowners . . . in the area around Gallatin City?"

"Well, Miss Ransdell," he began in a schoolmasterish way, "the rails are being brought east from Tacoma, but those coming west out of Dakota Territory are likely to arrive first. That will mean that landowners out east of town will have what a speculator would call 'prime real estate,' if you understand what I'm saying."

"I certainly do, Mr. Wells," Hannah said. She did not have to pretend to be interested.

"The direction up toward Confederate Gulch and the gold fields, that would pretty much end up as prime real estate as well. There is much more advantage in those points of the compass than in the west, for instance. The rails coming from Tacoma will have to cross several ranges of mountains . . . the Cascades, the Bitterroots, the main thrust of the Rockies themselves . . . so they'll be a long time coming to Gallatin City."

"If I was buying land . . ." Hannah began with a hypothetical tone.

"Then I'd say you were a year or so *too late,*" Wells chuckled with a raised eyebrow. "Those who bought before then will command a mighty pretty penny."

261

"My goodness," Hannah said. "I'll bet they will have doubled their money by the time the railroad gets here."

"Doubled and doubled," Wells said with a grin. "And doubled again after that . . . *at least.*"

"Making the land worth eight times what it was worth just a few years ago?" Hannah summarized.

"At least." Wells nodded. "The railroad will need to lay down rails on ground, and it will have to get that ground from them who own it."

If Hannah Ransdell had hoped for her research to put her mind at ease about her father, then she was disappointed. By way of the crimes perpetrated at the Blaine home, the rapidly increasing value of her father's holdings had doubled overnight. And the night of that doubling brought to her mind the most nagging of suspicions, the one which she longed not to have in her mind. He *might have* been there on that dreadful night, in harm's way, but he was *not.*

As she walked back to the bank, thinking the unthinkable, she felt tears on her cheeks.

"Are you all right?" Isham Ransdell asked as his daughter came in the front door and went straight to her desk.

"Yes . . . Why do you ask?"

"Your eyes are red and likewise the tip of your nose."

"It's cold today, Father," she said dismissively without looking up from the papers she was shuffling on her desk.

The dialogue might have taken further turns had Edward J. Olson not walked through the door at that moment.

He went straight to Hannah's father's office.

Though the door was nearly closed, she did catch fragments of their conversation. The bounty hunter was mentioned, and she heard Olson use the phrase "dead or alive."

CHAPTER 21

Jimmy Goode had been more dead than alive when he had been led, slumped over in his saddle, into the tiny former mining town of Copperopolis. When he rode out, he was more alive than dead — but just barely. As he watched Bladen Cole dig the stiff and frozen body of Enoch Porter out from beneath a pile of snow behind the city's jailhouse, he knew that this might have been his fate as well.

Goode's right arm was chained to his left just as it had been on the night of his escape, but today it was chained in that manner only as an anchor, because his right arm could never again be used for anything more. His hand was still there, and likewise a healed wrist, but he had no use of either.

They had waited out a storm and left before sunup on the second day following the doctor's pronouncement of Goode's being well enough for travel.

The storm having been more wind than snow, the ground was mostly bare as they climbed down out of the Little Belts and into more level country. It was, Cole thought, to keep with Natoya-I-nis'kim's analogy of his having taken on some spirit of the grizzly, like emerging from the hibernation of the snowy days spent in Copperopolis.

Descending out of the mountains, Cole hoped to pick up the headwaters of Sixteen Mile Creek and follow its canyon downstream to the Missouri. He had not chosen the main wagon road, which led down toward Diamond City, but a less used trail that promised a shorter distance to his final destination.

"You stupid pup," Porter said assertively as Goode fought with one hand to keep his horse from snatching a bunch of grass, exposed above the snow along the trail.

"Back atcha, Gideon Porter," Goode said defiantly.

In the days prior to Jimmy Goode's escape, the two prisoners had ridden mainly in silence — Gideon Porter brooding and angry, Goode silent and intimidated. After their days apart during Goode's moment of freedom and days of convalescence, the social dynamic had changed. For Goode, who had stared down death and still rode upright, Porter was no longer so imposing. He saw his onetime taskmaster as an increasingly disheveled man, his long-gone fancy boots replaced by a pair of simple moccasins that the bounty hunter had bought for him.

Cole chuckled to himself at hearing Porter's onetime lackey speaking his mind. All in all, though, he'd preferred the days of sullen silence to the incessant bickering that now filled the air.

"They're gonna hang us just for being part of this, ain't they?" Goode asked Porter.

"Shut up your mouth, Goode. I don't want you talkin' about that."

"I know I ain't very smart, but they wouldn't have sent a bounty hunter after us unless they was fixin' to string us up."

"I told you to shut up about that," Porter demanded. "You're too damned stupid to be thinkin' about that."

"Too stupid to be thinkin' about my *own neck*?"

"Ever since your mama dropped you on your head when you was a baby, you been tryin' to think," Porter said angrily. "And you ain't very damn good at it or you'd know that they can't hang nobody for a killin' that was done by somebody else."

"I hope that those friends of yours back in Gallatin City can . . ." Goode started to say.

"I told you to *shut up!*" Porter interrupted.

Cole wondered about Porter's friends in Gallatin City, and he wondered about them a lot. Long rides are an incubator for wondering, and this was a topic to which Cole's mind kept returning.

Cole had also done a lot of self-analytical wondering about his own motivations for wanting to deliver Porter and Goode alive, when delivering them dead would have been so much easier. Had he decided on the latter course, he would have been in and out of Gallatin City by now. It would be untrue to say that the idea of shooting both Porter and Goode had not passed through his mind on several occasions. He had certainly been handed opportunities with legitimate excuses.

He could have simply delivered three bodies, collected his money, and been long gone — yet there was something that made him crave justice and truth over expedience. It caused him some degree of fright to believe this to be symptomatic of some latent nobility within himself. Bladen Cole, noble? It could not be, he insisted.

Though his mind may have been seduced

into reflecting, Bladen Cole's senses were on his prisoners and on their trail. Five senses processed the routine sights and sounds and so on, but it was Cole's *sixth* sense that made him turn in his saddle and look back toward the route over which they had come.

The first reaction was the satisfaction that's always the product of surveying the miles you have put behind you on a long trip. Second came the realization that those miles behind were not unoccupied. Roughly two of those miles farther back, on a hillside in the distance, there was a lone rider.

Cole could see little at this distance except a blue coat and a brown horse, neither of which were distinctive, and neither of which he recognized. The rider was coming deliberately, but not quickly. He was visible for only a few seconds before he dropped out of sight behind some trees in the foreground.

The most likely explanation was that he was just another traveler, making his way along the same trail that Cole had chosen. It may have been a less traveled road, but it was not an *untraveled* road.

Was it simply and innocently this, or was this lone rider bent on the same intended mischief that had cost the lives of the man in the big hat and his companion?

Was the man a lone rider or was he merely one part of a whole gang who had gotten wind of Cole's passing through Copperopolis with prisoners who had a price on their heads?

Cole weighed his options. He assumed, or at least hoped, that he had the advantage of the man not knowing that Cole had seen him. The bounty hunter knew that if he had been riding alone, it would have been easy to leave the trail and double back, screening himself in the thick timber, to get behind his pursuer. With two cantankerous and sporadically bickering charges, this would be more difficult, perhaps impossible. It could also tip Cole's hand as having become aware that he was being followed.

"Let's pick up the pace," Cole demanded of Porter and Goode. "We have a lotta miles to cover."

"What does it matter if we hang on Tuesday or Wednesday?" Goode asked.

"Shut up, you good-for-nothing Jimmy Goode," Porter snarled. "I told you we ain't gonna hang."

Cole looked back, hoping to see whoever followed them. The man he'd seen was not in a hurry, and perhaps by getting Porter and Goode to speed up, he could put more distance between them and the unknown pursuer or pursuers. He hurried them across a broad, treeless area and paused when they had reached the stand of ponderosa on the far side. He was curious to see how many riders entered the meadow.

To Cole's relief, only the single rider appeared, and he was more than two miles behind.

Through the waning hours of the day, Cole managed to keep far enough ahead so that the man didn't seem to know he'd been seen.

Cole made camp quickly as the sun went down, choosing a place beside the trail in a V-shaped canyon where a man attempting to flank the campsite in the dark would find it impossible without making noise slipping across the shale that littered the hillsides.

Having made a fire, the bounty hunter positioned himself high on this hillside, telling his prisoners that he was going to take a "look around."

It did not take long afterward for the lone rider in the blue coat to emerge upon the scene of the camp. His eyes being fixed on the brightness of the fire, he would not readily notice Cole ensconced above in the shadows of late evening.

When viewed at close range in the firelight, the identity of the mystery man was revealed.

It was Sheriff Joshua Morgan.

He reined his horse to a halt and surveyed the scene briefly before he spoke.

"Looks like you got yourself in a considerably less comfortable state there than you had in my cell, Porter," he said, looking at his former lodger chained to a ponderosa trunk.

"Damn you, Sheriff," the man growled.

"Where's Cole?" Morgan asked, looking around as though he imagined the bounty hunter to be nearby.

"He ain't here," Goode offered, after a long pause in which the question went unanswered by the moody Porter.

"I can see that," the sheriff said. "That's why I was asking."

"Heard him go up yonder hillside," Goode explained. "Couldn't rightly see where on account of being chained here pointed t'other way."

"Here," Cole said from his perch.

"What are you doing way up there?" Morgan asked.

"I been watching a fellow trailing us all day, and I figured I wanted to be on high ground when he overtook us."

"That feller would be me, I reckon."

"Reckon so," Cole confirmed. "I never figured on you being one to be following us."

"Got to thinking," Morgan said. "Got to thinking as I watched you ridin' out that you might . . . could use a hand with these two scamps."

"Thank you for the thought, Sheriff, but I've come a long way on my own, and figure I can finish the job."

"I didn't mean to question your abilities, Mr. Cole," Morgan said apologetically. "I just wanted to offer my services. I hope you don't take offense."

"No offense taken."

"Good," the sheriff said with an exaggerated sigh.

"Sorry to have you come all that way for nothing," Cole said in a way that was not in the least apologetic.

"No need to apologize," the sheriff said with a smile, trying to lighten the mood.

"You're welcome to camp with us tonight before you head back to Copperopolis," Cole said, his offer framed not in the generosity of hospitality, but as a stern insistence that the sheriff clear out at first light.

Cole slept fitfully and arose before the others when the only indication of the nearness of morning was the position of the moon in the western sky. The others still slept, Porter and Goode chained awkwardly to separate trees, and Morgan on the ground near the fire. He snored relentlessly, his head of white hair bobbing in the moonlight with each breath.

Cole entertained thoughts of kicking him to try to quiet him but did not.

The bounty hunter had no reason to doubt the sheriff's intentions, other than that sixth sense which had caused him so much consternation the day before. Was this sixth sense, this disquieting streak of exaggerated distrustfulness, part of the curse of the grizzly's medicine?

"Coffee?" Cole asked as the sheriff rolled from his sleeping bag, a sputtering sound on his lips.

"It's the middle of the night," the older man said, rubbing his eyes and scratching the several days' growth on his chin.

Cole gestured to the sliver of light on the eastern horizon.

Morgan just nodded.

"Coffee?" Cole repeated.

"Yeah . . . obliged."

"I drank a lot of your coffee in Copperopolis," Cole said, shrugging congenially.

"You're up early," Morgan said, stating the obvious, as Cole handed him a tin cup.

"Got some miles to get behind us."

"I was thinking . . ." Morgan began. "Ummm . . . I was thinking . . . about what we was talking about yesterday . . . about my offering to help you take these two in . . . and about your saying you didn't need no help."

"Don't believe I do," Cole said succinctly.

"Well, you had one of those two fellers get away from you once . . ."

"He ain't going anywhere again," Cole interrupted, referencing Jimmy Goode's crippled state. He had not mentioned to the sheriff that *both* of the prisoners had made escape attempts.

"You never know," Morgan said, shaking his head.

"Now, Sheriff, I *do* appreciate your offer . . . and I *greatly* appreciate your hospitality in letting me store one of my prisoners at your jail . . . but I paid you an agreed sum for that, and I consider our dealings to have come to a close."

"Listen, young man," Morgan said, playing the elder statesman card. "I have been in and around law enforcement and the care of desperados since long before you were saddling your own horse, and I know a situation where two gunhands are better than one when I see it."

"I will certainly grant you the years of experience, Sheriff, but I am willfully determined that I'll be carrying on alone."

Morgan sat for some time, thoughtfully staring off into the distance. At last he spoke.

"Is there any . . . ?"

"Nope."

"What if I was to *ask* you politely to include me in this?" Morgan asked.

"No. I have gone through just about everything, including coming damned near being dinner for a grizzly, to get to this point, and I am not in a mood to share the reward . . . That's what it's about, isn't it? The reward?"

"Well . . . not that I know what that reward might be . . . excepting that I can imagine it to be a goodly sum . . . but I would be a liar if I said that the thought had *not* crossed my mind."

"That's what I *thought,*" Cole laughed sarcastically.

"I get barely more than room and board in Copperopolis," the sheriff complained. "I been there for years . . . ever since the town was *something* . . . and I ain't growing any younger."

"You were looking to sign on with me to bankroll a little change of scenery, then?"

"You could put it that way . . . I reckon," Morgan admitted.

"I just did," Cole said.

"I heard you talkin'. When we were sittin' around up yonder, I heard you talkin' about not liking to be setting in one place too long."

"I've been known to use those words," Cole said with a shrug.

"Well, you aren't the only one," the sheriff insisted. "I have spent the last many years committed to exactly the opposite, to being planted firmly in one place, but a man gets to thinkin'. A man gets to wondering . . . A man gets to wondering whether it might be true that you *can* set in one place too long."

"A man *does* wonder," Cole agreed.

"So I got to thinkin' that I ought to grab hold of whatever opportunity that might come along to get on to some other land-scape."

"So you rode out to give me a little sales pitch?"

"That I did."

"I see . . ."

"It ain't entirely about the money . . ."

"It ain't?"

"Well, I'd be a liar to say that ain't a *part*

276

of it," Morgan clarified. "But I'd be a bigger liar to say that that's *all* there is to it."

"Itchy feet?"

"A man gets to setting, and he stops wondering," the older man said, looking Cole in the eye. "If you stop wondering . . . you stop thinking about anything besides what's inside of your own four walls . . . and you stop being alive."

"That's a pretty drastic view," Cole replied.

"What I'm saying is that if you get to doin' nothing but setting around . . . pretty soon you ain't good for nothing 'cept setting around."

"I suppose . . ."

"I figured that at my age, I don't have many more chances to change away from setting around. At my age, the body isn't as limber as it once was . . . even a day's ride like yesterday's makes a man feel mighty stove up. If I don't get around to goin' *now,* I *never* will."

"Isn't there *anything* left for you in Copperopolis?" Cole asked.

"Don't reckon on nothing that is worth me staying for."

"What about Mary Margaret?" Cole asked, recalling a wistful look in her eye with regard to mention of the sheriff.

"Mary Margaret?"

"Yeah, Mary Margaret?"

"What about Mary Margaret?" Morgan asked, almost indignantly.

"About her having this sort of dreamy expression when your name came up."

"Can't imagine that to be."

"Let me ask you this . . . Are you interested in her at all . . . you know . . . in her as a *woman*?"

"She's got a look about her, I'll give you that," Morgan said, barely repressing a grin. "But as far as her and me . . . I reckon she'd never give me the time of day."

"You ever ask?"

"Of course not," the sheriff exclaimed.

"Why not?"

"A man don't ask a woman nothing unless he's damned sure of a positive answer."

"Yeah . . . I understand," Cole shrugged, "but I bet you'd be more likely to get a positive answer from Mary Margaret than you seem to think you would."

"Do tell."

"It ain't my place to tell a man that he *hasn't* been too long in a place," Cole said. "That would be against my nature . . . but I *will* tell you that I think you're wrong to say you got *nothing* left for you back in Copperopolis."

CHAPTER 22

The hierarchy of society in any community will have its center, its high and its mighty, and it will have its fringe. On the periphery of said fringe are the hangers-on, and the doers of odd and part-time jobs. Beyond that edge are the ne'er-do-wells, whose odd jobs are as often as not beyond the edge of what can be considered lawful.

In the hierarchy of society in Gallatin City, the latter caste certainly included the Porter boys, though they were not alone. Their names would be likely to come up in the same sentence with those of men such as Lyle Blake and Joe Clark, whom one might generously have characterized as losers.

For this reason, Hannah Ransdell did a double take when she saw Blake and Clark seated at the same table in the Big Horn Saloon with Edward J. Olson.

On her daily rounds, whether it be to the post office, or to Mr. Blaine's store for supplies, Hannah's route did not often take her on the boardwalk that passed the Big Horn Saloon. It was an institution that was not patronized by ladies — as the women who were seen inside the Big Horn were not considered to be "ladies" by the women of society's hierarchy who considered *themselves* to be ladies.

So long as she held to the pretense of her place in the hierarchy of Gallatin City society, Hannah avoided the Big Horn Saloon.

This is not to say that the place did not have a certain risqué allure, but she imagined that the allure of the laughter and the tinkling piano might not stand up to the reality of the stench of stale beer and tobacco smoke that often wafted beyond the swinging doors.

But for the company he was keeping today, Hannah would not have thought twice about seeing Edward J. Olson in the Big Horn — the rules of the hierarchy that governed ladies did not apply to gentlemen — but seeing him with Blake and Clark was surprising. What business did her father's "right-hand man" have with these lowlifes?

She wished that she could just stroll into the Big Horn, order a beer, feign surprise at seeing Olson there, and ask him point-blank

— but, of course, she *could not.*

She wished too that she could just stroll into the bank and ask her father what his "right-hand man" was doing at the Big Horn in the middle of the afternoon with Blake and Clark — but, of course, she *would not.*

Hannah did not, however, refrain from asking; rather she did so indirectly.

"What errands do you have Edward J. Olson doing for you these days? I haven't seen him in the office for a day or two."

"Some things out at the ranch," Isham Ransdell replied without looking up, giving a matter-of-fact answer to a matter-of-fact question. "Getting some men to rebuild the shed so we can bring in more hogs in the spring . . . Pork prices are on the rise again . . . good time to get into hogs."

"What do you hear from your bounty hunter?" Hannah asked, not commenting on the evasiveness of his reply.

"I've heard nothing since I got that letter postmarked out of Fort Benton," he said, looking up from his desk. "Why do you ask?"

"Just wondering. I heard you and Mr. Olson talking about it the other day."

"Yes . . . we were wondering ourselves," he replied. "The man said he was headed into Blackfeet country. There's no telling what might have happened out there."

"Do you reckon that he'll bring them back alive?" Hannah asked.

"One way or another, I hope he brings them *back,*" the banker said. "Could be that they'll *all* wind up under this winter's snow with Blackfeet arrows in them."

Hannah grimaced slightly at the thought of the handsome bounty hunter with the showings of a nice beard lying dead on the wild and distant plains.

"Do you prefer the Porter boys dead or alive, Father?"

"Well, wanting a man, even a *Porter,* to be dead, is not something a man likes to talk about with his daughter . . . but I will say that justice would be done either way."

Hannah Ransdell left work at her usual time. It was her custom to leave within an hour of the bank's closing in order to prepare supper for herself and her father, who usually remained at his desk until around seven.

As usual, the walk home took her past the Gallatin City General Mercantile and Dry Goods. Even all these weeks after the murders, people still called it "Mr. Blaine's store." If she needed something for the meal, she could always stop in and get it. Today, she had neither reason nor intention of doing so — until she saw Lyle Blake and Joe Clark walking into the place.

The embers of curiosity that remained from her having seen them in the Big Horn with Olson burst into flame. She impulsively followed them. Unlike the saloon, Gallatin City's largest store was frequented by those from all strata of the social hierarchy.

Hannah had no notion whatsoever of what she could or would accomplish by following Blake and Clark, but neither did she have any question that she should.

She inserted herself into a place where she would appear to be examining goods on the opposite side of a large rack from where the men were picking out beans and hardtack.

"Three days' ride, I figure," Blake said. "Gotta have enough provisions to go up and back."

Clark disagreed. "I reckon four."

His partner admonished him "That's 'cause you're a lazy sonuvabitch. Anyhow, I don't reckon on havin' to ride all the way to Copperopolis."

"You reckon they left by now?"

"Yeah . . . I figure they must have," Blake affirmed.

"One of 'em's wounded, though," Clark cautioned.

Hannah wondered who they might be describing. She remembered having heard once of a place called Copperopolis, but she could not recall where it was.

"They're not coming very fast if one of 'em's wounded," Clark continued.

"I figure we should get to 'em somewhere there on Sixteen Mile Creek," Blake said.

"We gotta . . . There's too much traffic comin' down from Diamond City once you get as far as the Missouri."

"You figure we gotta kill 'em all?"

Blake's question was not the sort one should be discussing in public in the afternoon, but the whiskey provided at the Big Horn Saloon, even with its presale watering down, had loosened his tongue considerably.

Far from being appalled by talk of murder, Hannah was only gripped by stronger yearnings of curiosity. Had they had more of their wits about them, they would have seen her craning her neck to hear them.

"Olson said that there is no way the Porter boys can show up alive in Gallatin City," Clark asserted. "Olson said there's no way they can be allowed to point fingers at them who can't have fingers pointed at them."

"What about the bounty hunter?"

"Guess he probably knows what Olson don't want told. I guess he's gotta get himself killed too."

From this exchange Hannah recoiled.

Talk of murder was one thing when it was in the abstract, like the plot of a dime novel, but quite another when the intended victims were the bounty hunter and the Porter boys.

Hannah Ransdell sat at her desk, staring at the notes she kept in her bottom drawer. Her head was spinning. After the conversation she had overheard the day before at the Gallatin City General Mercantile and Dry Goods, she could concentrate on nothing but her secret project.

She had found and followed the paper trail of the acquisition, and she had seen how the death of any member of the foursome would benefit his partners. She had calculated the value and confirmed that it would increase — if not eightfold as Richard Wells had estimated — at least *many* times.

Hannah had discovered that her father's net worth had at least doubled as a result of the murders. Had this been by coincidence or design?

She had dreaded the unthinkable hypothesis of her father's involvement in eliminating his partners on the eve of their jointly held land doubling and doubling in value, and then doubling again.

She had held out hope that it was all mere coincidence, despite the pronouncements of her overactive imagination. There had been no real and true reason to believe otherwise, despite the way it might *appear.*

That is, until she heard of her father's right-hand man ordering the deaths of the men who could point their fingers at Isham Ransdell himself. Lyle Blake and Joe Clark would kill the Porter boys and the bounty hunter, and with this, the fingers would never be pointed.

Her father.

Could it be?

How could he be involved in this?

Her *own* father.

"Hannah, what's wrong?" Isham Ransdell said as he came into the bank. "You don't look well."

She had gone to her room before dinner the night before and had left the house before him this morning. He had thought her to be ill, but in reality, she could no longer look him in the face without breaking into tears.

"I'm not," she stammered, "I'm not feeling well . . . May I go home?"

"Yes, of course," the banker said.

Once on the street, Hannah walked uncertainly in the direction of her home.

What should she do?

Conventional wisdom told her that murders and murder plots should be reported to the sheriff — but he was dead, gunned down by the same killers who had doubled the value of her father's land.

There was Deputy — Acting Sheriff — Marcus Johnson, but he was on light duty, recovering from wounds suffered in the same shootout that killed the sheriff. She could tell *him,* but what evidence did she have to offer?

None.

In the hierarchy of Gallatin City, what was the place of the daughter who accused her father of ordering brutal killings, and who did so without evidence?

What should she do?

What *could* she do?

She walked aimlessly, tossing the facts over in her mind and replaying the sequence of events.

Suddenly, it dawned on her.

She realized what she could do. She realized who she could tell. There was *one man* she could tell — the only survivor among the Big Four of the brutal assault on the Blaine home!

"Is Mr. Stocker in?" Hannah asked the clerk in Virgil Stocker's law office.

"Do you have an appointment?"

"No . . ."

Declining to go away and come back in an hour, she waited in the chair offered, watching the hands on the clock grind slowly around its face.

An hour passed, and then the better part of another.

"Mr. Stocker will see you now."

Finally.

The scarring on Virgil Stocker's face was still ugly, red and not fully healed. Hannah felt pity for a man likely to be disfigured permanently. She had seen him only a time or two since the murders, and then only at a distance, so the sight of the injury was jarring.

"Good morning, Miss Ransdell, how are you?" He smiled, standing up behind his desk as she entered his office.

"How are *you*?" Hannah asked, looking at his face. "Are your injuries healing?"

"As good as can be expected, I suppose," he shrugged. "How is your father?"

With the mention of her father, she could

not hold back the tears. The attorney leaped up to pour her a tumbler of water, which she accepted gratefully.

"Thank you for seeing me," she said when she had regained her composure well enough to talk.

"Of course."

"I have come to you on a grave matter."

"What is it?" Stocker asked sympathetically.

"It's about my father . . ." she said, breaking once again into tears.

"Is he all right?"

"I believe that he may have been involved," Hannah said between sobs. "I think that he may have been behind what the Porter boys did that night."

"That's impossible," Stocker said forcefully. "I've known Isham Ransdell for more than fifteen years . . ."

"*I've* known Isham Ransdell for twenty-five years," Hannah interrupted. "Nobody can be sadder about this than *me.*"

"What makes you think that it was he?"

"The will . . . Mr. Phillips's will . . . I learned that with this land that the partners purchased . . . the partners had right of inheritance."

"That's correct," Stocker nodded.

"I've learned that when the railroad

reaches Gallatin City, the land will be worth about eight times its original value."

"It is certainly true that the value will increase as the railroad approaches," Stocker said thoughtfully. "But the fact that an investment pays off is no motive for *murder.*"

"But the right of inheritance?" Hannah replied.

"Miss Ransdell, you have a superb head for calculation . . . for putting two and two together with respect to the value of the property to the railroad . . . but by your reasoning . . . by the inheritance issue . . . *I too* would have had a motive for the killings."

"But you were hurt . . . and my father *wasn't there.*"

"Yes, but that's just circumstantial . . ."

"That's what I thought . . . until . . ."

"Until?"

"Until I saw my father's right-hand man . . . Edward J. Olson . . . with Lyle Blake and Joe Clark . . ."

"I see," Stocker said. "They're not exactly the most upstanding citizens around these parts . . . but this is still what we would call 'circumstantial' in the eyes of the law."

"Until I overheard Blake and Clark in Blaine's store," she said, dabbing at the tears on her cheeks with her handkerchief.

"What did . . . ?"

"Edward J. Olson has ordered them to go *kill* the Porter boys."

"Why would he?"

"So they can't point their fingers at *my father.*"

"I think you're just jumping to conclusions," the attorney said sympathetically. "I'm sure that it's all a big misunderstanding. Your father couldn't possibly . . ."

"I just wish I could get away," Hannah said.

"Yes," Stocker agreed. "A change of scenery can always do wonders for a person's mood. Do you have anywhere . . . ?"

"I have a friend down in Bozeman who has wanted me to see her new baby," Hannah replied. "The child must be nearly walking by now."

"That sounds like a wise course indeed," Stocker said. "While you're gone, I'll look into the matter. I'm sure that there is an explanation, and I'll find it. Everything will be back to normal by the time you return."

Hannah Ransdell thanked Virgil Stocker and took her leave.

Yes, a change of scenery *was* called for.

Visiting Rebecca and the baby would be a welcome delight. However, under the present circumstances, when a mystery so vexing had to be resolved, she questioned whether she should, indeed whether she *could,* pamper herself with an activity carried out purely in the indulgence of her own pleasure.

As she went to the stage company office to purchase a ticket on the afternoon coach for Bozeman, the wheels were turning in her mind. She knew that she needed to keep her attention on the task at hand.

Instead of returning to the bank, she went home to pack her bag.

As usual, she set the table for dinner, but she set it for one. She left a note for her father on the dining room table, explaining that she was going out of town for a week to visit Rebecca, whom she had not seen in some time. She knew that he knew that it was not like her to go off on a whim like this, but men generally thought of women as impetuous, so she was merely fulfilling a stereotype. Hannah scorned the idea of filling the pigeonhole of the inexplicably impulsive girl, but rationalized that there was no harm in using the stereotype to her advantage. Certainly, she should be allowed to use every means at her disposal in the furtherance of the task at hand — that being the resolution of the conundrum that continued to haunt her at every turn.

Yes, a change of scenery *was* called for.

CHAPTER 23

Looking over his shoulder as he rode, Bladen Cole watched the rider in the blue coat grow smaller and smaller and finally disappear in the soft haze of gently drifting snowflakes.

He hoped that he had imparted good counsel to Joshua Morgan. He was not accustomed to the practice of giving advice in matters of the heart, and he was therefore unsure that telling a man to bet his future on a woman was something he was qualified to do.

Selfishly, he was relieved to have the sheriff out of his way. Even if Morgan did an about-face the moment he returned to Copperopolis, he would still be two days behind. Cole would never see him again.

Thankfully, the bickering between Gideon Porter and Jimmy Goode had slackened. They were exhausted after a short night and their uncomfortable sleeping arrangements.

Cole reckoned that Goode might even fall asleep in his saddle if given half a chance.

By early afternoon, they were within sight of Sixteen Mile Creek, snaking between patches of ponderosa in the valley beyond. Here and there, the smoke from a prospector's cabin rose into the windless sky. Random snowflakes still fell like feathers escaping from a pillow. It was as though the sky really did not want to snow but a few flakes had slipped through the crevices in the pillowcase of low-hanging clouds.

Hoping to avoid as many of the cabins as possible, Cole left the trail. He knew that once they reached Sixteen Mile Creek it would not be hard to find it again.

Nor was he especially worried about a chance encounter with a prospector. Whereas a bounty hunter and his prisoners might raise an eyebrow elsewhere, here this fact would only convince the prospectors that they were merely passing through and not here to cast an avaricious gaze upon anyone's claim.

As he rejoined the trail on the banks of the creek, Cole was pleased to see that no one had ridden this way since the snow had begun falling early in the morning. They passed a place where a man was panning for gold. He had his gear stacked near where he was working, with his rifle at the ready.

Cole waved.

The man waved back with uncertain hesitancy and watched the three riders only long enough to be sure that they were not claim jumpers, before returning to work. Even all these years after the big strike at Confederate Gulch, everyone panning gold on Sixteen Mile Creek was certain that the next pan of gravel would be his ticket to El Dorado.

As it was growing dark, they saw another man at work on a sandbar that paralleled a stream entering Sixteen Mile Creek from the opposite side.

The man hailed them, raising his voice loud enough to carry across the sound and distance of the creek. "Howdy, strangers."

"Hello," Cole returned with a wave.

"Say there," shouted the man, "I hate to bother you . . . but could I trouble y'all for a hand?"

"What did you say?" Cole asked.

"I could sure use a bit of help from you men," he repeated. "My sluice got drug too far into the creek and I need a hand gettin' it back."

Cole surveyed the scene. At first glance, it appeared as though the man had turned one bank of the side stream into a junk yard. All manner of boxes, pipes, and other stuff was scattered along it from where the man stood to a shack that lay about a hundred feet upstream. Two large dogs wandered about, looking idly at the man. Cole could see a sluice box that was about twelve feet from shore and sitting at an angle.

"I'll see what I can do," he shouted back to the man. His mind told him to expect a trap, but his instincts told him that this was not one.

"I ain't goin' in that goddamn water barefoot," Gideon Porter snarled angrily, having overheard the conversation.

"Oh, shut up," Cole said, more annoyed than angry.

"Some sonuvabitch gave my boots to a goddamn Indian."

"Shut up, Porter. You're not barefoot."

"Moccasins ain't no damn good in a stream."

Cole sent the two prisoners to ford Sixteen Mile Creek first and followed behind them as was his custom.

"Looks like you're ridin' with a couple of captives there, mister," the man said when he saw that Porter and Goode were chained to their saddles.

"Yep," Cole said, confirming the obvious.

"You a lawman?" the man asked.

"He's a goddamn *bounty hunter,*" Porter answered before Cole could say anything.

"I'll be danged to hell," the man said, looking at Cole.

"I'm just like you," Cole added. "I'm just trying to scratch out a living."

He then ordered the two men to dismount and stand next to the horses to whose saddles they were chained. The two dogs barked vigorously until the man hurled obscenities at them, whereupon they slunk away to eye the proceedings from a distance.

With Porter and Goode in a position in which an escape attempt would be awkward to the extreme, Cole directed his attention to the prospector.

"Name's Walz . . . Jake Walz," he said, extending his hand. He was an older man. He looked about sixty, though he may have been a younger man who had weathered to that appearance.

"Bladen Cole. These here are Porter and Goode. They got a date with the law down in Gallatin City."

"I won't ask why," Walz said. "Ain't in my nature to pry into somebody else's business."

"What do you need done?" Cole asked, looking at the sluice box.

"The current done moved my box out of

this here channel next to the shore and out onto yonder bar."

"I see . . . and you need to have it dragged back in the channel here."

"Yes, sir . . . I been trying to get it back. Workin' at it for more than a week. I had debated callin' out for help as I done with you, but . . . I'd be mighty obliged if you could help me."

"Let's figure the best way to do this," Cole said, studying the problem as presented. "You got a horse?"

"No, sir," Walz said with a degree of sadness. "I did have, but I had to sell her off. All I got's the dogs."

By his tone, he did not hold his canine companions in high esteem.

"Sorry to hear that," Cole said sympathetically. Apparently, prospecting did not afford the steady income that would allow a man the luxury of keeping livestock. "Guess we could use mine."

Walz waded into the frigid water to attach a rope to one end of the sluice box, while Cole anchored the rope to his saddle horn. The roan then pulled the sluice a few feet through the stream.

By repeating this process several times with the rope attached to various places on the cumbersome contraption, they were finally able to reposition it to the prospector's satisfaction.

When they were at last through, the sky was dark and snowflakes were falling heavier than before.

"Since its gotten too dark to travel, and since I've helped you out here, I was wondering if we could make camp up yonder in that clearing above your house?" Cole asked.

"Well . . ." Walz said thoughtfully as he stood on the shore shivering in his wet clothes.

He obviously prided himself on living alone. Most men in his profession tended to become hermits over time, regardless of whether they had any proclivity in that direction before taking up backwoods prospecting.

"Well . . . I reckon that would be all right . . . but I don't have no grub to offer."

"That's fine," Cole said. "We got our own . . . probably even extra that we can share with you."

The man smiled at that possibility and scurried up the hill to his hovel to dry himself.

Cole was pleased at the bartering he had done. The dried meat was easily worth a campsite off the main trail along Sixteen Mile Creek, guarded by two dogs. However lazy they were, they were unafraid to bark at strangers.

Having set up camp in a place sheltered by a dense stand of tall cottonwoods, Cole took his prisoners down to Walz's house, carrying some dried buffalo meat that had been part of Cole's gift from O-mis-tai-po-kah and his people.

Walz welcomed them into his home, which was warmed by a fire in an ancient stove as potbellied as its owner. The house had the strong odor of having long been shared with the dogs, but at least it was dry.

"Nice place you got here," Cole lied. "How long you been out here?"

"Since '69 . . . I came up from Confederate Gulch in '69," he said. "Mighty nice of you to share provisions with me."

"Mighty obliged for a place to camp."

"I ain't had buffalo jerky in years. There used to be an Indian fella came through trading it, but I haven't seen him in . . . I can't remember when. I get me a couple deer every now and then . . . an elk maybe . . . put in a patch of onions and taters every year."

"You got a regular farm up here," Cole observed.

"Where'd you get this meat?" Walz asked.

"From the Blackfeet."

"Whatcha doin' up in Blackfeet country?"

"Doin' a little hunting."

"Get anything?"

"Yup."

"What's it like up there? I've heard tell those redskins up there are truly untamed creatures."

"Depends on who's writing the definition of 'tame.' "

"Well, I reckon if you can come back with your scalp intact, that's sayin' a lot."

"Reckon."

"He had him a little squaw up there," Gideon Porter interjected. "Didn't you, bounty hunter?"

"You didn't say you was a 'squaw man.' " Walz smiled lasciviously.

"Ain't a squaw man," Cole corrected, scowling at Porter. "I was takin' her back to her place after roundin' up some horses."

"How *are* their squaws?" Walz queried.

"Wouldn't know," Cole said.

"He shot my little brother for wantin' to find out," Porter said.

"Your brother got himself shot for tryin' to cut up her face."

Walz looked at Porter in disgust. Even to a recluse who had lived beyond the edge of civilization for a decade, the deliberate disfigurement of a woman's face was viewed with revulsion.

"The placers are still pretty active up this way," Cole said, changing the subject.

"People do all right." Walz nodded.

"That's good to hear."

"You thinkin' about it, Mr. Cole?"

"I don't have the patience," Cole said with a smile. "I don't like to be too long in any one place. That takes a special kind of man to put in all the years required."

"I don't reckon to be here forever, myself," said the man who had worked this obviously marginal claim for a decade. "I fancy myself as kind of a wanderer."

"I see," Cole said, wanting to laugh at the irony.

"I've got my sights set on some place warmer . . . like down in Arizona Territory."

"I've heard of some pretty good strikes down there all right. How long you reckon you got on this claim?"

"Are you sure you ain't lookin' to nose in here?" Walz asked suspiciously.

"Absolutely not," Cole assured him. "I like it warmer myself."

"Ain't in my nature to pry into somebody else's business . . . but I suspect you do move around a lot in your line of work," the prospector observed.

"Yep . . . Colorado . . . Wyoming . . . Like

303

I said, I've developed a way of livin' that doesn't allow for staying around one place too long. I tried it down in Colorado and found out it didn't suit me."

"That's me too," the old man said thoughtfully. "I'm sure lookin' forward to gettin' a move-on myself."

"So long as you don't nose in on the bounty huntin' business."

"What?"

"That was a joke," Cole said. "I was just funnin' y'all . . . I would no more expect you to get into *my* line of work than I would expect me to get into *yours*."

"I see," the prospector said tentatively, before breaking into a broad smile. "Listen . . . can I let you in on something?" Walz asked in a hushed voice, dramatically leaning close so that Porter and Goode could not hear his words.

"Shoot," Cole whispered back.

"I'm gonna be outta here by fall."

"Fall's just past."

"I mean *next* fall."

"Oh."

"One more spring," Walz said confidently. "One more spring is all it's gonna take. You know how a placer works, Mr. Cole?"

"Well, I guess not exactly," he replied,

sensing that a good story was about to unfold.

"A placer gets its gold from the mother lode."

"Like the one out in California?"

"Yep. It's the mother that keeps the placers populated . . . year after year after year. Every spring there's more color . . . new gold in the placer. Next spring is gonna be the *one* . . . The mother is gonna give up *so much of her color* that it will put the Gulch to shame. I can *feel it in my bones.* I know it. I can see all the signs . . ."

CHAPTER 24

A bitter cold wind howled hauntingly through the trees. An hour after she ascended into the Belt Range, the reality of her situation dawned on Hannah Ransdell. The headstrong, single-minded woman remembered the impressionable young girl who had recoiled with horror at the terrible stories of "children lost in the woods" in these same mountains.

Hannah looked around at the thick forest, black and impenetrable, into which she had thrown herself. Her horse made slow progress, pausing to step over deadfalls and negotiate steep and slippery slopes. There were a few snowflakes in the air, but the only snow on the ground was in places where it had drifted deep in the storm a week ago and never melted.

With all the maneuvering and "going around" of obstacles that they had been doing, Hannah was sure that she and the mare would have gotten themselves completely and inexorably turned around if she hadn't had the presence of mind to pick up the old compass in the tarnished brass case which her father had given her so long ago.

Her father.

Her father.

Tears of anger came mixed with tears of sadness, and she wiped her cheeks on the sleeve of her riding jacket.

How could he have done this?

What would she say when she finally confronted him?

Would he say that he had done it for *her*?

Would he insist that he had done it for *her* long-term financial well-being?

Had she never known what he had done, her financial well-being would have eventually been greatly enhanced. He was far from being a poor man, but within a few years, he would be an extremely wealthy man, and she was his only heir.

Had it not been for her suspicious nature, things would be very different — and very much *easier* — at this moment.

Had she never known what she had learned in the long hours she had spent on her research, things would, indeed, be very different at this moment. She might be going home to a warm house, a warm meal, and a warm bath instead of riding though the dark forest that swallowed little children and impetuous young daughters of bankers.

What a fool she was to do this, she thought, as she listened to the moaning of the wind and the occasional whining *yip* of coyotes in the distance.

An unseen hand had snatched her and put her in this frightening place. That same hand now kept pushing her ever onward and pushing thoughts of retreat from her mind.

That hand, for better or worse, was her *own.*

Despite the leaden, overcast skies, she knew that it would soon be the hour of lengthening shadows. As it was, she knew that it would soon be the hour when darkness simply closed over these mountains like a black glove.

Part of her resolve demanded that she press on blindly. She was single-minded about following through once she had decided to do something. Her mother had called her "bullheaded."

When she had decided that Lyle Blake and Joe Clark *must* be stopped, she had asked the question of *who* would stop them.

The answer was that she would have to do it *herself.*

This was definitely "bullheaded."

Now that the reality of this course of action was setting in, she wondered if she was crazy for making this impulsively imprudent decision. Before she had grown into the "bullheaded" teenager who had become the headstrong, single-minded woman, Hannah had been the impressionable young girl who recoiled with horror at those terrible stories of "children lost in the woods" in these same mountains. The dangers here were not fairy tales, though. They were real. Throughout her childhood, there *were* children who *really* never came back.

Part of her resolve demanded that she press on blindly, but another part cautioned that if she did not soon make camp, the blindness that came with night would be her undoing.

Tethering the mare to a tree in a patch of dry grass where her horse could forage, Hannah unrolled her sleeping bag on the leeward side of the root ball of a huge ponderosa, long ago toppled in a storm. She had brought a fistful of matches, wrapped in wax paper to keep them dry, but starting a fire under these circumstances took more effort — and more luck — than she had remembered, and *keeping* it going in the cold wind took even more.

The thought occurred to her that she was

working up such a sweat starting the fire that she wouldn't need the extra warmth.

She thought this to be funny, and she laughed out loud.

The sound seemed so empty and so hollow when mixed with the deep baritone moan of the wind.

Her horse seemed not even to take notice.

She ate some of the bread that she had put into her saddlebags and wished she had brought more to eat. At least she had remembered the compass and the old Winchester rifle that was kept at the ranch.

As Hannah had boarded the stagecoach, she had made sure that her presence was noticed by many. If her father had inquired about her, the station agent would have confirmed her purchase of a ticket to Bozeman, and several others would confirm that they had spoken with her about the journey. Others had seen her waving as the stage pulled out of Gallatin City.

When she asked to be let out at her father's ranch, she was observed only by people who were headed to Bozeman. None would be returning to Gallatin City anytime soon. Even the stage driver would not be back for several days at the earliest.

From there, she had moved quickly, driven by adrenaline and that unseen hand. She saddled her own mare, whom she had named Hestia after the goddess of home and hearth, and who was kept at the ranch. She filled a canteen, tied a bedroll to the mare's saddle, took the compass and rifle, and headed north.

Instead of following a trail — for there was no human trail that led straight across these mountains — she had followed only the due north of her compass. She knew that this would take her to the valley of Sixteen Mile Creek, where Clark and Blake intended to intercept the bounty hunter and the Porter boys, and she hoped that the shortcut would get her there before either party.

Lying fully clothed in her sleeping bag with the Winchester beside her, she stared up at the sparks from her fire soaring upward to meet the snowflakes coming downward.

Hannah awoke with a jump, her dream quickly disappearing into her subconscious like a prairie dog down its hole. Hestia was snorting and sputtering and began pawing the ground nervously. Something was bothering her.

Hannah sat up and looked around. The snow had stopped falling. Here and there she could see shafts of moonlight and the moon itself through the trees. The fire had died down to embers, so she jabbed it with a stick, trying to bring it to life.

The mare was growing more agitated, and Hannah wondered what was amiss.

Suddenly, out of the corner of her eye, she caught a flicker of movement. Something was out there. She felt a nervous chill.

Hestia reared and stomped.

Then Hannah saw it, the glint of the firelight in a pair of eyes.

She pulled the Winchester from her sleeping bag and stared into the dark woods.

The pair of eyes, moving in and out among the trees, was low to the ground and about thirty feet away. It could be a coyote, or it could be a *wolf.*

Coyotes are scavengers. Wolves are predators.

Thoughts and fears cascaded through her mind.

Coyotes are skulking opportunists. Wolves are aggressors.

A wolf could attack her horse and leave her stranded on foot in the wilderness — or attack *her* and leave her dead or wounded in the wilderness. This was how people disappeared forever in these mountains.

She briefly wished that she had stayed to

a more well-traveled trail. This would have defeated her desire for a direct route, but it would have greatly diminished the likelihood of her present predicament. As aggressive as wolves are, they generally shun places that are frequented by people — but she was not now in such a place. She was in the dark woods that belonged to the predator.

Hannah shouldered the Winchester. She was familiar with this rifle. She had been firing long guns since she was nine, and this very one since she was a teenager. The recoil had knocked her down the first time, but she stood up and fired again, determined not to let a piece of steel and walnut get the best of her. Over the years, she had become quite good with a rifle, and even her father had remarked about her skilled marksmanship.

Her father.

If the wolf — if it *was* a wolf — was growling, it was not the only one that night in the woods.

Whatever it was, its eyes were no longer visible.

Maybe it was scared off by the fire being stoked.

Maybe it sensed that Hannah had upped the ante by adding a weapon to the equation. A quick kill of sleeping prey was no longer possible.

If it was a coyote, such suppositions were within the realm of the likely.

If it was a wolf, that would be an entirely different matter.

Hannah remained seated but eased herself back into the protection of the tree roots. Their snarled arms, rising eighteen feet into the air above her head, would protect her from an attack from behind.

After five minutes that felt like fifty, she suddenly saw another flicker of movement in the corner of her eye and turned. There were the eyes again. There was that cold chill on the back of her neck.

She aimed.

She squeezed.

The Winchester bucked in her hands as the .45-caliber lead ripped into the darkness.

The mare reared and whinnied.

Hannah blinked her eyes instinctively to wash away the effect of the muzzle flash on her pupils.

There had been no scream of pain or anxiety. She had not hit whatever it was.

There was a better than fifty-fifty chance that a coyote would have been scared off by the gunshot. With a wolf, the odds were much less.

Hannah took a deep breath and wiped her forehead on her sleeve.

Hestia continued to whinny and prance.

The monster of the dark was still out there, but she was no maiden in distress. She was armed with a Winchester. Of course, if she lost her horse, she would become a maiden in distress with a Winchester.

Time slipped by and Hannah felt herself relax. Gradually, she felt herself getting sleepy. Her eyelids grew tired.

Suddenly there was movement — *fast* movement.

Eyes — fierce orange eyes — eyes *coming*.

The rifle was more pointed than aimed.

The trigger was more pulled than squeezed.

The sharp *crack* of the cartridge being fired echoed into the night.

The scream was such as to curdle the blood.

Hannah felt the sharpness bite into her head.

A split second later, she realized that as she had instinctively jerked backward, a movement aided by the recoil, she had jabbed the back of her head on one of the gnarled roots.

She levered the Winchester to eject the

cartridge, looked into the darkness, and exhaled held breath.

She saw movement and fired again.

Again, there was a yelp of anguish.

She had hit it twice.

Then she saw the eyes again, and a face contorted with both pain and rage.

Barely a dozen feet away, she saw an enormous wolf, which her eyes told her was the largest she had ever beheld.

Hannah felt her own eyes growing larger than they had ever been.

The thing was skulking away, but moving with great difficulty.

It turned, bared its teeth in an angry sneer, then crumpled to the ground.

Hannah just sat there, still holding the gun, breathing deeply as though she had just climbed a steep staircase.

At last, she stood, comforted Hestia, and thought about the home and hearth for which the mare had been named. Hannah bit into an apple that she had put in the saddlebags, and shared it with her steed. She wished that she had thought to bring coffee.

As Hannah waited for the light of dawn to penetrate the woods sufficiently for her to resume her journey, she tried not to think about the dead animal lying in her camp

and cursed herself for initially forgetting
that wolves hunt in packs. Fortunately for
her, this one had come alone, or at least
had come with easily frightened cohorts.

CHAPTER 25

For Bladen Cole, the third day since he had left Copperopolis dawned as dark and gloomy as had the second, though the snowfall had taken a momentary hiatus.

He bade farewell to Jake Walz and his dogs, having poured the old man the first cup of coffee he'd had in months. Walz explained that his fear of claim jumpers kept him from straying far, and Cole wondered how he'd fare when he finally did leave here — *if* he ever left the side stream off Sixteen Mile Creek.

Cole hoped that the color really *would* run bright and plentiful for the man come spring — but he believed that it would not.

He could look into Walz's eyes and tell that they did not see the same world that others saw. He had seen the same look in the eyes of gamblers down on their luck. He had seen that gleam of optimistic madness that expressed their firm belief that the next hand, just *one more* hand, would make them rich.

The gaming tables were no different than Jake Walz's place, except that with the gambler, there was frequently a cardsharp to ease him onward with colorful promises. This thought made Cole think of Sally Lovelace and the look that had been put into *her* eyes by the guileful Hubbard down in Colorado. It was a disagreeable train of thought which Cole wished not to pursue, and he forced his mind back to the task at hand.

His father's watch told him that it was almost seven as they forded Sixteen Mile Creek to get back on the main trail, and the bounty hunter breathed a tentative sigh of relief. After today, only one more sleep separated them from Gallatin City.

There were tracks on the trail, laid down since the snow had ceased overnight, but they were headed the opposite direction. This, and the monotony and monochrome of the countryside were lulling. It was a landscape in black and white. The trees were black, and the thin covering of snow blanketed the hills and valley and merged into the clouds in a single shade of cold, bleak white.

Cole hated himself for having succumbed

to this hypnotic dullness — the split second that the first shot was fired.

Porter and Goode, both riding ahead of him, jerked their heads up from their own respective daydreams at the sound, glancing around instinctively, looking for the origin of the shot.

The men each saw it almost immediately, a bluish puff of smoke hanging in the still air high on a hillside slightly ahead of them.

The sniper had chosen well, training his weapon at a place on the trail where the terrain offered no cover his targets might run for.

"Hee-yaa . . . ride!" Cole shouted, kicking the roan into a gallop and swatting the flanks of Gideon Porter's horse with his reins — though the two prisoners needed no urging to spur their horses into a run. Like Cole, they knew that the best reaction in a situation with no cover was to make themselves a *moving* target, and one that moved as fast as possible.

If the sniper had done well in choosing the place of his attack, his execution left much to be desired. Having failed to hit anyone with his first shot, he waited too long to fire his second. By this time, his quarry was in motion. Only luck would guide his bullet now.

Cole, of course, had problems of his own. He had lost effective control over two prisoners at full gallop on a snow-covered trail. If any horse stumbled and broke a leg in a snow-covered hole, it would greatly complicate matters. Meanwhile, there was the danger that Porter and Goode would escape. Though their being lashed together with forty feet of rope lessened the chances of this, it could not completely prevent it. Desperate men did desperate things, and both of these men had recently proven this axiom.

By the third shot, they were out of range, and soon they had put the shoulder of a hill between them and the shooter. Cole was about to order Porter and Goode to slow their pace, when another shot rang out from a different direction.

He heard the whiz of a near miss from a gunman who was a better marksman than his partner.

"Dismount and take cover!" Cole screamed with as much authority as he could muster. At least there now was cover to take. He might have been a better shot, but fortunately, this second bushwhacker had not done as good a job in picking a place to do his shooting.

Cole remained on the roan until both

Porter and Goode had clumsily slid from their horses, then he grabbed his Winchester from his scabbard and leaped behind a nearby boulder, with his back to Sixteen Mile Creek.

As with the first sniper, the position of the second was revealed by bluish puffs of burnt powder and by the muzzle flashes of his rifle.

Having taken time to line up his own first shot, Cole squeezed the trigger.

The round impacted the rock behind which the second sniper was crouching, hitting close enough to spit up debris that the man no doubt felt on his face.

This apparently unnerved him somewhat, because he fired two shots in rapid succession which hit in the trees quite far from any of his targets.

Cole fired a second time but cursed when his bullet again hit the rock.

"Stay down," Cole growled when he saw Jimmy Goode start to move.

"He's gunnin' for *you,* not for us," Goode shouted back.

"You're wanted *dead or alive,* you idiot," Porter shouted. "You're worth as much to him dead . . . and you'd be a *helluva* lot less trouble dead!"

The impasse had the makings of a stand-off.

It had taken only a few minutes to establish that neither Cole nor the sniper could easily hit the other, but *both* were pinned down.

Over the ensuing ten minutes, each side fired only as often as he thought necessary to remind the other that he was stuck where he was until the impasse was broken.

Cole realized that this would happen as soon as the first bushwhacker appeared. If the two of them could get Cole into a cross fire, things would change abruptly in their favor.

The bounty hunter's eyes were compelled to constantly scan the hillsides all around for sign of the other gunman, while the second sniper had the good fortune of knowing where his targets were.

Changes of fortune often come in unexpected form.

As Cole was studying the surrounding hillsides, he caught sight of a rider. What confused him was that this black horse was moving among the ponderosa on the hillside *opposite* the direction from which the other sniper was likely to come.

It was hard to get a good look in the thick

trees, until the rider paused briefly in a small clearing slightly above the sniper's nest.

Cole couldn't believe what he saw.

The rider was a *woman*. By her narrow waist and the drape of her riding skirt, there was no mistaking this. She picked her way across the hillside with such ease that it made her seem to be simply taking a Sunday ride.

He was beginning to ponder the question of what a joyriding woman was doing out here when a gunshot answered his question.

She had a rifle, and she had fired on the bushwhacker.

As Cole had been watching for himself to be outflanked, it had been his opponent who was outflanked.

The sniper turned and returned fire.

As the woman was now behind the trees, Cole could not see exactly what was happening, but the gunman's attention had definitely been diverted.

Cole squeezed off another shot, coming frustratingly close without connecting.

Suddenly, the man broke from his position and started running.

Cole fired again and missed.

He heard another shot from up on the hillside, and the woman emerged from the trees. Cole watched her put her rifle to her shoulder and fire again.

The running man abruptly slowed to a limp.

One of the woman's shots had hit him.

Seconds later, though, he was on his horse and galloping away.

Cole watched as the woman squeezed off another shot and paused to study the terrain between herself and the fleeing sniper.

Cole watched her maneuver the black horse near a deep ravine and apparently decide that it could not easily be crossed in time for a her to undertake a useful pursuit.

She turned, looked down at where Cole was, and began urging her horse down the steep slope toward him.

Cole had just caught his roan and was leading the horse back to where his prisoners were standing when she rode up.

He recognized her immediately. It was Hannah Ransdell.

She wore a snug-fitting, long-sleeved jacket over her black skirt, and a stylish, narrow-brimmed hat with a floral-patterned ribbon on it. Dressed in what ladies in Virginia would have called a "riding habit," she did, indeed, have the look of a stylish lady out for a Sunday ride. Except for the Winchester '73 which she carried in her gloved right hand.

"You're in trouble," she said soberly. "Those men are out to *kill* you."

"Wouldn't have guessed," Cole said in a sarcastic tone.

"I'm serious," she said, bristling.

"I believe you, Miss Ransdell," he assured her. "By the way . . . you *did* arrive at a fortunate time. What brings you to these parts?"

"To stop them from killing you . . . *and* Gideon Porter."

"So far that plan seems to have worked," Cole nodded, looking at Porter, who for once appeared speechless. "But they are still out there."

"I know," she said, studying the hillside. "But at least there's two sets of eyes to keep watch . . . and two Winchesters to stop them if they show themselves again."

"You're pretty good with that thing," Cole said, nodding to the rifle, which she held muzzle high, the butt resting on her hip.

"You mean good for a *girl*?"

"Did I say that?"

"You thought . . ."

"What I *think* is that *you* hit a man while he was on the run," Cole interrupted.

She said nothing more on the subject but merely looked back at the hillside.

"What have you been doing to these poor men?" Hannah asked cynically as she observed Porter's scarred face and Goode's withered hand.

"These two fared better than Enoch," Cole said, nodding to the canvas-covered package tied to the last horse.

"I figured that was him," she said without emotion.

"We best get moving," Cole said as he mounted up. "Your hitting that one will not stop them, but at least it'll probably slow them down . . . and we'll want to get as far ahead of them as we can."

"We ought to be able to keep ahead of them if we stick to this trail," she said. "As I have learned from recent experience, riding across these mountains makes for very rough going."

"That ought to force them onto the trail, where we might have a better chance of seeing them coming," Cole suggested as he looked back down the trail. "But we need to get going and put some miles between us and them."

"Then let's make some miles," she said, touching the heels of her scuffed and muddied, though quite fashionable, riding boots to the flanks of her black mare.

■ ■ ■ ■

They rode the first of those miles, and most of the second, in single file because of the narrowness of the canyon, hurrying as much as possible without allowing the horses to get winded.

As the valley broadened, Cole reined the roan alongside the mare. He was curious to know what lay behind the auspicious appearance of Hannah Ransdell, especially in light of what he had concluded about her father.

"You said that you rode out here to save my hide and that of Mr. Porter there," Cole said without looking directly at Hannah. "How did you know that we *needed* saving? Who are those men?"

"Their names are Lyle Blake and Joe Clark," she said. "They're part of the same cesspool of town thugs that bred the likes of the Porter boys."

"How do you reckon that your friends were able to find us way out here?" he asked.

"They're *not* my friends," she snapped, glancing at him. "To answer your question, I happened to overhear them talking . . . talking about *you* headed for Sixteen Mile Creek from up north."

"How'd they know *that*?"

"They heard it from someone, who heard it from someone else, who saw you in a place called Copperopolis four days or so ago."

"So you followed them?"

"Not exactly," she said. "I came across the mountains. I wanted to get here first by taking a short cut. I *almost* did."

"How did you find . . . ?"

"It does not take a genius to figure how far someone would get after three or four days of riding from up at Copperopolis."

"Did your *father* send you?" Cole asked pointedly.

"My father certainly did *not* send me," she answered, her simmering irritability coming to a boil.

"When I saw you, I guessed that he might have sent you to check up on me . . . check up on how I was doing with this job he gave me."

"Well, I guess you guessed very, very *wrong,* Mr. Cole."

"Why *are* you here, then . . . making yourself the target of two men who aimed to kill us three and probably now aim to kill you as well?"

"Let's just say that I have a strong interest in seeing justice done," she said, looking at

329

him with disdain. "Unlike *you,* Mr. Cole . . . I am not here because of a substantial sum of money."

"Well, I won't say I'm *not* doing it for the money . . ." Cole began.

"That's because you *can't* say that," she finished, biting back. "At least you can't say it with a straight face."

"If the *only* reason I have for being in this situation is the reward money, then I would have made what I'm doing a helluva . . . pardon me for my language in front of a lady . . . lot easier."

"Apology accepted, though I've heard worse," Hannah said sternly without looking at him. "How?" Hannah asked after a long pause. "How, *exactly* could you have made this any *easier?*"

"The warrant says 'dead or alive,' " he began.

"Yes, I'm well aware of that detail."

"Then you can probably imagine how much *easier* it would have been for me to bring Porter and Goode back like old Enoch. Without going through all the details, my life would have been a helluva lot easier with these cantankerous fools dead rather than alive."

"Why then, Mr. Cole?" she asked. "Why did you decide to do it the *hard* way?"

"Let's just say that I *also* have a strong interest in seeing justice done."

The canyon narrowed once again, bringing an interruption to their conversation which left many questions yet unanswered.

CHAPTER 26

"Thank you, Mr. Cole," she said crisply, trying to maintain her facade of practical aloofness.

Late in the afternoon, the bounty hunter had offered her a slice of buffalo jerky. Hannah Ransdell was starving but tried her best *not* to appear so. She wished to deny him the satisfaction of knowing both how unprepared she had been for this venture and how much she appreciated his gesture.

She had lost her appetite after the anxiety of shooting Lyle Blake, but pent-up hunger had overtaken her and had dogged her for the past several hours. The meat tasted really good.

Hannah knew why *she* wanted Gideon Porter brought back alive, by why did *Cole*?

She had ridden to her rendezvous predisposed to his being merely a mercenary craving a reward, but his words suggested that there was more to it than she had believed.

It had surprised her greatly, and frankly confused her, that the bounty hunter had made a conscious decision to deliver at least part of the Porter boys' gang *alive* rather than *dead.* In this, his purpose coincided with her own — but she could not imagine *why.*

On the other hand, it annoyed her greatly to have heard him insinuate that she was the mere instrument of her *father* and that her motives in wishing to preserve the lives of Jimmy Goode and that detestable Gideon Porter were in the service of Isham Ransdell's interests — when exactly the *opposite* was true.

As the miles went by, the wind picked up, and with it a cold chill, although in its blowing it seemed to have parted the clouds, and there were now a few patches of blue showing.

"If it's any measure of consolation, Miss Ransdell," the bounty hunter said, "I don't think these men will try to attack us until after the sun goes down.

"Did I say that I needed consoling, Mr. Cole?" Hannah asked scornfully.

"The way that you've been biting at your lip when you look back at those yonder hills makes me think as much," he said with a slight smile.

As much as she resented the bounty hunter's verbal prods, she resented herself more for interrupting her resentment to admire the way his beard was taking shape.

"I would have to say that their presence in those hills concerns me a bit, as I suspect it does you as well," she said.

In fact, it troubled her greatly that Lyle Blake and Joe Clark were still out there somewhere stalking them. Her original plan, the plan which had taken shape back in Gallatin City when things seemed much simpler, had been to alert the bounty hunter and let him do whatever it was that gunmen did to relieve themselves of a threat. Instead, she too was now among the hunted.

"Yes, ma'am, I would be a liar to say that it is not a bother to me as well. Tonight worries me even more. Rascals like that are like the cowardly in the animal world who get their kills by attacking the unsuspecting under cover of darkness."

"I am *certainly* aware of that particular vexation," she said, referencing without describing her overnight wolf kill. She thought of mentioning it but decided such a tale would seem so improbable that he would take it as fabricated bragging, and it would therefore undermine the image of usefulness she hoped to cultivate in their mutual endeavor.

"I expect we'll have no shortage of vexations tonight, Miss Ransdell," he replied.

Afternoons don't last long in the months when the cold winds begin to blow, and the clouds through which the patches of blue had appeared were starting to take on the golden hue that would precede the dreaded twilight.

Below and ahead of them now lay broad, open country stretching down toward the confluence of Sixteen Mile Creek and the Missouri. They were now less than a day's ride from their final destination, and Hannah could see the sense of relief in the bounty hunter's eyes.

Her eyes followed his, looking back into the Big Horn Mountains and the canyon of Sixteen Mile Creek, as though they were putting a monster behind them.

"I half expected that your friends wouldn't let us get this far," he said, glancing at the surrounding hillsides. "Your description of them as 'cesspool-bred thugs' suggests to me that you're just writing them off as fools. I would not have thought that of them, given that their ambush showed a certain amount of foresight in the planning."

"I did not mean to suggest that they were

not wily in their conniving," Hannah clarified, "only that they were scum of the earth."

"Scum or not, I hadn't taken them for fools," Cole replied. "If the tables were turned, I would have thought it foolish to let us get this far."

"I thought you said that you didn't figure on them attacking us until after nightfall," she said.

"Didn't think it more than a fifty-fifty chance, so I didn't want to worry you."

"You didn't want to worry me?"

"No. Didn't much want to worry *me* either, I 'spect. We still got the most worrying time ahead of us. After nightfall will be the time when a man can slink up out of the darkness and not be seen coming on a distant ridge beyond rifle range."

"I don't appreciate your *keeping* things from me, Mr. Cole. I thought that we were in this *together.*

"We have both taken fire from these men, and we are *both* being hunted by them. I cannot abide you withholding information from me because you find me too fragile to take the worry."

"I don't much care for you keeping *me* in the dark either, Miss Ransdell," the bounty hunter replied with unexpected sharpness.

"What exactly do you mean by *that*?"

Hannah replied defensively.

"I mean that Isham Ransdell's daughter shows up out of nowhere this morning with a chip on her shoulder as big as all out-doors . . . and tells me all coy-like that she's here to 'see justice done' and nothing more. If this ain't something to make a man wonder, I don't know what is."

"I am not being *coy,* Mr. Cole, and I am not lying when I say that I *am* here to see that these men get back to Gallatin City alive. That is the *only* reason I am here. If I hurt your feelings by making you think there's a chip on my shoulder, that's just *too bad.* I'm certainly not here to shelter your feelings."

She could feel her face growing red with indignation.

"It would be a lot easier on my feelings to ride with a less ornery companion," he said with a smile, reacting to her suddenly flushed complexion.

"Nor am I here to brighten your day, Mr. Cole, but to do *my part* in seeing that our common purpose is accomplished."

"Then you can tell me the *whole* truth about what's going on, Miss Ransdell?" he said, the smile gone from his face. "I suspect there is *some* truth in what you've said, but I suspect it to be *half truth,* and half truth is

337

just the same as half *untruth*."

"I have *not* lied to you, Mr. Cole."

"Then tell me the part that's a half lie by its *not* being told."

"What do you mean by *that*?"

"I mean the part about you being Isham Ransdell's daughter . . . and him being absent from the room when those shootings took place."

Hannah felt as though the jaws of the wolf had seized her windpipe.

"What . . . makes you think . . . ?" she said, gasping and grasping for words as the tears welled up in her eyes.

Her father!

"Guess I touched a nerve," the bounty hunter said. "I can tell by your manner that we *both* know that the crazy notion that those people were shot over some trifle wrong that Blaine did to Gideon Porter is just a load of bull, and I will not apologize for strong language, because it serves my point."

"Which is?"

"That I figured out a long way back down the trail that Porter and his bunch got paid to do the shooting. And on his deathbed, Milton Waller *told* me so. I assume your daddy got my letter from Fort Benton?"

"Yes . . . There was nothing about . . ."

"Of course there wasn't," the bounty hunter said pointedly. "Would not have told your father what Waller said under any circumstance. But his words stuck with me since that night . . . and men don't tell lies on their deathbeds."

"What . . . ?" Hannah started to ask, fearing the worst.

"His words included something about a 'railroad,' and that there were four partners . . . three had to die . . . and only one could survive. We both know who among the four was *not* there."

Partners. Her father. The railroad again!

In the back of her mind, Hannah had hoped some evidence might emerge to the contrary of her worst fears, but instead, there was only this cold, hard confirmation, and also now the fact that the bounty hunter *knew.*

She turned her head, frantically wiping the tears from her cheek with a gloved hand.

"Once again, Miss Ransdell, why did your father send you out here?"

"Once *again,* Mr. Cole," she gulped between sobs as she reached for her handkerchief. "He *did not send me.*"

"I guess what I've just said comes as a pretty big surprise then," he said, taunting her, watching her wipe her face.

"No, Mr. Cole," she said, blowing her nose. "It does *not* come as a surprise. I too have seen evidence of my father's hand in this tragedy."

"Oh . . ."

It was his turn to be startled.

"Are you too blind to see that *this* is why I came all the way out here to make sure that those two men riding up ahead of us . . . hopefully hearing little of our conversation . . . that those two, especially Gideon Porter, did not die before they could point their *fingers* . . ."

"Point their fingers at your *father*?"

"At the *truth,* Mr. Cole. Point them at the truth . . . whatever it is . . . whatever terrible, sordid facts surround it. I cannot live or work with my father without knowing the *truth.*"

"The last time we crossed paths, you thought your father not being there was just a fortunate accident. What was . . . ?"

"What changed was the *damned* railroad . . . and I will not apologize to *you,* Mr. Cole, for strong language," Hannah said, regaining her composure. "The railroad will be coming to Gallatin City, and it will need land owned jointly by the four partners . . . whose arrangement has them inheriting the shares of partners who die.

I've uncovered the same facts which you uncovered at the bedside of Milton Waller."

"I see . . ."

"What I discovered was suspicious, but open to interpretations. It is, as the lawyers call it, 'circumstantial' evidence," Hannah admitted. "However, when I saw my father's cursed 'right-hand man,' Mr. Edward J. Olson, speaking to Lyle Blake and Joe Clark, within hours of their coming to kill *you,* this was the evidence which made the other evidence *damning* evidence."

"I reckon . . ." the bounty hunter said, "I reckon we both had the same reason for wanting those two to live long enough to see Gallatin City."

"I reckon that's so, Mr. Cole," Hannah said. "Now, are you going to tell me what you have learned from speaking with Gideon Porter? As I assume you have spoken to him on this matter."

"He has been even less willing to discuss it than *you* were earlier today," Cole explained. "Though he does insist that he has friends in high places who won't let him hang."

"Who? What *friends*?"

"Didn't say," the bounty hunter replied with a shrug.

"You didn't *press him*?" Hannah asked

341

with surprise. "Why didn't you press him to tell you? Weren't you the least bit curious?"

"You mean why did I not *beat* it out of him?"

"Well . . ."

"It's not my job. My job is to bring him in. It doesn't matter what he tells *me*. It doesn't matter what I say to anyone about what he told me. It matters what he says when he rides into Gallatin City. What matters is the look on their faces when he comes face-to-face with . . ."

"My father," Hannah said, completing his sentence.

"Yeah."

Hannah Ransdell felt a deep and brooding sense of foreboding as the sun sank into the clouds on the horizon and darkness rapidly enveloped what was left of the day. To have had her worst fears confirmed by the suppositions of the bounty hunter and the deathbed words of Milton Waller caused her great anguish and despair.

A person who has lost a parent often dreads the loss of the other, but to lose him to the gallows would cast a debilitating shadow across her own life.

Still, she had to know the truth. As much as she dreaded it and wanted to prevent the pain, she *had to* see the look in her father's eyes when he looked into the eyes of Gideon Porter.

Of more immediate concern were Blake and Clark and what the bounty hunter had put into perspective about the probability that they would strike before the sun rose again.

As they crested the last rise before the Sixteen Mile Creek trail dropped into the valley of the Missouri River, she breathed a sigh of relief to see a distant stagecoach making its way from Gallatin City to the territorial capital in Helena. It seemed to symbolize their passage from wilderness to civilization.

When they reached the broad plain through which the river flowed, the bounty hunter announced that he was going to look for a campsite.

"What about near the riverbank, where there's water," she suggested. "We'd also be near the road. If there are other people on the wagon road, they would be less likely to ambush us . . . wouldn't they?"

"Being near to water is useful, but unnecessary," he said. "Our canteens will hold enough water to get us through one night."

"Then where?"

"High ground," he said, studying the hills

that lay in the direction of Gallatin City. "I want to be where they got to show themselves to get close . . . *if* we have enough moon to cast light."

"It was pretty bright in the middle of the night where I was *last* night," she said. "But I don't like the looks of those clouds."

"We'll have to take what we get," he said, staring at the same gathering clouds and at the diminishing patches of deep blue twilight sky, touched by the first pin-pricks of distant stars.

As the bounty hunter chained him to his tree, Gideon Porter made a crude comment to Hannah, but Jimmy Goode just stared at her.

Noting that Cole had chained the two men to widely separated trees, Hannah decided to approach Goode with the purpose of getting the information that Cole had failed to elicit from Porter. She knew him, as many people in Gallatin City did, as the easily manipulated oaf who lived in the shadow of the Porter boys and strived for their esteem and respect.

"What have you got yourself mixed up in, Jimmy?" Hannah asked in a sympathetic voice, which she crafted so as to be inaudible to Porter.

"Nothing," he said, not looking at her.

"Don't you go talkin' to that goddamn hussy, Jimmy Goode!" Porter shouted from the opposite side of the camp. "Don't say a goddamn thing or I'll kick your fool ass from hell to kingdom come."

"Don't listen to him," Hannah said softly, trying to play a sympathetic card against Porter's threat. "He can't hurt you. He's chained to a tree."

"Not forever he ain't," Goode said in a low voice.

"What happened to your arm, Jimmy?" she asked sympathetically, sitting down on a log near where he was.

"Got shot."

"By who?"

"The bounty hunter . . . the goddamn bounty hunter."

"Why?" Hannah asked, startled. "What did you do to *him*?"

"Done got away."

"You escaped?"

"Yes, I did," Jimmy answered, looking at Hannah for the first time, and seeing her sympathetic expression.

"He shot you for *escaping*?"

"Yeah . . . sort of."

"Sort of?"

"Well there was sort of this homesteader . . . a whole family of 'em."

"Did you hurt the homesteaders?"

"No, ma'am . . . not one bit."

"What happened?"

"Well, I took the boy . . ."

"You took a boy? How old was this boy?"

"You know . . . eight or ten or something?
Goode answered, his voice expressing that
it had never occurred to him how old the
boy might be, and that he found it difficult
to guess.

"You *took* an eight-year-old boy? Whatever
for?"

"I dunno . . . Guess I kind of took him . . .
well, like a hostage."

"You took a hostage? Did you have a
gun?"

"Yeah . . . but I swear I did not shoot the
boy . . . I only wanted to flush him out when
he went to hidin'."

"The bounty hunter shot you for trying to
scare the boy, then?"

"No, I guess he shot me for trying to shoot
the boy's pappy."

"Did you?"

"I tried, but I got hit in the elbow."

Hannah just shook her head. What had he
expected for having kidnapped a child and
having tried to shoot the boy's father?
Really? At the same time, she was pleased

346

to hear that the bounty hunter had not shot the man merely for trying to escape.

"How did Gideon Porter get you mixed up in all this?" Hannah asked, continuing to feign sympathy.

"I was part of the gang," Goode said proudly.

"I know, but this shooting of people . . . at the Blaine home . . . ? That doesn't sound like *you*. Like you were saying, you are not one to shoot people."

"Got paid," he said. "Done it 'cause I done got paid."

"How much?"

"Thirty bucks."

"Who paid you?"

"Gideon."

"Who paid *him*?"

"I dunno."

"Do you know . . . ?"

"I don't know *nothing* . . . and I wish I didn't even know *that*," he said sadly. "Miss Ransdell, I really wish none of this would have happened."

"I can tell," she said with an empathetic glance at his limp forearm.

"Did Gideon say anything about my father?"

"Just that he wasn't there that night . . . course I knew that 'cause I *was* there."

"Anything else?"

"Not that I can remember, but I have trouble remembering sometimes . . . you know?"

"Yes, Jimmy, everybody's got trouble remembering sometimes."

"Miss Ransdell?" Goode asked after a pause. "Can I ask you something?"

"Sure."

"Are we gonna hang? Gideon says we ain't . . . but I figure since those folks got killed that we are."

"What makes Gideon think you *won't* be hanged?"

"Says he's got friends . . . friends who ain't gonna let it happen."

"What friends? . . . *Who?*"

"Gideon never tells me nothing."

Hannah smiled and stood up.

She walked away, regarding the man with a mixture of pity and contempt. What was it that made this man tick? Perhaps he didn't tick at all. Perhaps he was, as everyone had always said, really just "good-for-nothing Jimmy Goode."

"Soup?" the bounty hunter asked, handing her a cup.

"Thank you . . . much obliged," she said, noticing herself smiling at the man. "Aren't you having any?"

"I just did," he replied. "This is coffee."

She nodded. "Yeah, I could smell it. But it's kind of late for coffee, isn't it, Mr. Cole?"

"I don't plan on much sleep tonight . . . or rather I don't plan on *any* sleep tonight."

"It's almost night now," she said, looking out at the landscape.

He had picked a campsite on the side of a hill that was separated from other hills by at least half a mile.

"You can see almost everything from up here," she said. "You can see everything but the far side of *this* hill."

"From up there, I *can* see everything," he said, nodding to the top of their hill, which rose another fifty feet. "And I guess it's time for me to get to work."

"You'll be cold up there," she said, regretting her forwardness in expressing concern for his welfare.

"It'll keep me awake," he said, before he disappeared around a boulder into the nearly complete darkness.

CHAPTER 27

Bladen Cole surveyed the scene from his crow's nest high above the campsite. He watched the surrounding terrain as the moonlight brightened and faded with the passing clouds. Even when the moon slipped away, though, the contrast between the sheet of snow and anyone who walked on it was still stark. Cole saw a few deer at a considerable distance and was pleased by how well they stood out against the snow, even in the cloudy diffusion of the moonlight.

After so much overcast and snow in the preceding days, he was thankful for as much moonlight as he could get and thankful for it not to be snowing tonight. A snowstorm would have been ideal cover for the two gunmen attacking the camp.

He had built the campfire down below larger than necessary, intending to have it remain burning late into the night as a beacon to lure the bushwhackers into the trap that he intended to spring.

He thought about the grizzly and the feel of dreading the animal in the darkness. If he had, as Natoya-I-nis'kim believed, inherited the medicine of the grizzly, then he hoped that he would be a force worthy of such fear when the night brought the inevitable encounter with the bushwhackers.

Suddenly, Cole was jarred into the moment by the sound of something moving on the hillside below.

There was a little bit of a scratch, the tumbling of a small stone, then silence.

What was it? A ground squirrel?

Cole was certain that he had seen no animal larger than a deer approaching the hill from any direction.

He peered into the darkness and quietly raised his Winchester. Then he saw the movement, barely fifteen feet beneath him on the slope.

What?

Who?

At first he did not recognize Hannah Ransdell. She had undone the bun into which her hair was normally wound. It framed her face and tumbled across her shoulders.

"What are you doing, sneaking up . . . ?"

Cole hissed.

"Wanted to keep you awake," she whispered as she slid gracefully into a narrow hollow near where he had been lying.

"I almost shot . . ." Cole began.

"Shhh . . . I brought you some coffee," she whispered.

She had a cup in one hand and her rifle in the other. She had made the climb up from the camp with her hands full, and without making more than a trace of noise.

He took the cup with a nod. The coffee was lukewarm, but warmer than anything atop this hill, including his fingers.

Together, they crouched on the perch, scanning the approaches to their hill. He admired the skill and tenacity of this young woman. She was made of far hardier stuff than he might have imagined on that day when they strolled the streets of Gallatin City. Back on that day, he had found her attractive, dressed in lavender gingham, trimmed in lace — and with those three freckles on her nose which always drew a smile when he thought about them.

Tonight, dressed in black, with a Winchester in her arms and her long chestnut-colored hair cascading about her shoulders, he found her even more attractive, more exciting and untamed in her appearance —

not unlike that black mare she rode.

As they sat quietly on their perch, each studying the distance, awaiting the arrival of their foes, he occasionally allowed his eyes the pleasure of falling upon his companion. Once, he caught her sneaking *that kind* of glance at him. She briefly made eye contact, smiled, and looked away.

He thought about Natoya-I-nis'kim, and how there is something magical that is done by moonlight to the image of a beautiful woman.

The night was passing slowly, and naturally there were other things he would rather have been doing with a beautiful woman. He imagined feeling the softness of her smooth skin and tasting her lips, but he forced these distractions into the back recesses of his mind.

There were other things that must be done.

Cole consulted his father's pocket watch a time or two, more out of boredom than anything else. The news that it told was merely a reminder of how slow the hours were ticking by.

The laborious ticking had moved the passage of time closer to four than three, and Cole was stifling a yawn, when he saw it.

There was movement in the shadow of a

neighboring hill. Was it another deer?

He strained his eyes into the darkness until they saw the unmistakable glint of moonlight on a well-worn saddle.

He nudged Hannah, who was looking the other direction, and pointed.

She turned and nodded.

This was it.

Two men had dismounted and were creeping toward the fire, approaching so as to screen themselves behind the shoulder of the hill. The fire had died down considerably from its original roar, but it was still the brightest thing on the ground for as far as the eye could see.

One of the men, apparently Lyle Blake, was nursing a limp. Joe Clark would walk, get ahead of Blake, and pause impatiently.

Slowly, they made their way up the slope toward the ledge where the campsite was located.

Clark prodded Blake ahead, and he stepped into the glow of the fire first. He went into action immediately, firing a pistol round into Cole's bedroll, which had been previously arranged to appear occupied.

"You missed," Cole shouted from above.

Blake turned to look up at the sound of the voice.

His eyes were narrowed by the brightness

of the still flickering fire, and he fired wildly. This was his only chance at a shot, for he was promptly cut down by a bullet from Cole's rifle.

Clark, still in the shadows, fired at Cole's muzzle flash as Cole was ejecting the spent cartridge.

Hannah squeezed off a shot.

There was a loud curse, indicating a non-fatal hit, and Clark began to run.

Hannah fired again, as did Cole, but they both missed.

The moon was behind a cloud again, and Clark was moving quickly.

Impulsively, Cole set down his rifle, stood up, and ran down the hillside in pursuit.

Hannah watched as he slipped on an icy patch and fell, but managed to roll into an upright position and keep going.

She fired again and watched Clark hesitate slightly, giving Cole a chance to narrow the distance.

Clark reached the place where he and Blake had tethered their horses, glanced back, saw Cole coming, fired two shots from his pistol, and leaped onto his horse.

Cole dropped to the ground when he heard the first shot but was running again as Clark was mounting up. He pulled his Colt and fired one shot at the fleeing man.

Without a second thought, Cole grabbed the reins of Blake's horse and jumped on. He had left his Winchester behind because he felt that he could run faster without it. Now he wished that he had not.

The clouds had passed, at least for the moment, and the pursuit continued briefly at a gallop in the stark black and blue of a moonlit night.

As the open terrain abruptly gave way to one studded with more and more trees, however, both riders slowed, knowing that to run a horse in the dark over uncertain ground and through trees was dangerous. For a horse to trip, fall, and break a leg would be the end for the animal, but this would also put its rider at a great disadvantage.

The fast pursuit had become a hunt in which stealth, not speed, would be the deciding factor.

Cole stopped, straining his ears for sounds as he had earlier strained his eyes for a glimpse of Blake and Clark.

Above the heavy breathing of Blake's horse, he heard the light wind whining in the creaking branches of the low trees.

In the near distance, the unmistakable sound of a horse walking in the brush was the proverbial music to his ears for which he had hoped. It was impossible to move silently with light snow covering broken limbs and other objects that made noise when a hoof stepped on them.

Cole moved as quickly as he could, pausing periodically to listen. He heard Clark doing the same — moments of quiet, followed by the sounds of him continuing.

He thought of taking a shot in Clark's direction. The purpose would be only to keep him on edge, because the odds of hitting him in the darkness at this range were essentially nil.

He felt around on the saddle and found Blake's rifle, an old army-issue Henry, still in its scabbard. There was no way of knowing whether it was loaded and, if so, with how many rounds. Again, Cole cursed himself for not bringing his own rifle.

The thicker the woods became, the slower and noisier the pace became. Each man could hear the other, but neither was close enough for a decisive shot.

Crunch.

Crunch.

Snap.

Clunk.

Pause.

This could not go on all night — or could it?

I could walk *faster than this,* Cole thought.
Walk faster?

Of course he could.

At least he could walk more quietly.

Pulling the Henry from its scabbard, Cole slid off the horse, whacked him on the hindquarters, and watched him disappear into the woods.

He heard Clark, on the move again, adjusting his direction to match that of Blake's horse. The hunted was now the hunter; Clark was maneuvering to attack what he believed to be his still-mounted pursuer.

Moving carefully, and more quietly now that he was picking his own steps, Cole chose a path by which he could outflank his adversary.

Time stretched out like a reclining house cat.

How long has it been? Cole asked himself.

It may not have been longer than about ten minutes, but it really did seem like an hour since he had dashed down from his perch in an effort to catch Joe Clark.

Stepping as silently as possible — at least more silently than Clark's horse — Cole circled through the woods toward the place where Clark was aiming to intercept his prey.

Cole came over a small rise and peered

into the woods below.

He could see Blake's horse rather clearly now, and a short distance away, a shadowy object was moving toward it.

It was Clark's horse, and it too was *riderless.*

There was a brief exchange of snorting and whinnying. Without their riders, the two horses had sought each other's company.

Clark had the same idea as I did!

Cole realized this with alarm.

Which of us discovered it first?

The bounty hunter had to credit the man from Gallatin City's cesspool of ne'er-do-wells for being smarter than his pedigree suggested he should be.

Somewhere amid the blackness, Clark was either still circling to the rendezvous of the horses, or waiting for Cole to show himself.

There was the sound of snow falling from a branch, but it was a high branch, and it was not a man-caused event. Both men would have heard this, and each would have jumped a little at the sound against the stillness and the tension of the moment.

It was Clark who first broke the silence, who first tipped his hand.

"Hey, bounty hunter," he shouted. "I ain't got no beef with you. Let's just go separate ways."

Cole was tempted to shout back that if he had no beef, why had Clark been trying since yesterday to kill him — but he resisted this temptation.

By saying nothing, he did not reveal his position, and he therefore now had the advantage.

Clark had revealed not only his position — or at least the general direction of his position — but also the fact that he was nervous about a shootout and wanted to get away.

"See here," Clark continued. "There's nothin' personal . . . I'm just gunnin' for you for pay. You done shot Lyle . . . that should be enough for you to be satisfied with your night's work and be ready to let bygones be bygones . . . *I'm* willing to just let bygones be bygones."

Again, Cole chose not to reply.

Again, time seemed to slow to a crawl.

There was no sound but that of the light wind in the trees and the two horses scraping in the snow for easily uncovered bunches of grass.

At last, Cole could hear Clark walking through the snow toward the horses. He waited for sight of the shadow moving through the trees and took aim with the same Henry rifle with which Blake had

360

taken aim at him the day before.

He would not let Clark reach his horse.

Krrr-ack!

The sound of the shot shattered the peaceful stillness and impacted a tree very close to where Clark was walking.

Clark paused to fire a shot in the direction of Cole's muzzle flash.

Clark was nervous, and he was anxious to escape. To save himself, he ran.

As at the beginning of this misadventure, Cole again found himself running down a hill to pursue the man on foot.

They crashed and thrashed through the brush for a few hurried moments, then the woods fell silent. Somewhere up ahead, Clark had decided to make a stand.

Cole moved as quietly as he could, trying to close the distance.

K'pow!

Cole ducked.

The shot came from very close, and it was a pistol shot. Had he, like Cole at the beginning of the chase, left his long gun behind?

Cole squinted into the darkness and got lucky.

He took aim with the Henry on the silhouette of Joe Clark's bobbing head.

Click!

The hammer fell on an empty chamber.

Blake had left his Henry with just one round in it.

"I heard that," Clark shouted. "You're out of bullets!"

"I've been counting, and I think you're nearly down to none yourself," Cole shouted back confidently. "I know you got yourself nicked back at the fire. Why don't y'all just give up and we'll go back and sit by that nice warm fire."

In fact, he had *not* been counting and wasn't sure how many shots the man had left. It might be one, and he was sure it was no more than two. Meanwhile, Cole now had the advantage of Clark believing Cole had an empty gun, when he still had five rounds left in his Colt.

Cole braced himself.

The intuitive next step for a man facing another who was out of ammunition is to attack and finish him off.

Instead, however, Clark turned and resumed running. Maybe it was Cole's overconfidence, expressed in his invitation to the warmth of the fire, that made Clark believe that he was doomed unless he got away.

Cole jumped a downed tree that crossed his path, and gave chase. Maybe Clark really was almost out of bullets.

They came to an open area, and for a brief moment, Clark was exposed.

K'pow!

Cole fired once and missed.

He eyed a boulder in the middle of the clearing and ran toward it, knowing that Clark would turn and return fire as soon as he reached the dark woods at the far side.

K'pow!

Clark's shot hit the rock inches from Cole's hand. The shards of granite kicked up by the lead stung his flesh.

K'pow!

Cole fired again as Clark resumed running through the woods.

The pursued man grunted. Cole was unsure whether this meant that he had been hit.

The stillness of the forest was bisected by two men running as fast as the underbrush permitted.

Not far ahead, Cole heard the sound of feet slipping on loose gravel and the scrabbling noise of a man trying to keep his balance.

"Aargh . . . ahhh . . . eeyoooooh!"

Gasps turned to a single scream, which trailed off into the distance.

Suddenly, Cole found his own boots scruffling in the uncertain footing of gravel mixed with snow.

His feet went out from beneath him, and he fell on his back.

Briefly winded, he caught his breath, sat up, and looked around.

Barely two feet away, the ground dropped into a dark void. The patch of gravel on which he found himself seated was, literally, a slippery slope into nothingness.

The moon drifted out from behind a cloud, and Cole stared at the broad canyon that lay before him. He was at the top of a vertical cliff. Had he not slipped and fallen where he did, he would have gone over.

Grabbing a nearby tree root to steady himself, he stepped out to a rock outcropping where he could look into the chasm.

Far below, he saw Joe Clark, lying faceup and motionless on a slab of light-colored rock. The inky darkness spilling from his broken skull told the bounty hunter that he was never going to arise from this place.

CHAPTER 28

"Where's Clark?" Hannah Ransdell asked as she entered the campsite. She had remained in the crow's nest high above until she had seen Bladen Cole ride out of the woods.

"He didn't make it," Cole answered.

She didn't ask how or why. She did not really care. The day ahead demanded her attention more than did the last loose end from yesterday.

She had breathed a sigh of relief when she laid her peeled eyes on the bounty hunter and had come down from her perch to greet him. She was tempted to do so with a hug, but forced herself to remain focused on the business at hand.

For Cole, the first order of business was a perfunctory examination of the other bushwacker, who had not moved since Cole had drilled the man the night before.

"That's Lyle Blake!"

Gideon Porter recognized the body as soon as Cole rolled the corpse to face the gathering light of day. "What the hell?"

"Meet the man who's been trying to kill *you* since yesterday," Hannah said, holding her rifle in a posture that Porter found a trifle threatening. "Him and Joe Clark."

"They won't now," Cole said tersely.

"Why would they do this?" Jimmy Goode whined.

"Because somebody wants you *dead*," Cole answered. "It looks like Gideon's 'friends in high places' don't want to see you hang after all . . . they want to see you killed off *before* you get anywhere *near* a gallows."

"Gideon, is that right?" Goode shouted. Apparently, even after all the shooting on the previous day, it took the vacant stare of Lyle Blake to finally bring it home to Goode that someone was actually gunning for *him*.

"Shut up, damn you . . ." Porter roared back.

"If I'm not mistaken, these boys were paid by the same person who paid *you*," Hannah said.

"That would make you a loose end," Cole continued. "How does it feel to have your high-placed man turn on you and want you erased . . . squashed like a bug so that you can never talk?"

"But . . . he still owes me money."

"*Who* is it?" Hannah demanded. "Is it . . . ?"

"I ain't talkin'!" Porter shouted. "I ain't sayin' a word till I get to Gallatin City."

There being adequate rocks near the campsite, Cole put Porter to work in the construction of a rock pile mausoleum as the resting place of Lyle Blake. The flood of profanities that accompanied this task offended Hannah's sensibilities less than his stubbornness.

"That man is insufferable," she said, glancing at Cole as she saddled her mare and Cole stacked the saddles and tack belonging to Blake and Clark on top of the cairn.

"By this time tomorrow, he'll be somebody else's problem," he reminded her as he turned loose the horses that had been ridden by the late bushwhackers.

"I fear this will be a very long day," she said, revealing a trace of melancholy.

"Sometimes the last day of anything is the longest," Cole said. "But same as any day, they're all eventually over."

"Mr. Cole," she said, looking back at him.

"Yeah . . ."

"I'm really worried about today."

"After what we been through, what I've seen you able to take in stride, I can't picture you being too much of the worrying type."

"I've never had to face my father like this."

"I can't even imagine it," he said, betraying a shade of sympathy despite the overarching outrage he felt toward her father.

"Is your father still alive, Mr. Cole?"

"No, ma'am. He died in the war."

"I'm sorry . . ."

"It's been a while," Cole shrugged. "Lot of good men died in the war."

"I used to think of my father as a good man," Hannah said sadly.

"I'm sorry about that," he replied, trying not to appear cynical.

"Thank you . . ." she said, her voice trailing off.

She smiled, but he could see the tears in her eyes. He felt her hand close tightly on his wrist.

They were a curious contingent, this ragtag party making its way south along the Helena–Gallatin City wagon road on that cold, early winter morning.

The bounty hunter brought up the rear behind an assortment that included two well-worn men chained to their saddles and a ripening corpse that was beginning its foul decay even in the sub-freezing temperatures. Leading the way was a young woman. Despite a generous spattering of mud and dirt and her two mostly sleepless nights of camping in the wilderness, she still managed to present the manner and appearance of a lady out for a Sunday ride.

She cheerfully greeted a freighter whose wagon they passed on his way north toward Helena. He smiled and tipped his hat when she waved, but his jaw dropped a little when he saw the others. He was still looking back at them and scratching his head a quarter mile after they had passed.

Though he was tempted to breathe a sigh of relief at having gotten through the last night on the trail alive, Bladen Cole knew better. There was no guarantee that Blake and Clark were the only ones with a mandate to prevent Cole and his prisoners from setting foot again in Gallatin City alive.

Snowflakes drifted in the air more like paint flaking randomly from the white sky than harbingers of a serious storm.

About two hours from the campsite and the final resting place of the late Lyle Blake, Hannah Ransdell reined her mare into an about-face and trotted back to where Cole was.

"Did you see?" Hannah asked urgently.

"Yeah . . . three riders about a mile and a half out."

The three had dropped out of sight behind a low rise, but he too had been watching them for about ten minutes.

"I think I recognize one of them," she said.

"Oh yeah . . . Who?" Cole said cautiously.

"I think the one in the black coat is Edward J. Olson, my father's . . ."

"Yeah, I know," Cole nodded, instinctively tucking his long coat behind the holster that held his Colt.

"What should we do?"

"If we've seen *them* . . . they've certainly seen *us*," Cole said. "If we leave the trail now, they'll know that we have misgivings about crossing their path."

"Then we shan't leave the trail," Hannah said confidently. "We'll face them. I'll continue to ride point."

"Are you sure you want to do that?" Cole asked. "You're a good shot, but there's three of them, two of us, and we have a pair of caged pigeons to keep from getting killed."

"I don't mean for us to face them with *guns*," she said. "I mean to face Edward J. Olson with *words*. He *knows* me, and I think I can figure out what to say. He doesn't know that I know that *he* sent Blake and Clark out here, and there is no indication that we met up with those two. The best thing we have on our side is that he's in very big trouble if he lets anything happen to Isham Ransdell's daughter."

"He could say that you got hit in a cross fire," Cole said.

"Thanks for suggesting that comforting possibility," she said with an almost smile. "I'm betting there will not be a cross fire."

"I don't know . . ." Cole said hesitatingly.

"Do *you* have a better idea, Mr. Cole?"

The two groups of riders approached each other cautiously but deliberately, without overt demonstration of caution.

When they were within shouting distance, it was Hannah who spoke first.

"Good morning, Mr. Olson." she exclaimed with a merry smile, as though she were greeting Olson on the street in Gallatin City. "What a pleasure to see you."

His companions, whom she dismissed with a nod, were a pair of men she recognized as being among those who did occasional odd jobs around town.

"Good morning, Miss Ransdell," he replied, touching the brim of his hat. "I'm

371

surprised to see you out here this morning."

"It *is* such a nice morning, isn't it? A bit on the cold side, but it doesn't look like we're in for a lot of snow."

"No, ma'am. It doesn't look like much of a storm."

"Good morning, Mr. Olson," Cole said with a wave, riding up to a place near Hannah. Following her lead, Cole smiled broadly, though he kept his right hand close to his Colt.

"Mr. Cole," Olson said, nodding an acknowledgment of the bounty hunter. "I can see with great satisfaction that you have succeeded in your mission of rounding up the Porter boys . . . or at least *one* of the Porter boys."

"Enoch's right there," Cole said, nodding to the canvas-wrapped parcel tied across the saddle on Enoch Porter's horse.

"I can smell him from here," Olson nodded.

Olson was trying to appear cordial, but the two men with him had nervous, edgy expressions. Perhaps it was merely Cole's endemic distrust of Olson's employer, but it seemed to him that these two were keeping their gun hands at the ready.

Cole was sizing up how fast he could take them if they *did* draw on him, and which one to take first. Unlike the more seasoned and calculating bushwhackers of the day before, these two appeared very young and very inexperienced, the sort who were prone to being easily spooked into drawing weapons without adequate thought. That sort was, Cole knew, the worst kind.

Cole watched Gideon Porter exchange knowing glances with Olson. This man, as Olson's knowing nod and the expression on Porter's face revealed, was one of Porter's friends in high places.

"What are you boys doing out for a ride today?" Hannah said cheerfully. "Heading up to Helena?"

"No. Actually, we were riding out to meet Mr. Cole," Olson said warily. Whatever he was doing or saying that he was doing, he obviously had not in his wildest dreams expected to run into Isham Ransdell's daughter.

"Mighty good timing, I'd say," Cole smiled. "How'd you pick *this* morning?"

"There were some travelers who passed through Gallatin City a couple of days ago who had word of a bounty hunter with two prisoners who had been in Copperopolis about a week ago," Olson explained. "Figured it had to be you."

"Guess you figured right," Cole smiled calmly.

"Hadn't expected to see you out here, Miss Ransdell," Olson said, repeating his earlier words to her. "Does your father know you're out here?"

"Of course he does," Hannah lied with an innocent smile.

"He didn't say anything to *me* about you being out here on the road with this bunch."

"Well, you know Daddy," she laughed. "He doesn't necessarily tell everyone about *everything*. He often doesn't tell me about the errands he sends *you* on."

"He *sent* you?"

"Certainly," she said with a nod. "You don't think I'd come out here and associate myself with such riff-raff on my own, do you?"

"Well . . . I reckon not," Olson said. He had to admit that having his boss send her was the only possible explanation that he could imagine.

"Why do you suppose . . . um . . . Why did he do that?"

"Well, Mr. Olson, as Mr. Cole put it, he wanted me to 'check up on his bounty hunter.' Why do you suppose he didn't tell *you* that I was coming?"

Hannah wished immediately that she had

not made the latter barb, but she could not resist the temptation to insinuate that the right-hand man was not briefed on everything.

"I reckon he was busy with various affairs at the bank," Olson said weakly, trying to save face.

"Folks, if you'll excuse me, I've got some outlaws to move along," Cole interjected at this break in the conversation.

"Of course." Olson nodded. "But I must say that I'm certainly concerned to see Miss Ransdell being in harm's way like this, with these ruffians. Since things seem to be in order here, I'd like to escort her on ahead and get her back to Gallatin City as soon as possible, while you bring in your villains, Mr. Cole. I'll leave the boys here to give you a hand."

"Thank you *so* much for your offer," Hannah said. "There is really *nothing* I'd rather do right now than get away from this mess . . . especially now that Enoch Porter has started to reek with such an atrocious odor."

"I'm happy to oblige . . ." Olson smiled.

"*But* . . . and it pains me to say it, Mr. Olson, I would not be true to my father's instructions to accompany this motley crew if I were to do such a thing." Hannah smiled.

"I'm sure that if he were here, Miss Ransdell, he would . . ."

"He might or he might not." Hannah shrugged innocently. "But of course if he *were* here, he wouldn't have asked *me* to be here . . ."

"Okay, Miss Ransdell," Olson said, holding up a hand. "If that be your wish. Let us all hasten back to Gallatin City . . . together."

"You fellas work for Mr. Ransdell?" Cole asked innocently of Edward J. Olson's hands as they continued south toward Gallatin City.

While Olson joined Hannah in the lead of the procession, the other two had joined Cole in bringing up the rear.

"Ummm . . . yep," answered one. "Sometimes. Mainly do jobs for Mr. Olson."

"He sure seems to be surprised that Mr. Ransdell sent his daughter out to check up on me," Cole said in a casual, "making conversation" way.

"Does seem curious, I guess," the kid said. "But I guess he figured she was up to the job."

"She's a willful one," the other interjected.

"Too damned smart for her own damned good from what I've heard. Like some kind of filly bronc."

"Like to ride that filly bronc, though," the first kid said.

"Not me," said his partner. "I'm not rightly fond of uppity women. That one looks to be nothing but trouble."

"Still, she's a looker," the first insisted. "What do you think, Cole?"

"She's a looker, for sure," Cole said, nodding, in a casual, "making conversation" way.

CHAPTER 29

As Isham Ransdell unlocked the front door to the Gallatin City Bank and Trust Company and stepped inside, the big clock on the far wall chimed once. Half an hour until opening time.

Mr. Duffy was at his desk, hard at work under his green eyeshade. Hannah's desk was empty, of course.

"I wonder why Hannah decided so impulsively to take off for Bozeman," Duffy said as he noticed his boss staring at the empty desk.

"She has a friend down there who had a child recently," the banker replied. "But I do not know why she decided on this visit so abruptly. I have long ago discovered that the females of our species are given to flights of spontaneity. In any event, I looked forward to her return. I'm tiring of making my own breakfast."

"Maybe you'll hear from her by mail

today," Duffy said hopefully.

"When she travels, she usually drops a line to tell that she arrived safely, but young people often forget such things when they get busy. I hope she is having a pleasant visit."

Pouring himself a cup of the coffee which Duffy had made — more poorly, admittedly, than Hannah — he sat down to review a stack of papers that Duffy had placed on his desk for his signature.

After signing off on a couple of very routine documents, he leaned back in his heavy oak desk chair to take a sip of coffee. On the wall there hung a map of Gallatin City and adjacent parcels, with various properties marked with color-coded snippets of ribbon carefully attached with banker's pins. Red stood for mortgages, green for commercial loans, and so on. To the east of town, his eyes fell upon the tract of land that he and his partners had acquired some years back for practically nothing, and on which he and his lone surviving partner stood to make a fortune. Upon this reflection, he could not stifle a contented smile.

As the clock struck the hour, Isham Ransdell was raising the curtains and unlocking the front door. This was normally Hannah's job, but in her absence it fell to him. It was, he thought, only for the week. In any case, he was delighted, as always, to see a line of customers at his door.

Standing at the teller's window, performing the routine tasks of the bank teller — cashing checks, making change for the boy sent over by the mercantile, and so on — reminded him of his own early days in banking. He was glad, though, to have that part of his career behind him.

Isham Ransdell stepped into the cold morning. A few snowflakes were in the air, but there seemed no threat of a storm.

Not only had he been compelled to fill in at the teller's window this morning, but he now had to make the daily trek to the post office *himself*. He could have sent Duffy, but the man was more useful to the bank beneath his eyeshade working with his pen.

Standing in line, waiting for his mail, was another task Ransdell was glad to have behind him.

At last, he got his bundle, and he had stepped aside to thumb through it, when the door opened and in walked Virgil Stocker.

"What brings *you* to the post office, Virgil?" Ransdell asked with a smile.

"Same as you, I suppose," Stocker answered with a shrug. "My secretary is off today . . . Caught something . . . It's the weather, I suppose. These girls these days . . . they get the sniffles and suddenly they cannot work."

"Not like when we were starting out," Ransdell observed nostalgically.

"In those days, we'd have come to work with a broken leg."

"Indeed," the banker agreed, noting the injuries and scars that were still prominent on the attorney's face.

"Isham, I was thinking that if you are available, you and I should perhaps dine together at the Gallatin House, as we have *not* done in some time."

"That is a capital idea," Ransdell said, his eyes brightening. "What about this evening? With my chief cook and bottle washer off to Bozeman to call on her friend, dinner at my home is a lonely affair. Your company would be much appreciated."

"Excellent. We could make it an early dinner. We'd dine in my private booth, of course . . . perhaps around five?"

By now, Stocker had reached the head of the line and was rewarded with his own stack of mail.

Isham Ransdell was about to say "good

day" and leave his partner to look though his mail alone, when Stocker turned to him with a letter, addressed to "Mr. Virgil Stocker, Attorney," which he showed to his friend. It had been postmarked in St. Paul, Minnesota, and the return address was that of the Northern Pacific Railway Company.

Stocker looked at Ransdell and back at the letter.

"This may be what we have been waiting for," Stocker said, licking his lips.

"Are you going to open it?" Ransdell asked.

"I suggest that we open it *together*," Stocker said with a smile. "We *could* wait for dinner, but why don't we retire to my offices *now* and open it over a glass of something to warm us."

Neither man spoke as they made their way through the lazily drifting snowflakes to Stocker's law offices. The two men sat down, and Stocker ceremonially uncorked a half-filled whiskey bottle.

"Special occasions." He smiled, pouring generous portions for himself and his colleague. "I save this bottle for special occasions. I think you were here the last time . . . When was that?"

"Nearly a year ago, as I recall," Ransdell said, picking up his glass. "There were *four* of us on that day."

"Indeed, there were," Stocker agreed with sadness in his voice.

"Shall we drink to a satisfactory conclusion of a sad affair?" Ransdell said. "To the bounty hunter's having resolved the situation once and for all."

"To the end of the whole sordid mess," Stocker suggested, touching his partner's glass. "And to brighter days ahead."

"Hear, hear," Ransdell agreed with a smile. "Now, are you going to open the damned letter?"

"Indeed . . . after much adieu," he said, crisply slitting the envelope with a letter opener.

Isham Ransdell leaned forward as Stocker unfolded the missive.

Beneath the formal letterhead of the railway company, and above a signature that carried the legend, "on behalf of Mr. Frederick H. Billings," was a typescript containing more zeros than either man could have imagined.

"Jackpot," Isham Ransdell said. It was the only word that came to mind.

Stocker smiled after a long pause. "This is but their *opening* offer."

CHAPTER 30

Edward J. Olson found himself in the kind of situation his mother had always referred to as a "pickle." He never understood why, to her, a conundrum was like a canned vegetable, but the analogy had permanently stained his vocabulary.

When he had ridden north out of Gallatin City at the crack of dawn, he had expected to meet Blake and Clark on the trail with a line of horses bearing the bodies of the bounty hunter and the Porter boys. Just in case Blake and Clark had not accomplished their task, he had brought a further pair of hired guns to help him finish the job.

One way or another, he had expected to reach Gallatin City with a line of horses that represented a line of loose ends, each of them neatly tied off.

Then *she* appeared, unexpectedly, and as though out of *nowhere*!

When he had ridden north out of Gallatin

City at the crack of dawn, the *last* thing Olson would have imagined himself doing was riding back to Gallatin City beside Isham Ransdell's daughter — and with Gideon Porter still *alive*.

Where were Blake and Clark?

They must be out here *somewhere*. If *she* had found the bounty hunter, certainly they could have as well. Were they complete fools or had they been spooked into inaction by the presence of Isham Ransdell's daughter?

If they had done their job *before* she had showed up, then Edward J. Olson would not be in this pickle, but he *was,* and he knew he must either eat it or choke on it.

One way or another, Gideon Porter *could not* reach Gallatin City alive. If Gideon Porter pointed his filthy finger of accusation in front of everyone in Gallatin City, Olson himself would be in danger of the gallows. He cursed everyone involved in that fatal calamity at John Blaine's house and himself for agreeing to be part of it.

Her presence complicated everything. He *must* get rid of Gideon Porter, but he could not have her as a witness. He had to get her away so that his boys could take care of business.

"Miss Ransdell," Olson said at last, steering his horse close to Hestia. "May I have a word?"

"Yes, Mr. Olson," she said, smiling innocently.

"I'd like to beg you to reconsider my offer to ride on ahead with me. I would very much hate to see you get hurt if there were to be trouble. These men are dangerous criminals."

"They don't appear very threatening at the moment," she said, mocking him with a naive giggle. "They're both chained up. I don't see *how* they could hurt anyone in such a state."

"Miss Ransdell, I'm afraid that this is not something that is open to discussion."

"What?"

"As your father's right-hand man, I am afraid that I must *insist* that we get away from these men and that you allow me to escort you back to Gallatin City in safety. The men have the situation well in hand."

"As you should know better than anyone, sir, *his* wishes must be respected," she said, displaying a temper not previously in evidence. "I'm afraid that I cannot do as you've requested."

"This is not a request, Miss Ransdell," he said, displaying a temper of his own. "I must *insist.*"

"Then I *decline* your insistence, as I declined your request, Mr. Olson."

"You *will* do what you are *told!*" he said angrily. "I was your father's right-hand man when you were in pigtails, Miss Ransdell. If you will not obey me, I'll turn you over my knee as your father should have done long ago."

"I should like to see you *try* to do such a thing," she said antagonistically.

"You are a disrespectful girl demonstrating the behavior of a wench, young lady," he cautioned.

With that, he desperately grabbed for her reins.

She deftly sidestepped the black mare, and his grasp fell short.

"Aha," Hannah exclaimed, taunting him.

"Damn you," Olson said, turning his horse to get near to her.

The mare reared suddenly, but Hannah leaned into Hestia's neck and did not fall.

"What's going on up there?" Bladen Cole yelled from the back of the procession, having seen Olson make a grab at Hannah's mare.

Olson grasped again for Hannah's reins, and again he missed.

"What the hell are you tying to do?" Bladen Cole shouted angrily, as Olson glanced back toward him.

"Boys!" Olson shouted. "Take him *now*!"

The young man closest to Cole, the one who had described Hannah as a "filly bronc," went for his pistol.

Alerted by Olson's shout, the bounty hunter ducked as the first shot rang out, and fired the second himself.

As the man toppled from his horse, the one behind him reached for his gun.

The .45-caliber lead from the bounty hunter's Colt impacted just below the man's clavicle, ripping into his chest before he had a chance raise his gun.

Cole glanced once at his dying face and at hands thrashing clumsily in the warm, rapidly flowing blood, and turned the roan in the direction of Edward J. Olson.

As Olson was watching these events unfold, his gaze turned to Gideon Porter, the man who could, under no circumstance, ever set foot in Gallatin City.

He pulled his own pistol from the holster within his coat and took careful aim. Porter was so near, and so paralyzed with fear, that he could not be missed.

As he aimed his pistol at Porter, Olson felt what seemed to be a freighter's wagon crashing down on his head.

The sight of the near and vulnerable Gideon Porter melted into a dizzying grayness.

Turned awkwardly in his saddle, and spinning in dizziness, Olson felt his balance lost.

He had the sensation of the pistol tumbling from his hand as he reached out to break his fall.

The collision with the ground was nearly as painful as the blow to his head.

I must finish the job . . . Gideon Porter cannot live, Olson thought.

Through the dizzying grayness and the seeing of "stars," his eyes fell upon his pistol. He crawled and reached out to it as it lay on the ground in the light dusting of newly fallen snow.

"Don't do it!"

Someone was shouting.

K'pow . . . T'zing

A shot had been fired.

The bullet had ricocheted of the metal of the cylinder.

Something had hit him in the eye.

He rolled over and looked up.

With his other eye, he saw Hannah Ransdell, still on her mare, pointing a rifle at *him.*

"Put that gun down this instant," he demanded in a creaking, sputtering voice.

"Or what?" Isham Ransdell's daughter

asked. "Will you turn me over your knee?"

K'pow . . . T'zing

The second shot missed him by inches.

"That's for calling me a *wench,*" she explained. "Next time, I won't miss."

"Damn you, bounty hunter. He's the *one,*" Gideon Porter asserted as Bladen Cole rode up to find Edward J. Olson lying on the ground with Hannah Ransdell pointing her Winchester at him.

"One *what*?" Cole asked

"One what hired me to shoot those people."

"*Now* you tell us," Cole said. "After all these days of keeping your mouth shut about your 'friends in high places.' "

"Looks like he was not your friend after all," Hannah suggested.

"And not in such a high place at the moment," Cole added wryly.

"He told me he'd take care of it . . . said that he'd take care of everything," Porter insisted angrily.

"Looks to be that his plan was to take care of *it* by taking care of *you,*" Cole mused.

"You fool, you *stupid* fool," Olson said to Porter as he stood up and brushed off his hat.

"Is the fool *right*?" Cole asked. "*Did* you

hire him to do those murders?"

"You are *all* fools," Olson said emphatically, walking toward his horse. "This is not over yet!"

"Whoa, there, Mr. Olson," Cole said. "You're not dressed to ride just yet."

For Isham Ransdell's right-hand man, being "dressed to ride" meant the proper jewelry, specifically the manacles that then held Jimmy Goode to his saddle. Because Goode was without the use of his right hand, Cole decided to secure him to his saddle with rope and to use that set of irons for anchoring Edward J. Olson instead.

CHAPTER 31

As the banker entered the lobby of the Gallatin House, the hotel's big imported German clock was banging out the five measured beats of the hour.

He felt a tug at his sleeve and looked down to see John Blaine's widow.

"Mr. Ransdell, might I have a word?"

"Mrs. Blaine . . . I didn't see you. Good evening, ma'am."

"Mr. Ransdell, I must speak with you. Is there somewhere that we could talk . . . privately?"

"Certainly," Ransdell said. "Come by the bank in the morning . . . say around nine, before opening hours . . . you shall have my undivided attention."

"I'm afraid you don't exactly understand, sir," Leticia Blaine said in a hushed tone. "I must speak with you *now.*"

"I'm sorry, ma'am. I'm meeting Virgil Stocker for an early dinner at the moment."

"He should hear this as well . . . I have no secrets from my husband's associates . . . May I join you?"

"Well, I . . . uhhh . . ."

"Then it's settled," Leticia Blaine announced. "I don't see him in the dining room. When will he be coming?"

"*I* was to meet him at his private booth," Ransdell clarified.

"Lead the way then, sir."

Isham Ransdell was in no small way unnerved by the way that Mrs. Blaine had inserted herself into his evening plans, but politeness demanded that the widow of his former partner could not simply be dismissed and told to go away to mind her own business.

"Virgil, ummm . . . Mrs. Blaine has asked to join us," Ransdell said as he slid back the curtain and they entered Stocker's booth. "She has a matter of pressing urgency which she would like to discuss with *both* of us."

"Good evening, Mrs. Blaine, what a pleasant surprise," Stocker said, standing politely.

"Thank you and good evening to you, Mr. Stocker," she said, taking a seat at the table and seizing a napkin.

"Isham, I took the liberty of ordering a plate of oysters," Stocker said. "I know that you like oysters . . . Can't stand them myself, but I know that you . . ."

"I *love* oysters," Mrs. Blaine said, helping herself. "Thank you very much, sir."

Stocker poured a glass of claret for Ransdell and offered to pour one for his late partner's widow. She nodded.

"A fine evening." He smiled as he filled her glass and topped off his own. "No sign of snow yet, I believe."

"None that I could see," Leticia said, eating another oyster. Given the complexities of shipping to a location not yet reached by a railroad, oysters were rarely served here, and a prized delicacy.

Stocker offered the plate of oysters to Ransdell, who took it but did not put an oyster on his own plate.

"Now, what is the matter you wish to discuss with us?" Ransdell asked, getting to the point at hand.

"It is the matter of my husband's murderers," she explained.

"Yes . . ."

"It has been some weeks since you engaged that bounty hunter to track them down."

"Yes, that is correct." Ransdell nodded.

"I may be a foolish old woman, but it seems to *me* that a great deal of time has elapsed without his return. He was, as I recall, in pursuit of these scoundrels less than two days after they ran away."

"As I recall, that *is* correct, Mrs. Blaine," he said.

"In that case, may I be so impertinent as to ask what is *taking so long?*"

"These things do take time," Ransdell said in a reassuring voice. "As you recall, I *did* bring you up to date on that letter I received from Fort Benton."

"I do recall that letter, but as I *also* recall, that communication had been postmarked less than a week after your bounty hunter departed from Gallatin City. I *further* recall that your bounty hunter was headed into Blackfeet country, and you speculated that he and the Porter boys might come to their demise in that hive of merciless savages."

"Yes, I did," he said cautiously.

"Have you heard anything with regard to this?"

"I *have* had reports since then."

"And when were you planning to share these 'reports' with *me?*" She bristled indignantly. "I *am* the widow of your own partner, sir, not just another old woman off the street."

"The simple answer is that these are unconfirmed reports . . . which one might call hearsay."

"And what exactly did this *hearsay* have to *say*?"

"Some travelers who were passing through from up north claimed to have seen them in Copperopolis," Ransdell said in a confiding sort of way.

"Where on God's green earth is *Copper . . . opolis*?" Leticia Blaine replied, raising a eyebrow. "I don't believe I have heard of such a place."

"It's located across the mountains, this side of the Little Belts, up in Meagher County," Stocker interjected. "As you might surmise, it was once a mining town, but like so many mining towns, it withered practically to nothing after the easy ore played out. This would explain why you've never heard of it."

"A ghost town, then?"

"Practically . . ." Stocker said.

"And what in God's name was your bounty hunter doing in this place?"

"Apparently one of the Porter boys had been injured, and medical attention was being sought," Ransdell explained.

"*Medical attention being sought?* My husband was *murdered* by those thugs and *medical attention* is being sought?"

"That's what the reports tell us," Ransdell said. Her rage was making both of the men more than a little nervous.

"Mr. Ransdell, I was under the impression that the Porter boys were wanted dead or alive," she said angrily. "Is that not correct?"

Ransdell nodded.

"Why is it that your bounty hunter is wasting time to seek *medical attention* for a murderer who by all rights should be brought back to this city *dead*?"

"I do not know the answer to that," he said. "I don't even know whether it is true that it *really was* Mr. Cole and the Porter boys who were in Copperopolis."

"If it *is* the case, I hope that whichever of the Porter boys was sick has by now gone to follow Milton Waller to *Hades* . . . and that your bounty hunter sees the light and brings the others back *dead* . . . not alive."

"Believe you me, Mrs. Blaine," Stocker said. "My associate and I could not agree with you more that the lives of those nefarious criminals aren't worth saving for the luxury of a trial."

"Can you . . . Is there a way to determine whether this hearsay is true?"

"In fact, Mrs. Blaine, I hope to do exactly that," Ransdell told her with a smile. "This very morning, my right-hand man, Mr. Edward J. Olson, started north on the most likely route between Gallatin City and Copperopolis to investigate. I'm not certain what he will find, nor indeed, whether Mr. Cole and the Porter boys will be found at all, but at least we may know *something* within the next few days."

"I certainly, hope so, Mr. Ransdell," she said, not returning his smile.

The palpable tension in the private booth gradually dissipated as the steaks and boiled potatoes were served and conversation turned to other topics.

Mrs. Blaine seemed visibly relieved at having unburdened herself, and the claret seemed to have somewhat lightened the mood at the table.

"Would you care for some more horseradish, Mrs. Blaine?" Ransdell said, offering her the condiment.

"Yes . . . I mean no . . . I'm afraid . . . that I am not feeling well," she said, dropping her fork clumsily on the table.

She had suddenly gone pale and her eyes had glazed over.

"Here, take some water, madam," Stocker suggested.

"I don't feel well . . . I feel that I am about to be . . ."

She coughed as though about to vomit,

then gagged.

"Is something caught in her throat?" Ransdell asked.

As both men stood to come to her aid, Leticia Blaine began convulsing, then collapsed into a heap on the floor.

"I can't . . . breathe . . ." she gasped.

Pushing back the curtain enclosing the private booth, Virgil Stocker shouted to the head waiter. "Get a doctor! Quickly . . . *get a doctor!*"

CHAPTER 32

As the afternoon had slowly faded, the snow had come and gone. The closer they got to Gallatin City, the more traffic they met on the road. There were more wagons, and even the stagecoach headed up toward Diamond City or Helena. As they passed, people regarded this group of chained men escorted by a young woman and a bearded man with great curiosity, but no one said anything beyond exchanging simple greetings.

It was growing dark when they reached the crest of what both Bladen Cole and Hannah Ransdell knew would be the last ridge before Gallatin City. When he saw her pause and look down at the city, he ordered the others to stop and rode up to join her.

He looked at his father's pocket watch. It was close to six o'clock. The lights of the city were coming on.

"Are you ready for this?" Cole asked.

"No . . . of course not," she said bitterly. "Could I *ever* be ready for this?"

"Guess you'll just have to take it as it comes."

"Oh, oh," she said suddenly.

"What?" Cole asked.

"I just saw the light in the bank come on."

"Is that bad?"

"Actually not . . . I'd much rather this confrontation take place *there* than at home . . . with the memories of mother . . . and . . ."

Cole could see tears in her eyes.

"I understand," Cole said, nodding toward the city below. "We'll deliver this bunch to Deputy Johnson's jail, then we'll go over to the bank and . . ."

"No," Hannah interrupted. "I need to go to see him *alone.* I know that you will have to get your money . . . but I'll go to see him first, and I'll go alone. You won't need me with you when you deliver these people to the sheriff's office."

"But . . ."

"Don't argue with me." She smiled, glancing at Edward J. Olson. "You saw what happened to the last man who tried."

"Be careful," he said.

"I will."

"You don't know what may happen," he said.

"No . . . I do not," she admitted. "I'll be covering new ground."

"He may have more hired guns," Cole suggested.

"I don't know." She shrugged. "Probably, I guess . . . What a cheery thought."

"Let me give you something," he said.

"What?"

"It's a little something I picked up down in Green River," he said, reaching deep into his vest pocket.

"What is that?" Hannah asked. In the gathering darkness, she could not identify the small object wrapped in dark cloth that he had in his hand.

"It's an over-and-under Remington derringer," he said. "I got it from a man who has no further use for it. It's more discreet to carry than your rifle."

"I'm not planning to *shoot* my own father," she said, taking the little gun.

"Like we were saying, that which you *are* planning may involve people other than your father."

"Okay . . . I suppose it wouldn't hurt. Is it loaded?"

"Two shots, .41-caliber."

■ ■ ■ ■

Bladen Cole's long-awaited return to Gallatin City came just past dark, so few people noticed that the procession riding into town included three horses with men fastened to their saddles and three carrying men *across* their saddles.

They paused when they reached the intersection of Main Street and Cottonwood. Down one block on the latter, there was still a light on at the sheriff's office. Two blocks away on the former, they could see the light burning inside the Gallatin City Bank and Trust.

"Wish me luck," Hannah Ransdell said as she bade the bounty hunter good-bye. She reached for his hand, and he took it.

"Good luck . . . Stay safe," he said.

"You too . . . Bladen," she replied, calling him by his first name for the first time.

It was almost seven o'clock when Deputy — Acting Sheriff — Marcus Johnson heard someone knocking at the door of his office.

He was already in the back room, which functioned as his sleeping quarters, putting a pot on for his supper, and was ready to call it a day.

403

It had been a slow and quiet day, the kind that he preferred — that is, it had been until about an hour ago, when he had been summoned to the restaurant at the Gallatin House.

Poor Mrs. Blaine.

The recently widowed Mrs. Blaine had died a dramatic death on the floor of a private booth, and naturally the law must be summoned under circumstances where a clamorous demise occurs in a public place. However, the doctor, who was also summoned, ruled it a death from natural causes, so there was nothing for the lawman to do but tell the gawking onlookers that nothing could be done. You can't arrest an oyster for being tainted.

Now, back in his office, about ready to turn in for the night, Johnson was startled by the knock on the door.

"Who's there?"

"Bladen Cole . . . the bounty hunter . . . I got some wanted men for that jail of yours."

Johnson quickly opened his door, looked at Cole and up into the face of the infamous Gideon Porter.

Weeks had passed since the murders at the Blaine house, but the crime was still on the minds of the people of Gallatin City. So too, especially for Johnson, who was there when it happened, was the murder of Sheriff John Hollin.

"You done brought back the Porter boys," Johnson observed with satisfied wonderment. "Least one of 'em, or two, I guess, with Jimmy Goode here."

"Enoch's tied across that horse yonder," Cole said. "You better call the undertaker. He's started to rot. You've also got two others out there, but they're not nearly so ripe."

"Good evening, Mr. Olson," Johnson said, spotting Edward J. Olson sitting on his hitched horse. In the dark, he did not notice that the banker's right-hand man was chained to his saddle.

"Okay, you scum, let's dismount," Cole said, walking first to Porter's horse. Having detached him from his saddle, he handed him off to Johnson, who happily, though roughly, escorted the defiant outlaw to a waiting cell.

"What happened to you, Jimmy Goode?" Johnson exclaimed, looking at the man's debilitating injuries.

"It's what you get for kidnapping a six-year-old," Cole answered.

"Do tell," the sheriff said.

Goode glanced at him mournfully and looked away as he was led to a waiting cell.

"Here's the last of 'em," Cole said.

Having locked up both Porter and Jimmy Goode, Johnson turned back to the door, where Cole stood with Olson.

"That's Mr. Olson," Johnson said with alarm. "You got him in *irons*!"

"Yes, I do," Cole explained. "Meet the man who paid for the Porter boys' rampage over at the Blaine house."

"Damn right!" Porter shouted from his cell. "He's the one, all right."

"Mr. Olson?" Johnson asked. "But you are . . ."

"Nobody . . . none of you. Nobody understands the whole picture," Olson said angrily.

"And he tried to shoot poor old Gideon to keep him from talking," Cole added.

Johnson looked at Olson in disbelief and had an almost apologetic expression on his face as he closed a cell door on this erstwhile pillar of the community.

"I'll be damned if this bastard didn't try to shoot me," Porter shouted to Johnson. "Ain't that right, Jimmy Goode?"

"Damned right for sure," Jimmy Goode said. "Would have too, but for that Ransdell girl done whacked him . . . whacked him *hard*. I done saw it."

"The Ransdell girl?" Johnson asked, addressing his question to Cole.

"She came out to help me round 'em up," Cole said.

"What?" Johnson gasped incredulously. "Where is she now?"

"Over at the bank having words with Mr. Olson's employer," Cole explained. "I think that she is —"

His words were interrupted by someone rapping at the door.

"Who's there?" Johnson asked.

"It's Virgil Stocker, Sheriff."

CHAPTER 33

Hannah swallowed hard and took a deep breath, gently nudging Hestia down the street. She passed the post office, which she had visited routinely every business day for as long as she had worked for her father. She passed Blaine's store, where she had shopped since she was a little girl.

It was a street that she had traveled so often throughout her entire life, but tonight things were so very different, and they would never be the same again.

She peered into the bank. It was closed, of course, and the shades were drawn, but through a slit, she could see her father at his desk.

Having steered Hestia to a hitch rail in front of the closed store adjacent to the bank, she dismounted and made an effort to smooth her badly wrinkled skirt. She wished she had a mirror so that she could fix her hair, but she decided this was the

408

least of her concerns.

The bank's front door would be locked, but Hannah had a key in her jacket pocket.

Isham Ransdell looked up in alarm when he heard the front door open, wondering who it could be and whether he had forgotten to lock it.

"Hannah," he said in surprise.

To him, having no idea that she had been camping in the wilderness for two nights and on the trail for three days, his daughter looked terrible. Her clothes were wrinkled and dusty, her riding boots muddy. As he watched, she threw her hat on the counter and let her unkempt hair fall down across her shoulders.

"I'm so glad to see you," he said, standing up from his desk chair.

"Hello, Father," she said icily.

Her cold demeanor surprised and greatly disturbed him.

"You look like you've seen a ghost," Hannah said without emotion.

"Yes . . . I have," he said. "I just watched Leticia Blaine fall dead . . . less than an hour ago."

"What?"

This was a twist that Hannah had not seen coming.

"It was tainted oysters . . . over at the

409

Gallatin House."

"She's *dead*?"

"Yes . . . she's dead."

"There have been a lot of deaths in Gallatin City of late," Hannah said, her insinuation clear, assuming he chose to hear it.

"A lot has happened since you've been in Bozeman," her father said.

"I didn't go to Bozeman," she replied, still disallowing herself from expressing emotion, aside from a perfunctory bitterness in her words.

"But you said . . . you were on the stage . . ."

"It was a ruse," Hannah said, folding her arms.

"Why? Where?"

"I went up into the Sixteen Mile Creek country," she explained. "I took Hestia and went up to Sixteen Mile Creek to find the bounty hunter."

"Did you . . . ?"

"Yes, Father," she said. "I *found* the bounty hunter."

"Why?"

"Why did I go? . . . Or why did I go looking for a *bounty hunter*?" Hannah asked before proceeding to answer. "I went looking because I overheard *your* right-hand man — Mr. Edward J. Olson — sending

Lyle Blake and Joe Clark to *kill* the bounty hunter, and to *kill* the Porter boys. I went looking for the bounty hunter because I wanted to *stop* that from happening."

"But why would they . . . ?"

"Because, *as you know,* Father, dead men cannot point fingers," Hannah said angrily. "Can they?"

"Point fingers at what?"

"*Really?* Don't insult my intelligence, Father. I'm not your little girl anymore."

"I don't understand . . ." Isham Ransdell gasped. His daughter had never spoken to him like this.

"I know it *all,* Father," she asserted. "I know the whole, sickening story."

"What story?"

"*What story?*" Hannah repeated. "Let's start with 'Once upon a time there was a railroad that was coming to Gallatin City.' Then there were four businessmen who owned some land that was not worth too much until the railroad was coming. Do you know this part of the story, Father?"

"Yes, that's true, of course, but . . . ?"

"But it's not anything out of the ordinary, is it?" Hannah fumed.

"No . . . not at all," her father answered, becoming perturbed.

"Until you add on rights of inheritance,"

she said, counting one by one on her fingers. "And you add to *that* a series of *murders* . . . and *next,* the shares go not to families, but to surviving *partners.*"

"You can't believe . . ."

"I did not *want* to believe," she said, fighting back tears. "You asked whether I found the bounty hunter . . . and I said I did . . . and I learned what he *did not* write in that letter from Fort Benton."

"Which was?" Isham Ransdell demanded, his own ire growing.

"Which was Milton Waller's deathbed words. His *deathbed* words about him and the Porter boys being *paid* to go to the Blaine home that night. And *why* did they go there? Because there were *four* partners. 'Three must die,' Waller said, 'and only *one* can survive.' Who was the *only* man of the four who was *not* there that night?"

"I wasn't there, but . . ."

"*Exactly!*" Hannah shouted.

"What are you saying?"

"Gideon Porter knows, and Gideon Porter is *alive.* You sent the bounty hunter to bring him back, insinuating that you wanted him dead. *You* sent Blake and Clark out to kill them, and this morning, *your* right-hand man, Edward J. Olson, came *this* close to killing Gideon Porter until *your* little girl

412

slammed him across the head with the butt of a Winchester . . . but Gideon Porter is *alive!*"

"I did *not* hire Gideon Porter to kill *anyone,*" Isham Ransdell shouted back angrily, though he could tell that this woman who said she was no longer his little girl did not believe a word he was saying.

CHAPTER 34

The tall, impeccably dressed man with noticeable scars on his face stepped into the sheriff's office.

"Good evening, Sheriff," he said, though his eyes were not on Marcus Johnson but scanning the other faces in the room and the cells.

"Mr. Cole, when I saw you coming down Main Street a moment ago, I could see that you had done your job," he said, not looking at Cole, but directing his angry eyes at Gideon Porter. "And here is the mangy dog who did *this* to my face."

"Gideon kept sayin' he had friends in high places who were gonna get us off," Jimmy Goode shouted in uncharacteristic anger. "Now look at him . . . at *us.*"

For the first time, perhaps in his life, Jimmy Goode had spoken assertively without Gideon Porter denouncing him or telling him to shut up.

Looking at Stocker's face, Porter's expression changed from his usual countenance of bitter defiance to one of anxiety.

"And I see Mr. Olson here in a *cell*," Stocker said dramatically, as though he was performing before a jury in a packed courtroom. "Can someone explain to me how on earth a pillar of our community has gotten himself locked up?"

"These men have all said that Mr. Olson hired Gideon to do the shootings," Johnson explained.

"Edward?" Stocker asked, looking at the man himself.

Olson merely hung his head as Porter acrimoniously repeated his earlier assertion.

"The Ransdell girl stopped him from shooting Gideon . . . to keep Gideon from telling what you just heard he's already told," Johnson told the lawyer.

"*The Ransdell girl?*" Stocker said, having been caught off guard. "Where? She's in Bozeman . . ."

"Actually not," Cole said. "She rode with us down from Sixteen Mile Creek. Right now, she's over at the bank, where she's laying into the man Olson works for."

"She's *what?*"

"As you know, the man who hired Gideon Porter to do that to your face works for

Isham Ransdell," Cole explained. "Milton Waller told me on his deathbed that they were paid for those killings. It also seems that the only man not present that night stood to inherit some pretty valuable real estate."

"So you've surmised . . . that Isham hired Mr. Olson here . . . to hire Porter to . . . ?" Stocker said thoughtfully, recalling that Hannah had come to exactly the same conclusion.

"Haven't heard anything to the contrary," Cole interrupted.

"You were sure lucky, Mr. Stocker," Johnson added. "They was gunnin' for you too."

"I see," said Stocker thoughtfully. "So now we know the *whole* story . . . and we have *all* the perpetrators in custody. Wait, where's Enoch Porter?"

"He's out yonder," Johnson said. "He's settin' on his horse, but not upright."

"I thought I was smelling something pungent as I walked past," Stocker said.

"Now that everything is taken care of here, maybe I should mosey him on over to the undertaker's before it gets too late," Johnson said.

"That would be a very good idea," Stocker agreed. "We'd hate to have Gallatin City awake to his stench."

"Mr. Cole, I must commend you on rounding up the perpetrators of this crime," Stocker said after Johnson had left the office. "Including one — Mr. Olson — we had *not known* to be involved."

Cole merely nodded. His tired brain was fixed on a real bath and a good night's sleep in a real bed.

He should not have let his mind drift to such distracting thoughts.

"I commend you on figuring out all of the details . . . *except one,*" Stocker said with a smirk as he suddenly drew a gun and pointed it directly at Cole's head. "Now, please carefully unstrap your gunbelt and let it drop to the floor."

Stunned by this unexpected turn of events, Cole could do nothing but comply. To attempt to draw his gun would be a fatal mistake. The man had the drop on him, and he apparently knew how to use a gun.

"Now, kick it over to the cell containing the incompetent Edward J. Olson," Stocker demanded.

As Olson reached out and took Cole's pistol from its holster, Stocker tossed him the cell keys from Johnson's desk.

"It is quite amusing, Mr. Cole," Stocker

smirked, "that the *one* piece of the puzzle that you got wrong was believing that the straitlaced Isham Ransdell was the kingpin behind this affair. On one hand, I'm insulted, and on another, I find it a compliment that you *didn't* figure it out."

"If not Ransdell, then who?" Cole asked. *"You?"*

"Guilty as charged," Stocker confessed. As he laughed, the scars gave his face a macabre appearance.

"But Gideon Porter clobbered you bad with the butt of his gun," Cole said grimly.

"That was to make it look convincing, though Mr. Porter made it a bit *too* convincing," Stocker said, his leering grin fading. "While I *also* benefit from the right of inheritance, your eyes fell upon poor Isham because he was *absent* that night."

"That, and the fact that Olson is *his* man," Cole interjected.

"I also work for Mr. Stocker," Olson said, stepping from his cell and strapping on Cole's gunbelt. "Under the table of course."

"He really *did* hire the Porter boys to do the deed," Stocker added. "You had that part right."

"And I'm still owed another five hundred dollars for doing it," Gideon Porter asserted as Olson unlocked his cell.

418

"What do you mean?" Jimmy Goode whined. "You only paid me *thirty* bucks and you're gettin' *five hundred*?"

"That's 'cause I'm worth it, and you're good for *nothing,*" Porter growled, roughly cuffing Goode alongside his head as they were released from their cell.

"Calm down, both of you," Stocker demanded. "I believe that we all need to go over to the bank and see that everyone gets what's coming to him. Mr. Cole's diligence has presented us with an opportunity."

"What sort of opportunity?" Olson asked.

"A terrible thing happened at the bank tonight," Stocker said with exaggerated mock sadness. "You see, our Mr. Cole here decided that with the banker's vault wide open to pay the bounty, the rest of the bank's assets would be easy pickings for a robbery. He took you and me hostage and went to do his dirty work."

"I follow you," Olson said smugly. "And the banker dies in the shootout?"

"Exactly." The attorney smiled broadly. "And sadly, his daughter is killed as well. Of course, *we* . . . I'll let it be *you* . . . will save the day by killing the bounty hunter. *You* will become a hero by avenging your boss's death."

"I like it," Olson said, and smiled.

419

CHAPTER 35

"How could you, Father?" Hannah Ransdell sobbed.

"I told you, I *didn't,*" her father insisted firmly. "If Mr. Olson did as you have said, he *had* to be acting alone."

"Why?" Hannah demanded. "Why did he act alone? Why did he act *at all*? What did *he* have to gain? It was *you* who benefitted from . . ."

Hannah's tirade was interrupted by the front door of the bank swinging wide.

"You should remember to lock your door at night," Virgil Stocker said as he entered the room with four other men.

Hannah stared in astonishment. Bladen Cole had been disarmed, and Edward J. Olson was pointing the bounty hunter's gun around the room.

"What's going on?" Hannah demanded, looking at Cole.

"They will want you to believe that this is

going to be a bank holdup," Cole said. "But it's really a continuation of what started at the Blaine house . . ."

"Shut up!" Olson demanded angrily.

"Actually, I'm sad to say that he's right," Stocker said, looking at Ransdell.

"Virgil, can you *please* tell me what is going on here?" Isham Ransdell said. "This cannot be happening . . . This is *madness.*"

"Mr. Cole here has developed a fantastic theory, which is very nearly spot-on," Stocker said, pacing the floor dramatically. The tall attorney, with years of courtroom experience, was skilled at the art of dominating a room with his presence. "He has deduced that the four of us owned land with the right of inheritance flowing to surviving partners . . . and that the purpose of the unfortunate shootings was to get that inheritance flowing to *you.*"

"You can't be saying . . ." Ransdell sputtered.

"I'm afraid so," Stocker interrupted, feigning sadness. "The three of you . . . Blaine, Phillips, and *yourself* . . . were supposed to die that night. Because I was injured, and you were *not there* . . . and finally because *your* man Olson served as my intermediary with the Porter boys, Mr. Cole deduced that the guilt lay with *you,* not me, between the two of us who survived."

"I can't believe this," the banker said angrily. "Are you now intending to kill *me*?"

"Unfortunately, I must admit that tonight, your time has come," Stocker said, dramatically waving his hand. As a lawyer, he loved to pontificate with a theatrical flourish. "I had intended for your death to occur earlier this evening at the Gallatin House, in front of a room full of witnesses, but alas, poor Widow Blaine sucked down the oysters which were poisoned for *you*."

"You killed her *too*?" Ransdell said in disbelief.

"If it is any consolation, neither she nor Mrs. Phillips were *supposed* to die as part of this plan," Stocker said with a shrug. "Things just got a little out of hand."

"You weren't *supposed* to die either, missy," Olson said, smiling at Hannah.

"What are you going to do with us?" she demanded.

"As Mr. Cole has said, there is going to be a stickup tonight," Olson explained. "He has decided to take the opportunity of the bank vault being opened to pay his bounty . . . to well, empty that vault of cash, and disappear into the darkness."

"Unfortunately, Mr. Cole will murder the banker and his daughter in the process,"

Stocker interjected. "But, *fortunately,* the quick-thinking Mr. Olson will save the day . . . or the night, if you will . . . by killing this bounty hunter–turned–bank robber."

"What happens to us?" Jimmy Goode asked.

"Shot in the cross-fire, of course," Stocker said with a dismissive wave of his thespian hand.

"I'll be damned if I'll be a sitting duck," Goode shouted, bolting for the door.

"Stop!" Olson demanded, impulsively firing a shot into the darkness through the open door.

Even as he was feeling the buck of the .45 in his hand, Olson felt the body slam of Bladen Cole, jumping him from behind. The bounty hunter picked the moment of his distraction to send him crashing to the floor.

Virgil Stocker, meanwhile, took this same moment of distraction to do what he had come to do. Taking out his own gun, he aimed not at the bounty hunter, but at his former partner.

The wiry man with a narrow string tie and white sideburns looked back at the man with the scarred face, with whom he had dined as a friend that very evening.

Through Isham Ransdell's mind had run the humiliation of having lost the trust and respect of his only child, and *now* he was about to lose his *life* to an erstwhile friend who now eyed him over the top of a Smith & Wesson Model 3 with a businesslike "no hard feelings" expression on his face.

As Isham Ransdell stared into that scarred face, Virgil Stocker's head suddenly jerked sideways with a violent twist.

Isham looked then at his daughter and at the derringer in her hand.

Bladen Cole's gun slipped from Olson's grip as he fell to the floor. It bounced and cartwheeled across the polished surface, with both Cole and Gideon Porter scrambling after it.

Its trajectory had sent it flying toward Porter, practically as though fate wished to hand it to him.

He grabbed it, pulling it away from Cole's grasp by a mere split second.

Porter raised the gun and was working his forefinger into the trigger guard, when a sudden blast sent him toppling backward.

Bladen Cole looked up at Hannah Ransdell and at the derringer in her hand.

EPILOGUE

Nobody, not even Jimmy Goode himself, knew why he had chosen to run to find the acting sheriff at the undertaker's office instead of hightailing it to parts unknown.

Some said it was because he was the witless oaf who had *always* been called "good-for-nothing Jimmy Goode" and wouldn't have known where to *find* parts unknown.

Some said that it was because he was tired of living in the turbulent shadow of Gideon Porter and would do anything to get that terrible monster off his back.

Still others theorized that he was so exhausted, so spent, and so wasted by the experience of the previous weeks that he just could not go on.

Marcus Johnson, meanwhile, had heard the shots before Jimmy Goode found him, and had arrived at the Gallatin City Bank and Trust in time to hear the dying admissions of Virgil Stocker. The attorney had told the whole story as his onetime friend, Isham Ransdell, knelt over him, staring in disbelief. He told it in the form of an apology, and there were tears in his eyes when he took his last breath.

Those who were there interpreted his words as expressing not an apology for his terrible scheme, but only his sorrow that it had failed.

The only thing in Gideon Porter's eyes when he took *his* last breath was the reflection of an angry woman with an over-and-under Remington in her gloved hand.

Nobody shed a tear when the Porter boys were buried in a single unmarked grave. Their mother having long since died of a broken heart, there was not a soul in Gallatin City who would ever miss them.

Edward J. Olson was tried and convicted in the space of two days and was taken to the county seat to await the hangman.

Jimmy Goode got twenty years for his part in the whole affair. He might have gotten the noose, such was the mood of the jury pool in Gallatin City, but he did not.

Some say that his neck was saved by folks feeling pity for his limp and useless hand. Some say that it was because of his having gone for the sheriff that night.

Still others insist that it was because he

was the witless oaf who had always been called "good-for-nothing" Jimmy Goode, and therefore, nobody ever took him seriously.

Hannah Ransdell walked down Main Street, bound for the post office.

The snow had piled up considerably over the past few weeks, and she had to maneuver through the narrow paths that had been shoveled.

During those weeks, she had also been maneuvering through the narrow path of her relationship with her father. Saving his life had gone a long way toward rebuilding the relationship they once had, but only time would heal *all* the wounds inflicted by the penetrating distrust she had expressed that terrible night, if indeed they *ever* healed.

For Isham Ransdell, the memory of having a man considered to be a friend betray him so horrifically was a nightmare. Yet this nightmare was a mere trifle when compared to his having seen his own daughter, his little girl, say and — worse still — *believe* those things about him.

It was enough to make him yearn to have been one of those cold bodies on the floor of the parlor at the Blaine home on that *other* terrible night.

With the railroad coming, and him the sole surviving partner, he would sooner rather than later be a very, very rich man, but he would have gladly traded it all for a chance to sit down just once more with John Blaine and Dawson Phillips, or to have his relationship with his daughter back.

Stepping through the snow, Hannah passed the Gallatin House and the Gallatin City General Mercantile, the place that was still referred to as Mr. Blaine's store. She had been back to the Mercantile, long since stripped of the funereal black bunting, but she had not had an occasion to set foot in the Gallatin House since she had come back from her sojourn to Sixteen Mile Creek. She passed the building that once had held Virgil Stocker's second-story law office. Workers were carrying furniture out to load it on a wagon. She wondered who would be moving in.

She passed the intersection of Main Street and Cottonwood where she had parted company with Bladen Cole for the last time.

He had lingered in Gallatin City for a few days after collecting his reward money. They had spent some time together, and these were hours in which her heart had soared. She had finally indulged her secret desire to touch his black whiskers, and her secret passion to taste his lips. Even now, her mind returned often and happily to the memories of that time.

But they had parted. It was in his nature to be on the move, not staying long in any one place.

For a brief and fiery moment, born out of feelings kindled on that night on the hilltop near the mouth of Sixteen Mile Creek, she had imagined that same wanderlust to be in *her nature* as well. She had made up her mind that when Bladen Cole moved on, when he rode out toward far horizons on the roan, she and Hestia would be at their side.

She had decided that she would not *ask,* but that she would simply *tell* him: "Mr. Cole, you may ride anywhere you like, but you will *not* ride alone." In her replaying of this in her daydreams, he had replied with many diverse comments, but he had *never* said no.

If this fire for the vagabond life had been in her nature, as indeed it *may* have been, it was extinguished by her father's tears, when she finally took back all that she had said to him that night, and when he had tearfully taken her in his arms.

She had never, ever before, or ever since,

seen him cry.

No, her place was *not* beyond the far horizon.

As she thought about it later, she realized that the bounty hunter also recognized this, and with more sadness than he would admit to. They were each bound by their nature. Just as he knew that he must go on, he knew that she was bound to stay. She was still part of the world she had known before all of this happened.

When he said good-bye, she did not tell him that he would not ride alone. Nor did she ask where he was headed.

That night, her pillow grew soggy from her tears, a wetness she longed to be transformed into the sweat of his passion mixed with her own, but she awoke knowing that she was where she needed to be.

Hannah reached the post office, chatting briefly with a few of the regulars as she waited in the short line. As menial as it was, there was something comforting about the post office routine. It was *so* unlike the uncertainty and *wild exhilaration* of life on the trail.

When she returned to the bank, her father was in a good mood, which was gradually becoming more and more common as time went on. Time was, indeed, beginning its healing process.

As she was taking off her coat, he made an offhand comment about her being his "right-hand girl."

She froze for a moment with a lump in her throat. He had no idea of how she perceived the irony of this characterization, but that did not matter. It mattered only that he had articulated it, and this made her happier than almost anything he might have said at that moment.

Wounds would heal. She *now* knew this.

Hannah went to her desk and was sorting the mail when out dropped a letter hand-addressed to "Miss Hannah Ransdell, in care of the Gallatin City Bank and Trust Company."

It was postmarked Denver, and the return address was headed with the name, "Mr. Dawson Phillips, Jr."

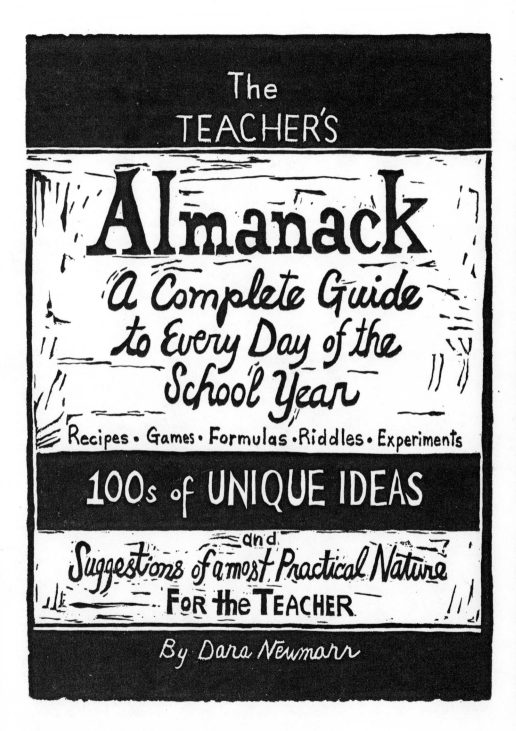

THE TEACHER'S ALMANACK
Practical Ideas for Every Day
of the School Year

Dana Newmann

The Center for Applied Research in Education, Inc.
521 Fifth Avenue, New York, N.Y. 10017

About the Author

Dana Newmann has been involved in elementary education for more than ten years as a classroom teacher and reading specialist. Her experience includes teaching in the public schools of Monterey and Carmel, California, and with the U.S. Army Dependents Education Group in Hanau, Germany. A graduate of Mills College with a B.A. in Fine Arts, Mrs. Newmann lives in Santa Fe, New Mexico.

a word of introduction

I remember very clearly how my grandfather would consult his almanac as a guide to the planting & farmwork. I've often thought how handy such a book would be for the teacher.

It would be so helpful to have a ready source of teaching suggestions geared to the seasons of the school year — a book that would primarily be a statement of ideas & recipes. You could open it to a day of the month & find a stimulating entry appropriate to that day. It would offer intriguing science experiments not requiring hours of preparation & practice; it would have a collection of _uncommon_ riddles; it would give historical anecdotes that make famous people come alive.

'The Teacher's Almanack' is such a book. You will find it a complete guide to the school year, containing unusual lesson suggestions for every subject & grade level. It covers such varied topics as: Rebus symbols, manipulative bulletin boards, Creative Writing self-starters, classroom cooking, formulas for art supplies & sources of free teaching materials. It gives the addresses, the formulas, the recipes so that you know _where_ to find them _when_ you need them.

A few of the teaching ideas included are standards that I use nearly every year, e.g. the directions for making an erupting volcano. I hope most of the suggestions will be fresh & novel to you as in many cases they are originals, e.g. games for helping & rewarding slow readers, an Interest Inventory to give you insight into the personality & interests of each child in your class.

I hope 'The Teacher's Almanack' helps this be the most rewarding year of teaching that you've ever had!

Dana Newmann

Table of Contents

11

Room environments, activities pertinent to October, e.g., original reading & math games; educational pumpkin projects; complete directions for a Halloween party that WORKS.

November   73

Calendar of important dates; etymology & quotations; historical background; activities related to:

Birth of R.L. Stevenson (76) . Birth of Robt. Fulton (79) .
Assassination of John F. Kennedy (79) . Thanksgiving (79) .
Birth of Jonathan Swift (89)

Room environments, activities pertinent to November, e.g., Indian finger puppets; suggestions to facilitate Parent-Teacher Conferences; crystal gardens; instructions for the organization of relay races.

December   94

Calendar of important dates; etymology & quotations; poetry; information & activities related to:

Birth of Eli Whitney (97) . Bill of Rights Day (97) . Birth of
Beethoven (97) . Wright Brothers Day (97) . 1st Day of Winter
(98) . Birth of Clara Barton (98) . Hanukkah (99) . Birth of
Pasteur (126)

Art activities & helpful hints for the month of December, e.g., historical origins of Christmas traditions; suggestions for a meaningful holiday party; complete guide to a joyous & creative Christmas season.

January   127

Calendar of important dates; etymology & quotations; ideas & activities related to:

New Year's Day (130) . Birth of Betsy Ross (132) . Birth of
Ben Franklin (132) . Birth of Edgar Allan Poe (134) . Birth of
Watt (134) . Birth of Ampere (135) . Edison's Electric-Light
Patent (135)

Games & ideas to spark-up the new year, e.g., 111 *uncommon* riddles; 28 plants from the kitchen; a complete guide to classroom printmaking; rainy-day games.

February   153

Calendar of important dates; etymology & quotations; information & activities related to:

> Groundhog Day (157) . Birth of Jules Verne (158) . Birth of Sir
> Francis Beaufort (158) . Birth of Thomas Edison (160) . Birth
> of Abe Lincoln (160 . Birth of Charles Darwin (161) . Valentine's
> Day (161) . U.S. Mail Established (167) . National Brotherhood
> Week (168) . Malcolm X Day (168) . Birth of George Washington
> (168) . Leap Year (170)

Ideas pertinent to the month of February, e.g., activities to help combat spring fever; directions for making new & novel valentines; a bulletin board that tells how we got our standards of length; sound exploration; haiku poetry.

March   176

Calendar of important dates; etymology & quotations; information & activities related to:

> Birth of Alexander Graham Bell (179) . Birth of Amerigo
> Vespucci (180) . Patenting of the Cotton Gin (180) . Birth of
> Ohm (180) . St. Patrick's Day (180) . Birth of J.S. Bach (183)
> . 1st Day of Spring (183) . Birth of Houdini (188) . Birth of
> Mies van der Rohe (190)

Room environments, activities & games pertinent to the month of March, e.g., science experiments with the Irish potato; all kinds of number and scientific magic tricks; a *Rebus Dictionary;* how to make 17 different rhythm instruments.

April   199

Calendar of important dates; etymology & quotations; information & activities related to:

> April Fools' Day (203) . Peary's Landing at North Pole (207)
> Birth of Jefferson (207) . Birth of da Vinci (207) . Ride of
> Paul Revere (208) . National Library Week (208) . Arbor Day
> (209) . Easter (210) . Public Schools Week (216) . Birth of
> James Buchanan (217) . Baptism of Shakespeare (217) . Birth
> of Audubon (218) . Birth of Monroe (219)

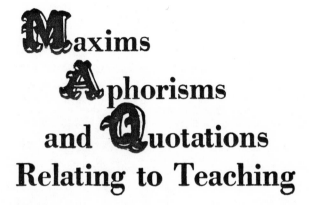

Maxims Aphorisms and Quotations Relating to Teaching

Who teaches, learns. *Anonymous*

Those who educate children well are more to be honored than they who produce them; for these only gave them life, those the art of living well. *—Aristotle*

What we like determines who we are and is the sign of what we are, and to teach taste is inevitably to form character. *—John Ruskin*

Education is not to reform students or amuse them or to make expert technicians. It is to unsettle their minds, widen their horizons, inflame their intellects, teach them to think. *—Robert M. Hutchins*

A great teacher has always been measured by the number of his students who surpass him. *Anonymous*

Only the educated are free. *Greek*

There is just one way to bring up a child in the way he should go and that is to travel that way yourself. *—Abraham Lincoln*

Kids need a challenge and a sense of achievement. There is no pride and no satisfaction in having things handed to you. *—Ann Landers, 4/29/70*

Perhaps the most valuable result of all education is the ability to make yourself do the thing you have to do when it has to be done, whether you like it or not.—*Huxley*

The teacher who is attempting to teach without inspiring the pupil with desire to learn is hammering on cold steel.—*Horace Mann*

Human history becomes more and more a race between education and catastrophe.—*H.G. Wells*

"The wisdom of nations lies in her proverbs which are brief and pithy. Collect and learn them. You have much in little; they save time in speaking; and upon occasion may be the fullest and safest answers."

(Edifying quotations appear throughout The Teacher's Almanack. Any of these which are appropriate for your class can be clearly printed on large rectangles of paper or card stock & posted about the room. Frequent changes will be especially effective in keeping the children's attention & interest.)

Patience and the mulberry leaf become a silk robe. *Chinese*

Think; do not guess. *Greek*

Better lose the anchor than the whole ship. *Dutch*

To silence another, first be silent. *Latin*

A little too late is much too late. *German*

Fear less, hope more;
Eat less, chew more;
Whine less, breathe more;
Talk less, say more;
Hate less, love more;
And all good things will be yours. *Swedish*

Good manners and soft words have brought many a difficult thing to pass—*Aesop, c. 620-560 B.C.*

Gratitude is the memory of the heart. *Greek*

A candle loses nothing by lighting another candle. *English*

The man who removes the mountain began by carrying away small stones. *Chinese*

> Sow a Thought, and you reap an Act;
> Sow an Act, and you reap a Habit;
> Sow a Habit, and you reap a Character;
> Sow a Character, and you reap a Destiny.

A Very Short History of the Calendar

(including a description of the major Jewish holidays)

> *Thirty dayes hath November*
> *April, June, and September,*
> *February hath xxviii alone,*
> *And all the rest have xxxi.*
> —Richard Grafton: 1562

Early man kept track of time by counting the suns & darknesses, by tying knots in ropes, making notches on sticks &, eventually, by noticing the changes in the positions of the sun, moon & stars.

Most of the holidays are in some way related to divisions of time—especially to the seasons. Primitive man celebrated the beginning of each of the four seasons; those early holidays exist today in differing forms throughout the world.

The Babylonians made the first calendar & based it on the moon, counting twelve lunar months to a year. An extra month was added about every four years to keep the seasons straight. The Greek, Semitic & Egyptian peoples adopted the Babylonian calendar. Later the Egyptians created a calendar that more nearly matched the seasons. This lunar calendar is used today by the Mohammedans & the Jews.

Therefore, the exact dates of the Jewish holidays vary from year to year. The Jewish calendar reckons from the year 3761 B.C., which is traditionally given as the date of the Creation. (Although most of the world now operates on a Gregorian calendar, which is a solar one, the lunar calendar is still of some contemporary significance. Your Jewish students celebrate holidays based on it.) The Jewish holidays include: Rosh Hashana, Yom Kippur, Sukkoth, Hanukkah, Purim, Pesach & Shabuoth. Each is noted in this book as it occurs during the school year.

In 46 B.C. Julius Caesar ordered a new calendar developed. This Roman calendar made use of the Egyptian year & encompassed 365 1/4 days, every fourth year having 366 days. There were twelve months in this calendar; Augustus & Julius Caesar each named one for himself, each taking a day from February, making August and July months having 31 days. (A complete historical description precedes each month as it is covered in the almanack.)

Pope Gregory XIII in 1582 requested that the error in the old calendar be corrected; the resulting Leap Year system is still in use today. The Gregorian calendar also made January first New Year's Day.

English-speaking countries began using the Gregorian calendar in 1752 & moved the calendar up eleven days. China adopted this calendar in 1912, as Russia did in 1914, & it is the standard in use throughout the world today.

Calendars for the Classroom

Lower grades. Stretch white oilcloth over a two-foot-square piece of lightweight wood. Screw 35 hooks into the board through the oilcloth as shown below. Each month, use rubber cement to affix cut-out paper letters in an appropriate color to the oilcloth at the top of the calendar. Keep 31 tagboard cards, each bearing a large, clear number, at the side of the calendar. Place the calendar upright in the chalk tray of the blackboard & each morning hang the card bearing that day's date on the appropriate hook.

Middle and upper grades. This calendar provides a striking bulletin board display & a fascinating class project that will motivate students to do extra research work. Each month, have every child research & illustrate one day's history of events. Allow pupils who have a birthday that month to illustrate their own date of birth. Illustrations may include drawings, photos, paper cutouts, objects & replicas. Use a large sheet of butcher's paper to provide a neutral background for the calendar.

Some First-of-the-School-Year Suggestions

On the first day of school have the children date a paper & write a few short sentences around a theme such as "What I Hope to Learn (or Want to Accomplish) in ____Grade." Put these finished papers in the bottom drawer of your desk & save them until Open House. At that time display each paper next to an up-to-date paper by the same child. The title of such a bulletin board might be "WOW! What a Difference a Year Makes!" or "See How Much My Penmanship Has *Improved*!" The children's morale will be given a boost by this concrete proof of their progress.

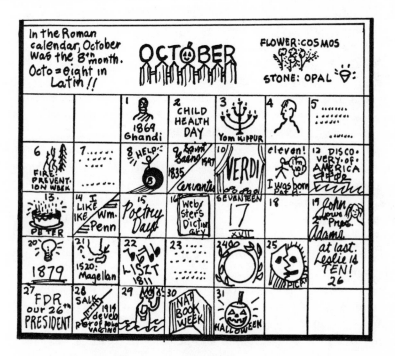

For the first few days of school, have several short periods in which the children practice the routines involved in passing out paper & handing in Spelling Tests, etc.

During the first week of school give the class a spelling "test" composed of words that the children have not been assigned to study. Such a list might include: "United States of America," the names of their city, state & school, the names of Presidents, an ocean, a nearby body of water, & any states that border theirs.

The results of this test will give you an indication as to the phonetic, capitalization & penmanship reviews needed. Save these papers until Public School Week & at that time have the children retake a test on the list of words. Perhaps the class will want to compare these two papers. Display some examples of extraordinary improvement.

Display a huge blowup of a correctly done homework paper, emphasizing heading, margins, paragraphs & placement of name.

Rather than presenting the children with an artificial confrontation of "Now we are going to write out rules for behavior at school," simply help the class to become familiar with the standing school policies ("No gum is allowed on playground," etc.). Then have the class set its own standards for conduct—as the particular problem arises.

A chart of the meanings of correction marks: $\wedge$ ¶ sp. $\frown$ _inc_. etc., could be permanently displayed in the room.

If there is a specific place for each working material (labeled drawers, boxes to fit and hold each size of paper used), classroom organization and cleanup will be facilitated.

Establish a general routine as to "cleanup." When planning allotment of time, include cleanup activities as a definite part of construction periods. Housekeeping jobs (watering the plants, closing the windows at dismissal, etc.) should be assigned to specific students each week. The last 10 or 15 minutes of each Friday* are set aside for cleaning out desks; try to keep *your* desk top uncluttered as a subliminal reminder if you wish to emphasize this type of organization.

Set aside time for a daily evaluation. A formal approach to discussion is helpful until the class is well organized. This daily evaluation will help alleviate the problem of students forgetting "what we did today" and should aid in getting the class to cooperate, function as a unit.

Always run through a science experiment yourself, at home the night before class, just to be certain that the experiment will be successful the next day. This saves time & patience. (And it's also a good procedure to follow if the class is to cook the next day; you'll find you have more confidence this way, too.)

---

*Why not try using a cooking timer which *audibly* clicks off these 10 or 15 minutes?

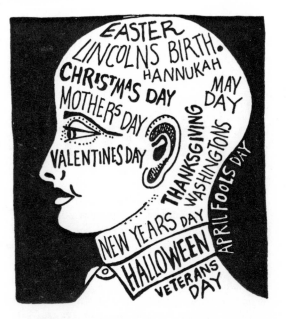

When presenting background information on each holiday, care should be taken to clearly distinguish between historic & legendary material. (Can the children?) It may be pointed out to the class that holidays are observed for specific reasons: to preserve a tradition, to mark a patriotic or religious event. (Can the children think of any other reasons?)

The use of holiday themes should not dominate a teaching program to the exclusion of other meaningful themes.

Be discriminating in your choice of the projects suggested here. Next year you can always try those projects which you were unable to fit into this year's schedule.

Allow the children to interpret these projects. In fact, different approaches to the same project should be encouraged whenever practical. Many times the children's variations will afford learning experiences that are especially fruitful.

September

Warm September brings the fruit,
Sportsmen then begin to shoot.

Note: The following dates, unless otherwise noted, refer to the birthdates of famous persons; dates within parentheses are the years of birth & death. This holds true throughout this book.

	First Monday of September is Labor Day.
1	World War II began, 1939.
2-6	Great Fire of London 1666 destroyed much of the city; c f. Sir Christopher Wren, Oct. 20, page 50.
3	Louis H. Sullivan (1850-1924), American architect. "Form follows function."
5	First Continental Congress met in Philadelphia, 1774.
	Jesse James (1847-1882), American outlaw.
6	Jane Addams (1860-1935), American pioneer social worker, winner of Nobel Peace Prize.
	The Mayflower set sail from Plymouth, England, for America, 1620.
7	Queen Elizabeth I of England (1533-1603).
8	Antonin Dvorak (1841-1904), Czech composer: *From the New World Symphony.*
	Richard the Lion-Hearted (1157-1199), King of England, Crusader.
	Peter Stuyvesant (1610-1672), last Dutch governor of New Amsterdam (New York).

9   Luigi Galvani (1737-1798), Italian scientist, discoverer of the metallic arc.

     William the Conqueror (c.1027-1087), King of England.

10   Elias Howe patented the sewing machine, 1846.

11   O. Henry [William S. Porter] (1862-1910), American author.

12   Henry Hudson 1st saw the river that now bears his name, 1609.

13   Walter Reed (1851-1902), American bacteriologist, conqueror of yellow fever.

14   Friedrich von Humboldt (1769-1859), German naturalist.

     Dante Alighieri died, 1321; 1st great poet to write in Italian: *Divine Comedy*.

     Great Britain and its colonies (America) adopted the Gregorian Calendar, 1752.

     "The Star Spangled Banner" was written by Francis Scott Key, 1814.

15   James Fenimore Cooper (1789-1851), American author.

     William Howard Taft (1857-1930), 27th President.

16   Tintoretto [Jacopo Robusti] (1518-1594), Italian painter.

17   Citizenship Day (Constitution Day); U.S. Constitution signed: Constitutional Convention, 1787.

18   Samuel Johnson (1709-1784), English dictionary-maker.

19   Washington issued his farewell address to the American people, 1796.

20   Alexander the Great (356-323 B.C.) crossed Tigris River to battle Darius for Persian Empire, 331 B.C.

21   First daily newspaper published in the U.S., 1784.

     H.G. Wells (1866-1946), English author.

22   Nathan Hale killed, 1776.

     President Lincoln issued Emancipation Proclamation, 1862.

22-23 Autumnal Equinox—fall begins.

     Euripides (484-406 B.C.), 3rd great tragedian of ancient Athens.

     Augustus Caesar (63 B.C.-14 A.D.), 1st emperor of the Roman world.

25   Vasco Nunez de Balboa discovered the Pacific Ocean, 1513.

     First American newspaper, *Publick Occurrences*, began publishing in Boston, 1690.

Alfred Vail (1807-1859), American co-developer of Morse Code.

Dmitri Shostakovich (1906-   ), Russian composer.

26 Johnny Appleseed [John Chapman] (1775-1847), American nurseryman and folklore hero.

George Gershwin (1898-1937), American composer of musical comedy: *Rhapsody in Blue.*

American Indian Day.

27 William the Conqueror landed in England.

Samuel Adams (1722-1803), American patriot and leader of the Boston Tea Party.

28 Cabrillo Day: Juan Cabrillo discovered California, 1542.

These Jewish Holidays may occur in September :

Sukkoth: The date of the Feast of Tabernacles or Booths varies from year to year. For 7 days in the fall, many Jews eat in palm-branch-covered dwellings; this is in memory of the 40 years that their people hunted for the Promised Land. It was during these wanderings that the Hebrews lived in huts of palm branches.

Rosh Hashanah: The New Year (September or October) lasting 2 days. It is celebrated as a solemn occasion, ushering in 10 days of penitence which lead up to:

Yom Kippur: The Day of Atonement (September or October). It is a day of fasting and prayer, asking for the forgiveness of one's sins.

September

The early Roman calendar began with March, therefore September was its seventh month; *septem* = seven in Latin.

SEPTEMBER QUOTATIONS

(Unless otherwise noted, the quotations are from authors born on the date under which they are noted.)

6 Civilization is a method of living, an attitude of equal respect for all men. (Speech, Honolulu, 1933)—Jane Addams

11   Love and business and family and religion and art and
      patriotism are nothing but shadows of words when a
      man's starving.— O. Henry

14   I despise mankind in all its strata.—Friedrich von Humbolt

      O, say can you see by the dawn's early light . . .
      'Tis the star spangled banner! O long may it wave
      O'er the land of the free and the home of the brave!
      ("The Star Spangled Banner")—Francis Scott Key

15   The cheerful loser is a sort of winner.—William Howard Taft

      Few men exhibit greater diversity . . . than the native
      warrior of North America. In war, he is daring, boastful,
      cunning, ruthless, self-denying, and self-devoted; in peace,
      just, generous, hospitable, revengeful, superstitious, mod-
      est and, commonly, chaste. *(The Last of the Mohicans)*—
      James Fenimore Cooper

18   The true art of memory is the art of attention.

      Few things are impossible to diligence and skill.

      Knowledge is of two kinds: we know a subject, ourselves, or
      we know where we can find information upon it.

      Dictionaries are like watches; the worst is better than none,
      and the best cannot be expected to go quite true.
      —Samuel Johnson

21   Were it left to me to decide whether we should have a
      government without newspapers or newspapers without
      government, I should not hesitate to prefer the latter.
      (Quotation of Thomas Jefferson)

      Human history is in essence a history of ideas.—H.G. Wells

22   I only regret that I have but one life to lose for my
      country.—Nathan Hale (before his execution: Sept. 22,
      1776)

23   A bad beginning makes a bad ending.

      Waste not fresh tears over old griefs.

      Second thoughts are ever wiser.

      Who so neglects learning in his youth, loses the past and is
      dead for the future.
      —Euripides

26   The lands are ours. No one has a right to remove us, because
      we were the first owners. The Great Spirit above has

appointed this place for us, on which to light our fires, and here we will remain. (To the messenger from the President, 1810)—Tecumseh, Chief of the Shawnees, 1768-1815

A little while and I shall be gone from among you, whither, I cannot tell. From nowhere we come, into nowhere we go. What is life? It is a flash of a firefly in the night. It is a breath of a buffalo in the winter time. It is as the little shadow that runs across the grass and loses itself in the sunset. (Last words of Isapwo Muksika Crowfoot, Chief of Blackfoot Confederacy, ?-1890)

SEPTEMBER EVENTS

• **Labor Day**

The first Monday in September is observed as "Labor's holiday" in the United States. The word "labor" comes from the Latin *laborare,* which means "to be tired." This is the day on which the workers of America are honored.

• **Birth of Luigi Galvani, 1737-1798   [9]**

Galvani was an Italian physician & physiologist. One day he discovered, by accident, that an electrical current would pass through the legs of a dead frog when two different metals were connected to them. When the metals were joined to set up a circuit, the electrical current would cause the frog's legs to jump. This leg movement could then be used to indicate amounts of electrical current. Galvani thought that his observations might mean that electricity is generated by living organisms. Galvani's metallic arc actually led him quite close to the theory of the electric battery which Volta (see Feb.) later discovered.

"Galvanometer," "galvanism," "galvanic electricity" are some electrical terms that come from Dr. Galvani's name.

We get our word "electricity" from the Greeks. They knew that when amber was rubbed it became magnetic. Since friction causes amber to give off sparks, this phenomenom was named "elektron" from *elektor,* "the beaming sun." This word passed into Latin as *electrum* & was turned into the adjective *electricus,* from which we get our word "electric(ity)."

- Adoption of the Gregorian Calendar   [14]

In 1752 there was no September third—at least not in Great Britain or in any of her colonies. The calendar was changed from Old to New Style by a parliamentary ruling that the day after September 2nd would be September 14th. Many people felt that their lives had been shortened by 11 days & that everyone whose birthdays fell between September 2nd & 14th was legally dead. Crowds of angry Englishmen ran after Prime Minister Henry Pelham, shouting, "Give us back our 11 days!"

Language Arts

It is good for one's perspective to realize that something as widely used as our calendar has come into existence only through the knowledge & efforts of hundreds of people of various races & backgrounds.

- Birth of Jacopo Robusti (Tintoretto) 1518-1594   [16]

Tintoretto was among the last great Venetian painters of the Italian Renaissance. His work later influenced that of El Greco & Rubens. Named Jacopo Robusti, he was called "Il Tintoretto," the little dyer, because his father was a dyer. Tintoretto was apprenticed to the great painter, Titian, who soon dismissed him. Some legends say the older artist was jealous of the talents of the young boy. Other rumors allowed that Tintoretto was of an extremely impatient temperament.* He was to become a prolific painter, in any event. The largest "Old Master" painting in the world was painted by Tintoretto; entitled *Paradise,* it measures 72'2" x 22'11-1/2" & contains 500 figures!

- Constitution Day   [17]

Discuss with the children: "What *is* a constitution? How & why is it important?" Talk about the enforcement of the Constitution, the roles of the police, the Supreme Court, the Civil Liberties Union. Invite a police officer, lawyer, or representative of a

---

*The word "temperament" recalls a belief of olden times; medieval philosophers felt that the 4 qualities of hot, cold, dry & moist blended in varying quantities were what determined the nature of things. The Latin word for this mixture was *temperamentum.* When someone becomes temperamental, it means, figuratively, that there is an imbalance in the mixture.

legal-aid society to visit the class WHEN the children have sufficient background knowledge to appreciate (& participate in) the visitor's talk or discussion.

A bulletin board might display a parchment reproduction of the Constitution, an illustration of the signing, a list of men present at the signing, & short, interesting biographies of some of the men. An incidental aspect of this display might be the description of the step-by-step procedure involved in the making of a quill pen. Such a pen could be shown with the reproduction of the Constitution. If turkey quills are available, the making of quill pens could provide an enrichment project for one evening's homework. Complete instructions appear in Edward Johnston's standard work: *Writing and Illuminating and Lettering* (New York, Pitman Pub. Corp., 1958), p. 20.

- **First U.S. daily newspaper   [21]**

The 1st known "newspaper" was a clay representation of a scarab* containing carved lettering. It was made & circulated in Egypt in 1450 B.C.

The 1st historically dated newspaper was a series of clay tablets entitled "Acta Publica" which were begun by Julius Caesar in 58 B.C.

The oldest printed newspaper, *The Peking News,* which began publication 950 years before the invention of movable type, is 1400 years old.

The 1st newspaper of modern form was published in 1566 when the government of Venice, Italy, issued handwritten news-sheets & exhibited them in the streets. They could be read by anyone who paid a small coin called a "gazetta." These "gazettes," as they came to be called, were so popular that they began to be printed.

In the United States, Freedom of the Press was established in 1735 when John Peter Zenger published in his *New York Weekly Journal* a report of election frauds & an exposure of graft & crime by the Royal Governor William Cosby. Arrested for "seditious libel," Zenger found his bail set so high that he was unable to pay it. Andrew Hamilton, ablest of the colonial lawyers, defended Zenger. He admitted that Zenger printed the charges, but con-

---

*There are more than 20,000 species in the widespread Scarab family. Probably the most familiar in America is the June-Bug or May Beetle. The most famous is the sacred Scarab of the Nile, described by J. Henri Fabre as "rolling that pellet of dung in which ancient Egypt beheld an image of the world."

tended that they were true. Zenger was acquitted & the Fourth Estate was allowed its freedom.

Language Arts

At the end of each day the children dictate to the teacher a summarization of that day's happenings. The teacher writes this on the board & it is copied the next morning by a volunteer. These daily records combine to make a class broadsheet, *Our Daily News.* It is the best record of the year's activities for it is written *as* the children's interest is highest. It will be of special interest to guests during Public School Week.

A class newspaper could be published (mimeographed) for wider reader-consumption. It might boast of stories (fact and fiction), puzzles, riddles, poems, jokes, comic strips, sports news, science fiction, a serial, word games, science experiments, rebus (see March), arithmetic word games or problems, interviews with local people of interest, biographies of the school secretary, librarian, etc.

To stimulate a Creative Writing lesson the teacher passes out an actual newspaper want ad to each child. These ads should suggest a situation in an office, store, home, or in someone's personal life, i.e., an accident seen, a pet lost, an article found. The children use these ads as introductions or as endings to their stories.

- **Fall begins [22] or [23] (Autumnal Equinox)**

Discuss with the children the meaning of "equinox": equal night & day, twelve hours of night & twelve hours of day. The sun rises directly in the East & sets directly in the West; at the equator the sun is directly overhead at twelve o'clock noon. Discuss the cause of the ensuing longer days, the process & importance of hibernation, migration, & the possible reasons that this season is sometimes called "Indian Summer." Talk about deciduous & non-deciduous trees.

> *Riddle:* Why is autumn the best time for a lazy boy to read a book? (Because autumn can always be counted on to turn the leaves for him!)

FALL BULLETIN BOARDS

General suggestions. Remember that a bulletin board is a learning device to reward & encourage outstanding work; it is NOT a decoration. Try the incorporation of eye-catching titles, lead phrases, unusual textures, photographs & actual objects. Place (written) materials at children's eye-level. Ask yourself occasionally if the displays reflect the *current* interest of the children.

Lettering suggestions. Try the use of unusual materials, i.e., wallpaper (from outdated sample books, free, from hardware or interior decorating establishments); pipe cleaners (both the slender & the thick, fuzzy types); cut synthetic sponge (used for initial upper-case letters of bulletin board titles).

Sheets of dark pressed cork, pinned by four long "hatpins" to the bulletin board area, are good for breaking up the total layout, introducing a dark tonal quality to the display.

Theme ideas. The children paint on a large sheet of butcher paper a mural depicting woods, pond, leafless trees, cave, hills, dried fields, piles of leaves, grey skies. When the mural is dry, flaps are cut in it to reveal the sleeping places of insects, rodents & mammals & the migration of birds. A short story written in the first-person (as though dictated by the animal) appears on the inside of each corresponding flap. A few camouflaged animals & birds could also be included on the mural. VARIATION: Instead of cutting flaps in the mural, pin four signs at the appropriate places: "In the Air," "In the Trees," "In the Water," "Under the Ground." The children collect specimens that they find in each of these areas. Drawings, photos, parts of objects, feathers, can also be used. Each object should be labeled by the child & then pinned or taped to the correct area of the board. This bulletin board encourages children to LOOK, to become aware of details.

As the season changes, discuss with the children the adjustments needed to keep their display up-to-date: ice forms on pond, ground turns hard, tree loses last leaves. Take off each object, discussing, "Where will it (the tree toad, acorn, garden spider) go now that it's winter?"

"Beauty of Form" offers a more sophisticated title for an upper grade bulletin board. Beneath the title display objects (characteristic of autumn) whose forms are in some way repetitious of one another: a dried sunflower, a pine cone, the center of a daisy. A biographical brief similar to the following would be shown also:

> About 1170 a boy named Leonardo Fibonacci was born in Pisa. He became one of medieval Europe's greatest mathematicians and contributed to arithmetic, algebra and geometry. One

of his discoveries was a curious set of numbers that appears very often in nature, especially in the arrangement of individual seeds in a pattern.

Here is the Fibonacci Series: 1, 1, 2, 3, 5, 8, 13, 21, 34, 55, 89, 144. . . . . Can you tell how these numbers are related to one another? HINT: It has to do with addition. . . . Look below for the answer.* Another sign might ask: Can you discover the ratios involved in the seed patterns of the natural forms shown here? [Pine cones have 5 & 8 rows; daisies, 21 & 34; & the common sunflower has a 55-89 ratio.]

It may also be pointed out that the relationship of these numbers to each other approaches the golden mean, i.e., 1 to 1.618, & is found in the dimensions of the chambered nautilus (display a shell or a photo of it, if possible) as well as in hundreds of other designs in nature. Examples of man-made designs that correspond to forms in nature—the folded plate in architecture & a jade plant, a piece of mushroom coral, the spore plates of a toadstool—could also be incorporated into the display.

Paper sculpture, original interpretations in color & design, might be an outgrowth of such a bulletin board. An excellent book to introduce to the class at this time is *The Anatomy of Nature* by Andreas Feininger (published by Crown Pub., Inc., N.Y., 1956).

To make a bulletin board pheasant, have the children collect & press brilliantly colored fall leaves; those of the oak & elm trees work especially well. Pin a large sheet of neutral-colored paper to a bulletin board area. Dab spots of rubber cement to the paper & to the back of each leaf when attaching the leaf to the board; two twigs form the legs. By adhering the leaves in this way, the children help the classroom pheasant to grow a larger tail with each day.

---

*The Fibonacci Series is that sequence of numbers each of which is the sum of the two previous numbers.

Language Arts

Once each season, if it is possible, take the class for a walk to a nearby hill or area of greenery. There the children sit & write down a few lines, phrases about their feelings. (No importance should be placed on rhyming.) The teacher may also write down her impressions. Once back in the room, the children should be encouraged to prune their sentences, keeping only those that they consider the best. It can be pointed out how editing is of great importance to all professional writers. Something worthwhile can be found in each child's efforts. The class may share their writings aloud if they like.

> Down, down
> Leaves of red & gold & brown
> Come falling down, down, down.
> Now the wind says,
> "Come & play."
> Outside our window
> The gull is gone.
> All is quiet.
> Only the swallows are heard.
> The green trees dance
> To the song of the swallow.

During their autumn walk the children can also collect twigs for sensitive line drawings, leaves to use for the Skeletal Leaf Science experiment & clippings to press & save for valentines.

After the walk the children can make a collective list of words describing natural forms, patterns, colors & sounds which they noticed while on their walk. This list may be permanently displayed in the room & may be used as a departure point for a science collection, creative writing, or haiku.

Natural form	Pattern	Color	Sound
water	ripples, repeating pattern	transparent magnifies moss,	rippling
rocks, stones	ripples, striations	reflects sky stones	plunk hitting water
leaves	ribbed	rust, grey green	whirling
bark	smooth, rough variations	golden rust	rasp as it is rubbed
tall grass	tall lines moving	shining when wet	slithering
sky (trees on skyline)	moving, clouds vary it	deep to light green ranging from light to darkest blue	rushing wind buzz of insects hum of cars

Fall Poetry

The melancholy days are come, the saddest of the year,
Of wailing winds, and naked woods and meadows brown and sere.

W.C. Bryant

The day is cold and dark and dreary;
It rains, and the wind is never weary;
The vine still clings to the mouldering wall
But at every gust the dead leaves fall.
And the day is dark and dreary.

H.W. Longfellow

AUTUMN FIRES

In the gardens
And all up the vale,
From the autumn bonfires
See the smoke trail!

Pleasant summer over
And all the summer flowers,
The red fire blazes,
The grey smoke towers.

Sing a song of seasons!
Something bright in all!
Flowers in the summer,
Fires in the fall.

R.L. Stevenson

Also appropriate: "Fog" by Carl Sandburg; "The Pasture" by Robert Frost; "September" by Edwina Fall.

Fall Science

Have the children observe & record seed travels. Have the class watch caterpillars spinning cocoons. The use of a magnifying glass or the less expensive reading-glass will be helpful. Place a cocoon in a box outdoors & wait for the emergence in the spring. (See May Science.)

Fall is the season to collect:

Seeds. Keep them in small labeled envelopes in a dry cool place until they are planted. Larger seeds & pods are excellent for printing borders, designs during an art class.

Buckeyes and acorns. Soak the buckeyes & acorns overnight. Put a few small stones in the bottom of each small flower pot, being careful not to block the draining holes in the bottom of the pots. Fill each pot with rich garden soil. Plant one (soaked) seed an inch below the soil in each pot. Put the pots in a dark place & water regularly until the shoots appear, then bring the pots into the light. Keep the plants dampened; try tapping the side of the pot, if it sounds hollow, add water. Also keep the surface soil loosened. Next spring the tiny trees will sprout leaves.

Buckeye

Any of the trees of N.A., resembling the horse chestnut, of the genus Aesculus. The large nut-like seed was used as medicine for horses. The tree itself was brought from Constantinople in the early 16th century.

Weeds & flowers.* Gather plants at noon of a hot clear day. Don't put them in water. Strip lower stalk of leaves. To trap their natural colors, hang them upside down by the stalks in a warm, dry, dark place for several weeks. These plants can be used in autumnal bouquets (November Art).

Lichens. These are a combination of a fungus & an algae living together. Their wide range of colors makes them a stimulating natural material for collages.

Leaves. To make *Leaf Skeletons* you will need: a canning jar, 1 quart of water, 2 T. lime, a small stick for stirring, a pan, a hot plate & a piece of soft cloth which is folded & tied over the end of a 2nd stick, a soft towel.

Put 2 T. lime in the jar & partly fill the jar with boiling water. Drop two or three leaves into the jar & allow them to remain there for up to 40 minutes. Slowly stir the water in the jar.

---

*An excellent chart of methods for "Preserving Flowers & Foliage" can be found in *Traditional American Crafts,* by Betsey B. Creekmore, Hearthside Press, Inc., 1968.

Take out one leaf; place it flat upon a table & gently rub it with the cloth-covered end of the stick. The green part of the leaf should be easily removed; if it doesn't come off completely, submerge the leaf a second time in the jar of boiling lime water. When one side of a leaf is clean, turn the leaf over & clean off the reverse side. Once the leaf is denuded, blanch it in 2 T. Clorox & 1 qt. water until leaf reaches desired whiteness. Rinse leaf; dry between paper towels & press beneath heavy books overnight.

Mount the leaf skeletons on black paper & use them in science study or art work.

Fall Art

During art periods, as often as possible, allow the class a freedom of choice: size, color, texture of papers, various colors of inks, paints. This encourages personal interpretation of each project & allows the child to explore, investigate, grow.

Seed mosaics. Children collect various seeds (pumpkin, apple, sunflower, corn, lentil, rice, peas, different kinds of beans) & sort them into (cottage cheese) containers.

Examples of mosaics, executed both by children & by adults, are shown to the class via filmstrips, art history books and art prints. The teacher elicits ideas as to the successful elements present in all of the examples: strong contrast of color, repetition of colors, balance of dark & light areas, definite composition.

Use corrugated cardboard pieces (10" x 12") for backings; cut the cardboard in varying proportions. The children draw a half-inch border all around the edge of the cardboard. The mosaics will be made within this delineation as the border facilitates display & protection of the finished piece. Children begin experimenting with the placement of various seeds on the cardboard. Usually the seeds themselves suggest an idea for a design. Squeeze-bottles of milk (casein) glue are used in the attachment of seeds to the cardboard backings. The seeds are pressed down firmly with the fingers & allowed to set for several minutes. Seeds can be scraped off if their placement is unsatisfactory. Large tweezers, toothpicks, or table knives are used to push small seeds into place. Patterned seeds should all face the same direction. The edge of a knife is used to make lines in the design clear & distinct.

After being allowed to dry for 36 hours, the seed mosaics can be sprayed with a clear (matte-finish) plastic coating.

Skeletal leaf collages. Abstract shapes of colored tissue paper are dipped into liquid starch. These shapes are overlapped, while still wet, on tagboard backings. Skeletal leaves (described in Fall Science) are gently pressed onto the wet tissue paper shapes. Compositions are allowed to dry completely before they are mounted on contrasting construction paper for display in the classroom.

Sand-casting. Each child removes one side from a half-gallon waxed milk carton. The cartons are filled three-fourths full of sand. Using a sprinkling or atomizer-spray bottle, the child dampens sand with water. Designs are then outlined in the sand with a small stick. Tablespoons are used to scoop out the sand within the confines of the design; a depth of two or three inches should be reached. Objects can be stamped firmly down into the dampened sand: (eucalyptus) seed pod or heavily veined leaf outlines are appropriate. After the impression is made, remove the object. If any decoration is to be added to the piece (small shells, colored glass, ceramic fragments, little stones, marbles, pieces of metal, etc.), these are pressed lightly FACE DOWN in the sand.

In a plastic waste basket the plaster of Paris is mixed (by the teacher) according to directions on the package. Using a plastic cup, each child pours the plaster carefully onto the moistened sand, making certain that each scooped-out area is filled with the plaster. A toothpick or broomstraw is inserted & withdrawn at random in the plaster's surface to aid in the escape of any trapped air bubbles. The plaster is allowed to dry undisturbed for several hours, if not overnight. Then the finished piece of sand sculpture is lifted out of the carton & any excess sand is removed from it by lightly brushing the sculpture's surface with a dry paint brush.

Veneer prints. Materials needed include: airplane glue; sheets of plywood of various dimensions (8" x 10"); different textures of paper, i.e. oatmeal, stencil, several grades of sandpaper; different textures of fabric, i.e. net, waffle-weave, embossed, Indianhead; yarn; string; toothpicks; masking & adhesive tapes; paper doilies & any textural materials that are flat & which the children find interesting. X-acto knives & linoleum block cutting tools are also helpful. Several brayers (a rubber roller with a handle), sheets of glass, linoleum block printing inks, turpentine & newsprint are needed for making the prints themselves.

A design is lightly drawn on the plywood with a pencil or is transferred to the plywood from a drawing. Flat textural materials (i.e. paper or fabric) are cut to fit the different areas of the design & are then glued firmly in place on the plywood. *All* edges of textural materials must adhere to the plywood. There should be some repetition of texture throughout the design. If the outline of any area is to be emphasized, glue yarn, toothpicks or string around the edge of that area. For negative lines & areas (which will appear white on final prints), an X-acto knife or similar tool can be used to cut away the surface of the plywood itself. Whenever possible the texture of the plywood should be utilized in the design, i.e. a sky, a background for a landscape, still-life or abstract. The textural areas of the plywood can be emphasized by repeatedly dampening the grain of the wood with a moistened sponge prior to application of the ink.

When the glue is dry, ink is applied to the veneered surface in the same way that it is applied to a linoleum block: ink is squeezed onto the glass pane from which the brayer picks it up & transfers it to the plywood sheet's veneered surface. The completely inked surface is covered with a piece of newsprint which is then rubbed gently but firmly with the heel of the hand, the fingers, & the bowl of a spoon. The corner of one edge of the newsprint is grasped & pulled diagonally toward the opposite corner, thus lifting off a copy of the finished veneer print.

The use of more than one color of ink can be attempted once the student is satisfied with his trial print.

Ink is removed from the plywood's surface, as well as from brayers and glass panes, by the frugal application of turpentine with soft cloths.

- **Birth of Alfred Vail, 1807-1859   [25]**

Alfred Vail was a friend of Samuel F.B. Morse & provided Morse with money for his experiments with the telegraph. Vail subsequently made numerous improvements on this invention & it was *he* who invented the dot & dash system for the telegraph.

Discuss briefly the invention of the Morse Code (see also Jan. 6, Marconi, & April 27, Morse). Distribute to the children mimeographed sheets bearing the code below.

A · —	G — — ·	M — —	S · · ·	Y — · — —
B — · · ·	H · · · ·	N — ·	T —	Z — — · ·
C — · — ·	I · ·	O — — —	U · · —	
D — · ·	J · — — —	P · — — ·	V · · · —	(.) · — · — · —
E ·	K — · —	Q — — · —	W · — —	(,) — — · · — —
F · · — ·	L · — · ·	R · — ·	X — · · —	(?) · · — — · ·

Then write the following message on the front board & see if they can decipher it:

/—/· · · ·/ ·/   /·—/·—/—/··/—/·· · ·/——/·/ —/·· ·/—·—·/

/· · · ·/———/——/·· /·——/———/·—·/—·—/

/·——/··/·—··/·—··/ /—··· ·/·/

Codes give the children practice in perceiving details.

Simple announcements can be written on the board with the vowels in each word omitted. This reminds the children that the vowels are "the mortar holding together the consonant-bricks of our words."

The children can experiment with creating their own codes.

- **American Indian Day   [26]**

Discuss the following exerpt from "Remarks Concerning the Savages of North America": (*Poor Richard's Almanack*, 1757)

At a treaty of Lancaster in Pennsylvania in 1744 the government of Virginia offered the Six Nations (Iroquois) a fund for the education of six Indian youth. One of the rules governing Indian politeness is that a public proposition not be answered on the same day it is made, as an immediate answer might imply that the proposition was being treated as a light matter. So it was on the following day that the representative of the Six Nations expressed a deep sense of kindness on the part of the Virginia government in making the offer: " ... for we know," says he, "that you highly esteem the kind of learning taught in those colleges, and that the maintenance of our young men while with you would be very expensive to you. We are convinced, therefore, that you mean to do us good by your proposal, and we thank you heartily. But you, who are wise, must know that different nations have different conceptions of things; and you will, therefore, not take it amiss if our ideas of this kind of education happen not to be the same with yours. We have had some experience of it. Several of our young people were formerly brought up at the colleges of northern provinces. They were instructed in your sciences, but when they came back to us they were bad runners, ignorant of every means of living in the woods, unable to bear either cold or hunger, knew neither how to build a cabin, take a deer, nor kill an enemy, spoke our language imperfectly, were, therefore, totally good for nothing. We are, however, not the less obliged by your kind offer, though we decline accepting it; and to show our grateful sense of it, if the gentlemen of Virginia will send us a dozen of their sons, we will take care of their education, instruct them in all we know, and make men of them."

Also discuss the quotations listed under September 26 Quotations.

Have the children listen to Buffy Saint-Marie singing "Now that the Buffalo's Gone," in the album: *It's My Way,* (Stereolab VSD79142, a Vanguard recording),* & then talk about feelings roused by the lyrics she has written.

If your class is interested in learning of a service project that they can undertake as a group to help Indian children living on a reservation, write, requesting information, to: American Friends Service Committee, 160 N. 15th St., Phila., Pa. 19102.**

Authentic American Indian recordings are published by the Folkways/Scholastic Records, 50 West 44th St., New York, N.Y. 10036 & may be obtained directly from them, or through record stores. ("Music of the American Indian, Southwest," 1420; &

---

*or "My Country, 'tis of Thy People You're Dying," in *Little Wheel Spin and Spin* (Vanguard: VSD 79211).

**Hereafter referred to as A.F.S.C.

"Music of the Sioux and Navajo," 1401.) Other long-playing records of tribal music may be obtained from the Music Division, Library of Congress, Washington, D.C. 20540. Write direct for price list.

Interpretive Art Forms

While listening to a record of American Indian music, the children can create interpretive art forms:

Leather collages (abstract or representational). Leather scraps can be obtained, usually at no charge, from any commercial tannery. Milk glue works well as an adhesive for the leather.

Sand pictures. Using a squeeze bottle, each child "draws" with milk glue on paper. A bit of sand is then blown onto the drawing. Parts of a design can be connected with solid lines of color & some areas may be filled in with tempera paint. VARIA-TION: (see November Art).

Soapstone sculpture. Soapstone (steatite) deposits are common in California, New York & North Carolina. This stone can easily be "mined" on a weekend & it is simple to work. A wood rasp, kitchen utensils & several grades of sandpaper are the only tools needed. A coat of wax is applied, after the finest sandpaper has been used, to bring out the subtle tonalities of the stone. When executing soapstone carvings, the children should allow the natural texture & veining of the stone to inspire the design of the sculpture.

If soapstone is not available, Girostone or Vermiculite (see Recipes for Art Supplies) also offer appropriate sculpture materials.

Educational materials & information pertaining to the American Indian are available through any of the following sources:

Publications Service
Haskell Institute
Lawrence, Kansas 66044

Superintendent of Documents
The Govt. Printing Office
Washington, D.C. 20402

The Museum Shop: The American
Museum of Natural History
Central Park West and 79th St.
New York, N.Y. 10024

Bureau of Indian Affairs
Dept. of Interior
Washington, D.C. 20242

Museum of the American Indian
Broadway at 155th St.
New York, N.Y. 10032

SEPTEMBER ACTIVITIES

Language Arts

Pen-pal projects. This is a good time to set pen-pal projects in motion. Bulletin board displays of pictures, coins, stamps (covered by sheets of clear acetate plastic to discourage the disappearance of valuables) can stimulate student interest in (international) correspondence.

Sources include:

The Parker Pen Co.	No charge; grades 4-10
Educational Service	Names, addresses of teachers
Janesville, Wisc. 53545	of similar classes are exchanged.
English Speaking Union	No charge; ages 10-17
Pen Friends	Enclose a self-addressed stamped
16 E. 69th, New York, N.Y.	envelope with each request.
10021	
World Pen Pals	35¢ apiece
World Affairs Center	ages 12-20
Univ. of Minnesota	
Minneapolis, Minn. 55455	

or contact your local Red Cross Chapter and inquire about their "School-to School Program."

A permanent classroom chart might be made to display these pen-pal writing suggestions:

When writing letters abroad, REMEMBER:

Answer promptly. You'll be most enthusiastic about writing on the day you receive a letter from your pen-pal.

Write legibly. You have to keep in mind that your penmanship will be unfamiliar to your pen-pal.

Tell all about yourself. Tell about your family, friends, school, home, hobbies, pets, favorite books, sports. Be careful not to sound as if you're boasting; be sincere about what you write; be polite.

Don't use slang. Foreign pupils will often not be familiar with slang (& as a rule children from other countries write in a more formal manner than we do).

Avoid controversial subjects. Don't talk about things that might make your pen pal uncomfortable, e.g. comparisons of religions, political views.

Suggest exchanges: Think about things you'd like to exchange— photos, coins, stamps, slides, drawings, shells, tape recordings.

Learn your pen pal's birthday: Be sure to send him a card or small gift.

The teacher can distribute a mimeographed sheet of leading questions to assist the writer in eliciting information from his pen-pal.

Handmade stationery. This is another pen-pal spur. On bright colored strips of paper, the children stamp a border design by using seed pods or a simply cut potato cut away & dipped into rather thick poster paint. The strip of paper is then adhered (with rubber cement) to the top of a sheet of plain white paper. The design can be printed directly onto the writing paper & the corrected letter re-copied onto the sheet of handmade stationery. Initials, or a design incorporating them, make a pleasing decoration for stationery.

Personalized greeting cards: These can be made of felt or fabric scraps or yarn pictures which are adhered to the card with milk glue. Tissue paper* may be dipped in liquid starch & laid on the card to form a collage; this makes a vibrantly-colored card. The starch acts as an adhesive & gives a varnish-like effect to the tissue.

---

*Crystal Craft Tissue®mfg. by Crystal Tissue Co., Middletown, Ohio, is available in beautiful brilliant colors & costs about $1 for a package of multi-colored tissues.

Science

Easy microscope. With a pin, prick a hole in a piece of stiff paper. Hold your eye close to the hole & look at a strongly lit object which is about one inch from the hole; you will be unable to see the object clearly if it is closer than one inch to your eye as the eye cannot focus on an object which is that close. The pinhole in the paper acts as a diaphragm & greatly increases the depth of focus. This same principle applies to the camera: the smaller the opening of the lens, the greater the focus.

Waterdrop microscope. Make a small *round* hole in a piece of light-weight tinplate or heavy aluminum foil. Hold the piece of metal absolutely horizontal & let a drop of water from the tip of a watercolor brush fall directly onto the hole; the water will remain in the hole & act as a lens. Under a strong light, try observing different objects (grains of sand, salt, sugar, parts of insects or pieces of fabric). Place each object an eighth of an inch below the waterdrop.

Experiment with different sizes of holes; the size of the hole determines the curvature of the drop. And it is this curvature which determines the number of times the waterdrop microscope will be able to magnify the objects.

Waterdrop microscope* No. 2. Cut a 4-inch strip of metal from a tin can; round off the corners by using emery cloth or a fine sandpaper, so that no sharp edges remain. Using a hand drill & a 1/16"-inch bit, drill a hole in the metal strip a half-inch from the end. Score two lines down the width of the metal strip: one at 2-1/2 inches & the second at 2-3/4 inches. Bend the strip along these lines.

Use the hand drill with a quarter-inch bit to drill a hole toward the end of one side of a cigar box. Place a 15-watt bulb so

---

*From Ronald Roos, "Waterdrop Microscope," *Child Life Magazine* (June-July 1967). Copyright © by Review Publishing Company, Inc. Reprinted by permission of the publisher.

that it shines up through the hole. Mount a large sewing thread spool over the hole in the box. The specimen on the slide (plain glass one inch square) is placed over the hole in the spool. By means of a small paint brush, make a drop of water fall onto the hole in the metal strip. Line up the hole in the metal strip with the one in the spool & observe the specimen, now magnified.

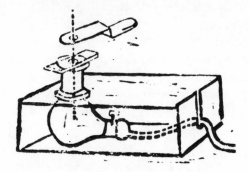

September Art

An excellent little magazine, *Everyday Art,* is free to (Art) teachers, & may be received by writing to The American Crayon Co., Eastern Office, P.O. Box 147, Jersey City, N.J. 07303.

Visual aids designed for classroom use are available from The Extension Service, National Gallery of Art, Washington, D.C. 20565. Ask for their catalog of reproductions & publications.

September P.E.* (grades 1-3)

Squirrel in the Tree. Divide the class into groups of three: two children hold hands to form a "tree trunk" & the third child stands in the middle of the ring & represents "the squirrel." Any extra players can be incorporated in the formation of "the trunk of a giant redwood tree."

At a signal from the homeless squirrel, *all* squirrels, including the homeless one, must change trees. The squirrel who finds himself without a tree becomes "the homeless squirrel." Game continues. Any player who has been "the homeless squirrel" twice

---

The Fun Encyclopedia, by E.O. Harbin, published by Abingdon Press (201-8th Ave. S., Nashville, Tenn. 37203), is a storehouse of games & would be especially useful to teachers of P.E. & dramatics.

The Encyclopedia of Games by Doris Anderson is a Pyramid Book (444 Madison Ave., New York N.Y. 10022) published by arrangement with Zonderian Pub. House. This is the definitive collection of games & will be useful to all elementary school teachers.

in a row automatically becomes a tree. Every child should have the opportunity to be "the homeless squirrel" at some time.

September Puppet (grades 1-4)

"Alexander" can become a regular feature of classroom activities; he may ask the class to please be quiet or to line up. He can enliven short review exercises, & he's always a dependable source of advice.

Stuff a three-year old's clothes with pieces of soft cloth; a straightened clothes hanger may be inserted through the middle of each appendage, as shown in the illustration. The hands are neutral-colored children's gloves & can be sewn in place to join the long-sleeved shirt. The head is papier-mâché modeled over a paper-filled sack. With poster paints apply a skin tone & facial features. When paint is dry, a clear mat plastic can be sprayed over the painted areas to protect them; adhere a large piece of (raccoon) fur to the top of the head. The finished puppet can wear glasses. Mainly, Alexander should express the personality of the teacher & *of her class.*

He may, when speaking, be made to sit on the teacher's lap. Lip movements need not be hidden while he is speaking; a change of voice, tonal quality, is sufficient. Because the children *want* him to speak—he can.

A hole may be made in the back of the torso so that by inserting a hand, movements of his head & torso will be achieved to further the illusion created.

Helpful Hints for Teachers

Fit 1 or 2 plastic containers for tableware into your top desk drawer. Use the little compartments for organization of, & easy access to, paper clips, pins, map tacks, tape, string, etc.

A picture file greatly simplifies the problems of bulletin board creation; collect large, clear, interesting pictures, photos. Make large tagboard folders to hold them & file them in alphabetical order (Animals, History, Holidays, Insects, Inventions, People, Sea, Weather, etc.). Obtain a large cardboard box, the top of which is cut on just 3 sides, forming a flap. The picture folders can be filed upright in the box & it can be kept in the classroom closet for easy reference.

There should be some stable month-to-month classroom activities, e.g. a nature walk, the recognition of students' birthdays, entries made in a Class Log or Diary.

For classroom book display: screw 2 metal coat hooks into a thick board.

From sturdy white cardboard, make 2 molar-shaped covers. Inside include at least as many pages as there are children in the room. Whenever a child loses a tooth, he has the honor of dictating "the whole story" to you: when, where, how. Type up the tale and include it in the book. Each story is signed by the child involved. This makes a Free Reading Time favorite, & visitors may enjoy it too.

One morning in the fall the children select a deciduous tree for year-round observation. They describe the tree in detail & record the date. Occasionally, throughout the year, they will visit the tree, illustrating & describing it & keeping a permanent record chart of it in the classroom. The height of the tree may be estimated (see March Science) on each visit.

It is always discouraging when a child arrives home & tells his parents that he has learned & done "nothing" in school that day. For lower-grade children, an aid-to-recall device can be set up beside the classroom door: a larger than life-sized paper scarecrow in September, witch in October, Indian in November—& each with outstretched arms. Every afternoon, as the class prepares for dismissal, it decides what the figure should hold in its arms, e.g. a penmanship paper, a science mimeo, a painting. As the work is attached to the figure by the teacher, she briefly discusses with the class their achievements of that day. This procedure need not take more than a few minutes & it has a calming effect on the group, sending each child home with a clear image of what he did in school that day.

Set aside in a classroom cupboard the materials & equipment for 1 or 2 specific projects. On a day when you need a pick-me-up, 1 of these projects can be brought out, & the enthusiasm it evokes will be natural. An example of such a lesson might be the experiment below.

Volcano experiment. Purchase some crystals of ammonium dichromate at a chemical supply store. From 2 colors of modeling clay, make a realistic-looking crater on a large smooth rock. The crater should be about 6" across at the base & 2-1/2" across at the summit. Hollow out the crater so that it can easily hold 1-2 teaspoonfuls of the crystals. Following a discussion of volcanic action, during which such words as *lava, magma, pumice, igneous, vent, molten, dormant, extinct* are introduced, have a classroom display of volcanic power. Encourage the children to watch for different aspects of an eruption: what happens to the lava that is initially thrown upward? Where is lava most likely to flow? How is pumice formed? . . . etc. Strike a wooden match & insert it into the mouth of the crater, igniting the crystals. Viewers should stand clear of volcano until eruption has ceased.

Make a large bar graph on the blackboard by listing each student's name. Give every child the same 3 addition problems & 5 minutes in which to work them. Allow the class to correct these problems, & then you put the results on the graph. Repeat this procedure with subtraction, multiplication & division problems. This is an appropriate lesson to present when the children have become tired of the routine Math period.

Occasionally prepare a mimeo of incorrect grammar, spelling, punctuation examples which you have taken from *their* written work. The fun of recognizing a sentence, identifying its author, will help to enliven language review lessons for your class.

Younger children are delighted to receive a little special attention on their birthdays. Buy a box of trick birthday candles (the type that re-light whenever they are blown out) from a magic shop. Announce to the class that this is a special birthday candle that cannot be blown out. Let the birthday child make a wish & blow out the candle. Verbally encourage the candle to re-light (or profess a lack of confidence in its powers). Once it has re-lit, the candle may be "blown out" a 2nd time or permanently put out by pinching its wick. Little children look forward to this "special attraction" each birthday.

# October

Fresh October brings the pheasant,
Then to gather nuts is pleasant.

1   James Lawrence (1781-1813), American naval officer in War of 1812.
2   Mohandas Gandhi (1869-1948), Hindu Nationalist leader, pacifist.
3   Child Health Day.
4   Jean Francois Millet (1814-1875), French painter.
     Rutherford B. Hayes (1822-1893), 19th President.
     1st artificial satellite launched by U.S.S.R.: "Sputnik," 1957.
5   Chester A. Arthur (1830-1886), 21st President.
6   Le Corbusier (1887-1965), Swiss architect.
7   Hans Holbein died 1543 (born c. 1497), German painter.
     Fire Prevention Week: always held during week of Oct. 9, anniversary of Great Chicago Fire, Oct. 9-11, 1871.
9   Camille Saint-Saens (1835-1921), French composer.
10   Guiseppe Verdi (1813-1901), Italian composer: *Aida, Falstaff, Il Trovatore.*
11   Eleanor Roosevelt (1884-1962), American diplomat, humanitarian.
     Columbus Day: San Salvador was sighted by Columbus on Oct. 12, 1492. (This holiday is celebrated on the 2nd Mon. of Oct.)
13   Molly Pitcher (1754-1832), heroine of the Revolutionary War.
14   William Penn (1644-1718), founder of Pennsylvania.
     e.e. cummings (1894-1962), American poet.
     Dwight D. Eisenhower (1890-1969), 34th President.

15   Virgil (70 BC-19 BC), Roman poet.
      Poetry Day.
      1st public demonstration of ether as an anesthetic: Mass. Gen.
        Hospital, 1846.
16   Noah Webster (1758-1843), American lexicographer: com-
        piled *Webster's Dictionary.*
19   John Adams (1735-1826), 2nd President.
20   Sir Christopher Wren (1632-1723), English architect.
21   Ferdinand Magellan 1st sailed into strait that bears his
        name, 1520.
      Katsushuka Hokusai (1760-1849), Japanese artist.
      Alfred Nobel (1833-1896), Swedish inventor of dynamite;
        established Nobel prizes.
      Edison invented electric light, 1879.
22   Franz Liszt (1811-1886), Hungarian composer.
      Veterans Day (3rd Monday in October) was traditionally
        Nov. 11, changed by Monday Holiday Bill.
24   United Nations Day.
25   Geoffrey Chaucer, died 1400 (born 1340), English poet.
      Johann Strauss Jr. (1825-1899), Austrian composer.
      Georges Bizet (1831-1875), French composer: *Carmen.*
      Pablo Picasso (1881-   ), Spanish artist.
      Adm. Richard E. Byrd (1888-1957), American Polar
        explorer.
27   Theodore Roosevelt (1858-1919), 26th President.
      Dylan Thomas (1914-1953), Welsh poet.
      Navy Day.
      Captain James Cook (1728-1779), English explorer.
28   Statue of Liberty dedicated, 1886.
      Jonas Salk (1914-   ), American, developed polio vaccine.
29   Stock market crash, 1929.
      Edmund Halley (1656-1742), English astronomer.
      John Keats (1795-1821), English poet.
      National Children's Book Week: last week of October.
31   Jan Vermeer (1632-1675), Dutch painter.
      Halloween.

October

In the early Roman calendar, October was the 8th month: *octo*= eight in
Latin.

OCTOBER QUOTATIONS

1   Don't give up the ship! (His dying command, now watch-word of U.S. Navy)—James Lawrence

2   If you think the world is all wrong, remember that it contains people like you.—Mohandas Gandhi

4   He serves his party best, who serves his country best.—Rutherford B. Hayes

14   Have a care where there is more sail than ballast. ("Advice to His Children")—William Penn

     Whatever America hopes to bring to pass in this world, must first come to pass in the heart of America. (Inaugural Address, 1953)—Dwight Eisenhower

     nobody, not even the rain, has small hands. ("Somewhere I Have Never Travelled")—e.e. cummings.

15   They are able because they think they are able. (*Aeneid*) —Virgil

19   I pray Heaven to bestow the best of blessings on this House and all that shall hereafter inhabit it. May none but honest and wise men ever rule under this roof.—John Adams: first tenant of the White House

25   A man doesn't begin to attain wisdom until he recognizes that he is no longer indispensable. *(Alone* "August: the Searchlight")—Richard Byrd

     Time! That's the thing. When it's gone, it's gone. No argument! Like a taxi meter ticking over. (*The Private World of Pablo Picasso*)

     When asked whom he considered the greatest painters of all time: "It depended upon the day."

                                 —Pablo Picasso

27   Speak softly and carry a big stick; you will go far. (Speech, 9/2/01)

     Free peoples can escape being mastered by others only by being able to master themselves.

     The things that will destroy America are prosperity at any price, peace at any price, safety first instead of duty first and love of soft living and the get-rich-quick theory of life.

                                —Theodore Roosevelt

28   Give me your tired, your poor,
        Your huddled masses yearning to breathe free,
        The wretched refuse of your teeming shore.
        Send these, the homeless, tempest-tossed, to me;
        I lift my lamp beside the golden door.
        (Inscription on Statue of Liberty) — Emma Lazarus (1849-
            1887)

29   A thing of beauty is a joy forever:
        Its loveliness increases; it will never
        Pass into nothingness.
        (*Endymion:* Book 1, Line 1)—John Keats

        National Children's Book Week:

            Something is learned every time a book is opened.—
            Chinese proverb

            May blessings be upon the head of . . . whoever invented
            books.—*Thomas Carlyle.*

            For a jollie goode booke whereon to looke is better to me
            than golde.—*John Wilson*

OCTOBER EVENTS:

• **Fire Prevention Week**

The 1st salaried fire department in America was that of
Boston in 1679; it used a hand-operated engine which had been
ordered from England & which required 13 men to operate it. The
1st volunteer fire department in the U.S. was founded by Benjamin Franklin in Philadelphia, 1736.

On October 8, 1871, at 9:00 P.M., Mrs. O'Leary's cow
allegedly kicked over a lantern & started the Great Chicago Fire,
causing $196,000,000 damage & leaving 98,860 homeless. Fire
Prevention Week always occurs near Oct. 8 in memory of this
disaster.

"Man the Bucket Brigade," a game that helps build coordination, may best be played outdoors. Each child, on the 2 or
more equal teams, has a paper cup. Each team forms a line. A
chair is placed at the head & at the end of each line. A water-filled
milk carton stands on the chair at the head of the line. An empty
milk carton is on the chair at the foot of the line.

At the starting signal, the 1st child on each team fills his cup
from the milk carton at his side. He then pours this water into the
cup of the child standing behind him, who pours the water into

the cup of the child behind him, & so on. The last child pours the water into the empty carton. The game continues until the container at the head of the line is empty. The winning team is that with the most water in the carton at the foot of its line.

> *Riddle:* What are the 3 main causes of forest fires? (Men, women & children!)

• **Columbus Day**

Social Studies

Columbus' voyages can be told in such a way as to include these 15 geographical references: Portugal, (Lisbon) Africa, Asia, China, Japan, India, Iceland, Europe, France, the Canary Islands, the West Indies, S. America, Central America, U.S.A., & Spain. Once each of these places is located by the class on the globe or wall map, Columbus' travels can be retraced.

Language Arts

Crossword puzzles. The letters in (Christopher) Columbus are used vertically as the backbone of the puzzle. Each child supplies definitions for each of the 8 words, e.g., Line 1 (7 letters): "the month in which Columbus sighted land." Line 2 (6 letters): "movement." Previously studied spelling words may be used. After the puzzles have been corrected, they might be recopied & exchanged between students.

Writing game. Each student is given a paper on which he is to write as many words as he can which have the word "ship" in them, e.g., friend*ship, ship*mate, craftsman*ship.* "At the sound of the bosun's whistle," writing begins. After 3-5 minutes, children stop & words are counted, results compared.

Dramatic play. This can be introduced at this time of year, using Columbus as the initial theme. Each month will afford opportunities for the use of this technique if you find it useful in working with your particular group.

> " ... [D]ramatic play in the classroom is an educational technique under which the children explore an area of human experience (1) by reliving the activities & relationships involved in that experience in their own way, (2) by acquiring, under teacher-guidance, needed information & skills & (3) by increasing the satisfactions inherent in play that is meaningful & extensive. Dramatic play encompasses the following procedures:

1. The introductory situation is an arranged environment planned by the teacher.
2. Children explore the arranged environment & are permitted to respond in their own way, to manipulate tools and materials & discuss them.
3. A story may be read by the teacher to further the interest of the children in the selected area & to provide initial data for use.
4. Children are invited to play out any part of the story or set their own situation.
5. First play is spontaneous & unguided, but is carefully observed by the teacher.
6. Play is followed by a sharing period in which satisfactions are expressed or dissatisfactions are clarified, under teacher guidance, into statements of questions & expressed needs.
7. Planning for meeting the expressed needs includes the processes of problem-solving, making of rules, assignment of work to be done. [Steps 8, 9 & 10 are particularly suitable to culminating of Social Studies units.]
8. A period of extension of experiences through such activities as research, excursions, firsthand processes & utilization of multimedia ensues before, & beside, further play.
9. Play proceeds on higher levels (involving more accurate activities & more interrelationships & interpretations) as a result of enriched experience.
10. This is a continuous & expanding procedure, progressing on an ascending spiral that may, in the upper grades, eventuate, after weeks of growth, into a structured drama."*

Dramatic play may be facilitated by collecting, & then keeping in the classroom, a box of small simple props such as assorted hats, costume jewelry, eye glasses (or frames), shoe-boxes, a flashlight, wooden spoons, coffee cans, a baby blanket, a few pieces of fabric, etc. The use of such devices as signs, drawings, guide-lines, crepe-paper (to indicate a stream or the sea), and notation of important facts & dates on the chalkboard can also enliven these sessions.

Etymology. Ancient maps were marked with lines of longitude & latitude just as contemporary maps are, except that long

---

*From Fannie R. Shaftel and George Shaftel, *ROLE-PLAYING FOR SOCIAL VALUES: Decision-Making in the Social Studies* (Englewood Cliffs, N.J.: Prentice-Hall, Inc., 1967), pp. 134-35. Copyright by Prentice-Hall Inc. Reprinted by permission of the publisher.

ago these lines indicated the length & breadth of a flat world. The Latin words *latitude* and *longitude* were derived from *latus* (wide) & *longus* (long), as the world was then thought to be only wide & long.

The Greek prefix *ge* means "earth" & *graph* means "to write or describe," so then, *geography* is "a description of the earth."

Riddles: What BUS crossed the Atlantic? (Columbus.) As Columbus sighted America on his right hand, what did he see on his left hand? (5 fingers.)

Columbus Day Poetry

Introduce your class to Joaquin Miller's "Columbus" with its famed "Sail on! Sail on and on!"

Columbus Day Art

Ship in a Bottle. The children familiarize themselves with various ships either via book illustrations or a bulletin board display, e.g., "The Evolution of Ships." Differences in hull-shapes, number & size of sails, masts & riggings can be emphasized. The structure of Columbus' ships might be studied. This should help young children eliminate the stereotyped ship from their drawings.

Each child cuts a large bottle shape from tagboard. Hopefully, a wide variety of shapes will appear. By cutting masts, sails, & hull from colored paper & then pasting these on the center of tagboard, the child constructs his ship in a bottle. The riggings are pieces of string cut & glued in place. Varying shades of blue & green paper are torn, or cut, & overlapped along ship's hull to simulate waves. The entire bottle is tightly covered with plastic wrap, creating a glass bottle effect. The ends of plastic are taped to back of bottle. A slice of cork, or brown paper to represent a cork, is glued to "mouth" of bottle. VARIATION: Cap the waves with foam made of thick white poster paint. Allow this to dry before covering bottle with plastic. Fluffy cotton clouds, a seagull, or waving banners may also add variety.

• Poetry Day   [15]

The following is a list of poets whose birthdates occur within the school year. You may wish to have appropriate samples of their work available (on a bulletin board or at a reading area), or even provide mimeographed sheets of poems for the students to enjoy during free times.

Matthew Arnold, W.H. Auden, the Benets, Wm. Blake, Eliz. &
Robt. Browning, Lord Byron, Lewis Carroll, Eliz. Coatsworth, e.e.
cummings, Emily Dickinson, Ralph Emerson, Rachel Field, Robt.
Frost, John Keats, Kipling, Longfellow, J.R. Lowell, Pasternak,
Poe, Sandburg, Shakespeare, R.L. Stevenson, Edna St. Vincent
Millay, Whitman, Whittier, Wm. Wordsworth.

An order form describing Caedmon recordings of special
interest to teachers may be obtained by writing to the Houghton
Mifflin regional sales office serving your school. These recordings
include "Carl Sandburg Poems for Children," on which the poet
discusses poetry & reads some of his own works.

• **Birth of Noah Webster   [16]**

Webster's 1st dictionary was published in 1828 & is used
today in a bigger & better edition. Children are often intrigued by
the mere length of words. Contrary to the belief of many children,
the longest word in the dictionary is NOT "antidisestablish-
mentarianism." This word was merely created as an example of a
string of prefixes & suffixes & it isn't in Webster's Dictionary. The
longest word in "common usage" in the English language is
"pneumonoultramicroscopicsilicovolcanoconiosis," the name of a
lung ailment that afflicts coal miners as a result of inhaling fine
coal dust. The children might enjoy dissecting "the longest word"
& breaking it down into syllables to better understand its meaning.

• **Birth of Theodore Roosevelt   [27]**

Your class can listen to the voice of this great American
President; his voice (& those of 40 other famous persons, e.g.,
Tennyson, Robt. Browning, Admiral Perry) has been re-recorded,
filtered & amplified from the original wax cylinders & 1st flat
discs. (Two LP albums & a descriptive book: "Forty-two Great
Lives"; $6.98; "Voices of History," 2025 Greenland Bldg., Miami,
Fla. 33054.)

• **Birth of Edmund Halley   [29]**

Halley observed a comet in 1682 & decided that it was the
same comet that had been known to re-appear every 76 years. He
predicted that it would again be visible in 1758 or 1759. It was.

A comet is described as a star with a tail; the original Greek
word *kometes* meant "wearing long hair."

Halley's Comet last appeared in 1910. Its head was approximately 161,000 miles in diameter & its tail was 27,800,000 miles long. This comet travels some 100,000 m.p.h.

Information source: American Astronomers' Assoc., 223 West 79th St., N.Y., N.Y. 10024.

• **National Children's Book Week**

Bulletin board suggestions: (Title: Books help make a friendly world where people live in peace.) Ask the public librarian for the use of some book covers illustrative of the bulletin board title. Pin these beneath title. It's important to question the children as to why each of the books represented is an appropriate choice. Discuss book titles that might not be correct to include in this display. Ask the class to give examples of ways in which the written word *has* worked (& can work) for peace in the world today.

Through Books We Discover
How Other People Think   How Other People Feel   How Other People Live

The children are asked to think of ways in which they could fill the areas beneath each of these subtitles; e.g., pictures of famous people could be used with balloons in which their thoughts & feelings would be expressed; exact quotations (as noted in this book) are possibilities. Under the 3rd subtitle, various dwellings (e.g., those of Heidi, Mowgli, Clara Barton, Sir Lancelot) could be shown, or examples of various methods used in different places to solve the same problem (transportation, acquisition of food, clothing, art, music).

Language Arts

Creative writing topics include: "Seven Books & Why I Own Them," "A Book That Changed My Life"; or ask the class to write a complete new ending to a book they've read, or to tell about the funniest, meanest or most daring book character they've met; or have the children pretend that they are to be exiled to an uninhabited desert island: "What (10) books would you choose to take with you—& *why?*"

Prepare a set of tagboard playing cards. On half of these print the titles of well-known books; on the remaining cards print the corresponding names of authors or book characters. Children may match the cards by themselves or play "Authors" with 3 or more players. Whitman & Co. produces an inexpensive card game of "Authors" which could be introduced to your class at this time.

When children write their own books, variety should be encouraged. Unusual formats could be shown to the class: samples of a scroll book, a Japanese accordion fold-out book (e.g., Sesshus' *Long Scroll: A Zen Landscape Journey*, $2.95: 1969, Charles E. Tuttle Co., Rutland, Vermont 05701) or books of unusual design. Suggest that the children include any of the following in their handmade books: marbleized paper fly-leaves (see Dec.), a complete title page with copyright date & place of publication, the name of person to whom the book is dedicated.

Older children might enjoy making individual readers, using a controlled vocabulary such as the Dolch 220 Basic Words List; these books could be donated to the school library or used by a student-aide during a 1st or 2nd grade reading class.

If you have your students make book reports, here are some suggestions for varying the forms throughout the year:

> This is a book for boys___ girls___ both___. Why do you think so? Give the main idea of the story in one sentence. Did anyone in the book overcome a difficulty or solve a problem? If so, what do you think about the way he/she did it? Why do you feel this book would/would not make a good movie? Would you like to change the ending? Why? Do you feel the author wrote this book for the reader's entertainment or to give the reader information? What makes you think so? If the book was non-fiction, tell 4 things you learned while reading it. What information did it make you want to know?

Etymology. In Old English, *boc*, from which we get "book," meant "Beech" as that was the bark on which words were then scratched. "Author" comes from the Latin *auctor*, meaning "he who originates or makes things grow."

Social Studies

A two-generation book display can be organized by having the children bring to class books which their parents read or used as children. As a contrast, display modern editions of the same titles or exhibit recently published children's books. Discuss any differences, similarities which the children discover.

> Information source: The Children's Book Council, Inc., 175 Fifth Ave., New York, N.Y. 10010

• Halloween   [31]

The Romans honored the goddess of harvest, Pomona, during this time of year. Druids of ancient England celebrated the New Year on the 1st of November, believing that on the last day of the old year, Oct. 31, the souls of the dead were allowed to return to Earth. The American Indian held special dances at this season. Our Halloween is a mixture of these celebrations. Traditionally, Halloween is the ancient holy, or hallowed, eve'n (evening) of All Saints' Day.

In pre-Christian England, disguises were worn to confound any spirit that might have been out looking for you; today costumes are worn "for the fun of it."

During medieval times "Soulers" roamed the streets of England, praying, singing hymns & asking for alms. In return for the money, the Soulers were to pray for the donor's relatives who might be in Purgatory. "Trick-or-treating" is an outgrowth of these Soulers' parades.

Bulletin Board Suggestions

For attention-getting titles, burn the edges of letters you have cut from construction paper or burn the sides of a sheet of paper on which lettering appears.

A display for older students is shown here. Appropriate vocabulary enrichment words are printed on the ghost shape. On the 2nd day of this display, definitions are made to float at the side of the ghost. By this time the class should be familiar with the words & ready to matchthem with correct definitions.

DO YOU HAVE the GHOST of an IDEA
what these words mean......

clandestine
lethargic
tenebrous
phantasm
ethereal
macabre

Using the title "A Witch's Guide to Gardening,"* you can achieve an interesting science enrichment display. Illustrate the following information with drawings or photos; not all of these plants need be included on the board at one time. (Older students may enjoy & benefit by taking the responsibility for the entire execution of this display.)

IMPORTANT: It should be noted that ingestion of most of these plants is dangerous & can be deadly. Any safety precautions deemed necessary should be taken.

Wild Angelica (the Holy Plant): Its name means "the angel-like herb." It is used as a flavoring & in medicines & perfumes. In olden days, it was hung over the front door of your house to ward off witches.

Mandrake: It was thought to feed on earth in which a murderer was buried. It is a deadly plant when eaten, & has a forked root which is said to resemble a man.

Wormwood: This plant was supposed to have grown in the track of the serpent as it slithered out of the Garden of Eden. It gives us absinthe, a drink that is harmful to health, but which was taken long ago "to counteract the bite of a shrew or of a seadragon." Its name has become a noun meaning "a bitter, mortifying experience."

Parsley: The most maligned of the plants. It was believed that it should only be planted on Good Friday in order to take off its curse & that it should *never* be transplanted. Plutarch wrote of a battle that was completely broken up as a parsley-laden mule crossed the path of a Greek army!

Belladonna: (Deadly Nightshade): A poisonous European plant (Atropa belladonna), it has purplish-red bell-shaped flowers. A tincture drawn from its leaves & roots is used to treat colic & asthma. Its name is Italian for "beautiful lady" & supposedly refers to its early use in cosmetics.

The Three Deadly H's: *Hemlock:* The Greeks administered capital punishment by giving a drink made of hemlock to criminals. Socrates died from drinking a cup of hemlock. *Hemp:* From its flowers & leaves, hashish, an intoxicating tobacco, is made.

*From Dorothy Jacob, *A Witch's Guide to Gardening* (Elek Books, London, 1964 and Taplinger Publishing Co., New York, 1965). Reprinted with permission of the publishers.

Henbane: A foul-smelling plant that is the bane (death) of hens—or any other bird that might eat it.

> Information source: Write to Geigy Agricultural Chemicals, Ardsley, N.Y. 10502 for a free folder, "Plants That Poison."

The following is not specifically a Halloween bulletin board, but it might be used at any time during this month. With the exception of the definitions which are hidden under flaps, the body of the information is printed on a large sheet of butcher paper. The definitions are printed on bright colored paper to contrast with the predominant tan of the board. Students raise flaps to verify or discover correct word meanings.

> OCTOBER was the eighth month of the early Roman calendar. *Octo,* or *Octa* (before a vowel) is a combining-form meaning "eight." Knowing this, can you figure out the meanings of these words?
>
> Octagon (*gonos* is Greek for "corners")
> Octopod (*pod* = "foot")
> Octopus (*oktopus* is Greek for "8-footed")
> Octogenarian (*octogeni* is Greek for "80")
> Octillion (*octo* + *mille,* the French word for "million")
> Octennial (*octo* + *annus,* the Latin word for "year")
> Octave (*octavus* is Latin for "eighth")
> Octet (*octo* + duet)

Classroom Door. Have the children make a large scary witch & attach her to the outside of the classroom door. In her hand place a sign that states: "Welcome to Room 7. Come in—if you dare!"

Language Arts

Halloween Surprise. 5-line compositions are written by the children in answer to the questions below (final stories need not be completely logical):

Sentence 1: Who? Where? When?
Sentence 2: What is the problem in this story?
Sentence 3: Why does this problem *have* to be solved?
Sentence 4: How do they try to solve it?
Sentence 5: What is the surprising outcome?

The variety shown in the finished compositions is a pleasant surprise in itself.

Ask the class to write the "Life History of a Monster," including such details as where he lives, what he does in his free time, how he gets friends or his food or clothing.

Have each child invent the imaginary origin of some superstition held today; e.g., the practice of saying, "God bless you" when someone sneezes, the belief that Friday the 13th is a day of ill-luck, etc. Encourage the children to include as many details as possible in these stories.

You can prepare for the following creative writing lesson the evening before presenting it. Cut as many pieces of 6" x 8" white (typing) paper as you have students. Fold each sheet in half—either crosswise or lengthwise. Using India ink (magenta is effective), apply several drops from the stopper along each side of the fold. Crease the sheet along the original fold & press firmly, rubbing with the palm of the hand. When paper is unfolded, a Rorschach-like pattern appears. Allow ink to dry completely. The next day, pass out writing paper to each child. Place the ink blot sheets, face down, on their desks. Advise students to listen to instructions before turning over ink-blot sheets. Direct them to look at the ink blot from any angle they like & let it give them an idea for a descriptive paragraph. Older students may be interested in hearing how Dr. Rorschach originated a method of analysis that utilized ink blots: his patients made up stories about what was seen in the blot & Rorschach interpreted these stories in much the way that Dr. Freud analyzed dreams.

When the paragraphs are corrected & recopied, they can be pinned up with their accompanying ink blots to make a quick display & fascinating reading.

A review spelling mimeo might direct the children to "supply

the missing letters in these $\mathcal{SKELETON}$ words."

Previously studied spelling words or words that your class frequently misspell might be included: The princip_1 helped the ch_ldr_n find th_r ball.

A classroom cave for dramatic play. Overturn a table, with its top to the wall; use butcher paper (painted gray) for the sides of the cave. The top is made by attaching the 4 corners of a sheet to the 2 uppermost table legs. Sew a long string to the middle of the sheet. By pulling up on this string (& tacking it to the ceiling) a tent-like structure is achieved. Drape it over with crepe paper vines & leaves.

Etymology. During the Middle Ages in England so many people died from the Black Plague that the bodies had to be burned every day in huge fires. These fires were called "fires of bones" or "bonefires." Later, when burning of heretics at the stake became common, these were also called "bonefires." Gradually, it came to be that any large fire was referred to by this name, but with a shortened spelling: bonfire. A costume is something that is the custom (from Italian *costuma*) to wear. The Latin *skello* means "to dry up," so a skeleton is a dried up body! Loot is a corruption of the Hindustani *lut,* meaning "something plundered."

> *Riddles:* How does a witch tell time? (With a witch-watch.) How can you get into a locked cemetery late at night? (Use a skeleton key!) Why is a haunted house a good place to play baseball? (There's always an extra bat handy.) What's the difference between a match & a black cat? (The cat lights on its feet & the match lights on its head.) Which burns longer: a black candle or an orange candle? (Neither—they both burn *shorter!*)

Halloween Poetry: This is a fine time to introduce your class to the image-eliciting "Windy Nights" by Robt. L. Stevenson.

Halloween Reading. An eerie introduction of new words can be achieved in this way: The night before the lesson, using a fine brush & evaporated milk, print each new word on a separate slip of paper. Each child in the reading group will have the chance to hold his "blank" slip of paper over a candle's flame & watch the "new word" appear. Once he can say the word, he shares it with the group, or the group may try to guess the word as it appears, letter by letter. The word will appear most quickly if the paper is held milk-side to the flame. This might best be used several days prior to Halloween, as the children will probably need little additional stimulation on the 31st!

Here is a reading game that gives the children the incentive to sound out unknown words: Make up tagboard cards, one for each child in the reading group. The instructions printed on the cards should utilize, & emphasize, whatever phonics the group is presently studying. Each child gets a card, reads it silently & prepares to perform. The other children watch until the performer is finished & then the group tries to guess the identity of the creature, & action portrayed, e.g.: "You are a little black bat. It is still daytime and so you are hanging upside down, sleeping. There goes the bell! Can that be seven o'clock already? It is seven o'clock and that means it's time for you to wake up! Stretch your wings. Now fly outside & swoop by the trees. Fly upward. Fly down again. Fly a———way."

Séance. This game can be played at any time during the year. It is basically a phonics-review device that affords the teacher a quick check on an individual student's progress. It also gives the teacher an opportunity to be *very* dramatic. A tagboard turban may be worn. An elaborate rhinestone earring can be attached to the front of the turban; the clip of the earring goes through the tagboard & is secured by tape to the backside of the turban. Fasten the ends of the turban with a rubber band so that the turban will fit any size head.

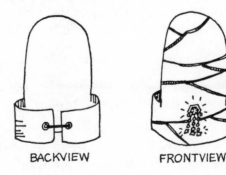

BACKVIEW   FRONTVIEW

Explain to the class that you are going to act as "a medium" & that they must be very quiet & concentrate as it demands a great deal of energy for you to make contact with the spirits. Stretch out your arms, & with just your fingers touching the table top (around which the reading group is seated) close your eyes & speak: "I'm thinking of a word that has the sound of 'oi' in it. This word means 'earth' or 'ground'; do any of you know the word? *Soil!* That's correct, Bob. Do you know how 'soil' is spelled? Absolutely right. . . . The next message I'm receiving is in the form of a word with a long 'A' sound. This word is a verb that means 'to lose consciousness' or 'to pass out,' " etc.

Sometimes the children themselves may be capable of conducting the séance. A new medium should be chosen only when he already has "a message" in mind.

These sessions, like all review-exercises, should be kept short: after a while simply note that the vibrations are growing weak & that you are very tired from the strain of transmitting these messages & so "now today's séance must end." By stopping a bit before the group grows restless, you will insure their being enthusiastic about having a séance at some future time.

Halloween Math:

Watch the Ghost Disappear (a flannelboard drill). On each piece of the ghost, which is made of felt, a problem is written in felt-point pen. Each child touches that part of the ghost which he wishes "to make disappear." If he gives the correct answer, he may keep the piece of felt; answers may be written on the back of each piece of the ghost. When the entire ghost has been taken from the board, children may work "to help make the ghost re-appear." VARIATION: "My Favorite Ghost." Children have the choice of 3 ghostly felt figures, each is devoted to a different multiplication table or math process.

Plus Cat (or Minus Cat)—a mimeo review sheet. Children fill in the differences at the bottom of the sheet, e.g.: left eye: 9 minus 5, 9 minus 8, 9 minus 2 etc. Following completion of the left eye, students do the right eye (11), nose (10), & mouth (12), each in succession.

Science Experiments

Bendable Bones. Soak a large clean uncracked chicken bone

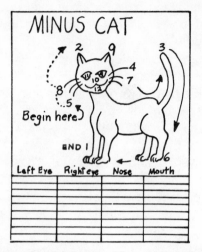

in a glass of vinegar for 12 hours. The acid in the vinegar dissolves the bone's calcium which gave it its initial stiffness. The resultant bone can be tied in a knot.

Halloween Art:

Discourage the stereotyping of Halloween motifs. Ghosts and devils can be presented as exciting, historically interesting phenomena. Nature can be personified, e.g., mountains that are watching you. It would be helpful if the children could observe from life in order to avoid generalizations, e.g., how a person, astride a broom, grasps the broom handle; how the leg of a cat comes out of the haunch; what happens to the back of a cat when he sits down.

Lesson suggestions. Let the children paint in accompaniment to Saint-Saens' "Danse Macabre," or "Night on Bald Mountain" by Mussorgsky.

Watercolor witchery. A red & orange watercolor wash gives a glow-like effect when applied over drawings of ghosts, goblins, witches done with white crayon on white paper.

Wet chalk drawings. Prior to the lesson, chalk may be soaked

in a solution of ⌇⌇ sugar & ⌇⌇ water; this mixture helps prevent chalk from rubbing off drawings. A water container (1/2 pint milk carton with top removed) may be placed on each desk; children can then repeatedly moisten their chalk while drawing.

During recess you prepare for this lesson by dampening large sheets of newsprint: hold each sheet under running water & loosely fold paper in halves or fourths; or submerge loosely folded sheets in basin of water. Pile dampened papers in large square plastic dishpan in order to transport them to the desks. Pass between the rows of desks, handing out dampened papers to children on either side of you. This procedure cuts down on confusion & wet floors. Designate an area at the back of the room where the children may lay their finished drawings to dry.

Witches. This lesson helps strengthen listening skills. The teacher may describe, in geometric terms, the pieces to be cut. In this way the identity of the witch is concealed as long as possible; e.g.: "Choose a long piece of the cotton yarn in any color you like (choices may include red, purple, green) and two partitions (egg holders) of an egg carton. Then return to your seat. Take out a black crayon and blacken the bottom (inside) of each of the egg holders; tear the holders apart from one another if they are not already separated. Now cut from black paper a medium-sized triangle (hat). Cut out a thin rectangle that is longer than the base of your triangle (brim of hat). Cut a very large triangle that's about 2 times as big as your 1st triangle (dress)," etc.

Arms, legs, fingers, high-heeled shoes could also be described in geometric terms for older children. Oral instructions continue until black shapes, egg carton eyes, yarn hair, are pasted in place on bright orange paper. Young children will add appendages with black crayon. A paper broom is optional.

Sculpted masks. Sheets of 12" x 18" construction paper or tagboard are used. Cut along dotted lines & fold in (or overlap) one piece, stapling it in place. Variations are countless.

Goblin mask. Children fold a sheet of 9" x 12" red orange

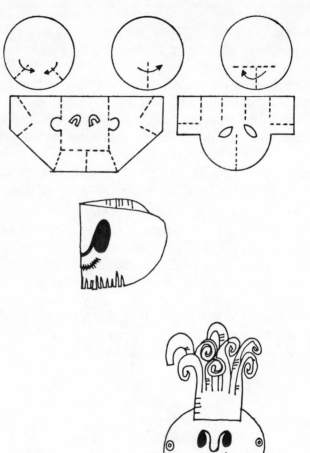

construction paper in half. Using scissors, they make the cuts shown.

Then they open the mask out flat & spread the teeth & whiskers with their fingers. A second piece of 9″ x 12″ construction paper is cut lengthwise & long slits are then made from these long strips. Using pencils, the children curl each strand separately, making some curl forward & some backward. This hairpiece is then glued to the goblin's forehead. Holes can be punched & backed with hole-reinforcers (this eliminates tearing of mask), & elastic or string ties attached.

| OCTOBER ACTIVITIES |

Plant Projects for October

Your name on a pumpkin. Cut letters from aluminum foil & attach them with petroleum jelly or waterproof glue to an unripe pumpkin. Put the letters on the side of the pumpkin which faces the sun. Since chemical reactions caused by the sun turn the pumpkin from green to orange, when the foil is finally removed bright green letters will stand out against the orange pumpkin skin.

Class pumpkins. If you are able to contact a farm-produce market, you can often purchase, or even order in advance, a tiny pumpkin for each child in your class. Then, armed with a spoon, each child can carve out his own jack-o'-lantern. You may walk around the room & slice off the tops of pumpkins with a knife, but usually the handle of the spoon can be used by the child himself to cut off the top. Newspapers are spread on each desk so that the seeds may be saved (recipe follows) & as an aid to clean-up.

As the pumpkins are scooped out, discuss the layers of the shell, the way in which the pumpkin grew from a blossom & the importance of water to the growth of the pumpkin.

The basic geometric shapes may be listed on the front board so that the children may use them as a guide to cutting features in their pumpkin. Also remind the children to bore a small hole with a pencil in the lid of the jack-o'-lantern in order to allow candle's smoke to escape.

Toasted pumpkin seeds. Thoroughly wash & clean the seeds. Drain them well on paper toweling. Sprinkle the bottom of a cookie sheet with a solid layer of salt. Arrange the seeds in a single layer on the salt. Place the cookie sheet in a moderately slow oven (300°) for 40-45 minutes or until the seeds are lightly browned. Allow to cool in the pan.

Flower bulbs. Now is the time to plant bulbs indoors. Hyacinths should bloom by Christmas; daffodils, tulips & mauve crocus are also usually successful. (Yellow crocus will not bloom indoors.) Plant bulbs in special fiber purchased at a nursery, or in a bulb jar (which need not be set in a dark place until roots appear, & therefore allows class to watch growth.)

October Puppets

Easy Witch Finger Puppets. Cut a circle from matboard. Tape a paper loop (the size of your finger) onto the back of the circle; on the front paste a witch's face. Black crepe paper taped beneath this head becomes the witch's cloak.

Matchbox Owl—October finger puppet. Attach an owl's head made of paper to the front of a small matchbox cover. Tape construction paper wings to the back of the box cover. Insert finger through opening to make owl move.

Halloween Party

Children, in committees, are encouraged to do the majority of the planning. A time schedule is set up as a guide for these committees, e.g.: 2:15, recess: children may be dressing in their costumes in the restroom or cloakroom. Supervision may be needed. 2:30, everyone is in his seat. 2:35, short games, a story. 2:55, ON THE DOT—refreshments (soft "spooky" music may be played as a calming device). 3:10, napkins discarded, everyone seated. 3:15, dismissal; clean-up committee remains in classroom (to wash paint off windows).

Decorations. The classroom windows have been painted with Halloween motifs, (a combination of kitchen cleanser mixed with poster paint). The cleanser facilitates window-washing on Friday afternoon. Torn tissue paper ghosts may have been lightly glued atop these paintings. Small scraggly tree branches have been suspended from light fixtures; brightly colored shapes (bats, owls, witches, moon) twirl on threads tied to these branches. The children can draw a large graveyard scene on the chalkboard, using only yellow & white chalks. This drawing might be done during free time on the day of the party.

Entertainment. Games should be kept fast-paced, quickly rewarding & controlled. This helps prevent younger children from becoming overly excited.

Each child is given an 8" x 8" square of yellow, gold, or orange construction paper. The children are asked to stand beside their desks. "Put the paper behind your back. Using no scissors & *without* looking, tear out an entire jack-o'-lantern. Now, remember, no looking!" When they bring out their finished pumpkins, the class will enjoy comparing results & choosing, perhaps, "the funniest," "the most realistic," "the most cleverly executed," etc. (These pumpkins can be quickly stapled, after school, to a vacant bulletin board for a cheery new 1-2 day display.

Pass out paper & see who can make the most words from the letters in (HAPPY) HALLOWEEN. Any word—proper noun, verb—counts, with the exception, if you wish, of abbreviations. It seems wise to state beforehand if searching in books for word suggestions will be permitted. Perhaps this might be allowed during the last five minutes. All writing of words begins at the same minute, e.g., at the next click of the classroom clock. The teacher may pass between rows giving spelling assistance, when needed. At the end of the game a winner is announced & the papers are collected. (A composite list of words cited by the class as a whole can be printed in large lettering after school & posted for the children to read the following morning.)

Finally, the teacher may read a short spooky story as the refreshment committee passes out napkins & treats.

Other entertainment possibilities include the "Halloween Science Experiments" or "Magic Experiments & Tricks" (see April & May).

Refreshments. Children can vote on the choice of food prior to their party. It need not be elaborate as, of course, an abundance of sweets will be consumed that evening. Treat suggestions include: hot or cold cider or orange Kool-Aid; cupcakes in which foil-wrapped fortunes & tiny prizes have been baked; or caramel apples; doughnuts with icing faces.

Two Notes to the Teacher. (1) Try to keep the day of the party as calming in mood, & as organized in method, as you can. (2) Bring an extra mask or two (or a sheet) for "that one kid who couldn't have a costume this year."

November

Dull November brings the blast;
Then the leaves are whirling fast.

1   All Saints Day.
2   Father Junipero Serra (1713-1784), Spanish explorer, founder of many Calif. missions.
    Daniel Boone (1734-1820), American frontiersman.
    Gaspar de Portola (1734-1784), discoverer of San Francisco Bay.
    James Polk (1795-1849), 11th President.
    Warren G. Harding (1865-1923), 29th President.
    Auguste Rodin (1840-1917), French sculptor.
    Election Day is the 1st Tuesday after the 1st Monday in November.
4   Will Rogers (1879-1935), American humorist.
5   1st black woman (Shirley Chisholm) is elected to the House of Representatives, 1968.
6   John Philip Sousa (1859-1932), American bandmaster.
7   Lewis and Clark sighted the Pacific Ocean 1805.
    Marie Sklodowska Curie (1867-1934), Polish-French physicist, co-discoverer of radium, received 2 Nobel Prizes: 1903 & 1911.
8   1st circulating library in USA established in Phila., 1731.
9   Sadie Hawkins Day.
10 Martin Luther (1483-1546), German theologian, leader of the German Reformation.
    William Hogarth (1697-1764), English painter.

US Marine Corps created by Continental Congress, 1775.

Stanley found Livingston, 1871.

11   Abigail Smith Adams (1774-1818), wrote persuasive, warm letters urging women's rights to her husband, U.S. Pres. John Adams.

Traditional date of Veterans' Day (now in Oct.).

12   Aleksandr Borodin (1834-1887), Russian composer.

13   Robert Louis Stevenson (1850-1894), British author.

14   Robert Fulton (1765-1815), American inventor.

Claude Monet (1840-1926), French impressionist painter.

Aaron Copland (1900-   ), American composer.

15   Articles of Confederation adopted by Continental Congress, 1777.

Pike's Peak was discovered by Zebulon Pike, 1806.

17   1st meeting of Congress in Wash. D.C., 1800.

18   Louis Daguerre (1789-1851), French inventor of 1st practical photography.

19   George Rogers Clark (1752-1808), American explorer— "conqueror of the N.W. Territory."

James Garfield (1831-1881), 20th President.

Lincoln delivered his Gettysburg Address, 1863.

20   Atahualpa, Inca of Peru, agreed to fill a room with gold for Pizarro, 1532.

21   Mayflower Compact signed, 1620.

22   John F. Kennedy assassinated, 1963.

23   Henry Purcell died 1695 (born c. 1658), English composer.

Franklin Pierce (1804-1869), 14th President.

Thanksgiving is the fourth Thursday of November.

24   Zachary Taylor (1784-1850), 12th President.

Carlo Lorenzini [Collodi] (1826-1890), Italian author of *Pinocchio.*

Henri Toulouse-Lautrec (1864-1901), French painter.

25   Andrew Carnegie (1835-1919), American capitalist, philanthropist.

26   1st national Thanksgiving proclaimed by Geo. Washington, 1789.

Sojourner Truth died 1883 (birthdate unknown); illiterate freed slave who became civil rights advocate, eloquent black feminist.

28   William Blake (1757-1828), English poet, engraver.

29   Louisa May Alcott (1832-1888), American author.

30   Jonathan Swift (1667-1745), English author, satirist.

Samuel Clemens [Mark Twain] (1835-1910), American author.

Winston Churchill (1874-1957), English statesman.

Children's Book Week varies from year to year (see Oct.).

Hanukkah: The Festival of Lights or The Feast of Dedication (November or December).When the Maccabees recaptured the temple in Jerusalem only one vial of sacramental oil (enough for one day's use) was found. However, this oil lit a light which lasted for seven days and allowed sufficient time for additional oil to be prepared. Each evening of this seven-day celebration a new arm of the menorah is lit in honor of the freeing of the Maccabees.

November

For the Romans, November was the 9th month: *novem* **= 9 in latin. ("November; n. The eleventh twelfth of a weariness": Ambrose Bierce,** *Devil's Dictionary***).**

NOVEMBER QUOTATIONS

4   A man only learns in two ways, one by reading and the other by associating with smarter people.

Don't let yesterday use up too much of today.

Everybody is ignorant, only on different subjects. *The Illiterate Digest*

I never met a man I didn't like. (Address, Boston: 6/30)

Will Rogers

5   I have been discriminated against far more because I am a female than because I am black.–Shirley Chisholm

13   Everyone lives by selling something. *Across the Plains*

To be what we are and to become what we are capable of becoming, is the only end of life. *Famous Studies of Men and Books*

The world is so full of a number of things, I'm sure we should all be as happy as kings.

–Robert Louis Stevenson

19   A pound of pluck is worth a ton of luck.

–James A. Garfield

25   Surplus wealth is a sacred trust which the possessor is bound
      to administer in his lifetime for the good of the com-
      munity.

                                                     —Andrew Carnegie

26   The man over there says women need to be helped into
      carriages and lifted over ditches, and to have the best
      place everywhere. Nobody ever helps me into carriages
      or over puddles or gives me the best place . . . ain't I a
      woman? Look at my arm! I have ploughed and planted
      and gathered into barns and no man could head me—ain't
      I a woman? I could work as much and eat as much as a
      man—when I could get it—and bear the lash as well! And
      ain't I a woman? I have born 13 children and seen most
      of 'em sold into slavery, and when I cried out with my
      mother's grief, none but Jesus heard me. . . . and ain't I a
      woman?

                                                 —Sojourner Truth, 1851

30   We shall defend our island, whatever the cost may be, we
      shall fight on the beaches, we shall fight on the landing
      grounds, we shall fight in the fields and in the streets, we
      shall fight in the hills; we shall never surrender. (Speech
      in House of Commons, 5/4/40)

      Never give in! Never give in! Never, never, never, never—in
      nothing great or small, large or petty—never give in
      except to a conviction of honor and good sense.

                                                   —Winston Churchill

      Supposing is good, but finding out is better.

      It is differences of opinions that make horse races.

      Don't, like the cat, try to get more out of an experience
      than there is in it. The cat, having sat on a hot stove lid, will
      not sit upon a hot stove lid again. Nor upon a cold stove lid.

                                                       —Mark Twain

      May you live all the days of your life.

                                                    —Jonathan Swift

---

NOVEMBER EVENTS:

• **Birth of Robt. L. Stevenson   [13]**

   Have children design their own Treasure Island maps, incorporating vocabulary words, e.g.: reef, cove, stockade, paces, grove,

westerly, marker, beneath, strides, doubloon, curse or Evil Eye. A story or journal may then be written to "explain" the map.

"Search for Treasure" reading game (2 teams): Distribute mimeos of sentences taken from the latest reading story; each sentence is missing a key word. Teams search for answers in their readers. First team to find all the answers "reaches the treasure."

Reading group Treasure Hunt, a culminating activity, e.g., a special reward for having mastered all of Dolch sight words & phonics, word-analysis skills. Schedule the hunt at the end of the day, the last 30-45 minutes on Friday. Eight participants, or less, work well. Advise them to come back to the room if they find they are having problems with any of the clues. Encourage them not to run as running causes accidents, & to keep their voices low because other children are still in class. Appoint one child to collect all the clue-papers & bring them back to the classroom wastebasket. (You will have taped clues in place during a recent coffee-break.)

Children wait outside classroom door initially. You tack up the map (brown paper bag wrinkled, dampened & ironed flat; then burnt around the edges) by piercing it through with a bloody-handled paring knife (red poster paint is applied to your hand before you grip knife's handle). When you are ready, call in the children. They find map & the hunt begins!

Sample clues (wording emphasizes phonics that have been studied by class): The 1st clue is taped to underside of the reading table: "This hunt is for fun, but still don't be loud & shout! No audible voices, please! To find Clue #2 go outside & look high up where Old Glory is raised."

Clue #2, taped to flag pole: "Clue #3 is at a place outlying from here, attached to a red & yellow fire-hydrant."

Clue #3, taped to the fire hydrant: "Look for a message tied to the handle of a broom at the top of the stairs. The broom is near a drain pipe."

Clue #4, tied to broom handle: "On the younger children's playground is a bench made of concrete. Look beneath it for your next clue."

Clue #5, taped to underside of bench: "The tether ball holds clue #6."

Clue #6, attached to tether ball chain or written on ball with felt pen: "Look on the ground for a number 3 and clue #7."

Clue #7, taped to number 3 which is permanently painted on playground black top: "Clue #8 is on a fountain. You must stoop to be able to see it, though!"

Clue #8, taped beneath water fountain: "Attached to a stick that is divided into 36 sections is your next clue. You're almost at the TREASURE!"

Clue #9, taped to yardstick which leans against nearby wall: "Go back to the classroom! Look in the book written by Webster. Look up 'oyster.' You're almost there!"

In an unconcealed dictionary at page on which "oyster" appears is this note: "Your treasure awaits you beneath a large table-like object. Look for the skull & cross bones . . . hee, hee, hee." (Signed with a skull & crossbones.)

You gauge, by watching their progress, when to bring ice cream bars from Faculty Room refrigerator & place them in "treasure chest" hidden beneath your desk. The chest is made from a large cardboard box & may be saved for future hunts.

Trunk is a corrugated cardboard box; lid is a piece of cardboard, curved & taped to inside back of box. The entire trunk is painted with a coat of tan opaque poster paint. When paint is dry, details (wood grain, metal hinges, lock) are added. A skull cut from white card stock is attached to lid. Stuff bottom of trunk with crushed butcher paper.

- **Birth of Robert Fulton   [14]**

    Fulton did *not* invent the steamboat; he was, initially, a painter & the inventor of machines for making ropes & for sawing marble! The steamboat was largely the invention of John Fitch in 1785. When Fitch died in 1798, he was poverty-stricken. Fulton studied all of Fitch's plans & all of the patents relating to it. With financial backing, Robt. Fulton built the Clermont in 1807 & consequently grew rich & famous.

- **Assassination of President John F. Kennedy   [22]**

    In World War II, Kennedy distinguished himself in the Navy, most notably when his torpedo boat was rammed by a Japanese destroyer. Rallying his crew on a few pieces of wreckage, Jack Kennedy got his men to safety & then towed a badly wounded sailor for 3 miles through shark-infested water with the man's life-belt strap in his teeth.

    There had never been a Roman Catholic President of the United States before John F. Kennedy.

    He worked hard for the Civil Rights Bill which would guarantee equal status for the American Negro. By doing this, he alienated the South, which usually voted Democratic, & partly to help alleviate this situation he set off on a tour of the Southern states. It was during this tour, & just after he had been in office 34 months, that on Nov. 22, 1963, in Dallas, Texas, the shots were fired that killed the youngest elected President our country has ever had.

    Etymology. 800 years ago Christian Crusaders were ambushed & killed by members of a secret band of Moslems who had worked themselves into frenzies by smoking hashish. Such fanatics were called "hashish eaters" or "hashashin." This East Indian word entered medieval Latin as *assassinus,* becoming the English "assassin" & so retaining its murderous history in its meaning.

- **Thanksgiving**

    "Harvest season is a time to be aware of the generosity and riches of nature and the effect of the productiveness of man. For thousands of years people in many lands, worshipping in different ways, have expressed joy and gratitude when their crops were harvested."* The Romans' Thanksgiving holiday was called "Cerelia"**& was dedicated to Ceres, goddess of harvest.

---

*From Days of Discovery, an A.F.S.C. publication.

**This is where we get our word "cereal."

The Pilgrims of Plymouth probably patterned their celebration after the Hebrew "Feast of Ingathering" described in the Bible (Exodus 23:16, Leviticus 23:33-44, Deuteronomy 16:13-15). The first Thanksgiving in America was proclaimed by Governor Bradford 3 years after the Pilgrims had settled at Plymouth. Here is a copy of that first Thanksgiving Proclamation.

To all ye Pilgrims:

Inasmuch as the great Father has given us this year an abundant harvest of Indian corn, wheat, peas, beans, squashes and garden vegetables and has made the forests to abound with game and the sea with fish and clams, and inasmuch as He has protected us from the ravages of the savages, has spared us from pestilence and disease, has granted us freedom to worship God according to the dictates of our conscience; now I, your magistrate, do proclaim that all ye Pilgrims, with ye wives and ye little ones, do gather at ye meeting, on ye hill, between the hours of 9 and 12 in the daytime on Thursday, November ye 29th of the year of our Lord one thousand six hundred and twenty-three, and the third year since ye Pilgrims landed on ye Pilgrim Rock, there to listen to ye pastor and render Thanksgiving to ye Almighty God for all His blessings.

(signed) Wm. Bradford, Ye Governor of Ye Colony

President George Washington proclaimed November 26, 1789, to be the first officially observed Thanksgiving in the U.S.A.

It wasn't until 1941 that Congress fixed a national date for Thanksgiving: the fourth Thursday of November.

Bulletin Board Suggestions

Try cutting out title letters from construction paper; texture these by gently tapping with a sponge lightly dipped in poster paint. Glue seed (pods) to letter shapes cut from tagboard. Or soak Indian corn, beans, fruit seeds, cloves in water; then when they can be easily perforated by needle (& before they begin to split), seeds are strung on heavy thread. Simply wind a long string of seeds around a straight pin outline of the first letters of the title of bulletin board display.

Where will your Thanksgiving dinner come from? Discuss typical menus. Explain the importance of including vegetables, fruits, grain, milk, meat on every menu. Talk about the sources of these foods (orchards, milk delivery, bakery, fields of pineapple, wheat, dairy farms, pumpkins from roadside stands, refrigerator R.R. cars & trucks, gelatine processing plants).

Illustrations may be made individually, or as a class mural, that emphasize how many people are involved in providing us with Sunday dinner. A short neatly written description can accompany each illustration. Arrows of red or orange may serve as connecting devices.

In a lower economic area—or in any school—the class might discuss "the story of the child (or family, town) that couldn't have a Thanksgiving turkey," talk about the meaning of the turkey as a symbol, the relative importance of the bird & of feasting. Stress the deeper meaning of the holiday.

Use "As Americans We Are Thankful For ... " as a topic. Children each choose an appropriate subject & write about it, illustrating their papers with photographs, actual objects or cut-outs. Written papers are backed with a square of red or blue & pinned against an all-white background.

Classroom Co-op Turkey. This activity for young children will facilitate small muscle control. Before introducing project, cut strips of tan construction paper (1" x 4" long). Pin a large tan turkey body to the bulletin board. Each tail feather, backed in orange, is a different color: tan, purple, green, grey, brown, blue. Eye is 3 circles: tan, purple, & the smallest is white. Red wattles, yellow feet & beak complete basic bird. Children curl & attach paper strips to bird's body. Curling is done by wrapping strips around a pencil, or by pulling them across the blade of a pair of dull scissors. This curling might occupy the 15 minutes prior to dismissal. Once bird is finished, children suggest a message for their turkey to convey. Individual birds can be made.

Language Arts

Prominently display a "November Remember Words" chart as a vocabulary & spelling aide. Such a chart could include: cornucopia, banquet, forefathers, endure, arduous, bountiful, Puritans, Plymouth. Words can be added to the chart as they come up during class discussions.

Have the children write down the first word they think of after they hear you read each of these stimulus words: life, freedom, school, food, America, our world, church, home, God, thanks. Their papers will indicate spelling needs & the phonetic weaknesses of the class. A bulletin board entitled "What Thanksgiving Means to Me" could be developed from such lists.

The class can practice their penmanship while writing thank-you notes to people who have been especially thoughtful or helpful, e.g., the school's secretary, nurse or librarian.

Classroom Game. "Why-When-Where?" facilitates spelling & noun study. One child leaves the room & a secret word, related to Thanksgiving, is chosen by the class. The children spend a few minutes getting sample answers in mind & then the player returns & asks each child in turn: "Why was it used? When was it used? Where was it used?" Each student must give a different answer to each question. The game continues until questioner guesses the secret word. If he can then spell it correctly on the chalkboard, he is allowed to choose the next questioner. If, however, he misspells the word, the teacher, after writing the word correctly, chooses the next questioner; the child who had especially thoughtful answers may be rewarded in this way. (Secret word suggestions: musket, prayer, feather, Bible.)

Dramatic play will be facilitated by having the children familiarize themselves with the historical details, background information of the 1st Thanksgiving. Children collect props & make simple identifying head-gear. Wigs for both Pilgrim men & Indians are made from crepe paper.

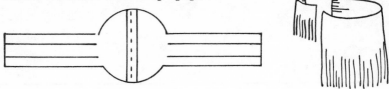

For Indian wigs, machine stitch a center reinforcing strip of tagboard. Children braid ends of crepe paper. Pilgrims wigs have bangs attached to cover forehead. Plays should incorporate historical facts & appropriate vocabulary.

Etymology. The word "pilgrim" is nearly 800 years old. As "pelegrim" & later in French as "pelerin," it dealt with traveling & wandering. The Latin *peregrinus* was a combination of *per* (through) & *ager* (field); a pilgrim was, originally, one who wandered through the fields on his way to the Holy Land. A banquet has come to mean a large feast, but in French it meant "the little bench" (on which you sat when you were seated for dinner). When the colonists arrived in America they sighted a large bird that reminded them of the guinea fowl of Turkey, so they named the strange new bird "Turkey-cock."

> *Riddles:* Exactly where did the Pilgrim Fathers stand when they landed on Plymouth Rock? (On their feet.) Who is never hungry on Thanksgiving? (The turkey: he's already stuffed.) What does everybody want on Thanksgiving, but they try to get rid of it as soon as they have it? (A good appetite.) What 3 letters spell the name of the first house built in America? (A T-P, the house of the Plains Indians.) Two Indians were standing on a bridge. One was the father of the other one's son. What relation were they? (Husband & wife.)

Thanksgiving Poetry

The classic "Over the River and Through the Woods" by Lydia Maria Child evokes the holidays of turn-of-the-century America.

> "So once in every year we throng
>   Upon a day apart
> To praise the Lord with feast and song
>   In thankfulness of heart."
>   Arthur Guiterman

Thanksgiving Reading

The following was adapted from a choral reading suggestion published by the A.F.S.C. in their Fall Guideposts series. As a group, the class compiles 3 appropriate responses wherever asterisks appear. Then the reading is practiced by the group, as a body, & ultimately taped (with appropriate music).

Leader: Thanksgiving is a time to thank. It is also a time to think. At this season of the year we think more than usual about our many blessings. We remember the gifts that we don't often notice just because they are all around us. They cost nothing. They can be enjoyed by everyone. Such gifts are 3 very precious ones: sound, color, & taste. They put gladness in our hearts.

Girls: We are thankful for sounds we hear:*(e.g., birds singing in the early morning.)

Boys: We are thankful for colors we see:*(e.g., orange pumpkins against black earth.)

Everyone:*(response.)

Boys: We are thankful for colors we see:*(e.g., scarlet maple trees.)

Repeat response.

Silence.

All: We are thankful for foods we taste:*(e.g., juicy grapes.)

Response.

All: We are thankful for foods we taste:*(e.g., spicy cookies.)

Response.

Silence.

Phonetic Drill

Farmer Jones' Turkey Ranch. Cut 8 or 10 medium-sized (6" wide) turkey bodies from tan paper. Details & color are added with crayon. A word-ending is printed on each turkey body.

Six or 8 bright colored paper feathers, with a blend printed on each of them, are tucked behind turkey body to form a fan-like tail. Turkeys are laid flat on the table & children in the reading group try "to pluck all the turkeys on Farmer Jones' Ranch. Each turkey (phonetic structure) is tackled in turn by each student; a child may have more than 1 try at a turkey, if necessary. Children withdraw each tail feather as it & word-endings are successfully pronounced. In this way turkey is "plucked." When a child has plucked 8-9 turkeys, he gets the chance to try his hand with "the toughest Tom," a difficult, tricky phonetic structure, e.g., "_ough," Once the toughest Tom is conquered, child earns the title "King of the Turkey Pluckers"!

Thanksgiving History Activities

Compare on a classroom map the different routes taken to the New World: that taken by Columbus & that by the Pilgrims.

Discuss with the children: Which people, according to skills, trades, professions, would have been chosen to come on the Mayflower? (There were 102 passengers on the Mayflower.) What food, tools, objects would the Pilgrims have chosen to bring with them? How might people have occupied themselves on the trip? (The trip required over 2 months: 10 times longer than it takes today.) In what ways did the advantages outweigh the hardships the Pilgrims were forced to face in the New World?

A classroom chart entitled "Now and Then" can be compiled by class: Pass out mimeographed sheets that list modern inventions, equipment or have class as a group compile such a list. Each child then fills in the Early American equivalent of each modern aid or appliance. There are innumerable "correct answers": if child can give a logical reason for giving a response, it's correct; e.g., hair dryer: wind & sun; clock radio: hour-glass, rooster or song bird singing at dawn; tape-recorder: handing down stories father to son. . . . A large class chart could then be made, displayed & added to throughout the year.

Thanksgiving Math Enrichment

Here are 2 recipes for classroom cooking experiences:

Young children can make Cranberry-Orange Relish (20 jars):

8 large cans whole cranberry sauce	4 pkgs. orange gelatin
8 fresh seedless oranges	2 cups hot water
(plastic wrap, ribbon)	20 small clean jars

Peel oranges & remove all the pith you can. Cut oranges into little pieces.

Add hot water to gelatin & stir until dissolved; add cranberry sauce to gelatin.

Add oranges to gelatin mixture. Ladle into jars. Cover jar

openings with pieces of plastic wrap. Refrigerate until children take relish home.

Tie ribbon around each jar top securing plastic wrap in place.

Secure a note (via a gummed sticker) to each jar stating how well this relish goes with turkey.

Older students may enjoy contributing a pint of homemade mincemeat to their holiday dinners. Here is a recipe (with modern equivalents) used by my Great Grandma Alden:

> Simmer 2 lbs. beef neck (or chuck) covered, in water to cover, until tender (about 3 hours). Cool. (This step might be taken the evening before; the prepared meat could be brought to school and the children could continue from here on.) Put meat through a food chopper, using the coarse blade. Mix 1/2 lb. ground suet with ground meat. Put these into a large kettle & add 3 lbs. (or more) red tart apples which have been pared & diced. Add the following:

1½ c. sugar	1 pint pineapple-apricot jam
1 pkg. currants	1 pint plum jelly
1 pkg. white raisins	2½ tsp. salt
1 pkg. dark raisins	3 tsp. cinnamon
1 pint strawberry preserves	2 tsp. allspice
1 #2½ can apricots (& their juice)	1 tsp. cloves
1 #303 can pineapple tidbits & juice	
1 #2½ can pickled peaches; remove seeds, dice (& add juice).	
1 #303 can red tart cherries: drain & discard juice.	

> Cover & simmer for 1 hour. When cool, mincemeat may be put into pint containers & frozen or into glass jars & sealed while it is still hot. *(Thank you, Mother.)*

Thanksgiving Art

Many children have never seen a live turkey. These children cannot be expected to draw or paint a personal impression of the bird; their work will, at best, be an interpretation of a photograph or drawing they've seen at some time. If a live turkey cannot be brought to class ("borrowed" from a poultry farm for an afternoon), perhaps a film featuring turkeys could be shown.

Turkey drawings. Ask the children how an emotion makes itself visually evident through posture, gestures, etc. Then have the children depict a turkey in an appropriate setting & have the bird express an emotion: fear, happiness, surprise, suspicion.

Collage turkeys. Have the class collect & sort magazine pictures into different colors, tonal groups: this helps children learn to recognize shades, tones. Feathers, neck, wattle, legs & feet are torn from appropriate shades of illustrations, regardless of subject matter. Background details are kept simple. Collage is glued to a piece of tan or light yellow paper. This type of lesson helps loosen up those children who always seem to need the security of using a ruler.

Giant Pilgrims & Indians. Have on display many reference illustrations showing differing dress, tools, footwear of colonists & Indians. This lesson necessitates use of newsprint, large sheets of colored paper, tape, glue, scissors & plenty of floor space. Children initially draw & color (on small sheets of newsprint) their interpretation of an Indian or Pilgrim man or woman. Next discuss briefly the sections of the body (head, neck, torso, legs & feet) & how the children should try to use as much of each sheet of paper as they can. (E.g., 1st a very big torso is cut out; then 2 legs to fit this torso; then feet to fit the legs, etc.) No pencils or crayons are used, if possible. Children try to cut shapes directly from the pieces of paper & refer back to their drawings as they cut out the sections of their figures. Rather than "dressing" the figures, clothes are cut out directly from colored paper & glued together (taped on underside). Once general form of figure is achieved, the addition of details, e.g., buckles, feathers, aprons, muskets, etc. (also cut from paper) should be encouraged. Finished Pilgrim & Indian figures may be from 40"-55" in height. Figures can be stored flat on top of a cupboard if more than one art period is required to finish this project. Staple the finished figures above the chalkboard; overlap their arms so that the Indians & Pilgrims will appear to be holding hands. Then they will look down on your class, watching over your November activities.

Quick paper-bag puppets. Draw facial features (of Pilgrim) rather high up on sack, using felt-tip pens. Fill sack with crushed newspapers. Insert a sturdy stick (dowel or ruler) into mouth of sack. Secure the sack to stick with rubber band &/or masking tape. Stovepipe hat or collar, made of construction paper, can be taped or stapled to bag. Children manipulate puppet with stick. Show puppets in a doorway, across the lower half of which a blanket is suspended, or turn a table on its side with its surface toward the audience; puppets pop up from behind the table top.

Thanksgiving P.E.

"Pilgrim Father" requires no equipment & emphasizes running, tagging. "It" (the Pilgrim Father) says to the Pilgrims standing on the goal line, "Come with me to hunt turkey." All the children fall in line behind him & march around in any direction he chooses. When he has led the pilgrims all away from the goal line he calls "BANG!" The children run back to the goal line; the Pilgrim Father catches as many as he can. These players become "turkeys" & are put in "a cage" & the game continues. Each Pilgrim Father has 3 turns & then he picks a successor from among the remaining Pilgrims. Turkeys leave cage & join game again; play continues.

Information sources:

Boys' Clubs of America
381 – 4th Ave., New York,
N.Y. 10003
"Crafts from Mayflower Times"
(35¢)

John Hancock Mutual Life
Insurance Co.

"Story of the Pilgrims"
(free)

Thanksgiving Culmination

Discuss a class gift project with your principal before introducing it to the class. Suggested outlets for classmade gifts include: hospitals & schools for children with special needs,* settlement houses, homes for the aged (all listed in the classified section of the phone book), or contact the local chapter of the Cerebral Palsy Assoc. or Council of Social Agencies; a staff worker can tell you of any special needs to be filled, e.g., the names, birthdates of children who would appreciate mail.

Discuss with your class: "Ways we can share with others who may not be as lucky as we are."

Two class gift projects. Have the children collect brightly colored, perfectly shaped autumn leaves. Press these between sheets of newspaper topped by heavy books. When the leaves are dry, spread them on newspaper & shellac them. Allow leaves to dry; then shellac reverse sides. A shut-in or hospital patient will be cheered by the sight of a bright autumnal leaf lying on his tray or pinned to the curtain. A.F.S.C.

---

*Write Mr. Kenn Kroska, Director, Volunteer Services, Faribault State Hosp., Faribault, Minn. 55021 to learn how your class may lend a helping hand.

Autumn bouquets. Using a bulletin board display of dried plants as a guide (& as a warning against poisonous plants), children collect wheat, Chinese lantern, bittersweet, cockscomb, milkweed, money plant & other appropriate weeds. Hang these plants upside down & allow to dry. Artistically grouped, these plants become decorative pieces & make kind, lasting gifts to shut-ins.

Bittersweet. A North American ornamental vine (*Celastrus scandens*); its small green flowers develop into yellowish tan capsules that burst, when ripe, to reveal brilliant orange seed coverings (the antils). Sometimes it is called "false bittersweet." Container suggestions: A small jar is dipped in Spackle, twirled, removed & allowed to dry (at which time it may be painted if you wish).

Using a funnel, children pour plaster of Paris into an attractively shaped soft drink bottle. Weeds are inserted into soft plaster. When plaster is hardened (& weeds secure), the bottle is placed in a heavy paper bag & held tightly at the neck. The bottle is smashed, leaving broken glass inside bag; the remaining plaster impression becomes "the vase."

- **Birth of Jonathan Swift [30]**

Ask children to choose one of the following to write about: "The adventures of Vegetable Man, " of " . . . a Flying Ghoul," " . . . an Imp Caught in a Bottle," " . . . a Spider Man," " . . . a Snake Woman," or of " . . . a Creature That Invades One's Sleep." Illustrations of these stories may be confined to 1 color, e.g., Veg.

Man: orange; Spider Man: brown, etc. If students are older, discuss with them the nature of satire, the lampoon.

NOVEMBER ACTIVITIES

Parent-Teacher Conferences are often scheduled during November. If the sample form given here is mimeographed & a separate sheet is dedicated to each student, you should find this a real aid to organization & a valuable post-conference guide.

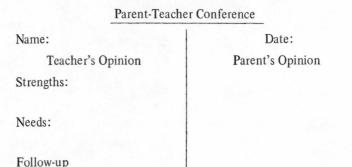

Parent-Teacher Conference

Name:	Date:
Teacher's Opinion	Parent's Opinion
Strengths:	
Needs:	
Follow-up	

November Poetry:

> ... No warmth, no cheerfulness, no healthful ease,
> No comfortable feel in any member—
> No shade, no shine, no butterflies, no bees,
> No fruits, no flowers, no leaves, no birds,
>   November!
>
>   Thomas Hood (19th c.)

Science

"The Study of Crystals" (a mimeo-sheet suggestion). "Do you know how grains of sand, salt, sugar, & a snowflake are all alike? (No, this isn't a riddle, but just a way of introducing you to the subject of crystals, for that is what sand, salt, sugar & snowflakes have in common: Each is a crystal.)

Crystals have flat faces & regular (geometric) shapes. This is because their atoms are arranged in an orderly & repeated pattern.

Each snowflake is actually made of many tiny crystals of ice. Snowflakes are always 6-sided & yet no 2 snowflakes are ever exactly alike!

Grains of sand are crystals of quartz, but the wind & water have battered them so long that their edges have been worn smooth.

Let's plant a Crystal Garden & then you can watch some crystals "grow" right before your eyes! You'll need small pieces of brick (the size of walnuts), small pieces of briquette, a fairly deep glass bowl (plastic cottage cheese containers work well)*, & 3 T. bluing, 3 T. water, 3 T. *uni*iodized salt, 1 tsp. ammonia, tiny twigs (toothpicks), & food coloring.

A few PRECAUTIONS : Ammonia is poison-

ous if swallowed (so wash your hands after using it). Ammonia also has a strong smell (it's a good idea to do your gardening in a room with the window open). Bluing can stain clothing, so push up your sleeves. And now on to the planting!

Place the brick & coal pieces in bowl. Prop the twigs, toothpicks between the brick & briquette. Add a little water to the bowl. Combine salt, bluing, ammonia, water in a cup. Mix well. *Slowly* pour this mixture over the broken coal & brick. To give color to your garden, sprinkle a few drops of food coloring over the mixture in the bowl. Place your garden in a warm place where it will not be disturbed.

In a short time tiny crystals will begin growing & in a few hours your crystal garden will have odd & interesting shapes. To keep your garden growing, just add 1 T. of ammonia to it once a week.

More fun with crystals (crystal candy). Each child will need a drinking glass, a pencil or ice cream stick, a piece of clean string 6" long, 1/2 cup of water, a paper clip & granulated sugar. Tie the string to the middle of pencil or stick. Tie the paper clip to the other end of the string. Put water in a pan & boil (on classroom hot plate). Add sugar, teaspoon by teaspoonful, until no more will dissolve in the water. Pour this liquid into each glass. Place the pencil across mouth of glass, with paper clip on bottom of glass. The glasses are then set in a warm spot where they won't be disturbed.

---

*Do not use aluminum containers, e.g., TV trays, frozen pie pans. The solution reacts with aluminum & causes tiny holes to develop in container.

In 1 or 2 days crystals begin to form along the string. After a week or 2 each child will have a large crystal candy suspended in his glass.

A very interesting Science publication:

Nature and Science $1.15 per child per semester or
$1.95 per school year (16 issues)
Natural History Press
American Museum of Natural History
Central Park West at 79th St.
New York, N.Y. 10024.

Art

Classroom frescoes. A mixture of sand, thick white tempera & a small amount of flour is applied to pieces of cardboard. Don't apply mixture too thickly. When dry, the cardboard is painted with tempera (water color), achieving a fresco-like effect.

Punched metal plaques. Display pictures of work by early tinsmiths, & point out how their designs served a purpose (radiation of light, air or heat) as well as beautified the object. Have the children collect a variety of lightweight aluminum containers. T.V. dinner trays, various sizes of frozen pie pans. With the aid of pencil, compass & ruler, a design is drawn onto the metal's surface. Then using hammer, different sizes of nails, a small chisel & adequate newspaper padding, the children perforate the aluminum along the pencil lines or in a designated area. Display the punched metal plaques in such a way that light is allowed to come through the holes (against a window) or against a dark-colored bulletin board.

November P.E.

Some suggestions for the organization of Relay Races: Relays are usually not introduced before the second grade. Never use relays before the skills involved have been practiced or learned. Initially, the children might want to walk through the procedure once before the race begins. Since the purpose of relays is the practice of skills & improvement of teamwork, competition is not overemphasized. Teams are of equal numbers of players. If necessary, the teacher can play, or 1 child could run twice, or extra children might be rotated into the teams. The starting line is specifically marked. Infractions are penalized by the subtraction of a point from that team's score or by sending the player back to the starting line (an infraction never disqualifies an entire team). Every team may receive points: 5 for 1st team, 4 for 2nd team, etc. The winning team is declared, in a classroom situation, when the whole team is seated, the last person over the line having also seated himself. (See June for additional relay races.)

Cranberry relay race. Divide children into 3-4 equal teams which line up at 1 side of the room. At the opposite side of the room are 3-4 empty bowls. The 1st child in each team has a sack containing 4 cranberries. He places these berries on the back of his hand & when the teacher calls "Go," he gives sack to 2nd player, runs to bowl, drops in berries, & runs back, tagging 2nd player. If any berries roll off a player's hand, they must be replaced BEFORE he may continue on his way to the bowl. The 2nd player gives sack to 3rd player, runs to bowl, puts berries on back of his hand & returns to the team putting berries into sack. This procedure is repeated until 1 team finishes first.

November Puppet

These are teacher-made finger puppets that can be re-used each year; they are introduced to enliven a drill period or as an aid to Language Arts work. The face, body, feathers are of colorful felt scraps. Hand-stitch the body down back. Glue ends of feathers about head shape. Glue black bias tape to encircle head shape; this adds rigidity & forms hair of puppet. Feather tips are also glued down to cover back of head. Facial features are glued to face.

December

Chill December brings the sleet,
Blazing fire and Christmas treat.

1   1st atomic nuclear reaction demonstrated 1942, Chicago.
4   Kandinsky (1866-1944), Russian painter: one of the originators of non-objective painting.
5   Martin Van Buren (1782-1862), 8th President.
6   St. Nicholas Day celebrated in Europe.
8   Eli Whitney (1765-1825), American inventor of the cotton gin.
10 John Smith began trip on which his life was saved by Pocahontas, 1607.
    Emily Dickinson (1830-1886), American poet.
    1st state, Wyoming, grants women the right to vote, 1869.
    Human Rights Day.
11 Hector Berlioz (1803-1869), French composer.
12 Marconi sent 1st radio signal across Atlantic from Newfdld. to England, 1901.
13 Sir Francis Drake started voyage around the world, 1577.
14 South Pole discovered, 1911.
15 Bill of Rights Day: 1st Amendments to Constitution ratified, 1791.
16 Boston Tea Party, 1773.
    Ludwig von Beethoven (1770-1827), German composer.
    1st rendezvous in space (U.S. Gemini VI & VII), 1965.
17 John Greenleaf Whittier (1807-1892), American poet.
    Wright Bros. Day: 1st successful aeroplane flight at Kitty Hawk, N.C., 1903.

18   1st colonial Thanksgiving celebrated, 1777.
Slavery abolished, 1865.

20   U.S. took possession of La. Territory, 1803.

21   Forefathers' Day: landing of Pilgrims at Plymouth Rock, 1620.
Winter begins.
Giacomo Puccini (1858-1924), Italian operatic composer.

24   Kit Carson (1809-1868), American frontiersman.
Matthew Arnold (1822-1888), English poet.

25   Isaac Newton (1642-1727), English mathematician, 1st person to identify the "law of gravity."
Washington crossed the Delaware, 1776.
Clara Barton (1821-1912), founder of American Red Cross.
CHRISTMAS DAY.

27   Louis Pasteur (1822-1895), French chemist, developer of the Pasteurization process.

28   Woodrow Wilson (1856-1924), 28th President.

29   Andrew Johnson (1808-1875), 17th President.
Charles Goodyear (1800-1860), American inventor of vulcanization process.

30   Rudyard Kipling (1865-1936), English author: *The Jungle Book.*

31   Henri Matisse (1869-1954), French painter.
Hanukkah (Feast of lights) may occur in December or November: 8 days. This holy day has been observed for 2000 years by Jews in many lands. (See page 75.)

December

This was the tenth month in the calendar of ancient Rome; in Latin *decem* is ten.

DECEMBER QUOTATIONS

5   The second sober thought of the people is seldom wrong and always efficient.—Martin Van Buren

10   There is no frigate like a book
To take us lands away,
Nor any courser like a page
Of prancing poetry.
("There Is No Frigate Like a Book")—Emily Dickinson

17   "Shoot, if you must, this old grey head,
      But spare your country's flag," she said.
          ("Barbara Frietchie": line 35)—John G. Whittier

      Success four flights Thursday morning all against 21-mile
      wind started from level with engine power alone average
      speed through air 31-miles longest 59 seconds inform
      press home Christmas. (Telegram to their father, Kitty
      Hawk, N.C., Dec. 17, 1903)—Orville Wright, Wilbur
      Wright

24   Where the great whales come sailing by,
      Sail and sail, with unshut eye.
          ("The Forsaken Merman")—Matthew Arnold

25   And the angel said unto them, "Fear not for, behold, I bring
      you good tidings of great joy which shall be to all people.
      For unto you is born this day in the city of David a
      Saviour, which is Christ the Lord." (Luke 2, v. 10-11)

      People say Christmas Day is too commercial. But I have
      never found it that way. If you spend money to give
      people joy, you aren't being commercial. It is only when
      you feel obliged to do something about Christmas that
      the spirit is spoiled.—Eleanor Roosevelt

28   The world must be made safe for democracy. (Address to
      Congress: Feb. 2, 1917)

      Liberty has never come from the government. . . . The
      history of liberty is the history of the limitations of
      governmental power, not the increase of it.
                                             —Woodrow Wilson

A General Word about December Events

Think through your ideas in response to the following
questions:

Can you state concisely what Christmas means to you? What
does it mean in our culture today?

What aspects of Christmas can be meaningful to your students
who are non-Christians?

How much of this can be part of your December teaching
plans? During this season outside activities accelerate & multiply.
How can you use the activities presented here to lessen or to

channel pre-Christmas excitement in young children? And which might be used to prevent older students from wasting December in a mounting spiral of over-activity?

DECEMBER EVENTS:

- ## Birth of Eli Whitney   [8]

It is said that while struggling to find an easier way than manually removing the seeds from cotton bolls, Eli Whitney happened to glance out the window & see a fox trying to snatch a hen from its coop. The fox clawed at the chicken wire pen & although he didn't get the chicken, he got plenty of feathers! This chance encounter gave Whitney the idea for the basis of his cotton gin—a metal claw that would pull cotton fibers through a strong wire mesh, leaving the seeds behind.

- ## Bill of Rights Day   [15]

Receive a free chart showing the Bill of Rights by writing to:

Standard Oil Co. of California
225 Bush St.
San Francisco, Calif. 94120

A free illustrated booklet is available from:

Boys Life
New Brunswick, N.J. 08903

- ## Birth of Beethoven   [16]

Beethoven was a lonely child who spent hours each day practicing the piano. He wrote great music for the piano, the violin & the entire orchestra. However, at an early age his hearing began to fail. By the time he was 34, he could no longer hear. Yet Beethoven lived to write his most wonderful symphonies AFTER he was deaf!

As December often needs a soothing classroom atmosphere, from time to time try playing excerpts from Beethoven's work (e.g., Moonlight Sonata). Children may draw while the music is playing, or simply listen for "pictures."

- ## Wright Brothers' Day   [17]

Read to the class from John Dos Passos' "Big Money" (published in 1936), an excellent short description of what led up to that famous flight.

Free packets of aviation materials:

Smithsonian Institution Press
Wash. D.C. 20560

United Air Lines   Air Transport Assoc. of America
P.O. Box 66141   1000 Conn. Ave., N.W.
O'Hare International Airport   Washington, D.C. 20036
Chicago, Ill. 60666

• **Winter begins   [21] or [22]**

This is the day of winter solstice when the sun is farthest from the equator & its apparent northward motion along the horizon ends. In Latin *sol*=sun & *sisto*=to stand still.

Discuss non-deciduous trees; make a collection of cone & needle samples: from these the children can learn to identify the 7 most common genera (Arborvitae, Pine, Yew, Hemlock, Fir, Spruce, Juniper). Emphasize the difference between the shapes of the trees. Use pictures from a seed or nursery catalog (see Jan. Science) to illustrate a mix-match quiz or a bulletin board display. Remind the children that the shape of the needles begins with the same letter as the name of the tree: the fir (& balsam) has flat needles; the spruce has square needles.

Talk about "cold" & its relativity. Discuss how snow, sleet, hail & rain are each formed.

Review the subject of crystals (see Nov.). Discussing how coarse salt is used during winter to melt the ice on northern roads can lead up to this simple set of experiments: Dissolve salt in hot water. Allow water to evaporate, revealing salt crystals. Repeat procedure, using sugar. Compare the 2 crystal formations under a microscope. Repeat procedure using borax. Next look at a piece of sandpaper (which is usually covered with quartz crystals) under a microscope. For further crystal investigation, obtain samples of alum, sulphur, & camphor crystals from a druggist. Let the children see if they can eventually identify the crystals by their formations.

"If winter comes, can Spring be far behind?"
P.B. Shelly: 18 c. English poet.

• **Birth of Clara Barton   [25]**

Clara was so shy as a child that her parents became worried that she would never be able to successfully relate to the outside world. They consulted a phrenologist who, after feeling Clara's head, assured the Bartons that the shape of Clara's skull meant that she would spend her life working for others. A lucky guess? Perhaps. Clara Barton grew up to teach school, tend the wounded of the Civil War & finally to persuade our government to sign the Red Cross Convention, organizing the American Red Cross—which is dedicated to helping humanity.

• Hanukkah

Hanukkah is a movable feast. Here is a cooky recipe that you might use as a math enrichment activity.

Hanukkah Cookies

Cream butter & sugar in a big bowl. In a second bowl beat egg & add milk & vanilla. Now combine these 2 mixtures in the big bowl. Sift together flour, salt, baking powder. Add these to the mixture in the big bowl. Refrigerate dough for 1 hour. Dust rolling pin & board with flour. Roll out dough to 1/4" thick. Cut into fancy shapes using cardboard patterns like those shown here. Place cookies on an oiled cooky sheet & bake for 12 min. in a 350° oven. (A.F.S.C.)

• Christmas   [25]

There have always been midwinter celebrations following winter solstice, when the days begin to lengthen & grow lighter. In ancient Egypt this time of year was celebrated with a Feast of Light; in Scandinavia they call it "The end of the Frost King's rule."

The American celebration of Christmas, as centered around the tree, its lights & presents, is a comparatively recent tradition. It arrived in our country via England, from Germany, after 1840. Until then Christmas in America was strictly a religious holiday.

Germany is generally credited as being the country of the Christmas tree's origin. Some feel St. Winifred created the first tree; others say Martin Luther, one Christmas Eve, envisioned a candle-lit tree as he gazed at the starry heavens. The 1st authenticated mention of decorated trees occurs in an Alsatian manuscript (1604). It is also recorded that the German soldiers in the British army decorated evergreens to celebrate Christmas in 1776 at Trenton, N.J. But it wasn't until 1841 that decorated trees became popular here & abroad. In that year Queen Victoria had a tree decorated for her children at Windsor Castle, at the suggestion of Albert, her German Prince Consort.

In pagan times bonfires were built to keep the waning sun alive during winter solstice. Christmas tree lights, fires & candles may be descendants of those primitive blazes.

In the 12th century, St. Francis of Assisi, Italy, wanted to make the Christmas story come alive for the people of his church. So he constructed the 1st creche scene. It was a doll in a simple manger set upon the grass near the church; live farm animals grazed by it. St. Francis also popularized carol-singing as he relied on the use of carols in the services held around the creche.

The word "holly" comes not from "holy," but from "holm oak," the leaves of which holly resembles. The Christmas wreath commemorates Christ's crown of thorns. Pre-Christian legends held that witches despised holly & that they would stay away from any house where it was hung (as a wreath on the door).

A pre-Christian custom dictated that Roman enemies were to reconcile with one another if ever they met under mistletoe!

Why do we have turkey at this time of year? Because James I hated boar's head. His taste for turkey at Yuletide became popularized when he became, in 1603, the King of England.

Legend says that one Christmas another English king found himself snowbound. His cook had no idea of what to prepare for a holiday meal. Then he had an inspiration; he collected all the supplies in the camp: stag meat & dried apples & plums. He threw in some flour, eggs & sugar & salt & wet these down with brandy & ale. Finally he took the resulting lump of dough, tied it in a cloth & boiled it. The outcome? The very 1st Christmas Plum Pudding!

Christmas Bulletin Boards

Lettering suggestions. Cut letters from holiday materials, e.g. gift-wrap, felt, ribbon.

Recipe for Fireproof Non-melting Snow: beat 2 cups detergent & 1/2 cup water, adding more soap or water until snow stands in peaks. Apply snow to cardboard letters or to fir branches, which may then be used as a bulletin board border.

Theme ideas. Cover a bulletin board with white butcher paper. Wind fluffy green nylon yarn around pins forming a large geometric outline of a Christmas tree. Below each branch, in felt tip pen print "Merry Christmas" in different languages. Include greetings from those countries which reflect the heritages of your students: Froeliche Weihnachten (Austria & Germany); Joyeux Noel (France, Switzerland & Belgium); Stretan Bozic (Yugoslavia); Buon Natale (Italy & Switzerland); Boldog Karacsony Unnep (Hungary); Glaedelig Jul (Norway & Denmark); Felices Navidades (Spain, Mexico); God Jul (Sweden); Wesolych Swiat (Poland); Kung ho shen tan (Chinese); Merry Christenmass (Scotland); Vrolyk Kerstmis (Holland); Um Feiz Natal (Portugal); S Rozhdestvom Christovom (Russia); Kala Hrystoughena (Greece); Glaedelig Jul (Norway); Nodlaig Mhaith Dhuit (Ireland).

Older students may enjoy studying lay-outs of the cities of Bethlehem or Jerusalem & topographical photographs of Israel. Resultant discussion topics might include how cities grow & change, & how nature imposes itself on the growth of cities.

Angel-inspired bulletin boards. Have the children collect &

bring to class any angel pictures they can find. Supplement these, if at all possible, with reproductions of Giotto's crying angels, Byzantine & Romanesque angels, &/or those of Signorelli, Memling, Fra Angelico. (The Christmas card catalog which can be purchased for 25¢ from the Metropolitan Museum of Art, New York, N.Y., is illustrated with small good pictures, many of which are of angels.) These may all be combined in a large class-made collage; pieces of colored foil can be used to highlight eyes, wings, halos.

After acquainting themselves with various illustrations of angels, the children are prepared to make their own artistic interpretations. Have them bring different types of musical instruments to class. Display pictures of instruments. Then let your class color & cut out pictures of angels playing different musical instruments. What easier way to learn the mechanics of drawing a flute, violin or trumpet? An angelic orchestra can then be assembled to herald the coming of the Yuletide.

A decorative bulletin board, a pyramid of angels: Each child receives a piece of white paper (6"x 8") & is asked to cut out an angel, using as much of the paper as possible. The finished cut-out is turned over to hide any pencil outlines that may have been made. Assemble these, with wings almost touching, in the following manner: base of pyramid is 6 equally tall angels pinned one next to the other. 5 angels are pinned above base, each cut-out supported by the wings of the 2 beneath it. Continue building pyramid, always using angels of equal height for each tier, arriving finally at the zenith with a gold star atop the shortest angel.

Just for fun & in a hard-to-fill area, display the following Mystery Xmas Trees: children lift up large printed tagboard labels in order to find answers. "The Oldest Xmas Tree" (a fossilized fern imprinted in clay); "The Newest Xmas Tree" (tree shape cut from Mylar or other newly developed substance); "The Youngest Xmas Tree" (a pine nut taped to tagboard).

Room Environment

Walls. A time-line based on Christmas carols, e.g., early 1500; "God Rest Ye Merry Gentlemen"; 1692, "O Come All Ye Faithful"; 1703, "While Shepherds Watched Their Flocks by Night"; 1709, "Joy to the World"; 1739, "Hark the Herald Angels Sing"; 1751, "Adestes Fideles"; 1833, "The First Noel"; 1849, "It Came Upon a Midnight Clear"; 1867, "O Little Town of Bethlehem." (Also see "Xmas Music" for additional carols). Let children choose the carols THEY want to include; this may lead to vocabulary & spelling word enrichment. Bring time-line up to date by including "Frosty" & "Rudolph" if children wish.

"The 12 Days of Christmas" mural. Divide class into groups. Staple a long sheet of butcher paper to cover one entire wall. Divide this paper into 13 equal parts, if title is to be in 1st space. (Title can be placed above mural, if you prefer.) Before beginning to draw, the class briefly discusses each of the 12 subjects: "What is a colly bird?* And a turtle dove?** How do the leaves of a pear tree look? How does a drummer keep his drum in place? What is a partridge, & a lord? And a French hen? How DOES a piper pipe?" (Later, you might explain how each came to be included in the song.) Children who enjoy being graphic technicians should be given the 1st, 2nd & 4th areas. Section 5 requires only 1 or 2 students while areas 8-12 require most of class. Have each group draw up their ideas on scratch paper. This plan may then be drawn on the butcher paper in LIGHT pencil. Children select colored papers from numerous piles of construction paper, including dull metallic gold & silver wrapping paper. These papers are cut out & glued in place on the butcher paper. Discuss with the group handling of the title: effective use of color; how title should tie up with, & NOT distract *from,* mural; different lettering possibilities. Those whose areas are 1st completed may begin careful cutting & pasting of lords or ladies.

Windows. Stained glass window effect can be obtained in several ways:

1. Draw a design on tracing paper; divide large areas into sections (mosaic-like effect). Lay newspapers beneath windows to catch any drips. Tape tracing paper to outside of clean windows. For each color required, pour 6 T. clear mucilage into a small container & add 2 T. food coloring. Test on window for intensity of color. Children paint all areas calling for one color before mixing (or using) a 2nd. A 1/3" strip is left between all areas to prevent running & to simulate leading of stained glass. A damp Q-Tip will help correct mistakes.

2. Cut shapes from lightweight colored tissue paper. Cut a

---

*The word "colly" used in England means "soot"; collybird is a blackbird.
**A slender European dove having a white-edged tail; some sources say that the 5 golden rings = 5 golden ring-necked pheasants.

piece of plastic film slightly larger than completed design will be. Heavy duty kitchen wrap may be used, or 12 gauge vinyl, $1.50 a yard at awning, auto seat-cover shops. A 9 x 12 plastic drop cloth ´is most economical, but is rather opaque & must be cellophane-taped to window. Brush shellac on plastic; smooth on 1st shape. Apply shellac between each successive tissue shape & on top. Allow to dry. Trim plastic around finished design. *Clean* window. Smooth on finished design. It will remain in place. If corners should at some time begin to peel away, remove design, wash it & window with water & then re-press design to glass.

3. Buy some clear plastic storm window covering; it is sold in 36" & 42" widths & easily cut with scissors. Felt-point pens work beautifully on it. (Vivid hues are obtained by squirting ink from felt point refill-can directly onto plastic.) Crayons give a rough texture; water colors mixed with Knox Gelatin give tints, pastels. To remove ink from an area, dip Q-Tip in shellac thinner & gently rub plastic. Finished compositions are adhered to classroom windows with double stick cellophane tape. You might mat small compositions & stand them along a window ledge.

Door. A cheerful Santa can greet visitors to your class. Tagboard or light tan (pink) construction paper is used for face. Score along & beneath eyebrows. Cut out eyeholes & make a slit along either side of nose. Pink cheeks are gently curved outward & then glued in place. Beard & hair are curled by gently pulling each paper strip along blade of scissors. Shaggy eyebrows, hair, & beard are glued to face. Eyes are glued behind holes. Red mouth is glued on the beard & a bushy mustache completes face. Bright pink,

orange or red paper is used for Santa's hat. White trim completes your paper sculpture. (Another paper Santa idea appears in "Let's

Have Fun," a free booklet copyrighted in 1966 by The Borden Co.)

Language Arts

Note: Check with your principal before presenting the following creative writing lesson as it could be considered too religious by some standards.

Have the children write stories based on the following:

"Each of the Animals Brought the Baby Jesus a Gift on His Birthday" (i.e., "Friendly Beasts"). Choose any animal, bird, fish, reptile, & tell about his gift & the travels he made to deliver it to the stable on Christmas Eve. VARIATION: Each child chooses & writes his impressions of an object that was present on the 1st Xmas, e.g., the star, the road, the straw, the inn, the barn, the night, a camel's saddle, frankincense, myrrh, gold, a piece of clothing worn by a Wise Man.

"Why We Use (or Have)_____at Christmas." Each child chooses an object & invents an imaginary historical background, developing this into a creative writing story. A list such as the following (in mimeo form, or written on the front board, may facilitate getting started): angel-hair, bells, holly, candles, wreaths, candy canes, fruit cake. Later you might briefly describe to the class actual historical data, comparing it with the stories they have written; an interesting tape-recording could be developed from the combined materials.

One day, as a change-of-pace activity, bring in a huge gift-wrapped cardboard box. Have young children suggest by pantomime (older students might write a descriptive paragraph) just what they think is in the box. (Contents? Tiny candy-canes for the class.)

Very young children may write about, or dictate to you, a story based on "The Time I Rode in Santa's Sleigh!"

An unusual spelling lesson can develop from asking the children to make up individual gift lists. These are handed in, & while you are correcting any misspelled words you can also be noting the specific phonetic review needed by each student. Any misspelled words become personal (extra credit) Spelling Words for the week.

The most frequently misspelled Holiday words: wreath, sleigh, icicles, poinsettia, reindeer, mistletoe, Bethlehem, creche, nativity, myrrh, frankincense, Jerusalem.

Etymology. "Angel" is from the Greek *angellos,* a messengeɪ or herald.

"Carol" stems from the Greek *choraules* (*choros* dance & *aulos* flute), which meant a flute player who accompanied the Greek choral dances.

"Christmas" is the celebration *maesse,* the Anglo-Saxon word for rite or celebration of Christ's birth.

"Creche" is a French word meaning crib.

"Noel" is also French, coming from the Latin *natalis* which means birthday.

"Poinsettia": This bright Christmas flower (which is actually tiny yellow flowers surrounded by brilliant red leaves) is a native of Mexico. It is named for Joel Poinsett who, when he was a special minister to Mexico, found it & brought it back to America.

"Xmas": the Greek letter *X* or *Chi* stands for "Christ" & so "Xmas" is an abbreviated spelling of "Christmas."

Yule is *Jol,* the Norse word for the Xmas feast, originally a pagan festival held at winter solstice. "Yule" was also influenced by the Latin *jocus* which means "a time of happy talking"!

> *Riddles:* What Xmas tree keeps you warm? (A fir tree.) What do we have in December that we have in no other month? (The letter *D.*) Which one of your toes can you never stub? (Your mistleTOE.) What do you fill every morning & empty every night except once a year, when it is filled at night & emptied in the morning? (A stocking.) What are some girls' names that you'll always find in a Xmas song book? (Carol, Merry, Angel, Holly, Joy, Noel, Chris, Bell[e], Beth [lehem].) What parts of the North Pole are in the United States? (The *N, T,* & *E.*) When does the postman bring you 29 letters in ONE envelope? (When he brings you a M-E-R-R-Y C-H-R-I-S-T-M-A-S A-N-D H-A-P-P-Y N-E-W Y-E-A-R card!)

Christmas Poetry

> Let's dance and sing and make good cheer,
> For Christmas comes but once a year.
>
> G. McFarren (prior to 1580)
>
> I heard the bells on Christmas Day
> Their old familiar carols play,
> And wild and sweet

The words repeat
Of peace on earth, good-will to men!
H.W. Longfellow

Also appropriate: "Carol of the Brown King" by Langston Hughes.

Christmas Reading

Try reading "The Christmas Mouse" (E. Wenning, Holt Publishing Co., 1959, $3.50) aloud to your middle-graders. It's entertaining & also explains the history of the carol "Silent Night." Older students may enjoy "A Child's Christmas in Wales," (as read) by Dylan Thomas. Some background & vocabulary build-up (i.e., jelly babies, etc.) will be most helpful.

Social studies topic suggestions. The manufacture of candles, the difference between mass-produced & individually created products, the production of stained-glass windows, Church Arts, a study of toys (their history & present-day counterparts; children each design a toy, e.g., jack-in-the-box), Xmas Tree Farms.

Christmas Math

Many children travel during the holidays. On the front board list the distances each child expects to travel. Let the children compute total mileage, (then you add your proposed mileage to list), average distance, greatest distance, shortest distance, 2nd greatest & shortest distances.

Let older students design & make tree decorations using ONLY pencil, compass, ruler, French curve, scissors & paper. Let children INVENT.

Help your class learn about postal rates for cards, packages, air-mail & parcel-post, & the meanings of 1st, 2nd & 3rd class mails. Have the children figure out various postage costs & then compare these in order to learn the most efficient way to dispatch their mail.

One day, for variety, let your class practice estimating by playing "Competent Consumers F.O.R.N." (Friends of Ralph Nader). To prepare for this game, cut out large pictures (from mail-order catalogs or magazines) of toys, food, tools, cars, books, furniture, appliances, sporting goods, musical instruments & pictures that illustrate a service, e.g., movies, gas, electricity, telephone, shoe-repair, water. Paste each picture to a piece of 9" x 12" tagboard. Beneath each picture indicate price of item (average monthly cost for a service). Mask-out price from view. Now children form "families" of 5-6 students (or "companies" of 10-12 students). You advise each group of its monthly income and the amount it may spend. A "salesman" holds up 1 of the tagboard cards & calls for estimates. Each family (or company) 1st discusses if they can AFFORD item & then each of group who wishes to is allowed 1 written guess at the cost. Price is then unmasked & item is awarded to the group whose bid was most nearly correct. At end of game children total up amount they "have spent that month." A "Competent Consumer" badge is awarded each member of the group with the most products or services (within their given budget). By playing this game, children become aware of how a toy may cost as much as a pair of shoes, a refrigerator costs less than a color T.V., & how a monthly income will go just so far.

Gingerbread for 45

15 cups flour	1 ²/₃ cups salad oil	3 tsp. cloves
1¼ cups sugar	5 tsp. ginger	5 tsp. salt
4 cups molasses	5 tsp. cinnamon	raisins or red hots
5 eggs	5 Tbsp. baking powder	for decoration

Children measure, sift & mix ingredients.
Chill dough well (15-25 min.).

Each child writes his name on a slip of paper & then receives a piece of wax paper for his desk top & a bit of flour. Using a large knife, cut dough into appropriate number of pieces. Once his hands are washed & his sleeves pushed up, each child gets a lump of chilled dough. Advise children to make men rather thin as fat men do not bake evenly. As each gingerbread man is completed, it is decorated with raisins or red hots & is transferred to an oiled baking sheet & the name tag is slipped under an edge of the man. Bake at 325° to 350° for 8-15 minutes depending on thickness of men. (Recipe may be halved.)

Christmas Science

The theory of electric currents can be demonstrated if you bring 2 strings of tree lights to class—a single strand (all bulbs go out when bulb burns out) & a double wire type. Electricity must make a complete circuit, a round-trip. The double set of wires gives electricity a round-trip to each bulb, while the complete circuit of the single-strand is interrupted whenever a single bulb burns out.

Christmas botany. American *holly* grows naturally from Massachusetts to Florida. In some places it reaches a height of 50'. At nurseries holly berries are sown & covered with mulch, & in the spring of the 2nd year the seeds germinate. Holly is evergreen, shedding its leaves every 3rd year.

Mistletoe. This is a parasitic air-plant growing on a host tree & manufacturing its own food. The roots of an air plant anchor it to the host tree; specialized rootlets of mistletoe delve into tissues of the host, drawing a water (& mineral) supply from it.

Christmas trees. *Balsam fir* has a symmetrical shape & its needles remain green even when dry. Its needles stay firmly attached, as they are arranged spirally on twigs & have no joints, brackets, at their bases. Its cones stand erect on the boughs, giving a candle-like effect. *White spruce,* while living, retains its bluish-green needles for 7 to 10 years! Once cut, it begins to shed. *Cedar* has short, scale-like needles. Long-needled pines are sometimes also used at Xmas.

This is a fine time for the children to work together on a class project such as "a gift for the birds." Such a lesson can induce quiet, thoughtful working conditions that may initiate meaningful ecological discussions. Consider for what type of birds you are making your tree & which of the following suggestions are appropriate fare for your birds:

Pine cones dipped in melted suet & rolled in seeds.
  Strings of popcorn.
  Balls of peanut butter, fat & seeds.
  Stale bread dipped in honey.

These are tied to the branches of a living or dried tree or bush. Incidentally, this is a traditional Christmas activity in Norway.

A Few Thoughts on Christmas Art

Year after year in their school experience, children have a Christmas Art curriculum; try to develop plans which will alleviate boring repetitions. What symbolic material comes with Christmas? Choose a symbol & explore its meanings & possibilities for use in the curriculum. What visual elements are especially a part of Christmas? How can these be used in developing sensitivity?

When choosing gift or decoration projects for your class, be critical of the possibilities afforded for individuality of expression. Ask yourself if the project will give deeper meaning or understanding of old symbols—or is it more likely to perpetuate the cliché? Finally, what is the value of a "clever" idea when it is the teacher who initiated it?

Christmas Tree Ornaments. These ornaments may also be hung from light fixtures or along window casing or used to form a bulletin board display. Of course, in all cases, they should not be distracting to your class.

Stars. Easy star: accordion fold a 10" strip of paper (or a paper soda straw) into 9 equal folds. Glue ends together, forming star. Insert thread through a small hole in topmost point of star.

Five-pointed star.

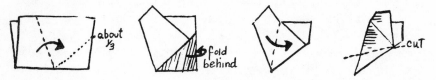

Six-pointed star. Fold a circle in half, fold this in half again. Fold this quarter of a circle into thirds. Cut on a slant as shown.

Any star at this point may have tiny holes & lacy edges cut, making snowflakes instead of stars.

Foam rubber snowflakes. Pattern is transferred to sheet of thin foam rubber (available at surplus stores). Cut out design.

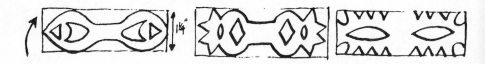

Fold lengthwise & cut out centers of designs. Using 4" lengths of wire or thread, bind 3 or 4 foam strips together at their centers.

Glitter may be adhered to finished snowflake with white glue. *Starbursts.* Cut several circles, 2" in diameter, from foil. Pinch foil at 1 side & crease to center of circle. Bring opposite side of circle over & lay atop crease, forming 2 small cone shapes. Join several of these shapes together by passing thread through points & pulling to form starburst cluster. VARIATION: Cut 3" diameter circles of foil or metallic paper. Fold in 1/2 vertically & horizontally & slantwise. Open circle out flat again. Cut along each crease to within 1/2" of the center of circle. Use pencil to make points of stars as shown. Thread through centers forming a cluster or starburst. VARIATION: Use 3" squares instead of circles. Fold in 1/2 vertically & horizontally ONLY. Continue as with circle starburst, making 1" slits from center top, bottom & left & right sides.

Hanging strands. From white paper cut small circles, bells, trees, or diamonds. Cut 2 identical shapes of each form. Fold each shape down the center. Apply paste to 1/2 of each shape & press 2 identical shapes together, forming a 3-sided figure. When dry, shapes are strung together using a long needle & thread. Hang strands so that they may gently twirl.

Beeswax ornaments from Mexico. Cut a basic shape from thin cardboard (star, bell, moon). Lay a sheet of beeswax atop cardboard, shape, & using your thumbnail (or a tableknife) gently trim wax to follow outline of cardboard. Soften wax slightly by placing it in the sun or near a heater & then press firmly onto cardboard shape. Using various colors of thin yarn & beginning at the outer edge of ornament, press yarn onto wax, eventually filling entire area. Wax may be re-warmed occasionally to facilitate adherence of yarn. Pattern should be uniform & variations in color of yarn used will create an intricate design.

Fish. Trace fish onto sheet of soft aluminum (sold at hardware, lumber stores). Cut 2 slits behind eyes. Fold in 1/2 lengthwise & bend each little strip down & forward. Also bend each 1/2 of tail a bit forward.

Danish string of bells. Trace pattern onto foil. Cut slits & curl paper around, forming bell-shapes. Glue paper in place. String of bells can be any length you wish. Size of bells may be varied also.

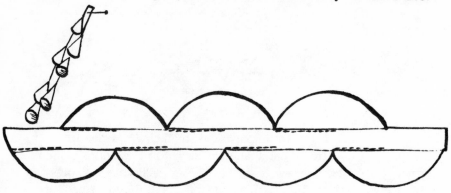

Dove. Insert body into wings. Let children design their own dove shapes.

 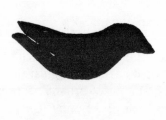

VARIATION: Wings of 1-piece dove may be slightly bent in opposite directions. Again, let children come up with their own personal bird shapes; variety will be pleasant.

Swedish angel. Cut shape out of white paper. Curve & tape dress back, forming skirt. Gently bend arms forward so that hands

appear to hold trees upright. Adhere wings to center of angel's back. Bend wings slightly forward. Unless enlarged, this angel had best be presented to older children with good small-muscle control.

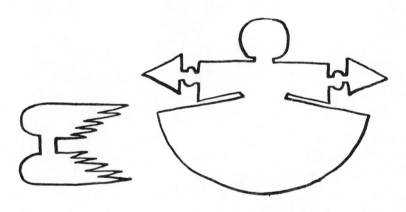

Snowy ornaments. Cut shapes from cardboard. Coat each with plastic starch. Shake in paper bag filled with soap flakes. Allow shapes to dry thoroughly before hanging.

Lasting Creations. For *a lasting ornament* which will be used each Xmas: Each child designs a basic shape (approx. 3" x 5"), e.g., snowman, toy, farm animal, bell, angel, etc. You cut these shapes from plywood, faithfully reproducing their original design. A jigsaw is used to cut plywood; each child sands his cut-out shape & then carefully paints it. Glitter may be sparingly used. If poster paints are used, the ornaments, when dry, may be sprayed with a protective coating of clear plastic.

Teacher's dowel-tree can be used each year in the classroom. May display ornaments made by children or God's Eyes interspersed with bright year tassels or bells—or Peppar Kakor, the thin crisp ginger cookies which the Swedes traditionally hang on just such a tree each Xmas. They also tie the trunk with a large bright bow, spear an apple on the end of each branch & festoon the top with a cluster of golden wheat stalks.

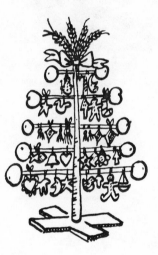

Gifts. *Teacher's gift to class.* Take your class caroling one evening (visit a local nursing home), & wind up at your house for hot chocolate & doughnuts.

Give the children a handmade piñata (as described in Christmas party suggestions later in this chapter).

Present your class with a set of holiday puzzles to be used during free time. Rubber cement a Xmas picture to tagboard. Press beneath books until dry. Paint the back of each puzzle with a different primary color to facilitate identification of pieces. Cut tagboard into pieces; each puzzle is kept in a hosiery box with a lid painted to match identifying color of puzzle it holds.

Class gift to school's principal &/or secretary. Candy or cooky-making can incorporate lessons in measurements, heat, & the action of leavening. Classroom cookery suggestions at the back of this book may be of help in preparing for this project. You might choose one of the recipes there or use the following gift recipe:

Toasted Coconut Chips

Pierce the eyes of fresh coconuts & drain off juice. Heat nuts in 300° oven for 1 hour. When cool, tap nuts with hammer until they crack into large pieces. Pry out meat, leaving brown skin on meat, & thinly slice with carrot peeler, the slicing side of a grater, or a slicing machine. Lay chips on cooky sheets & bake in a 200° oven for 2 hours or until chips are tan & crisp. Stir occasionally during baking. Sometimes an additional 1-1 1/2 hours baking time is required. Pack chips in airtight jars & wrap festively.

Children's gifts to parents. It seems wise to ask yourself if the gifts to be made by your class are appropriate, if they are likely to be used. Each child should have the joy of seeing that his gift is appreciated by his parents. Therefore, it helps to inquire as to how many children *have* fireplaces before making a gift for the hearth; avoid making ash trays in view of good health training & non-smoking parents. Personalize the gift: make it something that can be used each Christmas, something that will become a family tradition, e.g., an ornament, paper sculpture (see Bakers Clay recipe & suggestions at back of book), or a card that contains a Polaroid photo of the child. Have an easy-to-make substitute for the exceptional child who loses or breaks (or "hates") his gift at the last moment.

Classroom recipe books. Each child brings 1 of his mother's favorite recipes to class; variety should be encouraged. According to the abilities of the class, the teacher may (1) fold mimeograph master sheets in half & copy a recipe at the top of each side, leaving space at the bottom of each half for the contributing child's own signature & an appropriate drawing if he likes; or (2) have each child copy his recipe onto a paper which is checked for accuracy & spacing. If it is correct, it is transferred by the child to half of a mimeo master sheet. A second student will copy his recipe on the remaining half. Each signs his name at the bottom of his recipe & draws a picture of his mother, the reader, or of himself preparing the recipe in the kitchen, etc. A master-sheet bearing title page information is also designed & written up: "Our Christmas Recipe Book—Written by Miss Arter's Third Grade Class of River School, Christmas, 1973." Mimeos of the recipes & title page are run off for each student (& a few extras for your school librarian, the wife of your principal, etc.). Simple tagboard covers, secured by 2 brads, are added to the folded pages, completing your gift recipe books. In their free time, children may add color to illustrations.

Hot-dish trivet (a quick gift). Each child needs 15 ice cream bar sticks & a thick piece of cardboard. Eight of the sticks are painted with poster paints. When dry, the sticks are laid, alternating painted & unpainted, across the cardboard, forming a rectangle. Cardboard is cut to the size of this rectangle. Sticks are glued in place with milk glue. Weight is applied to trivet until it is completely dry. A light coat of clear plastic may be sprayed onto finished trivets.

Soap dish (for an easy gift). Neatly cut off the bottom sections of rectangular plastic detergent bottles. An awl is heated & used to make 5 holes for drainage in the bottom of each soap dish. Enamel paints may be used to add stars or polka dots around the edge of each dish. A bar of handmade soap might be a nice accompaniment.

Lemon soap. Mix 2 cups white soap flakes & 1/4 cup water. Add yellow food coloring & several drops of oil of lemon essence. Knead until well blended. Mold into lemon shape, packing tightly. Set aside to harden. A.F.S.C.

Key chain (another quickie)—for older children. Each child brings a smooth, interesting stone or shell to class. A light coat of shellac or clear nail polish may be applied to bring out deeper colors. Each stone or shell is snugly wrapped about with copper wire. On top is left a loose end, from which an inexpensive little key chain is securely attached.

Cryst-L Craze* bud vase. The children collect & bring to class

---

*Cryst-L Craze® spray is manufactured by Fry Plastic International Inc., Los Angeles 3, Calif.

a variety of interesting glass bottles. "Cryst-L Craze" is a relatively inexpensive solution sold in hobby shops. Following the directions on the bottle, the children can transform throw-away bottles into quite lovely vases. Re-cycling begins at school!

Tree ornament (for very young children). Teacher cuts out basic angel shapes from felt. Children choose fabric scraps, gold braid, buttons & yarn & decorate their angels. Glue the decorations firmly in place with milk glue. Weight is applied until angels are completely dry. Each child writes his name & the date in pencil along the bottom of his angel. Teacher machine stitches embroidery along name & date using bright colored thread—or you might use a fine pointed felt-tip pen.

Rose sachet. Have children gather & bring to class rose petals, geranium leaves, lavender. Spread these out to dry in a warm place. Using a dietetic scale, each child (if possible) weighs out the following: 4 oz. dried rose petals; 1 oz. dried lavender; 1 oz. geranium leaves; 2 oz. (granular) orrisroot; 1/2 oz. ground cloves; 1 oz. (granular) patchouli; 1 oz. benzoin (broken up). Mix these ingredients well by shaking them in a small paper bag, then spoon mixture into tiny silk squares. Gather up 4 corners & secure firmly with a pretty ribbon. Each sachet should be compact & NOT loose. (Makes 6 sachets.)

A gift for the hearth. Pine-cones tossed into a log-burning fire produce colorful flames. Have children collect & bring to class dried pine cones & small dry pine branches. Cones are dipped into a solution made by dissolving 1 T. of solid glue in 1 gallon of hot water. Skim out the cones & while they're still moist & hot, sprinkle generously with powdered chemicals:

For red flames: strontium nitrate
For bright green: borax
For orange: calcium chloride
For apple green: barium nitrate
For blue: copper sulphate
For emerald: copper nitrate
For yellow: common table salt
For purple: lithium chloride

Dry cones on newspapers for several days.

Easy gift wrap for cones, wood. The dried cones are put in new medium-sized brown paper bags. Neatly fold over opening & staple shut. Features of deer or bird are drawn directly on sack with felt tip pens. Cardboard appendages are painted, taped in place (brown paper tape works well). Deer's antlers are 2 appropriately shaped twigs.

Gift Wrapping Ideas. Other gift wrapping ideas include *marbleized paper.* Fill shallow (cooky sheet) pan with water. Mix left-over oil paints, enamels or lacquers with their thinners. Keep a bit of thinner in reserve for cleaning of pan. By snapping wrist or tapping brush, drop or spatter oils onto surface of water. If color immediately spreads out, you have added too much thinner. Stir water gently with a toothpick, causing a slight swirling of paint. Place sheet of paper lightly atop water, remove paper, "peeling" it off the water. Allow paper to dry face up on a flat newspaper-covered surface. Should globs of paint stick to paper, refusing to dry, you need to add more thinner to oil mixture. Two or more colors of paint may be used or a little bronzing can be sprinkled on the water (with a small salt shaker). The resulting papers are similar to those used as the end papers of books in the 19th century.

Hand holding gift. Each child wraps a tiny gift (i.e., key chain) in plain white or colored tissue. Child then traces around his hand on pink construction paper or tagboard. Hand is cut out & made to "grasp" gift. Double-stick tape or rubber cement holds hand in position.

Double-edged greeting. Wrap gift in a box covered with a solid color paper. Child writes "Greetings" in large letters along folded edge of a rectangular piece of paper. Bottoms of letters will touch fold. Letters are then cut around, always leaving some of the fold intact. The centers of the letters *G, E, & S* are cut out. Open out piece of paper. Adhere double-edged greeting to top of package. This idea can also be used on a card. A few sequins can be glued around edges of "Greetings." Older students will have the control of their scissors that is essential for this project.

Snowflake doily. Fold a round paper doily (according to the directions given for cutting a 6-pointed star, page 110). Starting at curved edge, cut INTO doily. Open out snowflake & glue atop gift package.

Cards or program covers (see "Jan. Printmaking" for other ideas). A handmade card is a thoughtful gesture to extend to your Room Mother & any other persons whom the children wish to remember at this time.

Standard greetings include: Joy; Peace; Noel; Rejoice; Season's Cheer; Happy Holiday; Glad Tidings; Yuletide Greetings. Children can be counted on to come up with personalized expressions of good cheer.

Card shape variations:

Gesso clay: Apply with a brush atop fine line pencil drawing. Gesso is diluted plaster of Paris & as such may be tinted appropriate colors. It may also be trailed from a squeeze bottle in intricate arabesque designs directly onto folded card. Rough textured paper (oatmeal paper) works well. Allow design to dry completely. Children may experiment with bronzing powder, blowing it on wet gesso. Dry designs may be lightly spray-shellacked for added protection.

Pine Print. Paint a small short-needled piece of pine with thick white poster paint. Press the pine carefully & firmly against a piece of dark green or blue paper folded into card form. Sprinkle print with mica.

Face in the window. Take snapshots of your students. Cut each photo to approx. 2" x 2" (including the head & torso of child). Hand out 7" x 8" sheets of tan tagboard. Pictures of varying house facades may be displayed. Have each child fill tagboard with a large detailed drawing of a house at Xmas time, including windows, one of which is 2" x 2". Houses are painted & carefully cut out. Photo of child is rubber cemented atop 2" x 2" window so that child appears to be looking out in greeting. Written date, message, signature may be added on back of card.

Inkblot Santa. Each child dips a big soft-haired brush into a rather weak solution of white poster paint. Tiny (2" x 2") pink construction paper cards are used. By touching brush to card, applying gentle pressure, dragging brush down, to left & up, a fat shape is produced with one sweep of the brush. Details are added with black felt-point pens. A wide variety of expressions should be the result.

Angels. Each child designs a simple angel (one that is flying) & cuts it out of a piece of inner tube which is then adhered to a hand-sized wooden block. Printing ink is applied to angel (using brayer) & angel is firmly pressed against folded card. Let children experiment with their prints; e.g., a slit is made above & below angel's hand and something is inserted. VARIATION: Each child stamps his angel somewhere on a bulletin board that is covered with light blue paper. A few soft cloud shapes are added. Each child, in his own way, designs & prepares a message of glad tidings for his angel to hold. This completed board becomes a classroom greeting. VARIATION (for older students): Each child folds in half, lengthwise, a piece of 3 1/2" x 5" gold foil-backed Japanese paper. Using sharp pointed scissors, the child makes cuts similar to those shown in the paper. Top corners are rounded off, paper is unfolded & glued atop a neutral colored card, e.g., oatmeal paper.

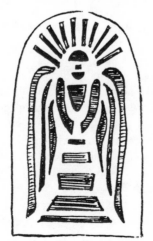

Xmas Music

In France they call Christmas songs "noels." In England & America they are called Christmas carols. The word "carol" comes from the Greek word meaning "to dance"; a true carol has a religious theme that is treated in a familiar, happy manner. Some of our Xmas songs are hymns rather than carols, e.g., "O, Little Town of Bethlehem," "It Came Upon a Midnight Clear." Carols date back to the 13th century (see Christmas Walls, page 102).

Historical backgrounds of 12 Xmas songs. What are some ways that your class might (re)-interpret this information?

Adestes Fideles: Origin unclear; scholars have spent years investigating 2 different claims—that it is Portugese & that it is English.

Away in a Manger: The German, Martin Luther, is said to have written this for his child.

Deck the Halls: Welsh; a very old melody which Mozart used for a piano-violin duet.

God Rest Ye Merry Gentlemen: English, traditional old song.

Good King Wenceslaus: Monarch of Bohemia, 928-935, this kind man was generous to the poor, especially on Dec. 26, the feast of St. Stephen. Carol, thought to be of Swedish origin, was 1st published in 1582.

I Heard the Bells on Christmas Day: This was written by Henry Wadsworth Longfellow at the time when America was involved in the tragic Civil War; peace on earth had, therefore, a special significance to Longfellow when he was composing this carol.

I Saw 3 Ships: English, traditional. Probably written in the 2nd half of the 15th century.

Joy to the World: Isaac Watts wrote this in 1719 when religion was at a low ebb in England. He paraphrased verses from the 98th Psalm & used music from Handel's *Messiah.*

O Little Town of Bethlehem: Phillips Brooks, a famous minister of Boston, promised his pupils a new Christmas song for the holiday. By Saturday he still had no song written. During the night he awoke. Suddenly a melody had come to him. He jotted it down & returned to bed. The next day he taught this new song to his children.

The Wassail Song: One of the oldest of carols. "Wassail" comes from the Anglo-Saxon "we shel" ("to be healthy"), & was used long ago as a toast ("To your health!").

The First Noel: French or English, it is the tune of medieval shepherds.

We Three Kings (1857); & It Came Upon A Midnight Clear: American.

Tell your class the story of *The Nutcracker Suite.* Let them hear excerpts from it while they paint.

Play Gian-Carlo Menotti's *Amahl & the Night Visitors.* Let the children follow the words being sung on the record by reading along with it a mimeo of the script of this opera. Discuss with the class how they might use this record as the basis of a puppet show to be presented to other classes or the sick ward of a local hospital—an appropriate gesture of thoughtfulness at this time of year. Take photos of the children involved in this activity & display these during Open House.

December P.E.

Your Left & My Right. Children are divided into pairs, all of which comprise 2 teams. Each pair of teammates is given a box, some wrapping paper (or newspaper) & ribbon or yarn, with instructions "to wrap the present." The only catch is that 1 child may use only his left hand & his partner may use only his right while cooperating in wrapping their package. Discuss, prior to playing, how class might insure that each player will use just 1 hand. The first team to successfully wrap all of its presents is the winner.

December Puppet

Quick Santa finger puppets. Each child designs his own Santa using a 3 1/2" Styrofoam ball for head, felt for hat & features, & yarn for hair & beard. Red corduroy is cut on the bias for his suit. White glue (or 2 straight pins) is used to adhere hat to head, facial features & head to suit, & edges of corduroy together. A little jingle bell may be sewn to the front of his suit, & a yarn tassel completes his cap.

Holiday Parties

Avoid chaos by being especially well-organized this month

Entertainment. Hand out to each child a paper on which the same sprig of holly has been mimeographed. Children make up original pictures incorporating the holly outline in any way they like; paper may be used in any direction. The class might enjoy sharing & comparing the variety of results.

Present relay. Children stand in 2 (or more) lines. Each child must run to a chair or table on which there is a "gift." He must un-tie, unwrap, re-wrap, & re-tie the gift. Then he runs back to his line, tagging 2nd player who repeats above activity.

A Mexican-inspired piñata. A piñata made from a heavy duty, double-thickness brown paper bag works well & it is quick to make. Its only drawback is that it usually rips when struck, rather than bursting apart.

Older children especially like the feeling of striking a more solid piñata. A corrugated cardboard box can be made into an animal piñata which offers a bit more resistance to the "swinger." Put a trap door in the bottom of a cardboard box. After filling the cavity with small inexpensive wrapped gifts, candy & gum, tape trap door shut. This door should fall open after a couple of direct hits by the blindfolded child. Box can be decorated to resemble a bird or animal. Rolled newspaper serves as a base for neck, legs, wings, or arms; use staple or masking-tape to fasten these in place. Fold crepe or tissue paper (10-12 layers) & cut long strips. Along edge of each strip cut many short vertical snips. Pull strips apart; glue them 2 at a time about body of piñata, overlapping cut edge atop uncut edge to achieve a feathered effect.

Spread blanket on the playground under a basketball hoop.

Piñata, firmly tied to a rope, is strung over the basketball hoop. Class stands behind edge of blanket out of range of blindfolded child who attempts to break the dangling pinata which you lower & raise by slackening & pulling on rope. When, after several tries, he is not successful, a new child is blindfolded & given the bat (or broomstick) with which he strikes at the piñata. Once smashed, the piñata spills its contents & the children rush forward to collect them.

Party place mats. These also make an interesting border design (for above chalkboard) in January when you return & the room is bare. So have the children make 2: one for the party & one for the border.

Each child folds 1 segment of "Tree-Saver" (recycled paper) or paper toweling in half & thoroughly moistens it with water. Excess water is carefully squeezed out. Towel is opened out flat. It is folded in half crosswise & then in half lengthwise. Then it is folded into a triangle as shown: Design is begun at pointed end.

With water colors children paint different types of lines across folded paper. Dots, stars, hearts, crosses may be added. Undo 1 fold & check to see if paint is sinking through. If the lines are too faint, they are carefully re-traced afresh. Undo a second fold & repeat process of re-painting, if necessary. Towel is opened out flat & allowed to dry.

Refreshments. The children would probably enjoy preparing their own refreshments (see Classroom Cookery, e.g., Nut Log) & this activity could take the place of exchanging purchased gifts. The money that would have been spent in that way could be collected & used for a charitable cause. (Save the Children Federation: Boston, Post Rd., Norwalk, Conn. 06852.) This is in keeping with the meaning of Christmas.

• **Birth of Louis Pasteur   [27]**

Pasteur discovered in the 19th century that fermentation could be prevented if a liquid were exposed to extremely high temperatures. Milk that has been treated this way is called PASTEURized!

January

January brings the snow,
Makes your feet and fingers glow.

1   New Year's Day.
    Bartolome Murillo (1617-1682), Spanish painter.
    Paul Revere (1735-1818), American patriot.
    Betsy Ross (1752-1836), maker of 1st U.S. flag.
    Lincoln issued Emancipation Proclamation, 1863.
3   Lucretia Mott (1793-1880), antislavery & women's suffrage
    leader.
4   Jakob Grimm (1785-1863), German author & collector of
    fairy tales.
5   George Washington Carver probably born on this date
    (1864-1943), American botanist.
6   Joan of Arc (1412-1431), French heroine.
    Carl Sandburg (1878-1967), American poet.
7   1st U.S. Presidential election, 1789.
    Millard Fillmore (1780-1874), 13th President.
9   Carrie Chapman Catt (1859-1947), American suffragist.
10 1st United Nations General Assembly, London 1946.
11 Alexander Hamilton (1755-1804), American statesman.
    William James (1842-1910), American psychologist, phi-
    losopher.
12 Charles Perrault (1628-1703), French author *(Cinderella,*
    Sleeping Beauty).

    John Hancock (1737-1793), 1st signer of the Declaration of
    Independence.

Jack London (1876-1916), American author *(Call of the Wild).*

John Singer Sargent (1856-1925), American painter.

14   Benedict Arnold (1741-1801), U.S. Revolutionary War traitor.

Albert Schweitzer (1875-1965), French doctor, philosopher.

15   Moliere (1622-1673), French writer of comedies.

Martin Luther King (1929-1968), American civil rights leader, winner of Nobel Peace Prize.

17   Benjamin Franklin (1706-1790), American inventor, statesman.

18   Daniel Webster (1782-1852), American statesman.

A.A. Milne (1882-1956), English author *(Winnie the Pooh).*

19   James Watt (1736-1819), Scottish inventor.

Robert E. Lee (1807-1870), Commander in Chief of Confederate Army, Civil War.

Edgar Allen Poe (1809-1849), American author *(The Telltale Heart).*

Paul Cezanne (1839-1906), French post-impressionist painter.

20   Inauguration Day: every 4 years U.S. President takes oath of office.

Andre Ampere (1775-1836), French physicist (developed science of electrodynamics).

American Revolution ended, 1783, after lasting 8 years.

Josef Hofmann (1876-1957), Polish-American composer.

21   Stonewall Jackson (1824-1863), Confederate general: Civil War.

1st Atomic submarine, "Nautilus," launched by U.S.A., 1954.

22   Lord George Byron (1788-1824), English poet.

Edouard Manet (1832-1883), French impressionist painter.

24   Gold discovered in California, 1848.

25   Dr. Mary Walker received the Congressional Medal of Honor 1866. She is the only woman to have received this honor.

26   Douglas MacArthur (1880-1964), Commander in Chief of Allied Forces in S.W. Pacific, W.W. II.

27   Wolfgang Mozart (1756-1791), Austrian composer.
      Lewis Carroll [Chas. Dodgson] (1832-1898), English author
      (Alice in Wonderland).
      Thomas Edison granted patent on incandescent light: 1880.
28   Jackson Pollock (1912-1956), American abstract-expres-
      sionist painter.
29   Thomas Paine (1737-1809), American Revolution patriot,
      writer.
      William McKinley (1843-1901), 25th President (assassinated
      in his 2nd term).
30   Franklin Delano Roosevelt (1882-1945), 32nd President.
31   Franz Schubert (1797-1828), Austrian composer.
      Explorer I launched 1958; 1st U.S. Earth satellite.

January

The name comes from Latin *Januarius,* after Janus the 2-faced Roman
god who was able to look back into the past &, at the same time, into
the future. Janus also busied himself with the beginnings of all
undertakings. The Romans dedicated this month to Janus by offerings
of meal, wine, salt & frankincense, each of which was new. The
Anglo-Saxons called January "Wulfmonath" because this was the
month in which hunger drove the wolves down into the villages.

JANUARY QUOTATIONS

1   No one ever regards the first of January with indifference.–
      (Charles Lamb)

      The American system of rugged individualism. (Campaign
      speech in New York 10/22/28)–Herbert Hoover

6   Shakespeare, Leonardo da Vinci, Benjamin Franklin &
      Lincoln never saw a movie, heard a radio or looked at
      T.V. They had "loneliness" and knew what to do with it.
      They were not afraid of being lonely because they knew
      that was when the creative mood in them would work.–
      Carl Sandburg

12   Every time I paint a portrait I lose a friend.–*John Singer
      Sargent

*Quoted in *The Treasury of Humorous Quotations* by Herbert V. Prochnow,
Harper & Row Pub. Co., 1969.

15   I have a dream. I have a dream that one day this nation will
      rise up & live out the true meaning of its creed: "We hold
      these truths to be self-evident: that all men are created
      equal". . . . I have a dream that one day in the red hills of
      Georgia, sons of former slaves and sons of former slave
      owners will be able to sit down together at the table of
      brotherhood.—Martin Luther King, Jr. 1929-1968

17   He that can have patience can have what he will.

      Early to bed and early to rise makes a man healthy, wealthy
      and wise.

      A little neglect may breed mischief: for want of a nail the
      shoe was lost; for want of a shoe the horse was lost; and
      for want of a horse the rider was lost.
          ("Maxims"—preface to *Poor Richard's Almanack:* 1732)

A few words about January. When the children return, you
may discuss their vacations by asking them to stop & consider:
"What did you *learn* over the holidays?" Thoughtful answers to
this question could be enlightening & would avoid extensive gift
discussion, the comparison of presents.

Talk about what your class would like to do, accomplish this
year. Do the students suggest any changes in rulings?

During this new year, try to help the children learn to savor
the moment—not always be preparing for "when I grow up." A
similar philosophy is not bad advice for a teacher either!

JANUARY EVENTS

- **New Year's Day**

This marks the beginning of the civil year. The date is
inherited from the Romans; Julius Caesar designated Jan. 1st as
the 1st day of the year, changing it from the traditional date in
early March (near the spring equinox). When the Romans, under
Constantine, accepted Christianity, New Year's Day changed from
a day of feasting to a time of meditation & fasting. Now—and for
the last 300 years—New Year's is, again, a time of feasting &
rejoicing.

Social Studies

On the 1st day back in class, older students are given paper on which they list every major news event they remember as having occurred during the previous year. These lists may be compiled, discussed, used as the basis for a graph giving an overview of historic events of the last months.

Discuss different methods of measuring time (see Page 0). Let each child make a (9" x 12") poster "publicizing" one of the days in January. The date should be shown in large numbers (in the upper left-hand corner); a pertinent quotation, birthdate of famous person, anecdote should be added; & an illustrative collage or drawing will finish this piece of personal propaganda. If research uncovers nothing historically important about a date, the child then supplies an original theme, i.e., a scientific fact, a meteorological comment. These posters are collected & put in chronological order. Each day the new one is posted, adding to that month's hall display.

Language Arts

Discuss "resolutions," their meaning & possible values. Talk about symbols: old Father time & the baby New Year, their clothing, the scythe & hourglass. Consider how in life it is necessary to have opposites, to have the *old* in order to have the *new.*

Talk about the almanac. Is it important today? How? Compare a current (i.e., Farmers') almanac with Poor Richard's. Perhaps the children will want to keep a classroom almanac of room information, anecdotes for Open House visitors.

Vocabulary enrichment words: resolutions, hindsight, fortuitous, predictions, serendipity, valedictory, prophetic, auld lang syne.

Etymology. The Italian word for candy is "confetti." Long ago during the fun-filled carnival days, Italians used to pelt one another with tiny pieces of candy. Then as time passed, little pieces of cardboard were substituted for the candies. Now, centuries later, we throw tiny pieces of paper "confetti" at one another—usually at 12:00 midnight, New Year's Eve!

Riddles: Why is a New Year's Resolution like a mirror? (Because it's so easily broken.) What is it that you can't see on Jan. 1st although it's right in front of you? (The whole new year.) Which travels faster in January: heat or cold? (Heat. It's real easy to catch cold in January!)

New Year's Poetry

> Ring out the old, ring in the new
> Ring happy bells across the snow;
> The year is going, let him go;
> Ring out the false, ring in the true.
>
> —Alfred Lord Tennyson

While the earth remains, seedtime and harvest, cold and heat, summer and winter, day and night, shall not cease. (Genesis 8:22)

New Year's Art

The ancient Romans thought Janus to be so alert & watchful that they kept images of him above their doors to guard their homes. Let the children create their own interpretations of the 2-faced Janus, some of which may become appropriate decorations for your classroom door.

• **Birth of Betsy Ross**   [1]

Mrs. John (Betsy) Ross was an expert seamstress who had an upholstery shop at 329 Arch St., Phila., Pa. George Washington, Robt. Morris & Col. Ross, all members of a committee appointed by Congress, went to Mrs. Ross & gave her a sketch of a proposed design for the American flag. It was Betsy who thought of making the stars 5-pointed. She demonstrated how it could be done with one snip of her scissors! (See Page 110 for directions for re-creating Betsy's demonstration.)

• **1st public demonstration of the telegraph   [6]**

On this day in 1838 Samuel F.B. Morse & Arthur Vail demonstrated the telegraph at the Speedwell Ironworks in Morristown, N.J. The word "telegraph" comes from the Greek *tele* (far away) & *graph* (writing), so it is literally "long distance writing"!

• **Birth of Benjamin Franklin   [17]**

Benjamin Franklin's prospective mother-in-law was hesitant to consent to her daughter's marrying a printer. There already were two printers in the United States & she was not at all certain that the country could support a 3rd. As it turned out, Benjamin Franklin lived to become a prominent statesman, scientist, philosopher, inventor, & writer!

Bulletin board suggestions. Under the title "What Do All

These Things Have in Common?" display pictures of a fire engine, metal rimmed eyeglasses, a copy of *Poor Richard's Almanack,* a library bldg., a Franklin stone, a lightning rod.

Across your room string a clothesline high enough up so as not to be distracting. From it hang sayings by Franklin (i.e.: Man is a tool-making animal; Time is money; God helps them that help themselves; Don't leave for tomorrow what you can do today; A penny saved is a penny earned; In this world nothing is certain but death and taxes). Such a display may lead to a discussion of cliches (their cause & significance & possible correction) that upper graders might enjoy.

Etymology. The Greeks knew that when amber was rubbed it became magnetic. Because friction could make amber give off tiny sparks, the Greeks named amber *electron* from *elector:* the beaming sun. *Electron* became the Latin *electrum* from which we have our word "electricity"!

Riddles: What did Benjamin Franklin say when he discovered electricity in lightning? (Nothing, he was too *shocked* for words.)

Fun with electricity. Ask the electric power company if your class may see a lightning arrester & be given an explanation of how it works. Explain how to read the electric light meter. Have the children read theirs on the 1st & last days of 2 months & then estimate the family light bills for these months. Explain why fuses blow, how to change a blown fuse (why NOT to use a penny in place of a fuse), & what measures help prevent blown fuses.

Your class might enjoy reading Franklin's self-written epitaph:

The Body
of
Benjamin Franklin, Printer
(Like the cover of an old book,
Its contents torn out,
And stript of its lettering and gilding,)
Lies here, food for worms
Yet the work itself shall not be lost,
For it will, as he believed, appear once more
In a new
And more beautiful edition
Corrected and Amended
By its Author!

• **Birth of Edgar Allen Poe   [19]**

Write & read to your class an original mystery story. Then show them a list of clues which you have previously written on tagboard or have hidden beneath the pull-down map at the chalkboard. Older children make deductions & write possible solutions to the mystery story.

Bulletin board ideas. Lettering might be in the form of a ransom note, with individual letters cut from magazines & pasted together to form a "warning" or notice.

MYSTERY THEATRE

Fold bright colored pieces (6" x 8") of paper in half length-wise; on the outside print an appropriate vocabulary word (i.e., somber, hypnotic, cataclysmic) or paste a picture to illustrate such a word (i.e., horrific, catatonic, foreboding). On the inside print the definition of the word & its syllabication. These folders are stapled on a bright background beneath title. Children try to guess contents before raising the curtain on each little mystery.

"Can you solve this week's mystery with Detective Don?" Post a short intriguing list of questions on which the children will try their sleuthing techniques. Emphasize the importance of the search (through use of reference books) to solve a mystery. Have 4-5 books (i.e., Guiness Book of World Records, the World Almanac, a science encyclopedia set, etc.) right near (beneath) bulletin board for immediate use in tracking down the answers. Children may also write to Detective Don & ask HIM questions.

• **Birth of James Watt   [19]**

James Watt did not invent the steam engine while watching his mother's tea kettle. He actually conceived the idea while on a Sunday walk shortly after having rebuilt a Newcomen steam engine for the lab at the Univ. of Glasgow. Over a period of 15 years Watt developed an engine that launched a new age.

"History of Horsepower" bulletin board. Power is the rate at which work is being done or the rate at which energy is being spent. Horsepower has no real relationship to an animal's strength or work. What we call "horsepower" is the outcome of experiments that James Watt did with big draft horses over a century ago. He wanted to find the rate at which a horse under average conditions will do his work. He decided on the round number 550 foot pounds of work a second or 33,000 foot pounds a minute. So 1 horse power is the energy it takes to raise weight of 550 lbs. one foot in 1 second. Watt realized that this was a high rate of work for the average horse to maintain over a full day's time. Watt set up the horsepower measuring unit as a means of promoting his engines.

Etymology. The "watt" is a unit of electric power named after James Watt.

A simple steam turbine. Take a syrup can with a tight-fitting lever lid & with a sharp nail bore 2 small (1/10") holes, one on either side of the can & at *an angle to the can.* This may be done by twisting the nail as far as possible to one side after you've driven it through the can. Put 1" of *hot* water in the can & tightly secure lid in place. By strong elastic thread, suspend the can from a button on a cord, as shown. Hang as shown over a candle's flame. Steam escaping from holes sets up a force of reaction which makes can move in opposing directions (e.g., as in a jet plane, the hot gases escaping backwards push the plane forward).

- **Birth of Andre Ampere   [20]**

    The Paris Electrical Congress of 1881 paid tribute to Ampere who had made great contributions to the science of electro magnetism. They named in his honor the current that 1 volt sends through 1 ohm: the "ampere."

- **1st patent by Edison on incandescent light   [27]**

    (Also see Feb. 11.)

    Riddles: What is the best & cheapest light? (Daylight.) Who was the most clever inventor of all times? (Thomas Edison. He invented the radio & the phonograph so people would stay up all night burning his light bulbs!)

JANUARY ACTIVITIES

Now is the time of year to take stock of your relations with your students. You know each student quite well, but it's very enlightening sometimes to listen to a child talk about himself. Give the following Interest Inventory to each of your students either by "interviewing" personally or by having each older student fill out the mimeo-sheet himself. Not all of these questions need be included. You can edit this Inventory to suit your needs.

Name_____ Age_____ Birth-
date_____(good as quick reference for classroom celebrations.)

—What do you want to do (be) when you grow up? Why?
—What is your favorite T.V. program?
—Do you have anything that you feel superstitious about?
—If you could be Teacher, what would we study in Science this month? (I.e., outer space, the physical body, insects, sea life, animals, flowers, science experiments.)
—What's the scariest (most frightening) thing you can imagine? (Or: Tell me something that you think is really scary.)
—If you had $10 to spend in a book store, what kinds of books would you buy—what would they be about?
—If you could be any animal or bird or fish or snake in the whole world, what would you be? Tell me WHY.

   (Note: the answer to this question often affords real insight into the child's self-image.)

—What do you think is the best part about school?
—If you could be Teacher what would you change?
—Is there anything in particular that YOU would like to learn more about this year?

Things to Make for Absentees

During the 1st months of the year, there is often frequent absenteeism. When one of the students in your class is ill, have the children make him something *other* than the perennial raft of get-well cards. Here are some ideas:

Sewing cards. Firmly glue a colorful picture or greeting (Xmas) card onto tagboard. Use a picture that is not too detailed. Outline the main figure with dots about 1" apart. Punch through dots with small-holed paper punch or carefully use a darning needle to do so. With the group of sewing cards include several pieces of bright heavy yarn. Dip the tips of the ends of yarn in shellac & allow to dry hard; this will facilitate the threading of each sewing card.

A flannel board. Tightly stretch a bright piece of solid-colored flannel (less expensive than felt) over a 15" x 20" piece of corrugated cardboard. Firmly adhere flannel's edges to back of cardboard. Now children cut a series of figures or objects from bright felt scraps. These may be the cast & props of a specific fairy tale or they might be various people, things around which the child may build his own stories. The class dictates a letter (which will be enclosed with the flannel board set), explaining how the board is like the child's own personal stage & he can now make up plays using the felt figures.

A yucca-day tree. Each leaf is made by a different child; he colors one side a shade of green & on the other side he writes a riddle, joke or cartoon. To facilitate things, a mimeographed sheet of riddles (see page 139) may be prepared. Cut this sheet apart, giving each child a different riddle to copy. Once the yucca-tree is finished, each child may share his riddle with the rest of the class. Following this, you may give each child a complete mimeo to enjoy on his own.

HERBUS YUCCUS

PicK a leaf when you want a Yuc!

A classmade surprise-ball. This can be appropriate for any age child depending on the surprises you include. Wrap a special little treat (Mexican jumping beans, a tiny clay whistle, jacks & ball) in a piece of cotton. Wind this round with a long thin strip of crepe paper. Continue winding crepe paper around this core. Occasionally wrap a small prize (balloons, coin, gum, tiny plastic toy, a magnet) into the ball. This is a good opportunity to use up any faded crepe paper you may have. When surprise ball contains 10-12 prizes (& little get-well messages written on strips of paper) the end of the last crepe streamer is fastened with a colorful sticker, or finished ball may be made to resemble a funny face.

A Wonder Box. This can be of great comfort to a child with a prolonged illness. Use a good sturdy box. Children cut out small colorful pictures of birds, flowers, insects (pictures that are appropriate for the child who is ill). These pictures are glued, overlapping, on the box & its cover. Every surface of the box is shellacked & allowed to dry. Wrap each of the following in a piece of colorful tissue: sea shells, a magnifying glass, small interesting rocks, a cocoon, a kaleidoscope, a small natural sponge & a package of grass or clover seeds. Place gifts in box. The following note is included with the packet of seeds: "You will find a sponge in this Wonder Box. Soak the sponge in water. Roll it in these seeds. Lay the sponge in a saucer of water & place it in a sunny window. If you keep the sponge VERY WET you will have a lovely green ball that's alive & growing." A get-well chain letter written by the class may accompany the Wonder Box. A.F.S.C.

Language Arts

A classroom serial. If *you* are feeling creative here is an idea to spark the new year, improve listening skills & stimulate creative writing. Each day after lunch read an installment of a class serial which you create. Incorporate occasionally into the story, names of children in your room. You might make the serial in the form of letters or the diary of someone caught in a time-machine or the memoirs of a person held captive by pirates on an unknown island. You may write in the 1st person. Include interesting science information. Don't begin reading the serial until the children are calmed down after re-entering the room after lunch. On days (& these are naturally few) on which you haven't written the continuation, you might bring in an old bottle with a note inside that says, i.e., "Sorry, the next installment has been delayed in the mails," or "Held up due to rain," etc. Once or twice when the children are very involved in the story, let them write the next installment themselves as a creative writing assignment.

Poetry. Let each student choose a color & then describe, in a stream-of-consciousness manner, his impressions of that color. Let him call to mind each of the sounds, smells, sensations, dreams, memories that this color elicits. When sharing the finished pieces, the children should be reminded how poetry often does not rhyme, that a poem tells you something in a beautiful or unusual way, that a poem lets you hear someone's imagination at work.

My Black Friend

Black is a ship, pirates and fun.
Black is night.
Black is a storm.
Black is a tree falling.
Black is blood trickling. . . .
Black smells like a shark washed ashore
And it's rattling.
Black is a person with a knife in her.
Black is BLACK and there is nothing like it.
Black is a dead tree and the lovely aroma of
A rotten whale.*

—Benjie Viljoen (1964)

An interesting bulletin board display can be made of these poems. Have each child make an illustration or collage using ONLY the color (its shades, tones) of his poem.

Roodles of Riddles. One of a myriad of uses of riddles in the classroom. This one is good for filling in those 5 min. pockets of time before dismissal. It may also be a godsend for the substitute teacher. Print riddles in large letters on 8" x 24" pieces of sturdy paper. Children read silently as you hold each card up (answer appears on back). Raised hands are recognized for guessing of answers.

1. What questions can never be answered YES? (Are you asleep? Are you perfect? Are you dead? What does "No" spell?)
2. What questions *make* you answer "YES"? (Are you human? Are you alive? Are you being asked a question? What does Y-E-S spell? Are you awake? Are you reading this? Are you a child?)
3. A barrel weighed 20 lbs. A man put something in it & then it weighed 10 lbs. What did he put in it? (A hole.)
4. If a man is born in Australia, grows up in Africa, comes to America & dies in France, what is he? (Dead.)
5. What famous man in history didn't hang up his clothes at night? (Adam.)
6. What is the best butter in America? (A mountain goat.)

*Printed with the permission of the poet, Ben Viljoen, Jr.

7. What is the smallest bridge in the world? (The bridge of your nose.)
8. What 3 things does a woman look for, but never wants to find? (A run in her stocking, wrinkles, a gray hair.)
9. How many hard-boiled eggs could the giant Goliath eat on an empty stomach? (One, then it wouldn't be empty any more.)
10. Why isn't your nose 12 inches long? (Because then it would be a foot!)
11. How long is a string? (Twice as long as 1/2 its length.)
12. What is yours & yet it's used by others more than by yourself? (Your name.)
13. What goes up & *never* comes down? (Your age.)
14. When is a boy like a pony? (When he's a little hoarse.)
15. What room can you NEVER go into? (A mushroom.)
16. What trembles at each breath of air yet it can bear the heaviest burdens? (Water.)
17. What asks no questions but requires many answers? (The doorbell & the telephone.)
18. Who always goes to bed with his shoes on? (The horse.)
19. What names of people read the same forwards as backwards? (Eve, Anna, Otto, Ava, Hannah.)
20. Name 4 things that never use their teeth for eating? (A comb, a gear, a zipper, a saw.)
21. What has a mouth & never eats? (A river, a pitcher, a jar.)
22. What fruit, plants will not grow in good rich soil? (Taffy *apples,* caramel *corn, cotton* candy, jelly *beans.*)
23. What's a good place to go when you're broke? (To work.)
24. Unable to think, unable to speak, yet it tells the truth to the whole world. What is it? (A mirror, or good bathroom scales.)
25. What can you keep, even after you've given it to somebody else? (A smile, a promise, your name & address, a cold or the flu.)
26. What has never been felt, seen or heard—in fact, it's never existed & yet it has a name? ("Nothing.")
27. What can be written in 3 syllables, yet contains 26 letters? (The word "alphabet.")
28. What's invisible yet never out of sight? (The letter "i.")
29. What's the best way to carry water in a sieve? (Freeze it first.)
30. Add 10 to nothing & what kind of animal will it make (Ox.)
31. Why does a maroon car never pay a bridge toll? (Because the driver pays it!)

32. What stays **HOT** in the *refrigerator?* (Horseradish, chilis, hot tamales, mustard, hot dogs, hot pastrami, chili sauce.)
33. What is the 1 thing you break when you say its name? (Silence.)
34. How many big men would you say have been born in *[the name of your city, town]* ? (None? only babies are born in_____.)

35. What's the easiest thing for a miser to part with? (A comb.)
36. Where can everyone always find "money" when he needs it? (In the dictionary.)
37. Where did Noah strike the 1st nail he put into the Ark? (On its head.)
38. What 3 letters will turn a girl into a woman? (A-G-E.)
39. What 8 letters will tell a girl named Ellen that she's pretty? (U-R-A-B-U-T-L-N.)
40. What 2 letters mean "not difficult"? (E-Z.)
41. What letter & number name an outdoor sport? (10-S.)
42. What are the 3 strongest letters in the alphabet? (N-R-G or TNT.)
43. What letter & number mean "conquered"? (B-10.)
44. What 2 letters spell "a wormlike fish"? (E-L.)
45. What 2 letters spell "to do better"? (X-L: excel.)
46. When a lady faints, what number will restore her? (You must bring her 2.)
47. Why is number 9 like a peacock? (Because without its tail it's nothing.)
48. What has 8 feet & sings? (A quartet.)
49. What animal never plays fair? (The cheetah.)
50. [Pull down the classroom wall map; point to it & ask:] Where are the Kings of England usually crowned?" (On the head.)
51. Name some times when a girl is not a girl. (When she's a dear [deer] or a bell [e] or a little pale [pail].)
52. What starts with a "t," ends with a "t," & in fact is full of "t"? (A teapot.)
53. What driver will *never* get a ticket? (A screwdriver.)
54. What does a person usually grow in his garden if he works very hard? (Tired.)
55. What word is usually pronounced incorrectly even by teachers? (The word "incorrectly," of course!)
56. What roof never keeps out the wet? (The roof of your mouth.)
57. What is the highest building in New York? (The N.Y.C. Public Library. It has, by far, the most stories!)
58. What man's business is best when it's dullest? (A knife & lawnmower sharpener.)
59. What is most remarkable about a yardstick? (Although it has neither a head nor a tail, it has a foot at either end & a third foot in its middle!)
60. What continent do you see when you look in the mirror in the morning? (You see Europe [you're up].)
61. What birds have 4 small feet & yellow feathers? (2 canaries.)
62. What kind of dog is a baseball dog? (Any dog that wears a muzzle, catches flies, chases fowls, & beats it home when he sees the catcher coming.)
63. Which is correct: "The yolk of an egg IS white" or "The yolk of an egg ARE white"? (Neither: the yolk of an egg is *yellow*!)

64. On which side of a church will you always find the cemetery? (On the outside.)
65. What 7 letters & a number did the Martian say when he met the little boy? (L-O-I-M-A-4-N-R.)
66. What Roman numeral can climb a wall? (I-V.)
67. What 4 letters would frighten a robber? (O-I-C-U.)
68. What has 100 legs & cannot walk? (50 pair of pants.)
69. I go out, but I can't come in; what am I? (A fire.)
70. What's the difference between an old dime & a brand new penny? (9¢.)
71. Why did the fly fly? ('Cause the spider spied her.)
72. What is ALWAYS behind time? (The back of a clock.)
73. How can you show that 1/2 of 12 = 7? (This way:)
74. Why is a man who runs a fish market likely to be stingy? (Because his business makes him sell fish [selfish].)
75. If butter is 50¢ a lb. in Chicago, what are window panes in Detroit? (Glass.)
76. If a mushroom is the smallest room in the world, what is the largest room in the world? (The room for improvement.)
77. Why is it dangerous to tell a secret on a farm? (Because the potatoes have eyes, the corn has ears & the beans talk [beanstalk]!)
78. What invention do we use to see through a wall? (A window.)
79. What is bigger when it's upside down? (The number 6.)
80. What is a bull called when it's sleeping? (A bulldozer.)
81. What did the jack say to the car? ("Can I give you a lift?")
82. What gallops down the road on its head? (A horseshoe nail.)
83. What starts with an E, ends with an E & only has 1 letter in it? (An envelope.)
84. What bird can lift the heaviest weights; (The crane.)
85. Name a liquid that *cannot* freeze? (Boiling water.)
86. What is the strongest creature for its size in the whole world? (The wasp: it can lift a 200 lb. man 3 feet off the ground.)
87. When is a ship at sea not on water? (When it's on fire.)
88. Why are fire engines red? (Fire engines are red because newspapers are read too and two & two are four; four times 3 is 12; 12 inches make a ruler; a famous ruler was Queen Elizabeth; The Queen Elizabeth sailed the ocean; the ocean is full of fish; fish have fins; the Finns fought the Russians; the Russians are Red—so fire engines are red because they're always rushin'!)
89. Why is a bad riddle like an unsharpened pencil? (Because it's dull & has no point.)
90. What in life is the end of everything? (The letter "g.")

Harder Riddles

1. An architect had a brother & the brother died; the man who died had no brother. Who was the architect? (A woman.)
2. What goes around a button? (A billy-goat. He goes around a' buttin".)
3. What 2 good tunes make everybody happy? (Good cartoons & good fortunes.)
4. What's the difference between the sidewalk & a taxi? (Taxi-fare)
5. If your uncle's sister is not your aunt, what is she? (Your mother.)
6. Why is an empty purse always the same? (Because there's never any change in it.)
7. What has every person seen & will never see again? (Yesterday.)
8. What is put on the table, cut, but never eaten? (A deck of cards.)
9. [Pull down wall map & ask:] "Where does Thursday come before Wednesday?" (In the dictionary.)
10. Name the make of a car that tells what the woman said when she bought a hen. ("Chevrolet?" [She-ever-lay?])
11. Can you spell "happiness" in 3 letters? (X-T-C [ecstasy.])
12. Can you spell a funeral poem in 3 letters? (L-E-G [elegy].)
13. Can you spell a drug in 3 letters? (O-P-M [opium].)
14. What is skinny at the top, fat at the bottom & has ears? (Mountains.)
15. When is a sailor not a sailor? (When he's aboard ship.)
16. How can you show that 2/3 of 6 = 9? (This way: $SIX = IX$.)
17. Why is a blotter like a lazy dog? (Because a blotter is an ink-lined plane, an inclined plane is a slope up, & a slow pup is a lazy dog!)
18. A father bought a ranch & presented it to his 3 sons. They planned to raise cattle for market, so they called the ranch "Focus." Why was this an appropriate name for their ranch? [*Note to teacher: Try to elicit the definition of "focus" from your group, i.e.,: It's the bringing of the rays of light together," etc.*] (Focus—That's where the sun's rays meet! [That's where the sons raise meat!])
19. Why didn't Moses take any bees into the Ark? (Because he hadn't been born yet; it was NOAH who took the creatures into the Ark.)
20. Can you think of a sentence in which all of these words are used: defeat, deduct, defense, detail? (Defeat of deduct went over defence before detail.)
21. What's the greatest riddle in the world? (Life: because in the end we all have to give up on it.)

Once shared with the class as a whole, the riddle cards might be stacked on a table at the back of the room where they may be re-read & shared during free time.

Science

Children can learn a good deal by watching the day-to-day growth of plants in their classroom; plants grow from different beginnings—seeds, cuttings, tubers, bulbs; but plants follow a definite pattern of growth. Baby plants will grow to be like the adult plants. Plants have different temperatures & require various amounts of water, sunshine, warmth & different types of soil. You can stock your classroom nursery with a variety of plants & at no expense; here's how.

Apple seeds. Seeds are not ready to be planted directly from the fruit. Put the seeds in a jar with damp moss. Refrigerate for 6 weeks (mark removal date on your classroom calendar). Turn them over periodically until they begin to sprout. Then fill a small pot with potting compost. Plant seed 1/2" down in compost. Keep in light, warm room. Keep moist.

Avocado pit. Place pit, round end down, in a small jar. Fill jar with water so that round end only is submerged. Then wait (for perhaps even 2-3 months). Keep adding water as it evaporates. When pit looks slimy & even moldy, do not despair; roots should appear any time. When root is 1/2" long, plant pit in a medium sized pot. Water it well when it is dry & give it food tablets from time to time.

Birdseed. Sprinkle on top of rich soil & then cover with 1/4" more of soil. Keep it moist!

Beet. Cut to within 1" of its top, retaining leaves. Trim foliage back. Plant beet top in sandy soil. Keep moist, not wet.

Broadbeans. Soak 2-3 hours until they swell. Cut & roll a piece of blotting paper & line a 1-2 lb. jam jar up to the mouth with the paper. Place bean about 1/2 way down between jar & paper. Pour 1" of water into jar. See that blotter remains WET. Place jar in dark cupboard until beans germinate, then bring jar into the light. (If you use 2 jars, placing 1 in cupboard & leaving 1 in the light, children will see which grows faster. Do they know why?) Lay sprouting beans on soil. Keep it moist.

Carrot. Cut, retaining 1" of foliage & 1" of root; set in a shallow dish filled with 1/2" of water. Add tiny pieces of charcoal to keep water sweet, or trim foliage; cut root 2" from top & hollow out center; hang upside down like a basket. Keep filled with water.

Corn. As a child in Illinois, my mother was taught to plant corn in this manner: "When sowing corn, plant 5 grains: 1 for the

blackbird, 1 for the crow, 1 for the meal worm, & 1 won't grow."
Date Seeds. These need lots of room. Plant seed in sandy soil.
When roots outgrow pot, break out bottom of pot & plant in a
bigger pot.
Grapes. Dry seeds. Put 1/2" of clean pebbles in the bottom of a
pot. Mix 1 part humus, 2 parts potting soil & a handful of
vermiculite. Put in pot. Water, allowing soil to settle. Plant 12
seeds 1/2" deep. Keep soil damp. Place pot where it will get just
1-2 hrs. of direct sun each day—until vine is 7" tall. Put a
re-enforcing stick beside vine for it to climb.
Grapefruit seeds. These do best if planted in February, I've read.
You can use the grapefruit shell filled with potting soil & sand as
the seed's initial holder. Soak seed overnight before planting. Sink
soil down close about seed. Later transfer young plant to a
sturdier container. The plant may grow for years. Keep earth
moist by spraying with water every day. Also water twice a week.
Kumquats. (See lemon seeds.)
Lemon seeds. Cover with 1/2" sand & potting soil, after having
soaked the seeds overnight. Keep earth moist (as described for
grapefruit).
Lentils. Spread in single layer in a saucer. Moisten, but don't float
lentils. Keep moist & in the sun. In 10 days they sprout & can be
planted like beans.
Mango seeds. These are difficult to start as they, like the avocado,
are slow in sprouting. Press seed into soil flat side down. Keep soil
moist.
Oats. Can be started in the following way: Line the bottom of a
pie tin with small stones. Add a layer of rich earth, then lay oats
on top of earth. Cover oats with layer of fine soil. Cover entire top
of pan with thin cloth (gauze); set in a sunny window. Sprinkle
cloth with water each day. Oats should sprout on 3rd day.
Remove cloth at this time. Keep soil moist.
Onion. Place pointed end up, in a small-mouthed jar. Cover 1/2 of
onion with water. Add small amounts of charcoal to water.
Orange seeds. (See lemon seeds.)
Peach seeds. (See apple seeds.)
Pepper seeds. These seeds, from tiny red peppers in pickling spice,
are spread out to dry on a paper towel. Punch small holes for
drainage in the bottom of cottage cheese container. Fill container
with soil. Barely cover seeds with soil. Keep soil moist.
Pineapple. Cut off 1 1/2"-2" from top of plant. Retain spiky

foliage. Allow pineapple to dry for 3 days, then place in sandy soil. Water lightly. Keep as warm as possible. In about 2 weeks (if roots have grown), re-pot in good sterilized soil. Keep soil damp, warm & near light. Your plant won't bear, but it is attractive.

Potato Porcupine. Slice off the top of an Irish potato. Carve out a hole, leaving plenty of meat on the walls. Insert 4 toothpicks as legs. Make eyes by attaching two small white paper circles with black map tacks. Fill cavity with earth (or moist cotton) sprinkled with grass seed. Keep watered for 10 days until Porky's spines sprout.

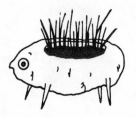

Plum. (See apple seeds.)

Pumpkin. (See pepper seeds.)

Sweet potato. Some are heat-dried & won't grow so ask grocer for a *fresh* one. If possible choose one with a few whiskers. Cut potato in 1/2. Insert toothpicks around potato below cut surface. Place potato, tapered end down, in a jar, suspended by means of toothpicks. Fill jar with water. Put jar in closet until roots sprout, then bring plant into the light. Plant will sustain itself on water for a long while, or you may plant the potato in soil, allowing green sprouts to remain above earth.

Squash. Follow directions for pepper seeds, except press squash seeds down 3/4" into soil.

Watermelon seeds. Plant directly in soil. Sprinkle lightly & often with water. Seeds sprout quickly & plant has abundant foliage. Continue watering as mentioned.

White potato. Cut into sections, each section containing an eye or two. Plant in rich earth & keep moistened. Let it have lots of sun.

Yam. Choose one that has purple eyes. Then follow directions for sweet potato.

Free seed catalogs to help children become better acquainted with a variety of plants:

W. Atlee Burpee Co.
Riverside, Calif. 92502

Wayside Gardens Co.
Mentor, Ohio 44060
($2.00, credited toward purchase)

Older children may enjoy learning about herbs & plants that are less common. Free catalogs are available from:

Nichols Herbs & Rare Seeds   Meadowbrook Herb Gardens
1190 N. Pacific Highway   Wyoming, R.I. 02898
Albany, Ore. 97321

Information on carnivorous plants & terrarium sets:

Armstrong Associates, Inc.
Box 127
Basking Ridge, N.J. 07920.

January Art

Printmaking. The most basic types of prints are made by applying ink to a flat surfact (i.e., a carrot sliced in 1/2), & then pulling a print (see Page 42). Children could compile Print Samplers, experimenting, searching for unusual surface possibilities.

Rubbings. These are easy to execute. Tape or firmly hold a piece of lightweight strong paper atop a rough surface. Rub the entire piece of paper with a carpenter's pencil, crayon, or liquid shoe polish on a cotton wad in the toe of a child's sock. VARIATION: Apply a rich wash of diluted poster paint atop a crayon rubbing. VARIATION: Cut several rubbings into pieces. Make a collage of these pieces. Colored construction paper might also be used in this collage.

Monoprints. Prepare the materials for making monoprints & then hand out the following mimeos: (Let the children read these to themselves.)

"Clear off the desk (table) in front of you. Be sure you have enough room in which to work. Lay down a large piece of plastic wrap* and tape it smoothly to the desk. Get some starch** and pour 1/3 cup onto the plastic wrap. Return the starch. Decide on the color of paint you wish to use and *carefully* sprinkle a bit of dry powder paint onto your starch. Return the paint. Take some sheets of white paper to your desk. Now ————————➤ Roll up your sleeves to the elbow. With *one* hand mix the starch

---

*Plastic produce bags, free at markets, may be slit, opened out flat & used in place of costly plastic wrap.

**This may be a commercial liquid starch (shake bottle WELL). Or you may prepare it at home the previous evening (from cornstarch) & bring it to class in plastic containers. (Keep starch quite dilute.)

& paint together. Try drawing in it. Use different parts of your hand & see what kinds of effects you can get. When you are happy with what you've done, take a sheet of paper (with your *dry* hand, of course) & lay it carefully on top of the starch-drawing. Pick up 1 corner of the paper & pull it sm-o-o-o-o-thly toward the opposite corner & off the starch. Turn the paper over & look at your results. Lay this print on the floor against the wall (where the newspapers are laid) at the back of the room. Try taking another print off the same starch by rubbing your hand in the starch and making a *new* picture or design. Or pull several prints off the same starch pattern.

When you're ready to clean up, untape the plastic wrap, roll it into a ball & place it in the waste can. Carefully wipe off the desk (and floor?) with a paper towel. Wash your hands & then read quietly or write a short story about an adventure that one of your monoprints might illustrate."

Linoleum block prints. (For older students.) Make an outline of linoleum block on tracing paper; draw your design within it. Turn your design over onto the linoleum surface of the block. Trace over the lines, pressing heavily so that the reverse of your design appears on block. Carve out all areas of block which you do not want to show on your finished print. Remember only the raised areas will take ink. Squeeze block-printing ink onto a small pane of glass. Roll brayer* back & forth through the ink until brayer is well coated. Roll brayer across face of block so that your design is fully inked. Carefully place paper on block; rub paper with spoonback or heel of hand to print design. Keep paper from moving. Starting at one corner, slowly peel the paper off toward the diagonally opposite corner. Allow ink to dry completely.

Prints from styro-foam meat trays. These are made by cutting or scratching design into foam tray. Ink is supplied & print taken as described above.

Veneer print-making. Described on page 37.

Felt block-printing. Children draw a basic design on paper. This is cut out & rubber cemented firmly to a piece of felt (from an old hat, etc.) & when dry, is carefully cut out with scissors. Trace around this basic design on the top of a scrap block of

---

*A brayer is a small hand roller used to spread ink thinly & evenly over surface of block.

wood. (Lumber yards are often happy to save such hand-sized blocks of scrap wood for you.) Apply rubber cement to *entire* paper-side of felt; apply glue or rubber cement to *entire* inner area of design drawn on wood block. When both rubber-cemented surfaces are dry, press felt to top of wood. Firmly attach felt to wood. Using a large (stencil) brush, apply poster-paint to felt design. Place paper to be printed atop a pad of newspapers. Then, holding paper in place, firmly press felt onto paper.

Foam-tape block-printing. Follow above instructions except use adhesive-backed foam-tape (used for weather-stripping). Child draws outline of a simple design on face of block; tape is pressed directly onto outline. Pour poster paint into flat cooky sheet; dip foam into paint & then stamp design onto paper. Child experiments with repetition of design & use of more than one color of paint at a time.

Silkscreen prints. Can be made by very young children in the following way: Purchase small (4''-6'' in diameter) embroidery hoops. Cut old nylon hose into pieces & stretch these taut in the hoops. Each child either cuts from newsprint a simple shape smaller than the hoop itself or, with wax crayon, draws directly onto the nylon, being sure to press firmly enough so as to fill the mesh with crayon. A tiny scraper, a "squeegee" (that can easily fit within hoop), is cut from a heavy cardboard. Thick poster-paint (or a liquid starch & powdered tempera mixture) is applied to the screen with a spoon. Use the squeegee to firmly scrape the paint over the crayon drawing & through the mesh of the nylon. If a cut-out paper shape is used, place it between the nylon & the paper to be printed. The paint, when applied with the squeegee, will adhere the cut-out to the screen, producing a negative image on the paper.

Older children can use this more advanced type of screen: Cut a window in a cardboard box lid or base. Stretch & staple slightly dampened cotton organdy or an old marquisette curtain over the outside. Keep material taut, placing 1 staple in the center of each side before stapling all around. On the inside of box tape the edge of the window to the material. Seal all the edges with masking or paper tape. Coat all sides of the box with the shellac. Child makes a design no bigger than the window, then he places the screen over the design. He proceeds to block out with a wax crayon all areas that are not to receive paint: he does this by thoroughly filling in the fabric's mesh. (Or he may place a dampened cut-out of newsprint under the screen as described in the preceding paragraph.) Child places his screen on paper to be printed. At top of screen pour a generous amount of finger paint. Using a cardboard squeegee slightly smaller than the window, at a 45° angle, the child draws the paint firmly across the full length of the screen. If he wants a 2-color print, he marks guide lines on the paper being printed for registering the 2nd screen. He then prepares a 2nd screen, identical in size to the 1st. From a sheet of newsprint the size of the window, he cuts away that part of the design that he wants printed a 2nd color. Screen is registered over 1st print, & 2nd color (which holds newsprint to screen) is applied.

January P.E.

Indoor games for January. Often the weather this month doesn't permit outdoor play. Here are some games to be played indoors.

Memory. Put an assorted collection of objects on a table, i.e., scissors, cork, comb, spoon, thimble, pen. Children observe objects for 2 minutes, after which a cloth is spread over objects & children see how many objects they are now able to list. Additional credit may be given for correct spelling. After lists are completed & objects uncovered, discuss different methods children used in order to recall objects, what tricks (i.e., counting number of objects on display) help a person remember large groups of things?

Nursery Rhyme Charades. Divide class into "acting companies." Let each child decide on a nursery rhyme & then act it out for others to try to identify. Pantomime & dialogue may be used if necessary. VARIATION: A fairy tale is chosen & child acts out a portion of the story (not the entire tale).

Who's the Leader? Players stand in a circle. "It" leaves the room. A leader is chosen. All children begin clapping until "It" returns & goes to the center of the circle. "It" tries to discover who is leading the group in its actions. Children try to imitate the leader's frequent changes of action (hopping on 1 foot, turning around, patting his head, etc.). At the same time children try NOT to be caught obviously looking at the leader. Once the identity of the leader is discovered, he becomes "It" & leaves room. A new leader is chosen & game continues.

Macaroni-Baloney. Dump a bag of alphabet macaroni onto the middle of a table, or distribute tiny paper cups of macaroni, 1 to each child. A topic is announced (animals, fruits, people, places) & each child tries to spell a suitable answer. After a certain time, children share their answers. Originality & correct spelling are verbally rewarded. Spelling errors should be unobtrusively corrected.

Geometric Figure-Fun. Children are shown, on the chalkboard, geometric figures such as triangle, pentagon, circle, rectangle, octagon, square; children design animals & figures or objects using ONLY geometric figures. Whole landscapes or cities may develop; perhaps a chronicle of these new worlds might also be created.

Mix & Match. Children are given a list of 10 capitals, inventions, historic deeds, etc. Children write in the corresponding state, inventor or historic figure. Additional information given is worth extra points. Any logical answer is correct (i.e., S.F.B. Morse OR Arthur Vail might be written in to correspond with "the telegraph"). The out-of-the-ordinary answer demonstrates real creative thinking & should be encouraged at every turn.

Categories. Hold up a card on which 1 letter of the alphabet is printed. Call out a category (i.e., plant, animal, country). First person to name object with that 1st initial gets the card. If he can spell the word, he retains the card intact; if unable to spell the word, he gets 1/2 of card & child with correct spelling of word gets the remaining 1/2.

Headlines. (A game for older children.) Cut out several newspaper headlines. Separate words & mix them up in a pile. Divide children into groups of 4 or 5. Each group takes 3-5 words from pile & arranges these in any order as to form a kind of plot around which they develop a short (5 min.) play or pantomime. An "announcer" may give a brief build-up before the presentation. Emphasize that ANY usage of words is acceptable.

January Balloon Puppets

Blow up a balloon. Firmly tie knot in end. Tie a 2" string to balloon. Using liquid starch & thin strips of newspaper, cover balloon with papier mâché. Hang balloon by string to dry; this may take several days. When dry, tape cardboard or tagboard to balloon to build up features. Cover entire head with papier mâche, using paper toweling strips & liquid starch. Hang up to dry. When dry, paint with·poster paints. When these are dry, lightly spray with Varathane. Add hair, eyes, hat, etc. Deflate balloon. Simple 2-seamed cloth body is stapled or glued securely within neck of balloon puppet.

February

February brings the rain,
Thaws the frozen lake again.

1 1st Supreme Court Meeting, 1790.
   Victor Herbert (1859-1924), American composer of light operas.
2 Groundhog Day.
3 Felix Mendelssohn (1809-1847), German composer.
   Elizabeth Blackwell (1821-1910), 1st U.S. female doctor. She applied to 29 medical schools before being accepted.
4 Charles A. Lindbergh (1902-   ), American aviator: 1st to make solo transatlantic flight.
5 Roger Williams (1603 [?]-1683), American teacher; founder of Rhode Island.
6 George "Babe" Ruth (1895-1948), American baseball player.
7 Charles Dickens (1812-1870), English novelist.
   Sinclair Lewis (1885-1951), American novelist.
8 Jules Verne (1828-1905), French writer of science-fiction romances.
9 William H. Harrison (1773-1841), 9th U.S. President.
   U.S. Weather Service established: 1870.
10 Charles Lamb (1775-1834), English essayist.
   Boris Pasternak (1890-1960), Russian poet, novelist.
   Race Relations Sunday: 1st day in week in which we celebrate Lincoln's birthday.
11 Daniel Boone (1734-1820), American frontiersman.
   Thomas A. Edison (1847-1931), American inventor; holder of 1,100 patents.

12   Abraham Lincoln (1809-1865), 16th U.S. President.
       Charles Darwin (1809-1882), English naturalist.
13   Grant Wood (1892-1942), American painter.
14   St. Valentine's Day (the day of his death, more than 1700
           years ago).
15   Galileo Galilei (1564-1642), Italian scientist.
       Cyrus McCormick (1809-1884), American inventor of the
           reaper.
       Susan B. Anthony (1820-1906), American feminist.
16   Ulysses S. Grant (1822-1885) forced the surrender of Con-
           federate troops at Fort Donelson in 1862.
18   Alessandro Volta (1745-1827), Italian physicist.
       Planet Pluto discovered by Clyde Tombaugh on photo-
           graphs he took 1/23-1/29, 1930.
       National Brotherhood Week.
19   Nicolaus Copernicus (1473-1543), Polish astronomer.
       Thomas Edison patented the phonograph, 1878.
20   U.S. Mail Service established, 1792.
       Lt. Col John Glenn, in "Friendship," was 1st American to
           orbit Earth: 1960.
21   Constantin Brancusi (1876-1957), Rumanian abstract sculp-
           tor.
       W.H. Auden (1907-   ), Anglo-American poet.
       Malcolm X day.
22   George Washington (1732-1799), 1st U.S. President. His
           birthday is celebrated on the 3rd Mon. in Feb. as directed
           by the Mon. Holiday Bill.
       Frederic Chopin (1810-1849), Polish composer ("Butterfly
           Etude" & "Funeral March:" Sonata Opus 35, B flat
           minor).
23   George Frederick Handel (1685-1759), British composer
           ("The Cuckoo & the Nightingale").
       Winslow Homer (1836-1910), American marine artist.
24   Wilhelm Grimm (1786-1863), German writer of children's
           stories.
25   Pierre Auguste Renoir (1841-1919), French impressionist
           painter.
       U.S. Income Tax established 1913.
26   Wm. Cody [Buffalo Bill] (1846-1917), American scout.
       John Steinbeck (1902-1969), American writer: *East of
           Eden, Cannery Row.*

27   Gioacchino Rossini (1792-1868), Italian composer.
      Henry Wadsworth Longfellow (1807-1882), American poet:
      "Hiawatha," "Courtship of Miles Standish."
29   Leap Year Day: occurs every 4th year.
      Purim: The Feast of Lots (February or March). It is a
      celebration of the casting of the lots which showed
      Haman to be evil and Esther to be good. The children
      often give plays commemorating the story of Esther; they
      dress up as Queen Esther, her uncle Mordecai, the villain
      Haman and the good King Ahasveros.

February

The name comes from the Latin word *februa,* an instrument of
purification which was used by the ancient Romans on Feb. 15th. This
was a day of atonement & ceremonial feasting. Numa, the legendary
2nd King of Rome, is said to have introduced February into the Roman
calendar.

FEBRUARY QUOTATIONS

4   I saw a fleet of fishing boats ... I flew down almost
      touching the craft and yelled at them asking if I was on the
      right road to Ireland. They just stared. Maybe they didn't
      hear me. Maybe I didn't hear them. Or maybe they
      thought I was a crazy fool. An hour later I saw land.–
      Charles Lindbergh

11   Results! Why, man, I have gotten a lot of results. I know
      several thousand things that won't work.

      I never did anything worth doing by accident, nor did any
      of my inventions come by accident, they came by work.
                                                    –T.A. Edison

12   No man has a good enough memory to be a good liar.

      To sin by silence, makes cowards of men.

      Die when I may, I want it said of me to those who knew me
      best, that I always plucked a thistle and planted a flower
      where I thought a flower would grow.
                                                    –A. Lincoln

13   The only good ideas I ever had I got while milking a
      cow.–Grant Wood.

15   Yet it *does* move. (Attributed to Galileo when being forced
       to recant his doctrine that the earth moves around the
       sun.)

       Modern invention has banished the spinning wheel, & the
       same law of progress makes the woman of today different
       from her grandmother.

       I am a full and firm believer in the revelation that it is
       through women that the race is to be redeemed.
                                        (1875)–Susan B. Anthony

16   Everyone has his superstitions. One of mine has always been
       when I start to go anywhere, or to do anything, never to
       turn back or to stop until the thing intended is accom-
       plished.–Ulysses S. Grant

18   (Nat'l. Brotherhood Week)

       How wonderful it is, how pleasant for God's people to live
       together like brothers. (Psalms)

       I am not an Athenian, nor a Greek, but a citizen of the
       world.–Socrates

       The world is my country, all mankind are my brethren, and
       to do good is my religion.–Thomas Paine

       Our true nationality is mankind.–H.G. Wells *(The Outline
       of History)*

20   Neither snow, nor rain, nor heat, nor gloom of night stays
       these couriers from the swift completion of their
       appointed rounds.–Herodotus (inscription on the N.Y.C.
       Post Office)

21   Mankind's history has proved from one era to another that
       the true criterion of leadership is spiritual. Men are
       attracted by spirit. By power, men are *forced.* Love is
       engendered by spirit. By power, anxieties are created.

       I just want to read it [the manuscript of his autobiography]
       1 more time because I don't expect to read it in finished
       form.

       For the freedom of my 22,000,000 black brothers and
       sisters here in America, I do believe that I have fought the
       best that I knew how and the best that I could with the
       shortcomings that I have had.
                           –Malcolm X *(Autobiography of Malcolm X)*

22   Liberty, when it begins to take root, is a plant of rapid
        growth. (Letter to James Madison 3/2/1788)

      I hope I shall always possess firmness and virtue, enough to
        maintain that which I consider the most enviable of all
        titles, the character of an "Honest Man."
                                            —G. Washington: *Moral Maxims*

27   The cares that infest the day
      Shall fold their tents, like the Arabs,
      And silently steal away.
                                            —Henry W. Longfellow

      Give me a laundry-list and I'll set it to music.—Gioacchino
        Rossini

FEBRUARY EVENTS

• **Groundhog Day   [2]**

      The woodchuck, or groundhog, is a small, blackish-gray
North American rodent. It was given this name by the Pilgrims
when they arrived in America, as it lived in the woods & reminded
them of the hedgehogs back in England. They also gave the
groundhog the responsibility of the hedgehog on February
2nd—that of predicting the date of spring. Tradition dictates that
on the morning of Feb. 2nd the groundhog comes up out of his
hole & looks about. If the day is cold & cloudy, he decides that
spring will be here soon & he emerges from his hole. If, however, it
is a bright clear day, the sun will cause his shadow to be cast—&
one look at his shadow sends the groundhog back into his hole &
continued hibernation for 6 more weeks, at the end of which time
it really *will* be spring.
      Discuss briefly with your class: How are traditions like this
born? What are some probable reasons for such a tradition?
      Science. Does the groundhog really come out on Feb. 2nd?
Research done at Pennsylvania State University over a period of 5
years & involving 4,000 groundhogs showed that a great number
of groundhogs *were* seen out of their burrows on Jan. 31, Feb. 1st,
2nd, & 3rd. Other scientists state that Feb. 2nd is the middle of
winter for a groundhog & so his hibernation should be at the
deepest point. If he is seen above ground, it must be accidental,

they say; he may have awakened to relieve himself. Scientists disagree on the answer, which indicates that more research on hibernation is in order.

• Birth of Jules Verne   [8]

In honor of the Father of Science Fiction, Jules Verne, let your class create fantastic stories based on 1 of the following topics. Emphasize how the inclusion of detailed descriptions is essential to any good science fiction story.

1. Make up a story surrounding the invention of some modern-day device (laser beam, atomic sub, rocket).

2. You have won a contest that allows you to travel FREE to any planet (known or unknown). Write about your choice, preparations (food, money, health precautions), take-off, weather, landing, the period of exploration, escape, rescue (capture), return trip, documentation of trip (samples of vegetation, soil; photographs), reception in America. This might be written in the form of a journal dated 2073 A.D.

3. Invent a country (or island, secret tower, room, attic, cave). Name it, after yourself, perhaps (i.e., Smithland or Smithtania). Describe its people, animals, plants, weather. What is of importance there? Do people live there? Why doesn't anyone else know of its existence? What do the people do? What do they believe? How are they similar to or different from Americans? Do they know about us? What do they think about us?

4. You have a friend from outer space. No one else knows about him (e.g., they can't see him, or they do not recognize him as an alien). You like each other very much. Tell about some adventures you have together. Tell how your friendship finally ends—if it *has* ended!

5. What discoveries (&/or inventions) would you most like to see by 2001 A.D.? Tell an imaginary story of how they came about.

• Birth of Sir Francis Beaufort   [9]

More than 150 years ago a British admiral, Sir Francis Beaufort, constructed the 1st practical anemometer & devised the Beaufort scale which appears below. An anemometer measures the force of wind which depends on the speed of air.

Beaufort Scale

No.	Description	Noticeable Effect on Land	Speed in m.p.h.
0	calm	smokes rises vertically	0
1	light air	wind direction shown by drift of smoke	1-3
2	slight breeze	wind felt on face: leaves rustle; flags stir	4-7

3	gentle breeze	leaves & twigs in constant motion: wind extends light flags	8-12
4	moderate "	dust & small branches moved; flags flap	13-18
5	fresh "	small trees in leaf begin to sway; flags ripple	19-24
6	strong "	large branches in motion: flags beat	25-31
7	moderate gale	whole trees in motion: flags extended	32-38
8	fresh "	twigs break off trees: walking is hindered	39-46
9	strong "	slight structural damage to houses	47-54
10	whole "	trees uprooted; much structural damage to houses	55-63
11	storm	widespread damage	64-75
12	hurricane	excessive damage	over 75

Word etymology. You know how a far-off hill can look like a cloud & clouds often have a hill-like quality. In Old English "cloud" was spelled "clud" & meant "a hill"! Typhoon comes from Chinese "tai-fong" which means "a great wind." Hurricane is from "huracan," a Caribbean word for "an evil spirit."

Science. Check with stores that carry balloons that are to be filled with helium. (Inquire at your local Army/Navy Surplus store to see if they have weather balloons available.) Have each child fill out an index card stating his name, age, date of launching & reason for launching. Have him ask who found the balloon, where, when, & how recovery was made. Have child put this card & a self-addressed (to school) postcard in a tiny plastic bag. Choose a day rating a No. 6 on the Beaufort Scale on which to launch your balloons. Obtain a tank of helium from a welding shop (look under "Gas-Industrial" in the yellow pages of your phone book). Each child gets a length of sturdy string. He ties his plastic package carefully & securely to one end of this string. As a balloon is filled, its end is tied in a firm knot & the free end of 1 of the children's strings is securely tied to the knot.

Bulletin board display. A fascinating display will develop as the post cards begin arriving. Thank-you notes can be written in which the children mention different places their balloons were found, mileage records, & what they have been learning in class about winds.

Information sources:

U.S. Weather Bureau
8060 13th St.
Silver Springs, Md. 20910

American Meteorological Society
45 Beacon St.
Boston, Mass. 02108

- **Birth of Thomas A. Edison   [11]**

Thomas Alva Edison was an inventor. He worked in his workshop. He worked in his laboratory. He worked in his mind. When he got an idea he looked at it from all sides. He never said, "That can't be done." When he was searching for the right' material to burn in a light bulb, he tried *6,000* different things before he found the one he wanted! In addition to the electric light bulb, he invented the phonograph & motion pictures! Thomas Edison changed the world!

Word etymology. *Phonograph* is a Greek derivative meaning "sound-writing." ("Phonograph; *n.* A vibrating toy that restores life to dead noises." Ambrose Bierce, from his *Devil's Dictionary*.)

- **Birth of Abraham Lincoln   [12]**

> Lincoln, six feet one in his stocking feet,
> The lank man, knotty and tough as a hickory nail,
> Whose hands were always too big for white-kid gloves,
> Whose wit was a coonskin sack of dry, tall tales.
> Whose weathered face was homely as a plowed field.
> —S.V. Benet*

Older students may enjoy this Lincoln's Day quiz:

How many of the following can you find on a Lincoln penny?

(1) a small animal (hair=hare); (2) a messenger (one sent=one sent); (3) a flower (two lips=tulips); (4) yourself (eye=I); (5) a drink (T=tea); (6) submarine (under the "C"=sea); (7) a snake (copperhead); (8) a fruit (date); (9) a part of a river (mouth); (10) a sacred building (temple); (11) long lines of soldiers (columns); (12) a part of the foot (arch); (13) result of game in which 2 teams have=score (tie); (14) an application of paint (coat); (15) a whole cob of corn (ear); (16) part of the mouth (roof); (17) a vehicle *(e pluriBUS unim);* (18) what Patrick Henry wanted (liberty); (19) a country (United States); (20) a statement of faith (In God we trust).

To assist them, you might explain that the answers to 1-6 are homonyms, 7-17 are nouns with more than 1 definition, 18-20 are straight (?) answers to the questions.

---

*From Rosemary Carr & Stephen Benet, *A Book of Americans* (383 Madison Ave., N.Y. 10017, Holt, Rinehart & Winston, Inc., 1933). © Holt Rinehart & Winston, Inc. Reprinted by permission of the publisher.

Etymology. Ancient Roman law prescribed a ceremony for the purchase of slaves: the new master laid his hand upon the slave's head. This was to fulfill the law of *mancipium:* "possession by the hand." Since *e* in Latin means "away," & *capio* means "taken," our word *emancipation* means "the master takes his hand off the emancipated slave."

"Freedom" comes from Old English & is related to a Norse word for "love & peace."

Information source: Lincoln Funeral Poster, Gettysburg Address in Lincoln's writing, Lincoln portrait formed from shading Emancipation Proclamation, & many other reproductions of Lincoln memorabilia are available from:

Pioneer Historical Society
Harriman, Tenn. 37748

The catalog, which costs 25¢, lists their many unusual, eccentric publications.

• Birth of Darwin [12]

The Darwinian theory of evolution holds that "all species of plants & animals developed from earlier forms by hereditary transmission of slight variations in successive generations." Surviving forms are those best adapted to the environment, e.g., survival of the fittest, or natural selection.

Two boys once thought they'd play a trick on Darwin. They carefully glued together several parts of different insects; they attached the head of a bee to the body of a butterfly & they glued to this the legs of a grasshopper. They took it to the famous naturalist & asked, "Do you know what kind of a bug this is?" Darwin examined the creature for a moment & then he asked, "Did it hum when you caught it?" "Yes, yes," the boys answered, thinking they'd fooled the famous man. "It's just what I thought," Darwin replied, "a humbug!"

• St. Valentine's Day [14]

Valentinus was a Christian priest during the days of the Roman Emperor Claudius II. It was a crime at that time to give aid or comfort to Christians. Valentinus was a good & kindly man, helping anyone in need. He was jailed by the Emperor & sentenced to death. Valentinus is credited with restoring the sight of the jailer's blind daughter, & according to legend & history, on the eve of his execution, Valentinus sent a farewell note to the little girl.

He signed it "From your Valentine." He was executed Feb. 14, 270 A.D. The practice of sending valentines grew out of an old belief extant even in Chaucer's day that birds began to mate on Feb. 14 & so this was an appropriate day for sending lovers' tokens. It is from Roman mythology that we have little Dan Cupid with his arrows dipped in love potion.

Bulletin board suggestions. A self-service post office makes a utilitarian display. Have each child paint a shoe box with white, pink, or red poster paints. Children stand shoe boxes upright & decorate them to look like mailboxes. Sturdy paper tabs for hanging are stapled to the insides of the top & bottom of box. A mail slit is cut in each box. Child's name appears near slit. Stapling these mailboxes in rows along a bulletin board facilitates the delivery of cards, cuts down on comparisons, & the bulletin board looks smashing!

Appropriate topics for bulletin boards this month include: "Valentine's Day Science" (information on the dove, the bluebird, flowers [forget-me-nots], the mechanics & function of the heart), "Let's Learn about Cupid" (historical, mythological background), "The Art of Archery" (examples of different types of quivers, arrows, bows, history of this sport, comic-relief by Dan Cupid shown making [in] appropriate remarks).

Language Arts

Ask older children to see how many compound words they, either individually or as a group, can list that incorporate the word "heart" (i.e., heartfelt, heartless, heartache, hearty, hearth).

Perhaps during your class party the students could try making words from the letters in the word "Valentine." Here are 89 possibilities:

vain, vale, valet, valiant, van, vane, vat, veal, veil, vein, vital, vine, vie, vile, Vienne, Venetia, Venetian, venal, venial, vent, vial, a, ale, ali, alien, aline, alit, Alvin, Ann, an, Anne, ant, Aventine, ate, anvil, Lee, Lea, Lianne, let, late, lie, lone, Latin, lean, linen, lint, enliven, let, live, alive, Elaine, Nat, Eve, Levi, Eli, Eva, Etna, net, neat, nave, navel, native, naive, nail, evil, event, even, entail, elite, elate; AND: ani, ante, Atli, len, Levant, lateen, lave, liane, lien, linn, linnet, vail, vela, velate, vina, ventail, anile, anil.

With your class discuss St. Valentine & what a valentine symbolizes (a message of love, laughter). Talk about the value of a valentine as a form of communication (discuss making an appropriate one for your principal, Room Mother, etc.). With older students you may criticize comic valentines, talk about their probable origins, purposes they served (as a reaction to the embarrassment at feeling affection for someone of the other sex, or as an outlet for hostility). Ask older students when they feel one should stop observing this day. Find out why they feel this way.

An appropriate haiku (see pg. 171), written by her child, would make a lovely valentine for Mother.

Convalescent patients, especially if they are elderly, would appreciate receiving handmade cards today.

Word etymology. *"Cupid"* is from Latin *cupido* (desire, passion). Our words *"friend"* & *"free"* probably both stem from one Indo-European base which means "to be fond of, hold dear," as the basic sense of "free" is probably "dear to (i.e., akin to) the chief" &, therefore, "not enslaved." The word *"flirt"* dates back to the 16th century! The early Frisian word for "a giddy girl" was "flirtje." It is also strongly influenced by the French word "fleureter" which means "to touch lightly; to move from flower to flower."

Vocabulary enrichment words: devotion, flirtatious, betrothal, affectionate, quiver, amorous, passionate, friendship.

A riddle for Valentine's Day: Why is your heart like a policeman? (Because it usually follows a regular beat.)

Poetry

My Valentine

I will make you brooches and toys
  for your delight

Or bird song at morning and starshine at night.
I will make a palace fit for you and me,
    Of green days in forests
    And blue days at sea.

                                —Robert Louis Stevenson

Also appropriate:

A Red Red Rose: Robert Burns
How Do I Love Thee: Elizabeth Barrett Browning

Reading (To review rhyming words & give aural practice:)

"Where's Your Heart?" Pass out to each child in the reading group a paper heart. These have been made by pasting together 2 pink, orange, red or white hearts of equal size. Between the 2 hearts is placed a slip of paper on which is printed a simple request, i.e., "Act like a frog." The children sit in a circle & the 1st child says to the child on his right: "Tell me, where's your heart?" The 2nd child answers with any ending he likes, i.e., "My heart's in a deep blue lake." The 1st child must now give a response that rhymes with "lake," i.e., "Well, don't let it get eaten by a snake." Each questioner is allowed ample time to come up with a rhyme (use an egg-timer as a guide), & then if he cannot think of one, he is told that this must really "break his heart." Whereupon he tears open his heart shape, reads the request (to himself) & fulfills it. Game continues.

Valentine's Day Art

Room decorations. Valentine banners offer a pleasant change from the usual Feb. 14th room decor. Students may paint with water color directly onto long strips of rice paper. VARIATION: Printing stamps are cut from a sponge or a potato. These are dipped in liquid tempera & printed on white or colored lengths of tissue or newsprint paper. VARIATION: Very basic shapes are cut from a variety of finger-painted & construction papers. These may be glued atop one another & then to a length of rice or newsprint paper. VARIATION: Colored tissue paper shapes are cut out & pressed with a warm iron between 2 long narrow strips of wax paper. A short dowel is glued or stapled to top & bottom of each banner. A small copper tack is inserted into each end of the top dowel. A short string is tied from these. A longer dowel, or straight stick for carrying the banner, may be tied to the string as shown, or banners may simply be hung from the strings. Hang these banners so that the light will shine through them. Hang them in festive groupings or clusters when possible.

Why not let each child make a dove. These doves, as a group, can be suspended in flight from a corner of your room. Or you might use them about the border of an appropriate bulletin board or above the chalk board. Let the children study pictures of doves, pigeons; point out how & where the wings are attached to the body, the way in which the neck is shaped & how the tail grows. Then let children cut, from white paper, doves of their own design. The following might be used as a basis of construction, but let the *children* come up with their own solutions, variants.

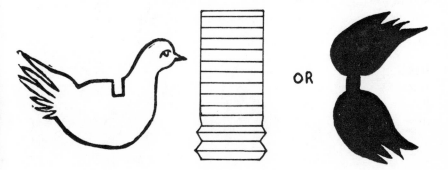

Valentines. In the 1st days of February, older children collect: several types of fern (clippings from a florist's), Queen Anne's lace, common clovers & any small leaves from bushes or trees that they may find available. These are pressed under heavy weights between sheets of waxpaper (which quickly accepts moisture) & then, in a week or so, are put between sheets of newsprint. Dilute milk glue with water. Apply it to backs of pressed plants, using a wide brush & large strokes. Arrange plants appropriately on the center of a doily-backed heart, or inside a card that carries a message on its cover.

Younger children make & collect flat materials that interest them (tiny paper cut-outs, sequins, glitter, tin foil, feathers, leaves, bits of fabric, lace, string). These are arranged in a pleasing manner on a piece of wax paper. A 2nd piece of wax paper is put on top & the 2 sheets are pressed together with a warm iron. Children cut a large heart-shaped piece out of a card. Then an area of their wax paper collage, chosen to go behind the heart-shaped hole, is cut & glued in place.

Individual folders to hold (& in which to carry home) their cards could be made in this way, too.

Traditionally, valentines had a lacy, almost fragile look. Besides using the commercially made white or gold paper doilies, the children can cut handmade doilies in the following ways:

(1) Fold square on dotted lines.

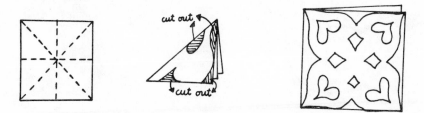

Paste doily onto card of a sharply contrasting color. Children may want to slip tiny pieces of foil or colored tissue beneath cut-out areas before doily is glued in place. This gives a more collage-like freedom to the valentine.

(2) Fold rectangular piece of paper in 1/2 lengthwise & then in 1/2 crosswise. Cut as shown; then fold diagonally & cut as shown:

(3) Fold rectangular paper as described in #2. Cut as shown. Then open out & fold over each corner & cut as shown below.

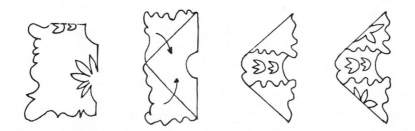

Doilies are opened out flat & carefully glued in place atop a folded card. The oval area in the centers of #2 & #3 is a perfect frame for a snapshot of the child, or for a tiny heart that opens revealing a secret, or as a space in which to print a message.

• U.S. Mail Established   [20]

We get the word "mail" from the Old French "male," the leather pouch carried by postmen. This word came into the English language in the 17th century when it was still correct to say a "mail of letters." *Litera* in Latin means "letter"; its plural means "a message." So it is that when you form a group of letters, you've written a letter!

In the Middle Ages couriers of the king rode *post*, a chain of stations that supplied fresh horses & men to deliver royal messages to distant places. The word "post" comes from the Latin *posita*, placed, as the original posts were placed at regular intervals along the 1st mail routes. The 1st postmen delivered only royal mail!

Riddle: What word is this?

Take away my 1st letter, I remain unchanged.
Take away my 2nd letter, I remain the same.
Take away ALL my letters & I continue unchanged.
What am I?   (The postman.)

- **National Brotherhood Week: Information sources:**

  Xerox Co. offers a series of booklets on Black History; these are sold by:

  Xerox Educational Sciences
  600 Madison Ave.
  New York, N.Y. 10016

  Nat'l. Conference of Christians & Jews
  43 W. 57th St.
  New York, N.Y.

- **Malcolm X Day** [21]

  A drop-out from school & an ex-convict, this man grew to become an American Black leader. Early in the 50's he joined the Black Muslims. After a decade of service he was suspended in 1963. An eloquent, provocative speaker, Malcolm X founded a new nationalist movement, "Afro-American Unity," in 1964. Hostility between the 2 groups developed & finally erupted into violence when Malcolm X was shot to death while addressing a rally of his followers.

  Etymology. A martyr is a person who chooses to suffer or die rather than give up his beliefs or principles. We get this word from the Greek *martyr,* or *martys:* a "witness."

- **Birth of George Washington** [22]

  We learn from his biographers that Washington was a Virginia gentleman who wore dentures made of wood, wire & elk's teeth; he kept detailed records of the money he spent; known occasionally to swear, Washington was not noted for a sense of humor. But it is not for these oddities that he is called the Father of Our Country. His was the strength & perseverance that kept our men fighting in a Revolutionary War that practically demanded surrender. And without Washington's leadership during the formative years of our country, America might never have existed.

Bulletin board suggestion

After discussing with your class the story of Washington, cover a bulletin board with blue paper. Make waves at the top as shown. Have the title "ride" the waves. If possible get a reproduction of the painting "Washington Crossing the Delaware." Pin this to one side of the title, giving the illusion of a tiny boat atop the bulletin board waves. Print the following questions below the title:

What did Washington take across the Delaware, beginning with A?
What did he use to cross, beginning with B?
What day did he go on, beginning with C?
Whom were they looking for, beginning with E?
What did his men carry, beginning with F?
Whom did they fight, beginning with H?
What did Washington's soldiers take, beginning with P?

To the right of each question have a series of waves covering the answer. Children lift up the waves to read the answers: A-army; B-boat; C-Christmas; E-enemy; F-flags; H-Hessians; P-prisoners. Washington also took B-bullets; C-cannon; P-powder; S-supplies; S-soldiers. His men took M-muskets; S-swords. They fought the T-Tories.

Word etymology. "Hatchet" comes from the French word "hachette," the diminutive of "hache" (ax), & so "hatchet" means "little ax." According to Roman writers, the cherry is named after the city Cerasus which was in the ancient kingdom of Pontus on the Black Sea. A pie is made by filling a crust with a mixture, a collection of a variety of things. "Pie" comes from the same Latin word *pica,* as does the word "magpie." That's because a magpie has the habit of collecting oddments, a jumble or mixture of things! "President" comes from the word "preside" which we get from the Latin *praesidere. Prae* means "before" & *sedere* means "sit." So our President is a man who presides by "sitting before this nation"!

Vocabulary enrichment words: honorable, dedicated, tenacious, persistent, affluent, literate, equestrian, monarchy, republic.

Riddles: Name the flower that tells what George Washington was to his country. (Poppy.) We have very good telegraph service to Hong Kong & to Paris & to Rome. Then why is it awfully difficult to try to send a telegram to Washington today? (Washington died in 1799!)

A Game for Washington's Birthday: "Cherry Pie" This game for younger children helps improve coordination & running skills. Children form a circle, holding hands. This is "the pie" & each child is "a piece of pie." "It" runs around outside of circle & holds his arms together outstretched, pretending to be a knife. He brings his arms down quickly between 2 children & shouts "I cut the pie!" Then he stands with his hands at his sides. The two children "cut" go racing in opposite directions outside the circle. The one who gets back to his place 1st, cries "Here I am, Cherry Pie!" He becomes the new knife.

• **Leap Year Day   [29]**

Of unknown origin is the custom that in leap years women may take the initiative & propose. In 1288 an act of Scottish Parliament permitted a woman during leap year to propose to a man & if the woman were rejected (unless he could prove that he was already engaged), the man had to pay her 100 pounds. In a few years a similar law was passed in France; in the 15th century, the tradition was legalized in Italy. By 1600 the custom was a part of common law in England.

Riddle: What's the best day for a kangaroo? (Leap Year Day!)

FEBRUARY ACTIVITIES

A very informative bulletin board can be made by collecting the following: pictures of animals (native to your state), their tracks or track-casts, pictures of common wild birds, their nests, bird feathers, pictures of local trees, their leaves & their winter twigs. Number each item. Children try to locate the numbers of matching pairs. Although this display does take preparation, once the items are collected, you can save them & use them again another year.

Social Studies

If your class has an encyclopedia at its disposal, have a group of children compile a list of important place names that have been in the news recently. The group selects 5-10 names in such a way that different volumes of your encyclopedia may be in use at 1 time. An atlas, a world globe & wall maps will also be used. Divide the class into groups, 1 for each place name on the list. Each group then selects the proper volume of the encyclopedia, finds their place name on the map & then completes a mimeo-sheet which you have prepared & which is headed "Where on EARTH is it?" It asks the children to locate their place name on a map of the state, nation, or the continent; list the bordering lands & waters, find the exact longitude & latitude; estimate how far it is from their home town to this place name; decide how important this place name is to its state or nation; decide what kind of life style the people living there may have.

Language Arts

"A Letter to My Teacher." Set aside a time during which the children will each write you a letter. Ask them to carefully plan the things they would like to ask or tell you. Explain that these letters are strictly personal & will not be read aloud or displayed. You might answer each of their letters separately, or you may post an open letter to the class in reply to their missives.

Haiku. This verse form has been written since the 13th century. It is a little Japanese poem of 3 lines. The 1st & last lines always have 5 syllables; the middle line has 7 syllables. Haiku are usually nature poems describing the season or explaining the feelings of the poet. A haiku does not rhyme. It paints a small, often exquisite picture in your mind.

> The patting of rain
> Mist gently on my window
> Then a pounding! Hail.*

Have your class read this haiku aloud together, clapping in unison at each syllable. Ask the students to describe the mental images they had while reading this poem. Then give the children the 1st two lines of a haiku, i.e.:

> At this time of year
> I am always thinking how
> . . . . .

Let them supply the 3rd line. Discuss their responses. Now with the aid of Webster & Roget (the thesaurus helps immensely in finding a synonym with the right number of syllables), let your class begin composing their own haiku.

Reading. Young students will enjoy reading in their spare time from the *"Magic Readers."* These are made by 1st folding a mimeo mastersheet in 1/2, crosswise. On one 1/2 of the sheet print a short story that directs the child to do something. ("Get blue. Make a thing you use. We can all use it. We can paint it now. Color it blue. We can paint it blue. Guess what it is.") On the

---

*Used with permission of the author, Elisabeth Tracy.

remaining 1/2 sheet print a story that is a description. ("He is good. He is not old. He is brown & white. He is for me. He likes to play. He & I play.") Once these are run off, each mimeo is folded in 1/2, book-fashion, & a piece of newsprint folded in 1/2 is inserted in the middle of the mimeo. A colored paper cover states:

Name_____

Magic Reader Number_____

Cover & pages are stapled together. Any object that the child wishes to draw is acceptable, as long as it corresponds to the description given. This way each child's Magic Reader may have entirely different illustrations.

Secret Messages. Each child in the reading group is given a small card on which appears a set of instructions. You create specific cards for each child emphasizing those word analysis skills that he needs, or which the group has recently reviewed. Or you may simply have a stack of cards, each child choosing one card. The group silently reads their cards to themselves. Then each child acts out the instructions on his card:

Catch a big fish. Be a rabbit; eat cabbage. Act like a bee; act as if you are going to a flower; get some honey from the flower. Walk to the window; look out the window. Act like a bird. Stand under a light; stay there until I call your name. Walk; find a hat; put the hat on your head; sit. Act as if you have lost something; act as if you found what you lost.

Older children may have more complicated directives:

Let us see you creep like a black sheep in the deep green grass. Then you seem to hear a bad noise. It is a FOX! Scram! Don't hang around. You keep on fleeing, but the fox gets you. So all you can do is weep.

The others in the group try to figure out what is being pantomimed. Finally the actor reads his card aloud to the rest of his group.

Math enrichment activities

(The following information, or a portion of it, could make an interesting bulletin board display):

How we got our standards of length. These came about in a natural way from parts of the body: fingernails, arms, feet, fingers—each became a unit of length. The cubit, 1st known measurement (about 20"), was the length of an Egyptian's forearm from the tip of his elbow to the end of his middle finger. A digit (which is from .72 to .75 inch) was the breadth of a Sumerian's finger. Even today "digit" still means "finger." A foot to the Greeks could be subdivided into 12 thumbnail breadths. This foot-unit passed on to Rome & so the invaders brought it to Britain where its division of 1/12 (or *unciae*) became "inches." In Britain the Anglo-Saxons had a measurement called the "fathom"—the length across two arms outstretched. Cloth was the Norman's most important trade. Under them half a fathom, the length from the middle of the body to the end of 1 arm outstretched, was used for measuring fabric. And *that's* how we got the yard. King Henry the 1st, in the 11th century, decreed that the distance from the tip of his nose to the end of his thumb should be the lawful yard. In 1325 Edward II passed a law that 3 kernels of corn taken from the center of the ear & placed end to end equalled 1". (This meant that a foot could be from 9 3/4" to 19"!) In the 16th century the length of the left foot of 16 men who were lined up as they came out of church on Sunday morning became the lawful rod!

A big chart to give younger children experience with the sequence of numbers & the counting of money. On a large piece of tagboard measure off 3 rows & divide these into 4 spaces each. Repeat these measurements on a 2nd piece of tagboard. Into each space on 1 piece of tagboard paste the picture of an object & its actual cost. Make a few of these objects humorous if possible. On the remaining piece of tagboard, cut 3-sided flaps that will cover objects & their prices. Glue this piece of tagboard in place atop 1st piece. Put under weights until dry. Then provide class with a pile of play coins, post the chart, & instruct 1st child to "lift up the 2nd window in the 3rd row & tell us what you see. In what ways could you pay for this 19¢ object? Give the 'store keeper' the correct number of cents."

Science

Sound Exploration. These activities would offer fine preparation for organizing a bulletin board display:

1. Keep a record of every sound you hear in 3 minutes.
2. Make a list: "The Uses of Sound."
3. Experiment: How many sounds can you make with a pencil? a comb? 2 bobby pins? a glass of water? Write up a record describing these sounds.

4. An ode was originally a poem to be sung. Write an ode to an animal, insect, fish or bird.
5. Listen to a recording of sounds, i.e., Folkway record 6115, "Bird Calls"; 6120, "Sound of a Tropical Rain Forest"; 6122, "Sounds of the American Southwest"; & 6170 & 6180, featuring noise of machinery, street traffic, applause, New Year's Eve in N.Y.C.
6. Paint to music, i.e., Cage, Stockhausen or Samuel Barber's *Piano Concerto.*
7. Talk about the sounds of fear. How are these different from fearful sounds?
8. Tell a story with sounds.
9. Give the class a bag of bones & rubber bands. Make up a tribal chant & its accompaniment using these.
10. Talk about the sounds of anger, of playfulness & of distress.
11. Man makes instruments from objects he finds in his environment (e.g., seed pods in South America, shells in Fiji, bones in Africa). What objects specific to *our* culture suggest musical instruments to you? Make a drawing of several such instruments.

February Game

What to do when it's too cold to go out & play: One night ask the children to write as homework a group of 10 statements on any historical place, famous person, or form of nature. Each statement is to help in the identification of the object. Then ask them to arrange these statements in order from the most obscure to the most revealing. Check over these lists yourself, then return them to the students. Divide the class into teams. Each team decides on a list (from those of teammates) to use. Each team will in turn present its list of 10 statements. Team decides on 1 guess they will venture: ONLY 1 guess a time. If a team gets the right answer after 1 statement, they receive 10 points. One less point is earned after each additional statement.

February E-Z Puppet

Child measures the length of his index finger against a toilet-tissue tube. One inch is added. Cut around tube. Roll a piece of newspaper into a small ball. Put this in the center of a folded single sheet of newspaper. Stand the tube atop the ball. Bring the newspaper tightly up over the ball & tube. Tightly wind string around the length of the tube. Tie string where ball meets tube, forming neck of puppet. Cover head with a piece of sheet, leaving enough fabric to go past neck. Fasten sheet in place at neck with rubber band or string. Make features on the face by gluing on felt, or by painting them with poster paints or a felt-tip pen. Now child is ready to make the clothing. He measures a piece of colored fabric 2 1/2 x the length of his hand & 1 1/2 x the width of his hand when his fingers are outstretched. Locate the middle of this fabric. Make a tiny slit & cut shoulders. Glue the shoulder seams together with white glue. Also glue the side seams together. Carefully push the head through the slit in fabric. Glue the neck of clothing to the neck of puppet. Tie a little necktie, bow, or collar around neck to cover glued area.

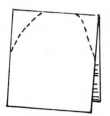

March

March brings breezes loud and shrill,
Stirs the dancing daffodil.

1   1st U.S. bank established, 1780.
2   1st round world non-stop flight, 1949.
3   Alexander Graham Bell (1847-1922), American scientist, inventor of the telephone.
4   U.S. Constitution went into effect, 1789.
5   Howard Pyle (1853-1911), American writer, illustrator.
6   Magellan Day.
    Michelangelo Buonarroti (1475-1564) [commonly known by his 1st name, Michelangelo], Italian painter, sculptor, architect.
    Elizabeth Barrett Browning (1806-1861), English poet: *Sonnets from the Portugese.*
    Fall of the Alamo 1836; captured by Antonio Santa Ana.
7   Luther Burbank (1849-1926), American horticulturist: developed over 200 plant varieties.
    Maurice Ravel (1875-1937), French composer: "Bolero."
    Alexander Bell patented telephone, 1876.
9   Amerigo Vespucci (1451-1512), Italian navigator after whom America is named.
10 Harriet Tubman (c. 1821, died on this day: 1913), American Negro abolitionist, called "Moses" by her people because she led 300 blacks to freedom (1850-1860).
    1st paper money issued in the U.S., 1862.
12 U.S. Post Office established, 1789.
13 Standard Time established in U.S., 1884.

14 Eli Whitney patented the cotton gin, 1794.

Johann Strauss (1825-1899), Austrian composer: "Blue Danube."

Albert Einstein (1870-1955), German-born American physicist, mathmetician.

1st transatlantic broadcast, 1925.

15 "The Ides of March" on which Julius Caesar was assassinated: 44 B.C.

Andrew Jackson (1767-1845), 7th U.S. President.

16 James Madison (1751-1836), 4th U.S. President.

George Ohm (1787-1854), German physicist.

17 St. Patrick's Day.

18 Grover Cleveland (1837-1908), 22nd & 24th U.S. President.

Nikolai Rimsky-Korsakov (1844-1908), Russian composer.

Rudolph Diesel (1858-1913), German engineer, invented the diesel engine.

20 Ovid [Publius Ovidius Naso] (43 B.C.-17 A.D.), Roman poet.

21 Spring equinox.

Johann Sebastian Bach (1685-1750), German composer.

Modest Mussorgski (1835-1881), Russian composer.

22 Anthony Van Dyck (1599-1641), Flemish painter.

Patrick Henry delivered his "liberty or death" speech, 1775 (see pg. 000).

24 Harry Houdini (1874-1926), American magician.

25 Gutzon Borglum (1871-1941), American sculptor, created Mt. Rushmore National Monument, S.D.

26 Robert Frost (1874-1963), American poet.

27 Nathaniel Currier (1813-1888), American lithographer, depicted manners, people of that time.

Wilhelm C. Roentgen (1845-1923), German physicist; discoverer of X-rays.

Mies van der Rohe (1886-1969), German architect.

29 John Tyler (1790-1862), 10th U.S. President.

30 Francisco Goya (1746-1828), Spanish painter.

Vincent van Gogh (1853-1890), Dutch painter.

31 Joseph Haydn (1732-1809), Austrian composer.

U.S. Daylight Savings Time began 1918 & lasted 2 years. It was repealed due to the violent protests from farmers

that their cows gave milk an hour after the milk trains
had passed. Following World War II it was re-established.
Holidays that may occur in March: Palm Sunday, Easter,
Passover, Arbor Day.
Pesach: The Passover (springtime). It is a celebration of the
freeing of the Israelites from Egypt. A traditional dinner,
"seder," is preceded by the reading of the Haggadah
which tells the story of the exodus.

March

In the Roman calendar, March was the 1st month of the year. This was
the season for the waging of war & so the Romans named this month
after Mars, the god of war. In 45 B.C. Caesar reformed the calendar &
March became the 3rd month. The expression "mad as a March hare"
evolved since "March is the mating season for hares & during this
month they are supposedly 'full of whimsy.'"

MARCH QUOTATIONS

3   Mr. Watson, come here; I want you. (1st words spoken over
      telephone, March 10, 1876 by Alexander Bell.)

6   It is only well with me when I have a chisel in my hand.
      Trifles make perfection, but perfection is no trifle.
                                        —Michelangelo Buonarroti

14   Imagination is more important than knowledge. ("On
      Science")

      Sometimes one pays most for the things one gets for
      nothing.

      I never think of the future. It comes soon enough.

      My political ideal is democracy. Everyone should be
      respected as an individual, but no one idolized.

      When a man sits with a pretty girl for an hour, it seems like
      a minute. But let him sit on a hot stove for a minute—and
      it seems longer than any hour. *That's* relativity.
                                        —Albert Einstein

15   Et tu, Brute? (You also, Brutus?)—Alleged dying words of
      Caesar

      Our Federal Union: It must and shall be preserved; [Toast
      at Jefferson's birthday banquet, 1830]—Andrew Jackson

18   I believe our Great Maker is preparing the world, in His own
      good time, to become one nation, speaking one language.
      (Inaugural Address 1893)—Grover Cleveland

20   The crop always seems better in our neighbor's field, and
      our neighbor's cow gives more milk.—Ovid

21   (1st day of spring)
      Grass is the forgiveness of nature—her constant benedic-
      tion—Forests decay, harvests perish, flowers vanish, but
      grass is immortal. —Ingalls (Speech 1874)

27   (Speaking of architectural design:) "Less is more."—Mies
      van der Rohe

      March Riddles: What is the worst month for a soldier? (A *long*
      March.) What can pass before the sun without leaving a shadow?
      (The winds of March!) What day is a command to move on?
      (March fourth.)

MARCH EVENTS

• **Birth of Alexander Graham Bell**   [3]

   He knew the pattern of vibrations made by sound in the
air, so he searched for an electric current that would follow the
same pattern. It took several years of experimenting before he had
refined his ideas & invented the 1st telephone.

   "The History of Hello" may be used as a bulletin board
display. Long ago people greeted one another by saying, "Hail."
This became slurred to "hallo" & finally was pronounced "hello"
in America. The French, German & Dutch still say "hallo" & the
Spanish say "Hola."

   In the early days of the telephone, people answered the
phone by saying: "Are you there?" (This is still used in England.)
It is said that Thomas A. Edison originated the practice of using
the word "hello" as the opening greeting in telephone conversa-
tions.

   Etymology: *Tele* is Greek for "far away" & *phone* means
"sound."

   Science. Mimeo-sheets are placed on a table along with
objects & materials to be used in experimentation. Each sheet has
space for child's name & the date, & is titled "Magnets." Beneath
this is written:

1. What will a magnet attract? Check one: (Yes & No columns are at the right side of sheet). Brass, Copper, Cork, Glass, Iron, Nickel, Plastic, Rock, Rubber, Seashells, Silver, Steel, Wood.
2. Will a magnet attract another magnet? Will it attract both ends of the other magnet? Can you find out why?
3. How can you make a magnet of a needle that is here?
4. How are magnets useful in the world today?

- **Birth of Amerigo Vespucci   [9]**

America was named by a young German geographer, Martin Waldseemuller. He included in his book of 1503 a map showing a region he called "New World." He had been greatly impressed by the writing of Amerigo Vespucci, who had himself referred to these lands as "new," & so Waldseemuller designated part of the land as "America," mentioning in the margin why he had done so. This enraged the Spaniards, who, jealous for their Christopher Columbus, refused to use the name "America" until the 18th century.

- **Eli Whitney patented the cotton gin   [14]**

"The yankee Eli Whitney, by inventing the cotton gin, perhaps made inevitable the Civil War. The yankee Eli Whitney, by popularizing (if not inventing) the principle of interchangeable parts, contributed heavily to the winning of the war by the Union."*

- **Birth of Georg Ohm   [16]**

G.S. Ohm discovered a unit of electricity & it is named after him: an ohm is a unit of electrical resistance equal to the resistance of a circuit in which 1 volt contains a current of 1 ampere.

- **The Feast day of St. Patrick   [17]**

Born in Britain, Patrick, at the age of 16, was kidnapped by Irish pirates & enslaved in Ireland. For 6 miserable years he tended sheep on the cold hills of Ballymena. He escaped finally aboard a ship to France (then known as Gaul). There he studied for the priesthood & in 431 A.D. was named a bishop. The next year he was sent by the pope to teach the gospel to the people of Hibernia—the same wild Irish tribesmen who had kidnapped him as a boy. Patrick spent nearly 30 years trudging up & down the

*Reprinted by permission of the publisher, from Thomas A. Baily: *The American Pageant*, 2nd Edition Lexington, Mass.: D.C. Heath and Company, 1965).

Emerald Isle, teaching Christianity. Few people today actually know who he was, or what he did. The Irishmen who knew him when he was alive must have loved him dearly for they have transmitted their affection for him to their descendants for 1,500 years.

Bulletin board ideas. Display pictures & information under the heading: March Is a Good Month to Learn More About Snakes. Though it's a *legend* that St. Pat drove them out of Ireland, it's a *fact* that Ireland has NO snakes today. Why do you think this may be true?

Make a large leprechaun; divide him in 2. On 1 side pin green word cards, on the other side pin corresponding white cards. These cards should be changed every few days & may emphasize homonyms, synonyms, antonyms, abbreviations, or vocabulary words. Children match the appropriate words.

Etymology. In Irish "seamrog" is the diminutive of "seamar," a clover. So shamrock is "a little clover." Because of its 3 leaves, it was used by St. Patrick to illustrate the Trinity, & in this way it became the symbol of Ireland. The potato is a native of Peru. The Spanish conquistadores discovered it in the Andes Mts. & brought it back to Europe. The potato was introduced to America in 1719 by a group of Irishmen & so we have the "Irish potato."

Vocabulary enrichment words: chartreuse, emerald, Kelly green, forest green, verdant, blarney.

St. Patrick's Day Riddles: What was the trick in driving the snakes out of Ireland? (St. *Pa*trick.) What's the name of an Irishman you'll find on every T.V. "talk" show? (Mike.) What kind of knee does an Irish traveling salesman like best? (*Blar*ney.)

"Going to Dublin," a rainy-day reading game. Make a large chart like that shown.* Children sit in a line or semi-circle. The head seat is "Dublin" & all the players are trying to get there. Starting at the foot of the line, each child in turn spins the arrow. He reads his directions & follows them. Two or 3 turns per child can constitute a game.

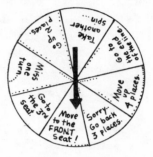

St. Patrick's Day Science. (For young children.) Bring a daisy for each child in your class. Put the flowers in a container of water to which the children add green food-coloring. As the daisies turn green, discuss how this happens (water travels to all parts of the flower, nourishing it). Let each child take a daisy home to Mother (& explain to her what has happened).

Try some starch detection experiments. Starch, a carbohydrate, is an important source of energy for humans. Starch is easily recognized by its reaction with iodine solution, when it turns blue. You will need: a medicine dropper, tincture of iodine, sugar, a slice of light & of dark bread, rice, beans, an apple, a lettuce leaf, corn, & an Irish potato. A hot plate & a pot may be used if you wish to cook the vegetables in the classroom. Boil uncooked food (rice, potato etc.) for a few minutes in order to release starch. Two or 3 drops of iodine are put on each food sample. See if the children can decide which foods will contain starch. Moisten cooked food (canned beans, corn) with a bit of water. See if the children can decide which foods will contain starch. Two or 3 drops of iodine are put on each food sample. When the dark brown iodine turns blue, this proves the presence of starch.

Help your class organize an Irish Rythm Band. (See pg.195 for instrument suggestions.) Teach them "Wearing of the Green" or "MacNamara's Band" so that they can really celebrate this day.

---

*If a small piece of corrugated cardboard is put between the arrow & the chart you may find that the arrow will spin more freely.

- **Birth of Johann Sebastian Bach   [21]**

As a child, Bach had to copy music in secret by moonlight so that his jealous older brother would not find him. It was this brother who tried to prevent Johann from becoming too proficient on the organ. But Bach grew to become a famous organist, choir leader, & composer who influenced Beethoven, Mozart, Chopin & Brahms!

Mention how at the same period in which Bach lived, Frederick the Great, Benjamin Franklin & George Frederick Handel were also alive. Indicate on the wall map the birthplace of Bach: Eisenach, Germany. Define & discuss the minuet; play "Minuet in G minor" by Bach; young children may enjoy improvising dance steps while the recording plays. The "Prelude" & the "Fugue" might be defined & presented in a similar manner.

- **Spring begins   [21] (Vernal Equinox)**

On this day there are just 12 hours from sunrise to sunset & 12 hours from sunset to sunrise. This is called the day of the "equinox" because that word means equal (day & night). In Greek mythology, Demeter & Zeus had a daughter named Persephone. One day Hades, the ruler of the underworld, kidnapped Persephone & married her. When Persephone left the Earth, the flowers died & the wheat withered. Demeter begged the gods to send her daughter back; the gods agreed to let her return for 2/3 of each year. When Persephone returned to Earth, life began anew. She corresponds to the Corn Spirit (of the American Indians) which died & was re-born each year.

Bulletin board ideas. Title: "A Collection of Fine Specimens." Display excellent papers done by children & intersperse these with 3-dimensional butterflies, the wings of which are cut from a variety of fingerpainted papers (*both* sides of which have color).

Two possible bulletin board titles (or writing assignment self-starters) for young children are: (1) "What did you see, touch,

smell, hear on your way to school this morning?" (2) "What are
the loveliest things you know (people not included)?"

As children have a tendency to grow restless at this time of
year, plan a class walk to see pollywogs, pussywillows & to LOOK
at spring's arrival. If your school is in a city, what signs of spring
CAN be seen, heard? When you get back in the classroom suggest
that each child make a drawing or painting that is "as fresh & new
as spring" (which may be the title for the display of this artwork)!

> *A Spring Riddle:* Why is it more dangerous to go out in spring
> than in any other time of the year? (Because in spring the grass
> has new blades, the flowers have pistils, the leaves shoot, the bean
> stalks, and the bulrushes [bull rushes] out!)

Spring Poetry

> Now every field is clothed with grass,
> And every tree with leaves;
> Now the woods put forth their blossoms,
> And the year assumes its gay attire.
>
> —Virgil

> For lo, the winter is past,
>   the rain is over and gone.
> The flowers appear on the earth,
>   the time of singing has come,
> and the voice of the turtledove
>   is heard in our land.
> —The Song of Solomon, 2:11-12

Also appropriate:

> "The Rain" by R.L. Stevenson
> "The Wind" by Christina G. Rossetti
> "Who Has Seen the Wind" by Christina G. Rossetti

Spring Science

The observation of nonpoisonous snakes can be an invaluable
classroom experience. Snakes are clean, quiet & aesthetically
pleasing. These reptiles are an important factor in the ecology of
our land. Although a 1st hand study of snakes can do much to
temper a generalized attitude of fear & suspicion, this classroom
experience is not for every teacher.

First check with your principal to get his permission.

Talk with your students to learn how each of them feels
about having a reptile in his classroom.

Then, if the reaction of the class is positive, set about choosing a snake with which you yourself feel at ease. It only perpetuates the cliche to present your students with an animal about which their teacher feels apprehensive.

Snakes can be collected in the spring months. They don't enjoy being handled, so children shouldn't over-do it. When handling a snake of less than 4 feet, let him move through your palms as you slowly go hand over hand along his length. This gives the snake the feeling that he is moving away. Grabbing a snake behind its head actually restricts the snake.

King snakes are the best snakes for classroom observation.* Adult gopher snakes are also good. Both are heavy-bodied, docile, eat well in captivity & are easy to handle. King snakes may lay eggs in captivity; gopher snakes over 3' long are of breeding age (3 years old), & gopher snakes breed well in captivity.

Keep snake in a cage that is as long as he is.

Using lots of hot water & Ajax, sterilize any commercially made cage & then put it out in the sun to kill mites (the sun dehydrates mites). A sterilized aquarium tank may be used, but don't use screening as a covering for its top as snake will rub his nose raw against wire screening. Instead, wrap a hardware cloth around a piece of screening cut to the size of top of tank. Snakes are natural escape artists, so any cage exits should be firmly secured.

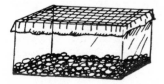

Put a piece of slate, bark, or a small box into cage so that snake may hide beneath it. Don't put plants into a snake's cage as plants may carry mites.

A Few Suggestions About Keeping Toads, Lizards & Snakes in the Classroom

Toads may be kept in a gallon jar, the lid of which has holes punched in it.

Toads will eat common earthworms & most soft-bodied

---

*The common garter snake may bite, has an odor, & won't readily eat in captivity.

insects (hairless caterpillars, meal-worms, adult & white crickets, termites & fly maggots). To obtain the latter, put some meat in a canning jar. When it is clear that flies have been there, screw on the rim, substituting wire screen for the metal disc. When flies hatch, dump the maggots, sans meat, into the toad's jar. (Adult toads will eat baby toads so they must be segregated.)

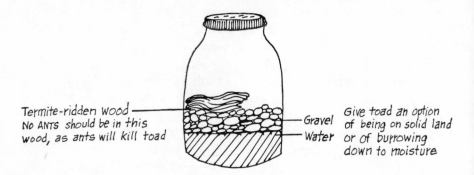

Termite-ridden wood — No ANTS should be in this wood, as ants will kill toad

Gravel
Water

Give toad an option of being on solid land or of burrowing down to moisture

Toads won't hibernate in the classroom as it is not cold enough there to trigger hibernation.

Some lizards require a lot of heat. Chameleons need 85°, & they may need their cages sprayed with water every day—& NO water dish left in the cage. Most other lizards need to have a water dish in their cages. Put a plastic vine in their cage for cover. Find out where your lizard came from & try to duplicate that environment.

Both snakes & lizards should have a coarse grade of gravel, NOT sand, in the bottom of their cages. Sand gets in their food & causes mouth rot. The aquarium gravel sold in pen shops is (as any gravel used *must* be) sterilized. After it has been used for several months, it can be re-sterilized by boiling it for a few hours or by baking it at 450° for 1 hour; this will save you the cost of purchasing new gravel every 2-3 months.

Give snakes water, but not enough to soak in (except during shedding period). If it gets too humid in cage, snake develops water blisters & starts cycle of ill health. Snakes periodically shed; 3-4 days before shedding, snake's eyes will turn blue. This is a good time to give him a bowl of water in which to soak.

Don't put 2 snakes in the same cage; it is an emotionally unhealthy environment for them. King snakes will eat 1 another, & infections can spread.

Don't place a snake's glass cage in sunlight. Glass blocks out the beneficial ultra-violet rays of sun & heat of direct sunlight will literally cook snake. The ideal temperature for snakes is 65°-85°. If the captive snake comes from the same general area as the school, there is no need to provide artificial heat. To heat a snake's cage do *not* dangle a bulb down into cage. A 15-25 watt bulb used as shown should work well. It's a good idea to have a thermometer to reassure one that temperature is 65°-85° within cage.

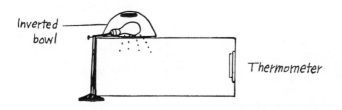

Feed snakes once a week. Most snakes will eat live mice, smooth-scaled lizards & *especially,* live frogs. If snake (especially a small one) doesn't eat for a month, set him free!

An easy way to differentiate between male & female: The tail of the male is longer & tapers more gradually. This is because the male sex organs are in the tail. The female's tail tapers suddenly to a point.

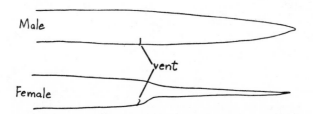

How to Recognize Dangerous Snakes & Lizards of the Continental U.S.A.

There are 5 different types of poisonous snakes: rattlesnakes, water moccasins, copperheads, coral snakes & rear-fanged snakes. *Rattlers, moccasins & copperheads* are all pit vipers, having broad heads & a pit under each nostril. (A rattlesnake has rattles at the end of its tail.) Rattlesnakes are found, mainly, in the mid & S.W. United States, though they are still common in some areas of the

N.E. & S.E. Copperheads are found in the E. part of the U.S. & moccasins are found in the South.

Coral snakes have conspicuous rings of red, black & yellow. An old saying warns:

> When Red touches Yellow
> You'd better RUN, fellow!

(The beneficial Kingsnake has rings of *yellow*, black, *red*, black, *yellow*, black, *red*, black, etc.)

The coral snake is found in the South & Southwest.

Rear-fanged snakes are small, rare & secretive. Their venom is very mild (equivalent to a wasp's sting). They are found in the Western U.S.A.

The Gila Monster, found in Arizona, & its Mexican cousin, the Bearded Lizard, are the only poisonous lizards in the world.

Spring Clue Charts

Let the children make personalized clue charts for the identification of trees & flowers (similar to Bird Charts—see pg. 218). Seeds, leaves, insects, & *plentiful* nature specimens may be included.

Revisit the class tree & study all the life around it. Talk about the changes brought on by spring. Watch for the 1st flowers, the 1st leaves, the 1st insects, & record these dates. Changing cloud forms may also be noted.

• Birth of Harry Houdini   [24]

Bulletin board suggestion: Title—"In Honor of Houdini and National Magic Week":

> YOU'RE the Magician. Sometimes don't you wish you could change things to suit YOURSELF? Well, here's your chance! Let's see how you'd change THESE things: What would you make bigger so that it would be more fun? What would you make slower so you could use it more often? What would you make sparkle so it would be more helpful? etc.

These might be answered on a mimeo-sheet or as a Creative Writing assignment.

Word etymology. The priests of ancient Persia had a word *magus* that meant "priest" or "fireworshipper." This word later became *magos*, meaning "a wizard" or "a juggler." From this came the word *magikos* which became "magic." Our "magicians" have generally retained all the original meanings implied by their name.

Reading for older students. None of the instructions are given orally; they are all written prior to class on large sheets of newsprint, or on the chalk board, in the following manner:

The Ashes Can Speak!

I am a mind reader! I have a few slips of paper to write numbers on. As I call you, come up & whisper a number for me to write down. I will fold each slip & put it in the tall can. Then I will ask someone to come up & pull out 1 slip of paper. He must not tell its number. The rest of the slips will be set on fire & burned up. Then I will read the ashes!

After slips have been burned in a tall metal can (wastebasket),* sift through the ashes slowly. Then announce that it's easy for you to read the remaining slip held by the student! Announce it (since you wrote down the 1st number you were told on *every* single slip of paper you can't go wrong). Pass out a mimeographed sheet that explains how & why the trick worked. This way the class *reads* the answer. Mention on the mimeo (& verbally impress upon the class) that this trick has *got* to be done in a tall metal can & with their mother's or father's O.K.!

Math enrichment

Number tricks. Ask each child to choose a number & keep it secret. "Double your number. Now multiply it by 5 & tell me the total." (Knock off final digit & you will have their secret number.) Why does it work? Children have actually multiplied numbers by 10. VARIATION: "Take a number. Double it. Now add 9. Subtract 3. Divide by 2. Subtract the number you started with. The answer you now have is 3!" (It will always be 3, because

$$\frac{2X + (9-3)}{2} - X \rightarrow \frac{2X+6}{2} - X \rightarrow X + 3 - X = 3.)$$

*Have a wet towel handy—just in case—to impress the class with your feelings about safety measures!

"Scientific" Magic Tricks

Magic Candle. Offer to light a candle without touching fire to its wick. First light a candle as you are explaining that *anyone* can light a candle *this* way. Blow it out. Light a 2nd candle & let it burn a minute. Hold 1st candle 3" above lighted candle in path of rising smoke. Flame travels up smoke & lights candle.

Magic Milk Bottle. Set bottle on table & drop a lighted match inside bottle. Place the small end of a peeled soft (but firm) boiled egg in mouth of bottle. Hold it there. The heat has created a partial vacuum & this sucks the egg inside. Once the egg is in, hold the bottle to your mouth with the small end of the egg in the neck of the bottle. Force all the air you can into the bottle by blowing, using the egg as a valve to let air in & to keep it there. When mouth is released from bottle, egg is forced out by air pressure.

Magic Needle. Drop a needle slantwise into a glass of water; needle sinks. Retrieve needle; dry it. Grasp needle at its middle & gently lower it to surface of water; needle floats. Explain how surface tension of water is supporting needle.

Information source:

The Society of American Magicians
93 Central St.
Forestville, Conn.

• Birth of Mies van der Rohe   [27]

Here is an art project that uses architectural forms as a basis: Each child is given a large sheet of 1/8" thick corrugated cardboard, the type that has a somewhat rough surface. Children draw their basically linear compositions on cardboard with pencil or chalk. Toothpicks are then glued to follow the general outline of the drawing. Thin balsawood (in sheets or sticks, available at hobby stores) is cut into appropriate lengths & used for outlining tiny areas & for giving a variety of textures. When glue is absolutely dry, a thin mixture of plaster of Paris is prepared & this is applied to the entire surface of the cardboard with the use of old, clean, wide brushes & various sponges; these last are used, again, for textural effects. Wherever toothpicks have been glued closely together, plaster must be applied with care so as not to clog area & make composition imprecise. Once surface is set, color is applied. Let the children experiment, using diluted poster paint applied with soft big brushes. A deep color, emphasizing the linear element, is applied, lastly, by brayer.

MARCH ACTIVITIES

Bulletin board suggestions. "March was named for Mars, the Roman god of War. Mars is also the name of a planet, 4th in distance from the sun. Let's learn some more about this planet. Mars is famous for its red light. Its circumference is 4,230 miles. (The earth's is 24,830 miles at the equator.) Its year is 686.9 days.

(Ours is 365 days.) ⚤ is the symbol of MARS (and also the symbol for MAN)."

Title: "It Happened in_____." Divide your class into the same number of groups. Each group decides on a historical date & place with which to complete the title. *Any* historical event (discussed in class this year) may be used. Each group works privately to complete their section. The completed display can be very interesting visually, & informative.

Title: "The Origin of the Umbrella." The umbrella or parasol originated in Asian countries* where it was used as protection against the glaring sun. "Parasol" actually means "for sun" (*para* = for + *sol* = sun)! It was introduced into England from Italy in the 18th c. Englishmen shunned it as being "women's wear" until Jonas Hanway, an English traveler, demonstrated its usefulness against rain. In 1740 when it was 1st used in America at Windsor, Conn., it was ridiculed; the townspeople made a line behind its poor owner & they paraded along carrying sieves attached to broomsticks!

Social Studies

A Biographic Movie. A group of these make an intriguing display for Public Schools Week. Have the children bring sturdy small boxes (shoe boxes are good). A rectangular hole for the "movie screen" is cut in the bottom of each box. Hole should not be cut right up to edge of bottom; a bit of bottom should remain as a frame. Cut a long strip of white butcher paper, a bit narrower than the width of the box (i.e., 10" x 24" long). Children choose a famous person in history. They divide paper into sections (leaving

---

*Umbrellas appear in Assyrian friezes of the 7th century B.C.

several inches free at top & bottom of strip) according to the number of "frames" they want in their "film." Titles for the film & an appropriate closing are designed. Balloons from the characters may be used or commentary may be printed atop each frame. Encourage ingenuity in the illustration of the films. The variety should be most appealing. Perhaps making a draft on news print 1st will save butcher paper & patience. Once the movie is finished, it is taped from its topmost edge to the wooden dowel (or if the box is big, to the paper-toweling tube). Dowel is then carefully inserted into 2 holes which have been made (& re-enforced) in the sides of the box somewhat above the top of the movie screen. By turning the protruding ends of the dowel, movie is rolled up until bottom edge is exposed. This is taped to the lower dowel (or tube) which has already been inserted in the lower 2 holes shown. Wooden spools or beads may be glued to the ends of dowels to facilitate turning of film.

Language Arts

Older children may enjoy the challenge of making "Lion" into "Lamb" by changing 1 letter at a time, forming a new word at each step: Lion, Loon, Lorn, Lore, Lone, Line, Lime, Limb, LAMB!

Cinquain. An unrhymed 5-line verse, Cinquain is a form of Japanese poetry. The youngest student can have success with this writing form:

The 1st line is 1 word, the title.	Kitten
The 2nd line is 2 words & describes the subject.	Brown cat

The 3rd line has 3 words, expressing action.   Runs in circles
The 4th line has 4 words expressing feeling, emotion.   Good to play with
The 5th line is 1 word, a synonym for the title word.   Pet*

Here's one way to help your class learn to be concise in what it writes. Discuss newspaper want-ads: what they are designed to do, why they must be concise. Then each child writes an appropriate newspaper ad for some inventor who has been discussed since fall (e.g., Edison, da Vinci, Watts, Bell, Carver, Franklin). These ads may be composed as though the inventor were trying to sell his patent or as if the invention had just been discovered today.

Weather indicators. March is a month of varied weather. Have the children observe natural change-of-weather indicators & make a collection of these (over a weekend). Such lists, when thoughtful & detailed, are usually also quite poetic. Here is such a list as found in a 19th century reference book:

> "Weather Indicators, Animal Creation: Rain is sure to come when the cattle snuff the air and gather together in a corner of the field with their heads to leeward; when sheep leave their pastures with reluctance; when goats go to sheltered spots; when dogs lie much about the fireside and appear drowsy; when cats turn their backs to the fire and wash their faces; when pigs cover themselves more than usual in litter; when cocks crow at unusual hours and flap their wings much; when hens chant; when ducks and geese are unusually clamorous; when pigeons wash themselves; when swallows fly low and skim their wings on account of flies upon which they feed having descended toward the ground; when toads creep out in numbers; when frogs croak; when singing birds take shelter; when bees leave their hives with caution and fly short distances; when ants carry their eggs busily; when flies bite severely and become troublesome in numbers; when earthworms appear on the surface of the earth."

Rebus. This is a kind of puzzle, the meaning of which is indicated by *things* rather than by *words*. Rebus offers a way to occasionally "candy-coat" review information or a homework assignment for your class. Rebus helps children analyze the written word in a new way. It's fun to try to invent new rebus symbols. Here is a good start on a Rebus Dictionary for your students' use!

---

*Written by a twelve-year-old student, Malcolm Garrard.

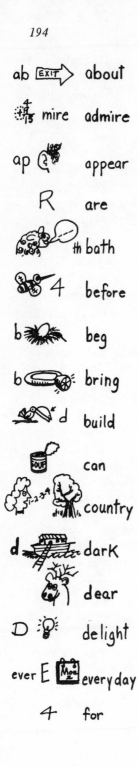

ab (EXIT→) about

mire admire

ap appear

R are

th bath

4 before

b beg

b bring

d build

can

country

d dark

dear

D delight

ever E everyday

4 for

ing going

8 great

h had

I

I learn

I k like

m my

n nice

O'c o'clock

(OFF) 10 often

or

pair

picture

T safety

salesman

saw

see

someway

t (or) st start

str 8 straight

sud LEE suddenly

t that

t then

t those

m time

tiny

t d turned

un until

w what

which

Y why

will

March Music

These instruments may be made by the teacher, by older students for a younger group, or by the students themselves:

Bass viol. Prepare a *large* tin can (an oil can from a gas station) by removing 1 end with a can opener. In the middle of the remaining end punch a small hole. Take a long piece of cord & thread it through the hole. Secure it in place by tying a button to it on the outside of the can. Tie a large button to the other end of the cord. Oil cord well with a candle stub. To play, child sits in a chair, grasps can between feet, holding cord taut by button with 1 hand & strumming cord with remaining hand.

Bongo drums. Stretch heavy plastic taut across open mouth of coffee can. Secure plastic in place with strip of inner tube or rubber sheet. Repeat with a 2nd coffee can. Bind 2 cans side by side with rope or masking tape.

Bell sticks. Saw 3/4"-1" dowel sticks (or an old broomstick) into 6" lengths. Nail (or staple) large jingle bell onto either end of stick.

Bottle xylophone. Fill 8 identical bottles with varying amounts of water to reproduce (approximate?) the 8 notes of a musical scale. Bottles are struck with pencil.

Cigarbox guee-tar. Stretch 4 rubber bands of varying widths & lengths over an open cigar box. Pick or strum bands.

Drums. Bases may be: #10 cans, nail-kegs, automatic transmission fluid cans, coffee cans, chopping bowls. Heads may be: heavy oilcloth or canvas which is coated, after attachment with clear Dope. Inner tube drumheads are more resonant; after attaching, hold tubing firmly to base by overlapping 6 (1 1/2") inner tube strips. Heads are attached to metal bases by strips of inner tubing & to wooden bases by tacking head all along 1 edge, pulling tight on the opposite side & tacking. Repeat until tacks are placed every 1" or 2". Child may hold smaller drum under 1 arm to play.

Ersatz bells. Have children collect & bring old keys to class. These or curtain rings strung on a string simulate, when shaken, the sound of bells.

Gongs. A bent metal rod or a heavy pot cover suspended from a pole is held aloft & struck with a wooden spoon.

Hand bells. Cut 2 pieces of elastic, 8" each in length. Make a loop of each & sew its ends firmly together. Sew bells onto that section of each elastic which will cover backs of hands. (Child slips hand into loop & shakes or claps hands to play bells.)

Kazoo. Cut several small holes in the middle of a paper-toweling tube. Cover 1 end of tube with a large piece of wax paper taped in place. Child places fingers on varying holes & hums or sings into open end. Of course, this instrument must, by its nature, be played by just 1 student. If several bazookas are made, children's names may be printed on each.

Knockers. Nail flat block of wood to dowel rod handle. Or drive nail down through center of wooden spool (handle) into 4" x 6" wooden block. Make 2 of each knocker.

Nail chimes. Hang nails from thick dowel & strike with small metal pipe.

Raspers. Staple sandpaper on underside of a set of knockers. Or notch the length of 2 thick dowel rods. These are then rubbed against 1 another.

Rattles. Scrub 6-8 ring-shaped bones of lamb shoulder or lamb chops. Dry well. String. Or nail a wooden dowel handle to a frozen orange juice can; put pebbles inside & cover top of can with vinyl & a rubber band. Or use small boxes or cans with snap-in lids (e.g., baking powder) & put rice or buttons inside. Or papier mache *heavily* over a large used light bulb: once covering is thoroughly dry, break bulb within.

Tambourine. Make tiny slits every inch or 2 along the edge of the round top of a cardboard container. Insert loop of sleigh bell through slit & secure in place from behind with a safety pin. Or cut 2 (1/4") circles of plywood (5" in diameter). Enamel the edges. Mark off the edges into 1/8" divisions. Flatten a number of soda pop bottle caps & punch a hole through each. Hammer a nail through each of the 1/8" marks in 1 circle. Place 4 flattened caps on each nail so that they may move freely up & down. Place 2nd circle atop nail points & hammer gently & firmly in place.

Tom-tom. Get a large hatbox or round wooden cheese box. Cut its lid in 1/2. Glue 1/2 of lid securely in place atop box. With string secure a 3" long flat stick to the middle of lid as shown. Tap on free end of stick to produce a tom-tom-like beat.

Xylophone. This affords a good lesson in fractions. Have the children collect cardboard mailing tubes. You will need strong cord & 2 wooden lathes. The proportions are: 1, 8/9, 4/5, 3/4, 2/3, 3/5, 8/15, 1/2. Tubes are struck with a dowel that has a cork nailed to its end.

March Games

Flowers in the Wind. Divide children into 2 equal groups, one being "the Wind" & the other "Flowers." The Flower group gets together & secretly chooses a specific flower as their group name Either end of the playing area is "Home"; the middle field is neutral. The members of the Wind spread out along their Home line. The Flowers walk up near to the Wind who, 1 child after another down the line, calls out the name of a different flower (pausing after each name), trying to guess the name that has been chosen by the Flowers. Once the correct flower is called out, all the Flower children race for Home, the Wind at their heels! Any Flower caught joins the Wind. Remaining Flowers choose a new name & game continues until every flower is captured.

Whip-Lash. Children form a circle except for 4 who stand in a line inside circle, with their hands on the shoulders of the child in front of them. The children in the circle have a ball & try to hit the final child in the line. Of course the line whips about protecting this player. When last child *is* struck, he goes & joins circle, & child who succeeded in hitting him becomes the new head of the line.

March Puppet: Shadow puppets & theatre

Figures (drawn in profile) are cut from tagboard or cardstock. An extra 4" or 5" is left at the bottom of the figure. Color is of no importance but detailed outline or cut-out areas add much to these puppets. Thumbtacks may also be punched into the figures, leaving tiny holes (textural areas) for light to come through. The extra inches at the bottom are folded over a dowel or stick & stapled in place. Let the children use their ingenuity to come up with solutions for how to show clouds, rain, wind, lightning.

Theatre is made from a large refrigerator box, the back side of which you have removed. Cut a large rectangular opening in the front leaving a 3" frame. Opening should be twice as tall as puppets. Staple a large piece of sheet (taut) to the inside of frame. Lay box, on its side, on top of a table. (Make sure that table is near a wall socket.) Set heavy-based lamp with a strong bulb inside box. Make sure cord is long enough to easily reach outlet. With masking tape adhere cord to floor to prevent any accidents. Place several bricks inside box to stabilize it, if necessary. Puppets may be inserted through a long opening cut on underside of box, in which case children will sit on floor beneath table & box front will slightly overlap table. Or long openings cut on either side of box will admit puppets held by students who stand beside theatre. Darken room. Children insert puppets behind screen & move them as they speak.

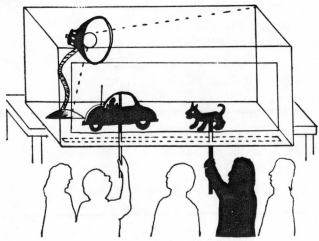

April

April brings the primrose sweet,
Scatters daisies at our feet.

1   April Fools' Day.
2   First U.S. Mint established, 1792.
      Hans Christian Andersen (1805-1875), Danish writer, collector of fairy tales.
      Sergei Rachmaninoff (1873-1943), Russian composer.
3   Washington Irving (1783-1859), American author: *Rip Van Winkle, The Legend of Sleepy Hollow.*
      John Burroughs (1837-1921), American naturalist.
      Pony Express began: 1860.
      Dorothea Dix (1802-1877), American humanitarian, reformer.
4   American flag adopted, 1818.
      Pocahontas married John Rolf, 1614.
5   Booker T. Washington (1856-1915), American educator.
6   Peary set foot on the North Pole, 1909.
7   William Wordsworth (1770-1850), English poet.
10   Beginning of U.S. Patent System, 1790.
12   Henry Clay (1777-1852), American statesman.
      U.S. Civil War began at Fort Sumter, 1861.
      Soviet Major Yuri A. Gagarin orbited earth, 1961.
13   Thomas Jefferson (1743-1826), 3rd U.S. President.
14   Lincoln fatally wounded by J.W. Booth; 1865. (Lincoln died at 7:22 the following morning.)
15   Leonardo da Vinci (1452-1519), Italian artist, inventor
      Henry James (1843-1916), American writer.

16   Wilbur Wright (1867-1912), American inventor.
     Earth Week.
18   Paul Revere's ride, 1775.
19   Patriots Day, commemorating the Battle of Lexington, 1775.
     U.S. Revolutionary War began, 1775.
     Adolph Hitler (1889-1945), German dictator.
20   Mohammed (570-632 A.D.), founder of the Moslem religion.
     Curies discovered the weight and properties of radium, 1902.
21   Legendary founding of Rome, 753 B.C.
     John Muir (1838-1914), American naturalist, writer; born in Scotland.
     Spanish-American War began, 1898.
     Birth of Queen Elizabeth II 1926; Queen of England since 1952.
     National Library Week.
22   Arbor Day (date varies in different states).
     Earth Day (Friends of the Earth).
23   William Shakespeare (1564 [disputed date] –1616).
     James Buchanan (1791-1868), 15th U.S. President.
     Sergei Prokofiev (1891-1953), Russian composer.
24   Guglielmo Marconi (1874-1937), Italian inventor.
     Wilhelm de Kooning (1904-   ,), American abstract painter.
26   John James Audobon (1785-1851), American ornithologist and artist.
     Walter de la Mare (1873-1956), English poet, writer.
27   Samuel Morse (1791-1872), American inventor.
     Ulysses S. Grant (1822-1885), 18th U.S. President.
28   James Monroe (1758-1831), 5th U.S. President.
30   President George Washington inaugurated, 1789.
     Louisiana Purchase (1803). Napoleon sold La. Territory to the U.S. for $15,000,000.
     Palm Sunday, Good Friday, Easter, Passover are movable Feasts; Easter occurs on the 1st Sunday following the full moon that falls on or after March 21st.
     Public School Week and Arbor Day may occur in other months; different states have different dates.

pril

No one knows for certain how our 4th month, April, got its name. Some sources state that it may have been named after Aphrodite, the Greek goddess of love. Webster's New World Dictionary (World Pub. Co.) says that April is akin to Latin *aprilis* which probably comes from the Indo-European root *apero*, "latter, 2nd," as April's original meaning was more than likely "the 2nd month." Other sources say that "April" may come from a Latin verb meaning "the opening." It is a fact that the Greeks called this season of spring "the opening."

APRIL QUOTATIONS

5   We are crawling up, working up, yea, bursting up. . . . There is no power on earth that can permanently stay our progress. *(The American Standard)*

No race can prosper till it learns that there is as much dignity in tilling a field as in writing a poem. *(Up from Slavery)*

–Booker T. Washington

6   The Eskimo had his own explanation. Said he, "The devil is asleep or having trouble with his wife, or we should never have come back so easily." –Admiral R. E. Peary (On his successful return from the North Pole)

7   The child is father of the man.

My heart leaps up when I behold
A rainbow in the sky.

I wandered lonely as a cloud
That floats on high o'er vales and hills,
When all at once I saw a crowd,
A host of golden daffodils.
    ("I Wandered Lonely as a Cloud")

–William Wordsworth

12   I would rather be right than be President! (Speech, 1850)–Henry Clay

13   The whole of government consists in the art of being honest.

Eternal vigilance is the price of victory.

If a nation expects to be ignorant and free, in a state of civilization, it expects what never was and never will be.

We hold these truths to be self-evident; that all men are created equal; that they are endowed by their creator with certain unalienable rights; that among these are life, liberty and the pursuit of happiness.

(Declaration of Independence)—Thomas Jefferson

14 *Sic semper tyrannis!* The South is avenged! (Spoken after he shot Lincoln, April 14, 1865. The translation of the Latin is "Thus always to tyrants!")—John Wilkes Booth

15 Iron rusts from disuse; stagnated water loses its purity and in cold weather becomes frozen; even so does inaction sap the vigors of the mind.—Leonardo da Vinci

16 I do not believe [the airplane] will surplant surface transportation. I believe it will always be limited to special purposes. It will be a factor in war. It may have a future as a carrier of mail. (Interview: March, 1906)—Wilbur Wright

18 Listen, my children, and you shall hear
Of the midnight ride of Paul Revere.

("Paul Revere's Ride": H.W. Longfellow)

19 Here once the embattled farmers stood
And fired the shot heard round the world.

("Concord Hymn": R.W. Emerson)

23 Suspicion always haunts the guilty mind.

There's nothing either good or bad, but thinking makes it so.

All the world's a stage,
And all the men and women merely players:
They have their exits and their entrances;
And one man in his time plays many parts. (*As You Like It)*
—William Shakespeare

If you are as happy, my dear sir, on entering this house, as I am in leaving it and returning home, you are the happiest man in this country. (Said to Lincoln, 1861)—James Buchanan

27 What hath God wrought! (1st message sent by Morse code: May 24, 1844)

28   The American continents . . . are henceforth not to be
     considered as subjects for future colonization by any
     European powers. (From his message to Congress,
     December 2, 1823)—James Monroe

April Riddles: Why should soldiers be tired on the first of April?
(They've just finished a March of 31 days!)
How is a crown prince like an April day? (It's very likely he will
reign [rain].)
Which is the worst month for rodents such as rats and mice?
(April: because it's always raining cats and dogs.)
Why can it never rain in April for 2 *days straight?* (Because
there's always a night in between.)

APRIL EVENTS

• **April Fools' Day   [1]**

Traditionally, on this day Noah sent the dove from the ark &
it returned, unable to find land. Some sources say that April
Fools' Day is a relic of an old Celtic heathen festival. In any case,
there are 18th century records of April Fools' Day celebrations
being held throughout Europe. In Scotland, if you're tricked
today, you're a "gowk" (Scottish for "cuckoo"); in France, you
become "un poisson d'Avril" ("an April fish"). In other words,
you're a person who's easily caught.

Some general suggestions. Write the date on the chalkboard:
"August 1, 197 " or "April 1, 1983"; asterisk the date & at the
foot of the board, in tiny letters, print: "April Fool." Set the
clock ahead (or back) & when this is discovered, use the opportunity to emphasize time-telling. Prepare a bulletin board or a
mimeographed worksheet titled: "Don't be April-fooled! Answer
the question & define the word!" Beneath this appears: "Would
you feel flattered if someone called you arrogant? enthralling?
vociferous? facetious? eccentric? insipid? rapacious? valorous?"

Another bulletin board suggestion. Display photos that are
greatly blown-up shots of portions of familiar objects or aerial
shots of the earth. These pictures have been collected by the
teacher from magazines & should be untitled; it is up to the
children to try to identify each photo. Listen as they say *how* they
came to identify each one; what types of clues they found; what
methods of deduction were used.

Language Arts. Point out the differences between a lie, a playful joke & a practical joke. Which is funny? The sense of (what is) humor(ous) differs from people to people: humor is partly a matter of culture. Talk about the role of jester in medieval times & his present day equivalent. Ask the children: *"Why* do we laugh?" Some possible answers: We laugh to release tension, anger, embarrassment, aggression, fear. We laugh to experience a sense of "togetherness," being a part of a group. Older children might give examples of different types of situations that illustrate different types of laughter.

Read aloud some Aesop's Fables in which animals get fooled. Then let the children write fables about creatures who get fooled.

Nonsense Stories, a card game. There are 4 piles of cards (green: nouns; red: verbs; blue: adjectives; yellow: adverbs). Each child picks (receives) 1 card from each pile. These cards are made into a nonsense sentence & upon this sentence the children build a nonsense story. Once the stories have been written, they can be read aloud &/or exchanged & read silently (& illustrated).

Word etymology. The Latin word *follis* from which we get "fool" means "a bag of wind"! Ambrose Bierce, in his *Devil's Dictionary,** defines April Fool as: "noun. The March fool with another month added to his folly." Vocabulary enrichment words: gullible, deceptive, fraudulent, ingenuous, guile, equanimity.

April Fools' Day Poetry.

Just As He Feared

There was an old man with a beard
Who said, "It is just as I feared!
Two Owls and a Hen, four Larks and a Wren
Have all built their nests in my beard.
      —Edward Lear: *Book of Nonsense*

Also appropriate: "Old Quin Queribus": Nancy Byrd Turner (from *Zodiac Town:* Little, Brown & Co.)

Reading

April Fool Tachistoscope. Ask the children in the reading group, "Can you tell what the jester says? Watch him speak!" or ("Take the words right out of his mouth!")

---

*Ambrose Bierce, *The Devil's Dictionary* (180 Varick St., New York, N.Y. 10014: Dover Publishing Co., 1958). © by Dover Pub. Co., Inc.

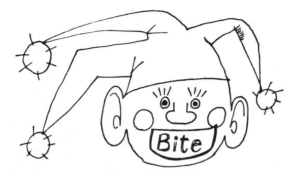

To help your class practice word analysis (& as a method of quick check-up), have each child fold his paper into 8 squares. (Teacher draws a similar pattern on the chalkboard & in each square prints a word that has an emotional connotation, i.e., furious, elated, astounded, etc.) Children draw a face in each square to reflect the word that appears in the corresponding square on the board.

Fishing with Simple Simon. Discuss the old rhyme: "Simple Simon went a-fishing, For to catch a whale; All the water he had got—Was in his mother's pail." Introduce a class fishpond (complete with bamboo or dowel fishing poles) to the reading group. Pond may be made from a large cardboard box painted blue with poster paints. Colorful cutouts of sea life are glued to the sides of box. Each child in the group goes fishing with his pole (to which a magnet on a string is tied); he tries to catch a new word (or a riddle or joke to be read aloud). Each card in the pond is made in the form of a fish (or octopus or jellyfish or old shoe) & has its message clearly printed on 1 side; the magnet on the fishing line is attracted by the large paper clip which is attached to each card. (Teachers' or Helpers' names might also be selected in this manner.)

Science

The following may be presented in the form of a mimeo sheet (to be done in free-time or as a part of homework):

"**Your Personal Science Experiments.**" (Be careful: don't be fooled!)

1 Make a tube out of a piece of paper. Hold your left hand up in front of your eyes, about 6" from your nose. Put the paper tube up to your right eye & rest the tube against the side of your left hand. Keep both eyes open and stare through the tube. What seems to happen to your left hand? Do you understand why?

2 How many pencils do you have? Tightly cross your 1st & 2nd fingers. Close your eyes. Now rub a pencil along the length between your crossed fingers. How many pencils do you think you feel? (Here's why: Under normal circumstances, the opposite edges of BOTH your index & middle fingers would not be touched at 1 time by a single object, so when such a sensation occurs, it is interpreted by your brain as coming from 2 objects.)

3 Your ♥ pumps the blood through your veins. With each "pump," the vein stretches a little. This stretching causes your "pulse." The rate of your pulse tells us how fast your ♥ is beating. You know that you can *feel* your pulse; well, here's how you can *see* how fast your heart's beating! Break a wooden matchstick or toothpick in 1/2. Stick the point of a thumbtack up into the end of the broken toothpick. It should look like this: Find your pulse: place the fingers of 1 hand along the wrist (below the thumb) of your other hand. With a felt-tip pen make a dot on the place where you feel a strong pulse. Now rest your arm on a desk or table. Place the head of the thumbtack on the dot on your wrist. Sit quietly. You should see the toothpick move with each beat of your pulsing ♥ !

The Mysterious Shoe-box. At some convenient place in your room, post the following sign & beside it place the esoteric box. "NOTICE!! You cannot IMAGINE what is in this box. You've never seen these things inside any box in your WHOLE life. But—beware! Once you look inside this box I will have April-FOOLED you! *[Signed]* Your teacher." Here's how to make the box: Tape a small hand mirror to the inside (end) wall of a shoe box. At the opposite end of the box, cut 2 small round eye-holes.

Cut a slit in the top of the box above the wall where the mirror is. Put lid on box & look through 2 round holes; if no adjustments to slit are necessary, firmly glue top of box onto bottom.

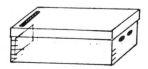

- **The date on which Peary set foot on the North Pole [6]**

   Word etymology. The Greek word *arktos* meant "bear." The Great Bear Constellation, which revolves about the northern part of the earth, is referred to as "arktikos." From this we get our word "arctic." The word "Eskimo" is said to be derived from the American Indian (Labrador-Algonquian) "eskimantik," eater of raw fish.

- **Birth of Thomas Jefferson [13]**

   He was described by his biographer, James Parton, as "The gentleman of 32 who could calculate an eclipse, survey an estate, tie an artery, plan an edifice, try a cause, break a horse, dance a minuet and play the violin."

   Jefferson himself wrote this epitaph for his grave: "Here was buried Thomas Jefferson, author of Declaration of American Independence, of the statute of Virginia for religious freedom, and father of the University of Virginia."

- **Birth of Leonardo da Vinci [15]**

   In order to protect his scientific discoveries, da Vinci described his inventions in his notebooks by the use of this "code": he reversed each letter & wrote his sentences from right to left. Your class may enjoy experimenting with mirror writing or you may occasionally write their homework assignment (on a mimeo sheet) using this technique: Print words in reverse order with each word spelled backwards & each letter reversed. Message is held up to mirror to be read. Up-side down mirror writing is produced by printing words in reverse order, each word spelled backwards & each letter printed upside down; only "s" will have to be reversed. Pocket mirror is held at right angle to message in order to "break this code."

- The date of Paul Revere's ride   [18]

    Bulletin board suggestion. Title: "Straight from the Horse's Mouth." (Perhaps title & the race-track origination of this expression should be discussed with class.*) Children list or write (in the 1st person) the impressions that Paul's horse gathered from that long night. What did he see, smell? Did anything frighten him? How did Paul speak to him? Was he tempted at any time to discontinue his mission? What were his after-thoughts? How did the other animals treat him after that night?

- Quotations for National Library Week

    A Book is a Garden carried in the Pocket.—Arabian

    Reading is to the mind what exercise is to the body.—J. Addison

    Books are ships which pass through the vast seas of time.—Bacon

    Few are better than the books they read.—Anonymous

    A man only learns in two ways; one by reading and the other by associating with smarter people.

    —Will Rogers

    To acquire the habit of reading is to construct for yourself a refuge from all the miseries of life.—Somerset Maugham

    Except a living man there is nothing more wonderful than a book! A message to us from ... human souls we never saw. . . books arouse us, terrify us, teach us, comfort us, open their hearts to us as brothers.—Kingsley

    "Little Theatre" constructions. Once his little theatre is built, each child peoples each of the 4 stages with the characters, scenery of 4 of his favorite books or 4 different events in 1 of his favorite books. These constructions can also be used for the dramatization of (reading) stories. To construct little theatres, each student gets 2 (8" x 16") pieces of cardboard & 1 (16" x 16") piece of cardboard. A slit is made to the middle of each of the 2 smaller pieces & they are then inserted into 1 another forming the 4 walls of the theatre; the slits may be reinforced with tape. The larger piece of cardboard is glued or masking-taped to the walls & the

---

*Presumably bettors at a race track like to feel that they are getting advice from people intimately involved with the stables; horses would, therefore, be the ultimate sources of authority.

construction is complete. Scenery may be painted, pasted on walls, & clay or paper figures moved about within it. Free-standing trees, buildings, etc., are possible. These theatres make an interesting exhibit on a table in the classroom.

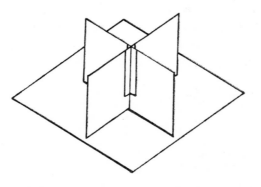

• Arbor Day [22]

J. Sterling Morton proposed to the Nebraska legislature the establishment of an Arbor Day to be observed on April 10, 1872. The date, in many states, is now fixed at April 22, coinciding with Morton's date of birth.

Math enrichment. To measure the diameter of a tree: with a tape, measure the girth of a tree. Divide this number by 3 (for an estimated measurement), or by 3.1416 (for a more exact measurement). To measure the height of a tree: with a piece of chalk, mark the trunk of the tree at 4 feet from the ground. Holding a ruler outstretched *at arm's length* before you, step back from tree. Close 1 eye & continue stepping back until the 1/2" mark on your ruler covers the area from the ground to the chalkmark on the trunk. From this exact distance measure the entire tree on your ruler. Multiply the number of 1/2" by 4 to get the height of the tree.

Sources of information:

Sierra Club
Mills Tower
San Francisco, Calif. 94104

U.S. Environmental Commission
Washington, D.C. 20460

American Forestry Association
919 17th Street, N.W.
Washington, D.C.

U.S. Forestry Service,
South Building
14th Street & Independence
Avenue, S.W.
Washington, D.C.

• **Easter**

The 3 principal events celebrated by those of Christian faith are the birth of Christ, His crucifixion & His resurrection. Easter commemorates the latter two.

Easter falls on the 1st Sunday following the full moon of, or after, the spring equinox (March 21). Its name & time of celebration indicate that it was originally a festival of ancient times celebrating the death of winter & the resurrection of the sun. Early Germanic peoples honored "Ostern," the goddess of spring, at this time of year; her name was also related to the East—in which the dawn appears.

Easter eggs. From earliest times the egg has been the symbol of the universe. It also stands for fertility; ancient Babylonians exchanged eggs at the beginning of each spring. Colored eggs symbolize re-birth; the Persians, Egyptians & ancient Chinese dyed eggs for their spring festivals. The origin of the *Easter egg hunt* is unclear. One source states that a noble woman was the 1st to hide colored eggs for the children.

Easter bunny. Our Easter bunny is related to the ancient Egyptian belief that the rabbit is the symbol of spring, the beginning of a new life.

Easter lily. There is also an original American Easter symbol! Towards the end of the last century, churches in America began having special Sunday services to help console those who had lost loved ones in the Civil War. The churches were filled with flowers, one of these being a Bermuda lily which was used in such profusion as to become associated with this season & which therefore has been named the Easter lily.

Vocabulary enrichment words: confections, apocalypse, resurrection, transfiguration, renaissance, crucifixion, Calvary.

Easter Rabbit Riddles: (These may be presented in the form of 3-4 Easter Rabbit Riddle Books, simply illustrated with colored felt tips, the answer appearing on the back of each riddle's page. Children may read these books during their free time.) How can you find the Easter Bunny when he gets lost? (Make a noise like a BIG carrot.) How can you buy eggs and be *sure* there are no baby chicks inside? (Buy duck eggs.) What kind of bush does the Easter Bunny hide under on a rainy day? (He hides under a wet bush.) What's the difference between a crazy rabbit & a phony dollar bill? (One's a mad bunny & the other's bad money.) There were 9 ears of corn in a field & a rabbit came each night & took away 3. How many nights did it take him to get *all* the ears? (Nine nights: each night he took his *own* ears when he left the field.) What goes up pink & comes down pink & white & yellow? (An Easter egg.) Which is correct: the yolk of an Easter egg *is* white or the yolk of an Easter egg *are* white? (Neither, because the yolk of any egg is YELLOW!)

Reading

Mimeos can be prepared using bunnies to emphasize words & word-skills appropriate to your group, e.g., "Circle the word that does NOT begin like the other 2 words in each bunny."

Using the puppet described on pg. 174 as a basis, add ears, tail & broom bristles for whiskers, to make a Reading Rabbit who will help introduce new words to your reading groups.

Easter Science

Science topics include the study of clouds, nests, rainbows, flowers & eggs.

Some Egg Experiments. "Can you tell which egg is the boiled egg?" Put a hard boiled egg on 1 saucer & an uncooked egg on a 2nd saucer. Place these on a table in front of the class. Ask if anyone knows how to tell which egg is the boiled egg. Spin each egg (sideways) on its saucer; the uncooked egg wobbles noticeably while the boiled egg spins smoothly. This is because the uncooked egg is filled with liquid. When spun, the contents of this egg, due to inertia, can't follow rapid motion smoothly. The inner part of the white of the egg slides over the outer layers of white, causing such friction that the egg wobbles & comes to a stop. Now spin the eggs again & this time quickly stop each one, immediately letting go of them. The uncooked egg will continue to spin for a bit; this is because its inner layers of white are still in motion.

"Can you suspend an egg in water?" Here's how: dissolve a great deal of salt into a jar that you 1/2-fill with water. Try putting an egg in this water; when enough salt has been dissolved, the egg will float on top of the water. Then carefully pour fresh tap water down the side of the jar until the jar is filled. The egg should remain suspended in the middle of the jar. This is because the salt water is heavier (it has a greater specific gravity) than an equal amount of fresh water. An egg (or any object) will float on top of the water only when it is exactly the same weight as the amount of water it is displacing. Between the fresh & salt water is an invisible boundary at which the egg will remain suspended.

"Do you know how to change a white egg to SILVER?" Completely blacken a hard-boiled egg with a heavy coat of soot from a candle. Carefully lower the egg into a glass filled with water. Suddenly the egg becomes a dull silver! This is due to the way that the light waves are reflected off the egg & through the water.

Easter Art

Cards. Supply each student with 2 or 3 buttons & a little piece of ribbon. They use these as the basis for an Easter bunny. The buttons are glued to the front of a folded sheet of colored paper & the rabbit is drawn around them. *Any* placement of the buttons is acceptable, e.g., buttons need not be used as shown.

VARIATION: Each child draws the side view of a *large* rabbit on the front of his card. A small slit is made in the upper torso (teachers may go around & make slits with razor blade; slip a small square of cardboard between cover & inside page of card in order to protect the latter). An arm is inserted as shown. A brad holds arm in place & allows rabbit to nibble at carrot or an Easter egg.

NOTE: Certain Christmas display suggestions (i.e., see pg. 103: stained glass window) are also appropriate for the class to make at this time of year.

    Easter baskets (see pg. 226, May baskets, for further ideas). Mimeograph an enlargement of this basic outline onto sheets of construction paper or tagboard. Children add design of *their invention.* You might discuss how basket's sides could be a rabbit's head, a brooding hen, a basket with decorated eggs showing, etc. Then children cut out baskets & glue or staple sides in place.

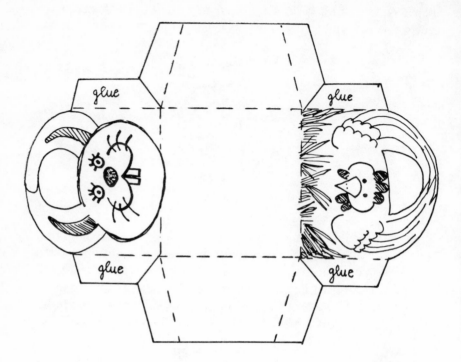

Easter eggs. Pioneer children dyed their eggs in the following way: with thread, they bound the outer gold or purple skins of onions to eggs which were then boiled. Bits of log wood bark were boiled with eggs to produce lilac, deep purple; vinegar was added to water to produce red. Once colored, these eggs were rubbed with butter or sweet oil & then polished to a bright glow.

It is not always practical to use hard-boiled eggs in the classroom. You may want to show your students how to blow out eggs & ask them to collect these empty eggs for use during class time.

Easter egg characters. Egg is dyed an appropriate basic color. Paper appendages are designed, cut out & glued in place. Tiny glass (seed) beads may be used for eyes or noses, brush bristles glued to eggs for whiskers, & yarn glued in place for a mouth or tail. Four burnt match sticks glued to egg become legs of animal. Let the children use a myriad of scraps of felt, trim, beads, sequins, papers, glitter, plastic to invent their own characters. Here are some ideas:

Eggs are made to stand by the use of a tube of construction paper as with bunny, or by sticking a small piece of modeling clay to underside of egg as with fish, mouse, octopus, frog & mermaid.

Collage eggs. By gluing overlapping tiny pieces of colored tissue, children cover egg's surface. Final effect should be almost like stained glass.

Older students will be able to produce eggs like those made in Poland & Yugoslavia. *Polish Easter Eggs:* Tiny long strips of glazed paper are folded in accordian pleats & cut to produce a chain design effect, i.e.,

or tiny squares of glazed paper are folded & cut to make geometric shapes, i.e.,

These are carefully covered with rubber cement, as is area where they will be on egg. When all cement is dry, tiny shapes are secured to egg's surface. Excess cement is *gently* rubbed off egg.

Yugoslavian Easter eggs: Using kitchen tongs, blown egg is immersed in pan of melted paraffin. Entire surface of egg is covered with wax & this is allowed to dry. Children use orange sticks (toothpicks) to incise designs with lines wide enough to accept dye. Egg is dyed & allowed to dry. (If more than 1 color is desired, 1st color must be a water-proof ink, applied heavily.) Wax is washed off with very hot water. Finished egg is oiled & polished.

• **Public School Week**

Some suggestions for preparation of your room: Display the children's work by subject matter but *don't* label groups as "Our Best Work" unless *all* the students have papers exhibited. Every child should have several examples of his efforts on display; some papers can be taped to windows if these are at eye level.

There can be a *large* book of drawings & stories covering many subjects. Classroom plants can have little signs noting dates seeds were planted. Try emphasizing the foreign language taught (if any) by labeling all the common objects about the room with the foreign names which the children have learned. Post examples of comparative writing efforts (Sept. & April); include 1 sentence that is the same, if possible (i.e., "This is my very best penmanship"), or short paragraphs written especially for this display ("What I Love About My Parents," "The Funniest Day in 4th Grade," "Why I Think I Want to_____When I Grow Up"). Display many different types of artwork, labeled as to medium used: tempera, collage, silkscreen, rubbings, etc. Have a small group of photographs taken each month covering as many subject areas as you can. Set out the microscope with slides THEY'VE made.* On the Science table have an experiments display: list purpose, materials, procedure, results, conclusions; have the experiment's materials set up in the center of the table.

Have a pile of mimeographed sheets for parents to take home; these might cover: Characteristics of the (i.e., 4th) Grader—physical, emotional, intellectual, etc. Enliven presentation of learning projects, study materials & students' work with tape recordings (at a labeled "Listening Post"), or by having an

---

*Boxes of unprepared slides (& directions for their preparation) are available through scientific supply houses.

automatic cartridge of slides shown in one corner of your room. Post this proverb & discuss it with your class: "Remember: it was the North Wind that made the Vikings."

For parents of older students, prepare a mimeographed sheet of objectives for each subject covered at your grade-level. Word these concisely; avoid using educational jargon, generalizations. Note areas to be covered, projects & enrichment work, e.g.:

> *Reading:* Continuation of the developmental reading program. In addition to this, a study of vocabulary, root words, structural & phonetic analysis is emphasized. Recreational reading ("reading for fun & profit") is encouraged through the library program. Subject matter reading is stimulated through assignment of projects in Science, Social Studies & other academic areas. Your child will be encouraged in many ways this year to develop a life-long interest in reading!

- **Birth of James Buchanan**   [23]

While studying law, James became engaged to a beautiful young woman who was sensitive & shy. She heard some gossip about her sweetheart & wrote him, breaking their engagement. Shortly after, she died. Many years later he told a friend that he had only gone into politics to distract him from his grief. Buchanan, who wanted to be a married lawyer, lived to become a lonely, childless man & 15th President of the United States.

- **Date of baptism of William Shakespeare**   [26]

The actual birthdate of Shakespeare is unknown. However, his baptism took place at Stratford-on-Avon on April 26, 1564.

Bulletin board suggestion. Mount a picture of Shakespeare on a brilliant piece of paper; cut from white paper a large comic-strip balloon which will connect with Shakespeare's mouth & will have printed within it the title: "What's in a Name?" (A 2nd balloon might state: "A rose by any other name is STILL a rose." Yet our names do link us to our ancestors & tell us something about them: the *work* they did, *where* they *lived,* or how they *looked!*) Spot about the board, brightly backed papers that tell the derivations of the surnames of every student in your class. A book of name origins will be a help; give the derivation of the given name, if the surname cannot be traced. Older children might do their own research. Here is a start:

> *Archer, Bowmen:* a man who used arrows to do battle. *Chester,–cester:* from Latin *Castra* (camp); means your ancestors lived near

a fortified Roman site in England. *Crump:* round-shouldered. *Dexter, Dyer:* A man who teased the wool before it was made into yarn. *Fitz—:* "son of," dates back to Norman invasion of England. *Fletcher:* a man who made or sold arrows. *Hill, Dale, Moore:* described the land he lived on. *Latimer:* from "Latiner," one who could translate a strange tongue into a universally understood language. *Lightfoot, Ambler, Trotter:* described the way a man walked. *Mac—:* Scottish, "son of." *O'—:* Irish, "son of." *Pollard:* a bald man. *Quincey:* you are the descendant of the Normans who invaded England 900 years ago! *Scrivener, Scriver:* a scholar. *Schearer, Sherman:* a man who worked on the nap of the wool cloth (13th c). *Smith:* not all were blacksmiths; many worked in gold, silver, copper, tin; or it may refer to a man who lived *near* the forge. *Tailor* (and *Taylor*), *Weaver, Webster, Webb:* weavers of wool: 13th c.

• Birth of John James Audubon   [26]

Audubon spent his life painstakingly recording, in beautiful watercolors, the wild birds of 19th c. America. Many states celebrate Audubon's birthday; in some places Audubon Day & Arbor Day (see pg. 209) are celebrated as one.

Have the children observe birds. Help them learn to discriminate as to size (relative to the robin, starling, & sparrow), color (markings), & shape of body & bill. With experience, children will learn to make finer discriminations. (How does it fly? How does it get its food? Does it run or hop? What are its nesting habits? Of what value are these birds, ecologically?)

Science

Have each child accumulate clues for his own personal bird chart; each child's chart should be completely different from the other children's. Divide large sheets of tagboard into sections entitled: Size, Shape, Color & Markings, Special Characteristics, Location Where Seen, Flight Pattern, Song, & finally, NAME. Children may illustrate any section with a drawing; "the song" should be in terms of how it impresses the *child;* the size section should compare each bird to a robin, starling, & sparrow.

Sources of information:

Nat. Audubon Society (Jr. Program)
1130 Fifth Ave.
New York, N.Y. 10028 (free materials & information)

"The Community of Living Things": a set of 5 books written

with cooperation of National Audubon Society ($6 each; $30 for set). Write for information to: Creative Educational Society, Inc., Mankato, Minn. 56001

• **Birth of James Monroe** [28]

Word etymology. "Doctrine" comes from the Latin word *docere,* to teach. A doctrine is a theory based on carefully worked out principles & *taught* by its adherents. The Monroe Doctrine stated that the U.S.A. would regard as an unfriendly act any attempt by European powers to interfere with American affairs or to increase their possessions on the American continents.

APRIL ACTIVITIES

Bulletin Board Lettering Suggestions. In order to attract attention to displays try making titles from unusual materials, i.e., bent cellophane straws glued to a vivid background color, fabric remnants cut with pinking shears, aluminum foil letters glued to a color that is in strong contrast to silver. One important (& at the same time short) word in the title can be spelled from toy building blocks; you may wish to re-paint each of these letters in a bright poster paint.

Title: FACE IT! Teacher &/or children collect all kinds of pictures of faces. From these each child chooses 1 & writes a history of this person: where he is, what he's doing now, what he wants from life, etc. Each theory, part of the history may be proven by details noted in the photograph, e.g., worry-lines, make-up, expression, hair-style. Children hypothesize what each face is thinking at the moment it was photographed. These compositions & their corresponding photos make fascinating reading & an intriguing display.

Language Arts: Creative Writing "Self-Starters"

1. One dark night an owl flew by your house. He landed on the window ledge & looked into your living room. Describe *every* thing he might have seen.
2. Take a simple human interest (animal) story from a newspaper or the S.P.C.A. Newsletter (i.e., involving the rescue of a wild animal). Have the children write, speculating as to how the animal got into its predicament, what might be done to help it & then what becomes of it & why.
3. If you could take a trip to any place in the world, describe your

itinerary, activities, possible adventures, how this trip might change your life. This could be written as a satirical Baedecker or "_____ on $____ a Day."

4. You find a bottle on the beach. A note is in it. What does the message say? Because of the note, what do you do? What finally happens to the bottle & its contents? How has finding this bottle changed your life?

5. Teacher holds up a large sheet of newsprint on which is written: "One day I got up & went & looked at my face in the mirror. I let out a LOUD cry because I was so surprised & upset. . . . "

6. Children write an autobiography of an animal, vegetable or mineral, e.g., "My Life as a Hunk of Coal."

7. Display 3 large random photos (of persons, animals, objects) in the chalk tray. Children are to write a sentence incorporating the 3, i.e., "The dog stopped beside a stream because he thought he heard a fish calling his name." Children are asked to complete the stories which these sentences introduce.

8. Without identifying them by name, describe the largest &/or smallest thing(s) you noticed during recess.

9. Discuss the term "x-ray." Emphasize how details are essential to a good adventure story. Ask the children to write about: "If I had X-ray Eyes (Vision)."

10. "My Most Popular Day Dream."

11. "I was a Caveman in 40000 B.C."

12. "Lost and Found (and Lost Again)."

13. Teacher brings to class a good reproduction of a famous painting. Children are asked to write, answering "What kind of person do you think made this painting? How did he happen to paint it? Did he like it? What did other people say about it? What became of it after the artist died? How did it get to be recognized as a masterpiece?" (After children finish writing, teacher might tell them, via mimeo sheets, the actual historical answers to these questions about the painting.)

14. Let each child choose a new name for himself & tell *why* he likes it, what it makes him think of, why he would (would not) like to *legally* have this name, how it might make his life different.

15. Ask each child to choose an emotion or state of mind. Then have him put it in the blank space & finish the sentence with a story: "I feel _____ when(ever) _____."

16. "I Wish Grown-ups Would STOP _____."

17. "The _____ Person I Know."

18. Think about something that really scares you. Try to think back to the very 1st time you got scared by it. How did it happen? Why did you feel that way? In what ways does(n't) it make sense to be afraid? How would you handle this fear in your *own* child?

April Poetry

Sweet April showers
Do bring May flowers.

—Tosser: "500 Points of Good Husbandry"

For as the rain cometh down, and the snow from heaven, and returneth not thither, but watereth the earth, and maketh it bring forth and bud, that it may give seed to the sower, and bread to the eater.

—Isaiah 55-10

Be still, sad heart, and cease repining;
Behind the clouds is the sun still shining;
Thy fate is the common fate of all,
Into each life some rain must fall,
Some days must be dark and dreary.

—Longfellow: "The Rainy Day"

April P.E.

Mystery Man: Children line up along the home base line. They close their eyes & keep their hands behind them. Teacher goes down the line, behind the children, pretending to deposit a penny in each child's hands. Children immediately clench fists when teacher has passed them. Child who actually receives coin does not let this be known. When entire line has been covered, children open their eyes & begin to move out onto playground. After a few minutes the teacher calls out, "Mysteryman! Mysteryman! Catch them all if you can!" Everyone runs for the home base line. Child with the coin calls, "I will! I can! I'm the Mysteryman!" & he tags as many children as he can before they cross home base line. Once everyone has gotten to safety, "Mysteryman" counts up the number of his victims, just to get the record straight. Children form line & "Mysteryman" goes behind it, depositing the coin in some unsuspecting person's hands. And so game continues. *VARIATION:* Children stand in a circle, hands extended in front of them. "It," who is inside the circle, goes to each child & pretends to put a penny into his extended hands. Each child acts as if he *may* have penny. Child who actually gets penny breaks away from circle & runs to cross a goal line. Whoever catches him becomes the new "It." If no one catches him, he is then "It."

**April Puppet: Very Simple Hand-Puppets
Made from Rubber Gloves**

A black rubber glove with cut-out paper features quickly becomes a spider. A pink rubber glove, treated in a like manner, becomes an octopus. Features are attached with rubber cement. To make a butterfly or snail, cut out a set of cardboard wings (or a cardboard snail shell); staple to it a wide elastic band that slips over a gloved hand. The 1st 2 fingers are entended, becoming antennae, & thumb grasps remaining fingers beneath puppet. Eye spots or a face may be painted on antennae or glove. A curtain secured to either side of a doorway becomes an adequate "stage" in lieu of an actual puppet theatre. These puppets, while limited in their range of actions, are appropriate for reading group practice sessions or as a little something special for a rainy day.

May

May brings flocks of pretty lambs,
Skipping by their fleecy dams.

1   May Day.
2   Catherine the Great (1729-1796), German-born empress of Russia.
3   Niccolo Machiavelli (1469-1527), Italian statesman, author.
5   Karl Marx (1818-1883), German philosopher.
    1st U.S. sub-orbital space flight by Alan B. Shepard, 1961.
6   1st postage stamp, "the penny black," issued in England, 1840.
    Sigmund Freud (1856-1939), founder of psychoanalysis.
    Robert E. Peary (1856-1920), American arctic explorer.
7   Robert Browning (1812-1889), English poet, husband of Elizabeth Barrett.
    Johannes Brahms (1833-1897), German composer.
    Peter Ilich Tchaikovsky (1840-1893), Russian composer.
8   Harry S. Truman (1884-   ), 33rd U.S. President.
9   Capt. Kidd was tried for piracy, 1701.
10 Completion of the railroad across the U.S., 1869.
    Mother's Day: 2nd Sunday in May.
12 Florence Nightingale (1820-1910), English nurse; regarded as the founder of modern nursing.
13 1st permanent U.S. settlement (by English): Jamestown, Va., 1607.
14 Gabriel Fahrenheit (1686-1736), German physicist.
15 Pierre Curie (1859-1906), co-discoverer of radium.

17   Dr. Edward Jenner (1749-1823), discoverer of vaccination against smallpox.
18   Walter Gropius (1883-1969), German-born American architect.
19   1st Ringling Bros. Circus: 1884 at Baraboo, Wisc.
20   Dolly Madison (1768-1849), official hostess at the White House for widowed Pres. Jefferson & later for her husband, Pres. Madison.
      Charles Lindbergh's flight: 1st non-stop transatlantic solo, 1927.
21   Albrecht Durer (1471-1528), German painter, engraver.
      1st bicycles imported to U.S. from England: 1819. These were called "swift-walkers"; when pedals were invented, the name changed to "bone-crushers."
      Clara Barton (1821-1912), founder of American Red Cross.
22   Alexander Pope (1688-1744), English poet.
      Richard Wagner (1813-1883), German composer (Wedding March from *Lohengrin*).
23   Franz Kline (1910-1962), American abstract-expressionist painter.
25   Ralph Waldo Emerson (1803-1882), American poet.
26   1st steamship to cross the Atlantic: U.S.S. Savannah, 1819. (She made it largely with the help of her sails.)
29   Patrick Henry (1736-1799), American statesman.
      John F. Kennedy (1917-1963), 35th U.S. President.
      Memorial Day (the 1st one was in 1869), 4th Monday in May: Monday Holiday Bill.
30   Joan of Arc burned at the stake in Rouen, France, 1431.
      Hernando de Soto, Spanish explorer, landed on Fla., 1539.
31   Walt Whitman (1819-1892), American poet ("Leaves of Grass," "Song of the Open Road," "I Hear America Singing").
      May is "Be Kind to Animals Month."
      Shabuoth: The Festival of Weeks or Pentecost (end of May, seven weeks after Passover). It is in commemoration of the bringing of the Torah to the Hebrews by Moses & is also in celebration of the beginning of the grain harvest.

ay

Probably named for Mai Majesta, the Roman goddess of spring, May

was also dedicated to the goddess of grain, Ceres. In the N. Hemisphere, corn, the favorite grain of Ceres, is planted in May. The corn-growing Navajo Indians of N. America called May "the month of tiny & tall leaves."

MAY QUOTATIONS

5   From each according to his ability, to each according to his need. —Karl Marx

7   Words break no bones; hearts, though, sometimes.

The year's at the spring
And day's at the morn;
Morning's at seven;
The hillside's dew-pearled;
The lark's on the wing;
The snail's on the thorn:
God's in His Heaven—
All's right with the world.
(*Pippa Passes*, Part I)
—Robert Browning

8   Sixteen hours ago an American airplane dropped one bomb on Hiroshima. . . . It is a harnessing of the basic power of the universe. The force from which the sun draws its powers has been loosed against those who brought war to the Far East. (Aug. 6, 1945)—Harry S. Truman

12   Too kind—too kind. (When handed the insignia of the Order of Merit on her death bed)—Florence Nightingale

22   Fools rush in where angels fear to tread.—Alexander Pope

25   The reward of a thing well done is to have done it.

Fear always springs from ignorance.

Life is short but there is always time for courtesy.

A friend is a person with whom I may be sincere. Before him I may think aloud. ("Friendship")

Write it on your heart that everyday is the best day in the year. He only is rich who owns the day and no one owns the day who allows it to be invaded by worry, fret and anxiety. Finish every day and be done with it. You have done what you could.
—Ralph Waldo Emerson

29   Ask not what your country can do for you; ask what you
       can do for your country. (Inaugural Address: 1/20/61)
       If we all can persevere, if we can in every land and office
       look beyond our own shores and ambitions, then surely
       the age will dawn in which the strong are just and the
       weak secure and the peace preserved. (Address to U.N.
       9/25/61)

                                                              —John F. Kennedy

       Is life so dear or peace so sweet as to be purchased at the
       price of chains and slavery? Forbid it, Almighty God. I
       know not what course others may take, but as for me,
       give me liberty or give me death! (2nd Va. Convention:
       3/22/1775)—Patrick Henry

31   And the narrowest hinge in my hand puts to scorn all
       machinery—Walt Whitman

       May Riddle: If April showers bring May flowers, what do May
       flowers bring? (The Pilgrims.)

MAY EVENTS

● **May Day   [1]**

    This is 1 of our oldest holidays. Over 2000 years ago
the Romans honored Flora, the goddess of flowers on this day.
The tall marble columns in Flora's temple were twined with
garlands & the children danced about them praising the goddess;
such is the history of *the May pole.* The Pilgrims brought from
Europe the custom of giving *May baskets,* which are a secret
message of friendship & celebrate the arrival of spring.

Language Arts

    With older children discuss the relative importance of this
day in relation to other holidays; why has it lost importance
through the years?

May Art

    Baskets: Quickie. Make a slit at the center of each end of a
rectangle of construction paper. Lap over ends & staple or glue.
Attach handle.

Paper doily. Doily is folded in 1/2 & rolled into a cone. Glue edges together & let dry thoroughly. Attach handle of pink construction paper. *Fruit basket* may be painted, if it is wooden, with colorful stripes of poster paint. If basket is plastic, strips of a contrasting color of paper are woven in & out between slats of basket. Staple handle in place. *Tiny paper basket* may hold a few flowers & a haiku, or a few pieces of candy made in class. Each child folds an 8" square of paper in 1/2 horizontally & then in 1/2 vertically. This is then folded in 1/2 along a diagonal line. Cut as shown. Fold across tip. Open out & overlap each section with the 1 next to it. Rubber cement sections in place. Add handle.

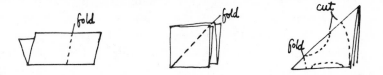

A Conservationist's May basket. Using 6" x 9" pieces of paper, children design their own flowers to fill this basket. Once colored (or painted or cut & glued), basket of flowers is cut out & paper is formed into a circle & glued. A 1/2" x 13" strip of paper becomes handle. A variety of leaf & flower shapes help this to become a very pleasant & personal May basket.

Completed baskets may hold cookies made in class (see suggested recipes at back of book) & "delivered" to an older person or a shut-in. Teacher might arrange in advance to give baskets to a local convalescent or rest home.

- 1st U.S. Sub-orbital Space Flight   [5]

Language Arts

As a class effort, a Space Age Dictionary is compiled; children collect both pictures & terminology & draw illustrations when they cannot find appropriate photos. A large inexpensive scrapbook may be used & its edges indexed to speed location of words.

Reading. "Man in Space" is a game for reviewing facts. Students are told that each of them represents "a man in space." At the front of class is a globe representing the Earth, & the teacher represents "Houston" (or "Controls" or "Cape Kennedy"). Each time teacher holds up a drill card, she waits a moment before calling the name of one of the men in space; this commands attention of class & allows each child to prepare an answer. When his name is called & he answers incorrectly, child leaves his seat & "returns to Earth where he is quarantined" (goes to stand by globe). When teacher next calls out the name of a man in space, the earthbound student attempts to answer 1st; should he succeed & also give the correct answer, he returns to space & the other student becomes quarantined. Game continues this way.

Information sources (for Free Air Age teaching materials, pictures, bulletins):

Lockheed Aircraft Corp.
Public Relations Director
Burbank, Calif.

Aerospace Industries Assoc. of
   America
1275 DeSales St., N.W.
Washington, D.C.

American Institute of Aeronautics & Astronautics
1290 Avenue of the Americas
New York, N.Y.

Nat. Aeronautics & Space
   Administration
400 Maryland Ave., S.W
Washington, D.C.

• **Birth of Sigmund Freud** **[6]**

Psyche is a Greek word meaning "breath, soul, or spirit." *Psycho-* is a combining form meaning "the mind." *-Logy* is a combining form coming from the Greek *-logia* & meaning "a theory of, a science, or study of." From these we derive our word "psychology." "Psychoanalysis," developed by S. Freud, is a method of studying a person's "mental life" in order to help treat disorders of the mind.

• Mother's Day

President Woodrow Wilson proclaimed this day as a national observance on May 9, 1914, but it has roots far back in history. In pre-Christian times the people of Asia Minor worshipped Rhea, the great mother of the gods, as she was called. When Christianity took the place of these ancient rites, the Virgin Mary became "the Mother of the Roman Catholic Faith" & the "Mother Church" idea developed. During the Middle Ages in England this Mid-Lent Sunday was called "Mothering Sunday." It was the custom for each person to return to the place of his birth & attend his mother church. As everyone was in his home town, after church services people would go & visit their parents, bringing cakes & gifts to their mothers.

Language Arts

Have the children, as a group, dictate sentences (which you quickly record) based on their ideas & feelings about "Mothers." The teacher organizes these & prints them, in large letters, on a piece of butcher paper that nearly covers a bulletin board. A colorful paper border outlines the composition for which the class should choose a title. This is also an appropriate time for improving public relations by writing your Room Mothers notes of thanks; perhaps you might organize a small party for all the mothers of your students.

Mother's Day Cards

Pop-up card. Make by folding a piece of 8" x 10" paper in 1/2 lengthwise & cutting out a 3" x 3" notch as shown. The portion that is left jutting out from card is folded inside & pops up when card is opened. Children modify pop-up shape (oval, heart) or draw a face, a bouquet or a jack-in-the-box on it. Cover of card is designed so as to accommodate "cut-off" top left-hand corner.

Talking card. Each child cuts a small (2"-4") square of white paper in 1/2, diagonally. Each triangle is then folded as shown. Finally, a rectangular piece of white paper for the card itself is folded in 1/2 lengthwise, the 2 modified triangles are placed at the center of the inside fold, & flaps 1 & 2 are glued down to card. Child draws a face around these "lips": it may be a self-portrait that answers "ME" as his mother opens the card. Message on front of card might then be: "Who wishes you a HAPPY MOTHER'S DAY?"

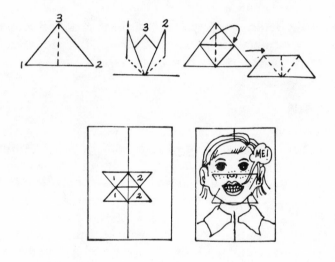

Mother's Day Gift

Suggestions. A plant grown in class from a seed or carrot top, class-made cookies or other sweets (see recipes at back of book).

A decorative tile. This can be made by using the encaustic technique: Heat unglazed tile on a hot-plate or in an oven. Apply a line drawing or decorative pattern with wax crayons, or scatter shavings from wax crayons on heated surface. VARIATION: Dissolve crayons in Amaco Brand Glaze Surfacer* (or *turpentine*) & apply to *un*heated bisque tile as you would tempera. Spray (or brush) design finally (once design is dry) with glaze surfacer or a fixative for a semi-gloss protective coating.

Clay slab dish. Each child finds & brings to class a 3"-8" smooth oval stone; these are scrubbed clean. On a table across

---

*Available from the American Art Clay Co., Indianapolis, Ind. 46222.

which an old sheet has been stretched & tacked in place, children 1st pound clay to "wedge" it, breaking up any locked-in air bubbles. Wedged clay is pushed down with the heel of the hand until surface of clay is 1" thick. Then, using rolling pins, cut-down broom handles or sturdy mailing tubes, children roll out clay into a smooth slab. Each of these is placed over a stone & molded to fit snugly. Keep top edges wide, erase any cracks by smoothing clay with moistened fingers. Sturdy feet or a cube base may be added by 1st scratching area on dish where feet will be & *then* attaching them. This scratching helps prevent the breaking off of appendages. Large dishes are removed from stones when clay is sufficiently dry to retain its shape. Clay edges, when leather hard, are smoothed with fingers. When completely dry, edges may be gently sanded, if you like. If there are no facilities available for firing clay, "Marblex," a product of the American Art Clay Co. (Indianapolis, Ind., 46222), may be used by the students. This self-hardening clay dries firm & durable without being fired in a kiln. (See "December Gifts" for other ideas.)

Lavendar Sachets. Students mix the following ingredients & put them in cambric bags, tied with pretty little bows: 2 oz. dried thyme, 2 oz. table salt, 1 oz. ground cloves, 1 oz. caraway seeds, 2 oz. dried & ground mint, & 1 lb. dried lavender flowers.

Clove

An East Indian evergreen tree (Eugenia aromatica), the unopened flowerbud of which is dried & used as a spice. The oil from clove trees is used in medicine & perfumery.

• **Birth of Gabriel Fahrenheit   [14]**

Most inventions are the products of the labors of many men. For instance, both Galileo & Sir Isaac Newton experimented with thermometers, using water & alcohol with some success. But it was a manufacturer of weather instruments who built the 1st mercurial thermometer that allowed temperature changes to be seen & recorded. Gabriel Fahrenheit was German & yet the Germans do not use the fahrenheit thermometer. Instead, they use the centigrade thermometer, which is named after Celsius, its Swedish inventor!

● **Memorial Day**

This was originally called Decoration Day & had its 1st formal observance on May 30, 1868. In the South, after the Civil War, mourning friends & relatives of slain soldiers put flowers on the graves of both Southern & Northern soldiers. The news of this gesture traveled north & soon most of the states honored the war dead on this day.

● **May is "Be Kind to Animals Month"**

"Animals are such agreeable friends; they ask no questions, pass no criticisms."–George Eliot

Science

Let each child make an Animal Chart (similar in lay-out to the Bird Chart described in "Science," pg. 218). These charts may be based on any 1 of the following groups of mammals: Farm, Zoo, Forest, Jungle, Arctic, Local, or Household Pets. Categories would cover: Comparative Size, Shape, Coloration, Track Prints, Food, Habits, Family to Which It Belongs, & Ecological Value (how it fits into the "Web of Life").

Information sources:

Nat. Wildlife Federation
1412 16th St., N.W.
Washington, D.C.

American S.P.C.A.
441 E. 92nd St.
New York, N.Y. 10028

American Humane Assoc.
P.O. Box 1266
Denver, Colo., 80201

Publishers of *Nat. Humane Jr. News,*
a newsletter for children; free copy
for teacher

MAY ACTIVITIES

Bulletin board title: "What kind of May flower will grow, if you plant": Beneath title are listed a dozen "exotic seeds" & following each of these is a large flap beneath which appears a full color photo (from a seed catalog) with its identity printed clearly under it. Children, in attempting to answer riddles, will familiarize themselves at the same time with a variety of May flora. These are the 12 unknowns: (1) "A couple" plus "part of your face"? (Tulip.) (2) A vehicle & all the people of a country? (Carnation.) (3) "The expensive spread" & "a drinking vessel"? (Buttercup.) (4) A whole lot of sheep? (Phlox.) (5) A liquid & an Easter decoration? (Water lily.) (6) The name of a man & a part of a feather? (Jonquil.) (7) A word that means "just fine" & the king of all beasts? (Dandelion.) (8) Anger & the singular form of the verb "to be"? (Iris.) (9) A Xmas decoration & a part of a pig's leg (or a word that means "to leave something at the pawnshop")? (Hollyhock.) (10) A fib & a word that means "not having enough"? (Lilac.) (11) A bird & something a cowboy wears? (Larkspur.) (12) The opposite of "sour" & a common green vegetable? (Sweet peas.)

Lettering suggestions. Cut letters from unwanted finger-painted papers. Make simple letters in a short title from toy plastic clothespins glued to a contrasting color of background paper.

May Social Studies

In honor of Florence Nightingale, whose birthday is May 12, invite a nurse to visit your class. Before she actually arrives, talk over with the children types of questions that *they* would be interested in asking her. Help them to cover a wide range of topics; encourage them to take full advantage of this opportunity to interview a professional in the field of medicine. (Just for fun to help break down pre-conceptions, you might sometime invite a male nurse.)

At the front of the class, display a long line to which is tied a variety of kitchen utensils (e.g., wooden spoon, pancake flipper, egg timer, vegetable grater, pastry brush, kitchen shears, rubber spatula, etc.). Ask each child to choose a utensil & to keep its identity a secret. Now ask the students to thoughtfully outline the probable history of this utensil, describing how it may have been (& looked when it was) invented. Were equivalent utensils used by cavemen, ancient Mayans, Egyptians, early Christians, etc.? What famous people in history probably used an ancestor of this utensil? Describe 1 such historical incident. Each child might anthropomorphize his utensil & have it tell of its birth, youth, complaints, desires, attitudes now. Encourage students to cite as much historical data as they can in writing these papers.

Language Arts

"When it is dark enough, men see the stars" (Ralph Waldo Emerson): discuss this quotation with the children. This month affords many opportunities for short talks about thoughts, ideas of famous men (e.g., Whitman, Browning, Kennedy, Patrick Henry).

May words. Pass out to each child a mimeo sheet of May words: mayor, maybe, Mayflower, Maypole, mayhem, mayhap, May Day, May Queen, Maying, Mayflowers, Maynard, mayonnaise, dismay, manger, mail, maiden, male, make, maze, Mabel, mate, matron, mason, mane, main, maple, maniac. Discuss any word on the list which seems unfamiliar to a student. Then ask children to write a story or poem incorporating as many of these May words as they can.

The literary forms include: adaptation (condensed version), adventure fiction, allegory, autobiography, ballad, biography, essay, fable, feature article, folk tale, haiku, historical fiction, legend, limerick, mystery story, myth, parody, picture story (i.e., *Life* magazine), poetry, satire, science fiction. Ask the children to identify, describe those with which they are familiar. Then ask the students to list for each style 3 types of experiences that would provide good backgrounds for an author wishing to write in each of these styles.

Vocabulary enrichment words. Maternal, bouquet, beneficent, compassionate, protective, magnanimous.

May Poetry:

May

May be chill, may be mild,
May pour, may snow,
May be still, may be wild,
May lower, may glow,
May freeze, may burn,
May be gold, may be gray,
May do all these in turn—
May May.

—Justin Richardson, in "The Countryman"*

---

*Quoted in *New.York Herald Tribune* & subsequently in *The Reader's Digest.*

(He is) as fresh as the month of May.

Chaucer 1340?-1400 *(Canterbury Tales)*

Reading

Ask each child in a reading group to outline in 5-6 sentences the life history of a famous person (or the historical background of a holiday) about which they have learned this year. Once these sentences have been checked for accuracy & grammar, they are carefully printed on sheets of tagboard. Each group of sentences is cut apart & placed in an envelope on which is written: "These sentences are mixed up. Arrange them to make a story." Envelopes are used by class during periods of free time.

May Science

An informative bulletin board may be made based on the following: "A mosquito & a bee make different noises. What causes the difference?" "The wings of a mosquito are much smaller than the wings of a bee. The mosquito's wings go up & down much faster than the bee's. The faster a thing goes up & down, the higher the sound it makes. And so a mosquito makes a higher sound than a bee!"

Word etymology. *Entomology* is the study of insects. This word comes from the Greek *entomos* which means "cut-up." Insects have segmented or "cut-up" bodies. Our word "insect" comes from the Latin *insectum* which means "cut up." It is simply the Roman word for the Greek *entomos! Metamorphosis* is from the Greek; *meta-* means "changing" & *morphe* means "form." Metamorphosis means "a change of form or shape."

The Study of Insects. This study can be introduced by taking the class for a walk to a nearby vacant lot, if 1 is extant. Pencils, paper, sticks & string are taken along. There each child stakes out a 1-foot square claim of earth; he may even drive 4 ice cream sticks into the 4 corners & bind it round by a piece of string. Then he examines every inch of his claim, recording every single thing he finds; he may even dig into the earth if he wishes. When they're back in class, students compare notes, see who had the richest claims & who they feel "struck it rich." A bulletin board record of this walk may be titled: "Have you ever really seen a *vacant* lot?"

Before collecting or exhibiting any insects, ask the class one day during an art period to draw or make a butterfly. Then ask them to make a moth. Elicit answers to such questions as "How are moths & butterflies different?" The children may not look at any photos in books but they may ask questions that can be answered by "yes" or "no." These drawings should be kept for a few weeks & then returned to the children who, by then, should have a much clearer idea of how each insect looks. The children will, additionally, be able to see how they have improved their scientific knowledge.

Once the class has begun collecting insects, the following sign might be posted: Do you get moths & butterflies confused? Here are some ways to tell them apart:

Moths	*Butterflies*
night-flyers	day-flyers
thin, hairy feelers	club-shaped feelers
short, fat bodies	thin bodies
spread out wings when lit	fold up wings when lit

Trapping insects. Lay towel or open out umbrella beneath bush; beat bush with stick. At night collect moths from about neon signs. The grills of cars sometimes afford undamaged insects. Bury a topless tin can, its upper edge flush with the soil; pour a little molasses into bottom of can. Place a large stone *over* can (but *not interfering* with access to *rim* of can); beetles should crawl toward sweet smell & be trapped in can. Lightly bury a cookie sheet in soil; put a dead mouse or baby chick (some pet shops sell these frozen) on top of the soil-covered sheet. Scavenger insects should appear beneath animal after a few days.

Rearing insects. Children can experiment with raising various sorts of insects:

Beetles are kept in large gal. mayonnaise jar that is fairly high in humidity (see De-nested & Mealworm).

Butterflies can be raised from *larvae,* from *pupae* or from *eggs.*

Crickets are raised in a 1 gal. jar, the bottom of which has 2" of soil spread on it. Put a watch glass* (or plastic container lid), filled with water, on top of the soil. Mouth of jar is covered with wire mesh. Make certain that watch glass keeps filled with water. Crickets eat old mashed potatoes, tiny shreds of lettuce, corn meal

---

*A 1/2"-1" deep glass receptacle used in science studies.

mush or bread soaked in milk; once in a while give them a little library paste or peanut butter for a special treat!

De-nested beetles are caught as they are attracted by a piece of cheese children have left outdoors in warm weather.* Placed in a screen-covered jar, they are given the dried carcass of a dead mouse. Class may study *osteology* at the same time ("Osteon" is Greek for "bone") as beetles clean off carcasses, exposing skeletons beneath.

Grasshoppers are raised in a 1 gal. jar, the bottom of which has been lined with a 2" sod of grass. This is watered from time to time & provides food & an egg-depository place for grasshoppers.

Larvae (caterpillars) are raised in a wooden crate that has its bottom knocked out & its sides covered with screening. Box is stood on end & potted "feedplant"** with larvae on it is placed in box; or line bottom of aquarium with 2" of moist soil into which are planted "feed plants," (or jars of water with stalks of "feed plants" are placed in tank). Put larvae on "feed plant." Cover top of aquarium with "Stretch & Seal." The more airtight the larvae's cage, the longer his food supply will remain fresh, edible. There's little chance of suffocating larvae as they use very little air to live.

Mealworm beetles cultures can be obtained from a biological supply house if no one is able to find any in seldom-used box of cereal, corn meal or flour. Fill gal. jar 1/2 full of All-Bran, atop which you lay a piece of crumpled newspaper. Put 1/2 a potato on top of the newspaper; this affords moisture & food. Place culture in jar & cover jar's mouth with screening. Put jar in a warm place. Replace potato when it dries up.

Moths can be reared from larvae, from pupae or from eggs.

Praying Mantises are carnivorous & eat live insects; give a baby mantis aphids to eat, while an adult mantis will eat houseflies, roaches; if not fed enough the mantis will turn cannibalistic. Spear tiny piece of liver on a toothpick if no live

---

*Beetle cultures may be purchased from a Biological Supply House (i.e., Scientific Center, Santa Clara, Calif.). Cricket cultures are available from Wards Natural Science Estab., Inc., 316 Cannery Row, Monterey, Calif. 13940.

**The real secret to successful rearing of larvae is to keep them well-supplied with their "food plant": each adult female lays her eggs on a specific plant which will provide the food for emerging larvae. These larvae will usually *not* eat *any other* plant & so most captive larvae in the classroom starve to death amidst heaps of grass & green leaves. So it is essential to identify the "food plant" of larvae, e.g., either take note of plant on which larvae is found & get it & keep it fresh for larvae or use Frank Lutz's book: *Field Book of Insects of U.S. & Canada* (New York: G.P. Putnam's Sons, 1948) to help identify food source.

insect food is available. Eggcases must be collected in the fall or winter,* brought indoors & placed in jar (as described under Roaches). Babies emerge in 2-4 weeks.

Pupae: Larvae will molt several times & then stop eating. They may go beneath soil in jar to pupate. Don't bother them. Keep pupae to watch adult emerge (or children may collect cocoons & bring them & branches of the "food plant" to class). Put 1" soil in bottom of large jar; stick branches in soil & with a few drops of glue attach cocoons to sticks. Cover mouth of jar with screening. Once a week spray soil & pupae with water to keep air in jar humid (but never to the point of producing mold or mildew). If kept in a warm room, cocoons will produce adults in a few months; these will die if their host plants are not in leaf & available. If you wish to raise eggs & larvae from the adults, you must prevent their emergence until the spring. To do this, place jar between regular window & storm window on northern side of the school building. (To make certain that you get fertile eggs, you'll need both sexes of moth from pupae. A newly emerged female attracts males, so just put her in a cheesecloth covered jar & set this outside of an evening—males should arrive any time!

Insect-inspired art. Ask children to make a *painting* from a "bug's-eye view" (i.e., the huge, slightly transparent leaves overhead, etc.). Have children create an imaginary environment (& a *written description* of it) for an imaginary insect. Use an insect's wing to inspire a *stabile;* use the segmented body, legs to point out *balance in designs.* Use insect markings or microscopic view of insect to inspire an *all-over design* or an *abstract cut-out:* fold piece of newsprint from insect to edges of paper. Keep paper folded & cut out insect; open out paper & mount on contrasting paper.

Yarn pictures. Ask younger children to make a large pencil outline of a moth or butterfly on cardboard. Glue is applied to

*Or you may purchase praying mantis cocoons (3 for $2, 5 for $3) from Bio-Control, Route 2, Box 2397, Auburn, Calif. 95603. Each cocoon contains *many* young insects.

entire inside of this drawing & yarn is carefully laid in place, wound about, always touching edge of previously placed yarn, & coiled in this way until entire area of insect is made of yarn. Wax paper is put over picture & heavy book put on top to insure adherence of yarn to board. Different colors, textures of yarn should be used. Background may be filled in carefully with poster paint.

May Art

This month freshen up your room by developing a Creative Corner in the classroom. Here children, when they have free time & the inclination, may sit quietly & experiment, inventing new toys, games, constructions, ways of seeing things. The Creative Corner should be functional but not elaborate, containing a table, chairs & a *few* of the following objects. (As the days pass, objects will be changed; specific areas of interest shown should be noted & capitalized upon when new objects are added): tiny boxes, scraps of Lucite or colored plexiglass, film-tins, a large magnifying glass, colored toothpicks, Styrofoam, geometric wooden shapes (scraps from lumber yard), Plasticene (modeling clay), interesting buttons & seeds, a small flannel board & colorful felt scraps, scissors, a small piece of pegboard & yarns & Mexican hemp, golf tees, a broken alarm clock, sea shells, negative & positive shapes cut from cardboard (some reproductions of Arp),* durable toys from different countries & made of different materials, small wheels of different sizes, organic materials (i.e., blown-out egg shells). From time to time a book might also be put on the table (e.g., a book of African masks, mythical creatures, folk art etc.). After a while children may decide on a special name of their own for this corner, in which case it could be printed in large bright letters on a sign that is posted above table. Experimentation of all types should be allowed; what might appear to be dawdling can often lead to the most inventive results &, of course, not all results will be material.

*Jean Arp (1887-1966), French painter & sculptor.

May P.E.

Paper-cup relay: Divide class into teams of equal numbers. Each team forms a line. At a distance from each team is a chair on which stand 2 paper cups, 1 of which is filled with water. (Each team's cup holds the *same* amount of water initially.) At a given signal, the 1st player on each team runs to the chair, carefully pours water into empty cup, replaces cup on chair, runs back & tags 2nd player, who repeats this procedure. The team who finishes 1st, retaining the most water in a cup, is the winner.

Spiders & Flies.* A game for young children. The "spiders" stand in a long line facing away from the "flies" who creep softly up on them, until teacher calls out "Look out or the spiders will get you!" at which the spiders whirl about in pursuit of the fleeing flies. Any flies caught before reaching safety are taken back to the web & become a new arachnid. Now flies turn *their* backs & spiders creep up on them, etc.

May Finger Puppets

Child places his hand on a sheet of paper, fingers touching the edge, & 1st 2 fingers slightly apart. He draws around the 1st 2 fingers. The rest of the figure is drawn in proportion to these 2 "legs"; distance from tip of finger (foot) to middle knuckle (knee) is equal to distance between "knee" & "hip," "hip" & "shoulders," & "shoulders" & top of "head." A circle is drawn & cut out at base of each leg to allow entrance of fingers. At least 3/4" margin is left beneath these 2 openings. A gathered fabric or crepe paper skirt may be glued to waistband to heighten effect. Tiny modeling clay slippers or little bows tied on 2 fingers complete the illusion.

---

*From Doris Anderson, *The ENCYCLOPEDIA of Games* (1415 Lake Dr. S.E., Grand Rapids, Mich. 49506: Zondervan Pub. House). Copyright © 1955 by Zondervan Publishing House. Reprinted by permission of the publisher.

June

June brings tulips, lilies, roses,
Fills the children's hands with posies.

2   Thomas Hardy (1840-1928), English author: *Far from the Madding Crowd.*

3   Jefferson Davis (1808-1889), American statesman, President of the Confederacy.

Dr. Charles R. Drew (1904-1950), "Father of Blood Plasma."

4   Henry Ford drove 1st successful Ford down streets of Detroit, 1896.

5   Socrates (469 B.C.-399 B.C.), Greek philosopher.

Adam Smith (1723-1790), Scottish author, economist: *Wealth of Nations.*

1st public ascent of a balloon, France, 1783.

6   Nathan Hale (1755-1776), American patriot.

7   Mohammed died, 632 A.D.

Gwendolyn Brooks (1917-   ), 1st Negro to receive Pulitzer Prize, 1950 *(Annie Allen).*

Children's Day.

8   Diego Valasquez (1599-1660), Spanish painter.

Robert Schumann (1810-1856), German composer.

1st vacuum cleaner patented by Ives W. McGuffrey, 1869.

Frank Lloyd Wright (1869-1959), American architect.

9   Peter the Great (1672-1725), Czar of Russia, responsible for the westernization of Russia.

1st ballistic missile submarine launched, 1959.

11   John Constable (1776-1837), English painter.

Richard Strauss (1864-1949), German composer: *Der Rosenkavalier.*

12 Henry David Thoreau (1817-1862), New England author: *Walden.*

14 Flag Day: Continental Congress adopted official American flag, 1777.

15 Magna Carta granted, 1215.

Rembrandt (Harmensoon van Rÿn) (1606-1669), Dutch painter.

Edward Grieg (1843-1907), Norwegian composer: *Peer Gynt Suite.*

16 1st extra-terrestrial flight by a woman, Jr. Lt. Valentina Vladimirovna Tereshkova; orbited Earth 48 times in 2 days, 22 hrs. & 50 min., 1963.

Father's Day (the 3rd Sunday in June).

17 Discovery of Mississippi River by Louis Jolliet & Father Marquette, 1673.

Bunker Hill Day, 1775.

18 Igor Stravinsky (1882-1971), Russian composer in America: *The Rites of Spring.*

19 Blaise Pascal (1623-1662), French philosopher.

Arrival of the Statue of Liberty in N.Y.C., 1885.

20 Adoption of design of Great Seal of U.S. by Congress, 1782.

21 Jacques Offenbach (1819-1880), German-French composer: *The Tales of Hoffman.*

Summer begins.

23 Treaty with Indians signed by William Penn, 1683.

U.S. Secret Service established, 1860.

Henry Hudson died after 6/23/1611: set adrift, without food or water, by a mutinous crew, Hudson wasn't seen again after that date.

25 Custer's Last Stand, 1876.

26 U.N. Charter signed by 50 nations, 1945.

27 Helen Keller (1880-1968), American author, speaker; blind & deaf since infancy.

1st demonstration of color television, 1929.

28 King Henry VIII (1491-1547), established Church of England.

Peter Paul Rubens (1577-1640), Flemish painter.

John Wesley (1703-1791), English minister, founder of Methodism.

Battle of Monmouth, Revolutionary War, 1778.

30   1st demonstration of transistors, 1948.

June

May have been named for the great goddess Juno, protectress of women, although some Romans felt that its name came from the Latin *juniores,* in which case June would be a month dedicated to the young. Some scholars believe that "June" is derived from Junius, a Latin family to which the murderers of Julius Caesar belonged.

JUNE QUOTATIONS

3   All we ask is to be let alone. (Inaugural Address as President of the Confederate States of America, 1861)—Jefferson Davis

5   Know thyself.

Courage is knowing what not to fear.

Nothing can harm a good man, either in life or after death.

The nearest way to glory is to strive to be what you wish to be thought to be.

                                —Socrates

6   I only regret that I have but one life to lose for my country. (Last words, 9/22/1776)—Nathan Hale

8   The physician can bury his mistakes, but the architect can only advise his clients to plant vines. *(New York Times* magazine, 10/4/53).—Frank Lloyd Wright

12   In the long run you hit only what you aim at. Therefore though you should fail immediately you had better aim at something high.

Our life is frittered away by detail. . . . Simplify, Simplify. ("Where I Lived and What I Lived For")

                          —Henry David Thoreau

19   Man is but a reed, the weakest in nature, but he is a thinking reed.—Pascal

Give me your tired, your poor,

Your huddled masses yearning to breathe free,
The wretched refuse of your teeming shore,
Send these, the homeless, tempest-tossed to me:
I lift my lamp beside the golden door.
    (*The New Colossus,* inscription for the Statue of Liberty)
    —Emma Lazarus

27   Security is mostly a superstition. It does not exist in nature, nor do the children of men as a whole experience it. Avoiding danger is no safer in the long run than outright exposure. Life is either a daring adventure or nothing.— Helen Keller

28   (About Rubens): "The fellow mixes blood with his colors."—Guido Reni

Cleanliness is next to Godliness.—John Wesley

June Riddle: What's a good thing to keep in summertime? (Cool.)

JUNE EVENTS

A few words about June: Try to plan these last weeks of school so that the inevitable restlessness of the children will not be compounded. Let the children work with the encyclopedia, tracking down answers to questions the class raises as a group. Bring in large, sturdy puzzles of the U.S.A. or of the world. Bring to class a set of wildlife books for free time reading. Construction paper scraps need to be used up so encourage the making of collages, torn paper compositions, or a scrapbook of magazine & student-made pictures for a hospital children's ward. The classroom will have to be cleaned (on the last day of school). This may be facilitated by dividing older children into 4 groups, each assigned the responsibility of thoroughly cleaning 1 side of the classroom. Make sure that all things to be accomplished in each area are clearly noted (where to put old papers, etc.) before you announce (by blowing a whistle) the beginning of house cleaning. First group successfully finished is rewarded in some small way. This may mean 5-10 minutes of noise but at the end of this time your room should sparkle!

• **1st successful drive by Ford of his car   [4]**

Many people believe that Henry Ford invented the automobile. This is incorrect. Karl Benz, a German, built the 1st Benz, a 3-wheeler, in Mannheim. Although it was greatly ridiculed, he was driving this car down the "autobahn" in the fall of 1885—11 years before Henry drove his Ford through the streets of Detroit. Information sources:

Automobile Mfrs. Assoc. 320 New Center Bldg. Detroit, Mich 48202	Am. Auto. Assoc. 1712 G Street, N.W. Washington, D.C. 20006
Society of Automotive Engineers 485 Lexington Ave. New York, N.Y. 10017	Museum of History & Technology Washington, D.C.

● **Patriots Day   [6]**

The ancient Greek term *patrios* meant "founded by the forefathers" (*pater*=father). For this reason *patriotism* is the quality of one devoted to his family, who is prepared to defend the country of his forefathers at any cost.

● **Flag Day   [14]**

When he taught in Wisconsin in the early years of this century, Dr. Bernard J. Cigrand, each June 14th (in honor of the anniversary of the day in 1777 when the U.S. flag was adopted), would fly the American flag over his school. In 1916 President Wilson officially designated June 14th as Flag Day.

Bulletin board suggestions. Paper chains of red & white are made by the class. These are alternated to fill an entire board. The deep blue rectangle is filled with 50 stars also designed & cut out by the children.

Creative writing topic: "What America (My Flag) Means to Me."

Vocabulary enrichment words; halyard, pennant, flagstaff, banner, hoist.

History. Each day as the children salute the flag, they should understand the true meaning of the words they speak. Why not (with the assistance of the children & their dictionaries) paraphrase the salute to the flag, e.g., "I promise (myself) that I'll be loyal to the American flag & to the United States, whose power belongs to the voters, a country which, believing in God, cannot be divided & offers liberty & justice to everyone."

Occasionally set aside 5-10 minutes prior to the pledge, in which you discuss a topic such as: how are flags made commercially? Who wrote the Pledge of Allegiance? What is the Flag

Code? (June, 1942, U.S. Congress.) Who were Barbara Frietchie, Betsy Ross?

Flag Day relay race. At the opposite end of the playing area are 2 chairs. On each chair is a lump of clay in which is stuck a tiny American flag. Class is divided into 2 equal teams. First child of each team runs to chair, snatches flag, bringing it back to 2nd child who takes it & runs back to chair & sticks flag into clay again. Throughout relay flag is *always* held upright. 2nd child runs back to line, tags 3rd player who repeats procedure until 1 team finishes.

● **Birth of Rembrandt   [15]**

A painter of the Dutch school, he produced many remarkable portraits & figure paintings outstanding for their masterly technique. He was also an etcher of high ability.

Information source:

Publications Distribution Section
Smithsonian Institution Press
Washington, D.C. 20560

(Free catalogs & papers, Rembrandt's etching technique: an example, by Peter Morsel, is #61)

● **Bunker Hill Day   [17]**

Read to the class the long narrative poem "Grandmother's Story of Bunker Hill," by Oliver Wendell Holmes. (It can be found in *The Golden Treasure of Poetry,* edited by Louis Untermeyer & published by Golden Press, New York, N.Y., in 1959.)

● **Father's Day (the 3rd Sunday in June)**

Mrs. John B. Dodd & her 5 brothers & sisters had been raised by their father after their mother's death. One spring day in 1919, while listening to the Mother's Day sermon, Mrs. Dodd had an idea. She thought how she would like to honor her father & other men like him, & so, after the sermon, she spoke to her minister. He agreed with Mrs. Dodd & drew up a resolution for her, proposing that June 10, 1919, be set aside as Father's Day. Three years later, on the 3rd Sunday of June, America celebrated the 1st national Father's Day.

Although Father's Day usually falls after the closing of school, a small gift made in advance would undoubtedly be welcomed by Daddy. (See December: Christmas Gifts, pg. 114, for suggestions.)

Ask the children to finish: "My Daddy is. . . . ." & illustrate these pages.

Combed finger paintings. These afford an unusual, colorful gift wrap for Father's gift. Cut a notched comb from cardboard 2½ x 4"-8". Comb is drawn through application of wet dark-colored finger paint. Variation in notches (wide, deep, shallow) will vary texture of patterns produced.

* **Summer Solstice   [21] or [22]**

In the Northern Hemisphere, the sun appears at its highest point in the sky on June 21. On this day the sun's rays shine directly on the Tropic of Cancer, an imaginary line north of the equator, which encircles the globe. This line goes through Havana, Cuba; Calcutta, India; & Hong Kong, China. People living in these 3 cities see the sun directly overhead on June 21.

* **The Battle of Monmouth during U.S. Revolutionary War [28]**

Read aloud to the class "Molly Pitcher" by Kate Brownlee Sherwood (also found in *The Golden Treasury of Poetry*, Golden Press, New York, N.Y., 1959). Older students may read poem silently.

JUNE ACTIVITIES

Bulletin board lettering suggestions. Cut letters from corrugated cardboard; use these themselves, or cut letters in reverse from corrugated cardboard, paint these &, while wet, stamp letters of title on a long strip of white paper.

Title: Who Are We? What Are We Doing? A manipulative bulletin board. Children mix & match pictures of famous people & balloons with quotations in them. Quotations & dates of historical events might also be used.

Game of Presidents. Write (can be a mimeo-sheet)—*What President* was called: Tippecanoe? (Harrison); was the son of a President? (John Quincy Adams); said "I do not choose to run"? (Coolidge); was called Old Hickory? (Jackson); was called "the Sage of Monticello"? (Jefferson); outlined a foreign policy with S. America? (Monroe). What 2 Presidents died on the same day? (Jefferson & John Adams.) What 4 Presidents were assassinated? (Lincoln, Garfield, McKinley, Kennedy.)

A blown-up balloon is tied to the end of a slender stick of balsa wood which is anchored by a lump of clay beneath the paper figure. Felt pen lettering on balloon directs children to read books on table in their free time.

Language: want ads. Have children bring last night's paper (the same edition) to class. Study the classified section for wording, abbreviations, prices. Have children compose want ads for historical figures; ads may advertise for something to rent, lease or swap; may describe a lost/found object; may be in the category of "personals" or services-to-be-rendered. These ads are printed up on the primary typewriter for an interesting bulletin board or as a mimeo which the children will read to themselves. VARIATION: Hand out pictures of inventions you've mentioned in class during the year & ask each child to describe his in an ad (e.g., an almanac, reaper, phonograph, balloon, sewing machine, movie camera, tank, steamboat, telephone). VARIATION: Older students design full-page magazine lay-outs incorporating photos, lettering, border.

Penmanship practice—imaginary postcard correspondence: Each child is given a piece of tagboard cut in the shape of a postcard. He is asked to pretend that he is already on vacation & that he is sending the teacher a picture postcard. On 1 side he draws or pastes a collage of a picture of a vacation spot; he may show himself in the picture. On the reverse side he writes a note to the teacher & her address (which is clearly printed on the front chalkboard). Humor & ingenuity are encouraged.

At the end of the school year have the children write a class letter thanking the Room Mother. Each child designs & cuts out of colored paper a tiny bird, flower, butterfly, heart or angel & these are pasted all around the letter, in its margins. Letter is rolled up & tied with a pretty ribbon, each tail of which each has

a pasted on it.

Poetry

> And what is so rare as a day in June?
> Then, if ever, come perfect days;
> ... We may shut our eyes, but we cannot help knowing
> That skies are clear and grass is growing.
> —James Russell Lowell (19th c.)

Also appropriate is "The Seed Shop," by Muriel Stuart.

Reading

Pictorial review. Make a large book with cover & pages of tagboard. On the left hand pages draw or paste 2-4 pictures depicting famous people, historical events discussed in class during the last few months. These pictures may also stress sequential order. On the right hand pages cut slits to hold oaktag sentence slips which describe pictures. Children insert slips (which, initially, appear as a group in front of book) in correct positions throughout book.

A wheel of fortune. This helps break the routine of drill sessions in the reading group. Pointer of tagboard wheel is spun & number designates pile of cards from which "fortune" is chosen. This card is read aloud by child & may indicate small prize, poem, puzzle or penalty. (Reading instruction may be involved in "deciphering" of fortune.)

On finishing a reader. Ask the children to think back over the stories they have read & choose 1, giving it a different ending (beginning)? Ask how each character might have behaved differently in that case. VARIATION: Go through the reader & choose sentences at random from different stories. On slips of tagboard print 2-3 sentences that might begin or end a story. These slips are drawn from a box by children. Each child thinks for a few moments & then tells his original story, based on these sentences, to his group. Children may enjoy trying to identify the story in reader from which sentences were actually taken.

End of the year reading mimeo for older students. This may be done on the last day of classes; its vocabulary should be adjusted to the children who will be using the mimeo.

1. If blackberries are still green when they are red, write *H* in the left hand margin. If not, write *Z.*
2. If brown cows give white milk which makes yellow butter, write *A* in the left hand margin. If not, write *W.*
3. If paper can be made out of wood, write *V* at the left. If not, write *3.*
4. If Leap Year has 366 days, write *E* at the left. If not, write *A.*
5. If a ground hog is a pig that lives in the earth, put an *8* at the left. If not, write *A* there.
6. If the letter "M" comes before the letter "K" in the alphabet, write *R* at the left. If not, write *G.*
7. If the Atlantic Ocean is the largest ocean in the world, write *P* at the left. If not, write *O.*
8. If Beethoven was deaf the last years of his life, write *O* at the left. If not, write *T.*
9. If basketball is a major sport, write *D* at the left. If not, write *S.*
10. If the 1st day of summer is called the Spring Equinox, write *K* at the left. If it is called Summer Solstice, write *S.*
11. If seventy is larger than seventeen, write *U* in the left margin. If not, write *T.*
12. If Edison invented electricity, write *P* in the left margin. If not, write *M.*
13. If Francis Scott Key wrote our national anthem, put an *M* in the left margin. If he didn't, put an *X.*
14. If Mr. Gettysburg wrote the Gettysburg Address, put *B* in the left margin. If not, put *E.*
15. If the Pilgrims had never seen corn until they came to America, put *R* at the left. If they *had,* put *Z.*
16. If this is the final question in this quiz, put *!* at the left. If not, put a *?*

When children have correctly answered each question, "HAVE A GOOD SUMMER!" appears in the margin.

June Science

Grasses are among the most useful of all plants. They flower in summer but do not ripen until late July, August or September. Wild grasses include timothy, rye grass, meadow foxtail, cock's foot & common quaking grass. Cultivated grasses include wheat, barley & oats. The flower-head of grass is called the "ear" or "panicle." The flowers that develop are called "spikelets."

Classroom cacti may flower in June. Give them a bit of water once a week if the weather is dry.

Nature Quiz. This may be used for Classroom Baseball, which is played as follows: Divide class into 2 equal teams. Players come to bat as in regular baseball. They tell the pitcher (teacher) the type of "ball" they want. Teacher pitches that type question at batter. If batter answers correctly, he makes a hit & gets on base (designated on blackboard or elsewhere in room) & 2nd player comes up to bat. A team completes an inning when it has missed 3 questions. According to their difficulty, questions are labeled as being singles, doubles, or triples, or a home-run. For older children, extremely easy questions could be called "double-play balls"; if any men are on base, 2 outs are made if batter answers incorrectly. Teacher will evaluate questions according to the ability of the class. Prior to "pitching" question, teacher announces type of question involved, i.e., "This question is for a home run!"

1. What does "equinox" mean? (Equal night & day.)
2. What planet, discovered in 1930, is named after the god of the lower world? (Pluto.)
3. Who discovered the Pacific Ocean? (Vasco Nuñez de Balboa.)
4. How does a deciduous tree differ from a non-deciduous tree? (A deciduous tree sheds its leaves annually, while a non-deciduous tree is "evergreen.")
5. Who invented the telescope? (Galileo.)
6. Explain why the whale is a mammal & NOT a fish. (It is warm-blooded, breathes air, bears its young alive & feeds them milk.)
7. How many legs has a spider? (8.)
8. Do snakes close their eyes when they sleep? (No.)
9. Why don't they? (Snakes have no eyelids.)
10. What do sugar, sand, salt & snowflakes all have in common? (They are all crystals.)

11. What planet, discovered in 1846, is named after the Greek god of the sea? (Neptune.)
12. How long would it take to drown a grasshopper by holding its head under water? (It would starve to death 1st, as a grasshopper breathes through apertures on its sides.)
13. How long is a year on the planet Mercury? (3 months.)
14. Explain how it rains. (Water from the earth evaporates into the atmosphere where it is condensed & falls back to Earth as rain.)
15. Name a marsupial found in the U.S.A. (The opossum).
16. Who invented the phonograph? (Thomas Alva Edison.)
17. Name the 1st man to walk on the moon. (Neil Armstrong.)
18. When Wilson Bentley photographed 1000s of snowflakes, what 2 discoveries did he make? (Each snowflake has a hexagonal pattern. No 2 snowflakes have the exact same pattern!)

History Culmination

Help the children learn to draw conclusions by giving them some "problems" to discuss & answer, e.g.: I think Henry David Thoreau was a great man because _____; If I had come on the Mayflower, I would have brought _____, etc.; If Franklin (Lincoln, Booker T. Washington) had never lived, the world today would be different in these ways _____.

June P.E.

Relay Races (See November P.E. for organization suggestions.)

Hopping. The trip to goal is made by hopping 1st on 1 foot & then the other OR by taking 5 hops on 1 foot & 5 on the other.

Hurdle Relay. Divide each team into couples. Have the couples line up 1 behind the other at arm's distance between pairs. The 1st 2 children of each team are given a broomstick (yardstick). Holding this near the ground as they go, they run down the length of their team. Each couple must jump the hurdle as it passes. When the end of the line is reached, the 2 children who are now at the head of the line run back, grab the broomstick, run up to head of the line & continue the race until every couple has held the stick.

Jump rope Relay. At a given signal, 1st child of each team begins jumping rope toward goal line 40 feet away. Once there he turns around & continues jumping rope back to the starting line where he gives rope to the 2nd child on his team, who repeats procedure.

Run and POP Relay. Brown paper bags (1 for each player) are laid on 2 chairs at goal line. A wastepaper basket stands between the chairs. 1st child of each team runs to his chair, takes bag, blows it up, pops it (with his fist), throws burst bag INTO wastebasket & runs back & tags 2nd child, who may *not* leave starting line until he is tagged.

Cottonball Relay. Each player is given a soda straw. At goal line is a bowl with 2 little cotton balls in it. 1st child of each of the 2 teams runs up to bowl. Holding his soda straw in his mouth & sucking in, he causes a cotton ball to adhere to his straw. In this way the ball is taken from bowl & child runs back & deposits ball into a bowl that is on a chair next to his team. 2nd child repeats procedure. NO HANDS are allowed throughout relay; should cotton ball fall en route to destination, it must be rescued without aid of hands.

Pea-picker Relay. Children are divided into equal teams. 1st child of each team is given a round-ended plastic picnic knife (or butter knife or tongue depressor). Near each team is a bowl filled with a given number of dried peas (or beans). At the goal line are empty bowls, 1 for each team. At a signal, 1st player of each team goes to his bowl, scoops up as many peas on his knife as he can & proceeds to goal line where he empties peas into his team's bowl. (Warn children not to run with upheld knives as speed is NOT the idea of this relay!) He then tags 2nd player who repeats procedure. Dropped peas are not counted or retrieved. Team with most peas in bowl at goal line is the winner.

Summer Vacation Mimeo

A summer vacation mimeo for parents might be extremely helpful. This mimeo could include suggestions for how to make a summer trip educational; the selection of educational souvenirs; reminders about vaccinations, swimming lessons, poison oak prevention. You could list suggestions for use of free time: local hobby shops, educational films, T.V. shows to watch for, recreational facilities. You might list games that can be played without equipment, activities that can be done alone, short trips the family could take together, summer art lessons offered (by a local museum). Instructions for simple hand crafts, i.e., Spool Knitting which can be done by 6 yr. olds, might be included:

To start

> Four finishing nails are hammered into top of spool. Thin yarn is threaded up through spool & wound about nails as shown. Loop A is picked up & drawn over B & top of nail. Repeat at each nail in turn. Long knitted roll develops. This roll can be handstitched to form purse, doll clothes, a mat.

Summer vacation mimeo to parents might also include a list of appropriate summertime reading suggestions, summaries of things accomplished during the year, e.g., "Math Facts I Know," "Words I Know How to Read," "Words I Can Spell." Review of these pages during the summer will provide materials for playing school & will help children retain their skills over vacation months.

A list of activities which children may enjoy while traveling in a car might be appreciated.

Prepare a recipe box of suggestion cards from which the children will draw when they can think of nothing to do. Only 1 card at a time should be drawn from the box, & once selected, the suggestion should be followed. Suggestions should not include things the children would normally think of themselves. A few suggestions:

—Act out a favorite story.
—Make & cut out a set of paper dolls.
—Make a hat from an old newspaper & become a pirate hunting for treasure.
—Make a sampler by using a big needle & bright yarn on a piece of burlap.
—Draw a picture of your entire family.
—Make a clay model of your right foot.
—Make a hand (finger) puppet from a piece of an old sheet, felt-tip pens, felt & feathers, & then give a puppet show.
—Play doctor & pretend that you are making a round of house calls.
—Tell Indian legends around a make-believe bonfire.
—Make a map of your neighborhood, including buildings, plants & main landmarks.

—Close your eyes & feel the things around you; make a list of the different textural qualities you feel.

—Design a perfect bedroom for yourself.

—Using a stack of old magazines, go through them & collect an entire alphabet of capital letters & objects illustrating each; use these to make an alphabet book.

—Using tagboard, a big needle & yarn, make a sunglasses holder similar to the one shown here.

Classroom Cookery

During their Social Studies reading, the children may learn of unusual or interesting foods prepared in other countries or areas. As these foods are mentioned, the teacher could prepare some for the students to taste. This allows the children an opportunity to see the food in a raw form as well as in its cooked state. Tortillas, succotash, poi, maple sugar are a few possibilities.

Six of the following recipes require no cooking. The few utensils necessary can be kept in a classroom cupboard: wooden spoons, plastic or metal measuring cups, measuring spoons (which have been separated one from another), a plastic wash basin for mixing ingredients (preferable to glass bowls which are awkward for children to handle & can accommodate only one child at a time), cooky sheets & wax paper. A sponge & a 2 lb. coffee can of warm water will facilitate quick clean-ups. Several men's shirts, worn buttoned down the back, will make excellent aprons.

Each recipe can be so organized as to involve each of the children (in the reading group) in some aspect of the preparation. This preparation of food in the classroom will give the children experience with volumetric measures & will impress upon them (as nothing else may) the importance of careful reading. After clean-up, children may be asked questions based on the set of directions which a recipe represents.

Classroom cooking also offers a chance to break down the stereotyped idea which children may have that it is only *women* who belong in (or more subtly, can function in) the kitchen.

If a hot plate is available for classroom use, many other creative cooking experiences, including the making of art supplies, are possible. With the addition of a double-boiler & a candy thermometer to their store of cooking utensils, the children will be able to prepare any of the following recipes.

Culinary Word Etymologies

For many centuries Latin words have poured into our language. One of hundreds which we have adopted without even a spelling change is "recipe."

It is from *dactylus,* the Latin word for "finger," that we get our word "date," as that fruit was once thought to resemble a human finger.

In 496 B.C. a terrible drought afflicted the Roman countryside. The priests brought forth a new goddess, Ceres, & the people were told that if they immediately made sacrifices to her, rain would fall. Because Ceres was successful in ending the drought, she became "the protector of the crops." The Latin word *cerealis* meant "of Ceres," & gave us our word "cereal."

"Currants" were named for the corrupt city of ancient Greece, Corinth.

In the first century before Christ the Roman legions were in Germany. Whenever anything was sold to the semi-savage tribes found living there, the Latin name for the object went with it. In this way many Latin words found their way into German. Some centuries later German invaders brought nearly a hundred Latin derivatives into Britain—& into English; "butter" was one of these.

"Walnuts" means "foreign nuts." The Anglo-Saxons called them *wealhhnutu* (*wealh*="foreigner" & *hnutu*="nuts"), as these nuts were unknown to England before the arrival of invading armies.

"Yolk" is a derivative of a Middle English word *yolke* or *yelke*, through an Old English word *geolea,* from *geolu,* all of these words meaning "yellow."

Sometime in the year 850 A.D. a goatherd named Kaldi became puzzled by the strange actions of his goats. He noticed that they were nibbling at the berries of a certain bush. When Kaldi tried some of these berries himself he was amazed at the feeling of exhilaration he experienced. He rushed off & told the other goatherds of his discovery. The Arabs learned to boil the berries of these bushes, calling the brew "gahve." The Turks introduced it to the French who called it "cafe," & in this way we got our English word, "coffee."

Coffee

Trees of the genus Caffea, native to Africa & E. Asia, bearing fruit containing beans used in making coffee. The green coffee bean is freed from the pulp & dried in the sun.

"Vinegar" is actually *vyn egre* meaning "sour wine," & comes from Old French.

The Latin word *gelo* means "to freeze" or "to congeal," & it led to the French word *gelee*, "a jelly," & in English this became "gelatine."

Under William the Conqueror, in 1066, the Normans (North-men) conquered the Germanic tribes who, in turn, became their servants. The vocabulary of these conquered peoples was of the field & kitchen & from it we get such words as "house," "hearth," "oven," "pot," "stone," "wheat" & "milk."

The Mexican Indians called the tree from which the cacao seed comes, "caucauatl." The invading Spanish had difficulty pronouncing this Indian word & shortened it to "cacao." In English it became "cocoa." Another Mexican Indian word, "chocolatl," meaning "bitter water," gave us "chocolate."

The word *"coconut"* (also spelled "cocoanut," thanks to an error by Dr. Samuel Johnson in his dictionary), comes from the Spanish & Portugese word *coco* which means "a grimace." The three holes in the bottom of the coconut were thought to resemble a grimacing face & so "coconut" actually means "funny-face nut."

Candy Recipes:

(All starred recipes require no cooking whatsoever.)
Egyptian hieroglyphics show that in 1566 B.C. candies made of honey, flour, almonds & figs were being sold in the market places.

*Greek Candy: Karridakia (makes 20)

1 c. dried figs	1 c. shelled walnuts
1 c. pitted dates, apricots	1/2 c. powdered or granulated
or raisins	sugar
	1 t. cinnamon

Chop figs, dates, walnuts (by running them through a meat-grinder). Mix thoroughly. Roll into balls 1" in diameter. Mix sugar & cinnamon. Roll balls in this mixture until well coated. Store in tight jars. ("Hi Neighbor": Book III UNICEF U.N. New York, N.Y.)

*Algerian Lemon Fondant

1/3 c. soft margarine	1 t. lemon extract
1/3 c. light syrup	4-1/2 c. sifted confectioner's
1/2 t. salt	sugar
	yellow food coloring

Blend margarine, syrup, salt & extract. Add sugar all at once. Then add a few drops of food coloring. Stir. Knead. Turn out onto a wax-papered surface. Knead until smooth. Shape into cherry-sized balls. ("Days of Discovery" packet: American Friends Service Committee, 160 N. 15th St., Phila., Pa. 19102.)

*Orange Fondant Balls

2 egg whites	1-1/2 T. orange flavoring
1 T. cold water	4 c. sifted confectioner's
	sugar
	orange food coloring

Beat egg whites & water until well-blended. Add sugar gradually until mixture becomes stiff. Add flavoring & coloring. Knead until smooth; then shape into balls. (Ibid. American Friends Service Committee.)

Ann G.'s Recipe

2 c. sugar	dash of salt
1/2 c. milk	1/2 c. peanut butter
1/4 lb. margarine	1 t. vanilla
3 T. cocoa	4 c. oatmeal, uncooked

Put sugar, milk, margarine, cocoa, salt in a pan; bring to a rolling boil. Remove from heat. Add peanut butter & vanilla. Pour this mixture over oatmeal. Drop by teaspoonfuls onto wax paper lined cookie sheet. Cool. Enjoy.

Simple Crispies

corn flakes or crisp	(coconut or chopped nuts)
rice cereal	cupcake liners
milk chocolate candy bars	

Put candy bars in pan & place over hot water until melted. Stir cereal (& coconut or nuts, if desired) into chocolate until cereal is completely coated. Place a spoonful of mixture in each cupcake liner. Let stand 5 minutes.

Fudge-in-a-Minute (makes 18)

8 squares semi-sweet	1t. vanilla
chocolate	1/4 t. salt
2/3 c. sweetened condensed	
milk	

Melt chocolate in milk over low heat, stirring to blend. Add vanilla & salt. Spread into an oiled 4 x 8 pan. Chill until firm. Cut into squares. (Simple yet satisfying.)

Fantastic Fudge (makes 30)

2-1/4 c. white sugar	1/4 c. butter
3/4 c. canned milk	1/4 t. salt
4 c. tiny marshmallows*	1 c. chocolate bits
1 c. chopped nuts	1 t. vanilla

In a pan mix sugar, milk, butter & salt. Bring to a boil, *stirring constantly.* Don't let it stick on the bottom of the pan! Boil & stir for 5 minutes. Stir in chocolate bits. Stir until melted. Stir in nuts & vanilla. Pour mixture onto an oiled plate. Cool. Cut.

(This is wording that can be read by young students themselves. A good recipe.)

*Or 16 marshmallows cut up into little pieces.

*No-Bake Chocolate Walnut Balls (makes 40)

36 chocolate wafers, crushed fine   1 c. confectioner's sugar
1/2 c. finely chopped chocolate   1/4 c. orange juice
   bits   1/2 c. finely chopped walnuts
3 T. corn syrup

Mix crumbs, bits, sugar & walnuts. Add syrup & juice. Mix well. Form into 1" balls. Roll in confectioner's sugar, cocoa, or finely chopped nuts. (Store in tight container & allow to ripen.) These are nice enough to be given as gifts.

Chocolate Raisin Clusters (makes 30)

1-1/4 c. chocolate bits   1/2 c. coarsely chopped nuts
1 c. seedless raisins

Melt chocolate bits in top half of double boiler. Stir until syrupy. Add raisins & nuts. Stir until they are coated. Drop by teaspoonfuls onto wax paper lined cookie sheet. Chill 10 hours.

Mr. Nelson's Peanut Brittle (makes 18 1" x 1")

2 c. white sugar   1 t. baking soda
1 c. white corn syrup   1 T. butter
                            1-2 c. peanuts

Put sugar & syrup in large cast-iron skillet. Stir to mix. Bring to hard boil. Boil 5 minutes. Add butter; stir in & wait until mixture darkens. Add peanuts. Wait until it boils again. Add soda. Stir in & immediately pour onto oiled cookie sheet. Cool for 15-20 min. Crack with hammer.

Plain White Pull Candy

1/4 c. water   1-1/2 t. butter
1-1/4 c. granulated sugar   1/4 t. baking soda
2 T. mild vinegar   1 t. vanilla
                            candy thermometer

Oil platter. Place water, sugar, vinegar, butter in pan. Stir over low heat until sugar is dissolved. Increase heat until thermometer reads 268°. Remove from heat. Add vanilla & soda. Stir just enough to blend. Pour onto platter; let cool until a dent can be made in top with finger. Gather into a lump & pull with oiled fingers until candy is light & porous. Dip fingers in cold water often. Roll candy in long strips & cut into 1" pieces. (Place candy in tightly covered tin if creamy quality is desired.)

VARIATION: Molasses Pull Candy

Follow the same procedure, using these ingredients:

1 c. molasses	1/2 c. granulated sugar
1 T. butter	1/4 t. baking soda
2 t. vinegar	1 t. vanilla

The history of cookies & cakes is the history of bread—& bread is as old as Man. The early nomadic peoples had to carry nourishment with them as they traveled. They made a meal by grinding grain & seeds & added water as a cementing agent. The resulting rock-like loaves were the earliest forms of bread—man's first manufactured food.

Gateau a la Brochette

3/8 c. evaporated milk mixed with 3/8 c. water (or a bit less)	
3/8 c. salad oil	1/2 t. baking soda plus
3/8 c. CRUSHED walnuts	1 t. cream of tartar
5 egg yolks	1 c. honey plus 1/2 t. soda
2 c. plus 4 T. sifted cake flour	3/4 t. salt

Mix oil, yolks & nuts together. Sift together: salt, flour, soda, & cream of tartar. Add to nut mixture. Now stir in honey combined with soda. Add half of milk, a bit at a time. Once flour mixture is moist, beat batter 250 times. Add remaining milk & beat 120 times.

Put a lump of dough on an oiled brochette (skewer); turn brochette until dough clings to it. Hold brochette in front of an open fire & keep brochette constantly rotating. From time to time, add more dough to that on skewer until (after 2-3 hours) a cake, eight inches in diameter, has been produced.

When cake is thoroughly cooked, carefully slide it off brochette. (This recipe is included only as a curiosity & is adapted from one found in THE ARTISTS' AND WRITERS' COOKBOOK, by Beryl Barr & Barbara Turner Sachs, eds. (Sausalito, California: Angel Island Pub., 1961), p. 273.

Cookie Recipes:

That old favorite, "Marshmallow Treats"

1/4 c. margarine	5 c. Rice Krispies brand cereal
4 c. tiny marshmallows (or 40 big	1/2 t. vanilla
marshmallows cut up into pieces)	

Melt margarine in a pan. Add marshmallows & cook over LOW heat, *stirring constantly,* until marshmallows are melted. Add vanilla. Add cereal & stir until it is well coated. Press warm mixture into an oiled pan. Press down firmly. When mixture is *cool,* cut into squares.

And now, The Quickies (makes 30)

1 can sweetened condensed milk (1 1/3 cups)
1/2 c. peanut butter
1 c. chopped nuts, 3 c. shredded coconut, or 2 c. raisins

Blend all ingredients well. Drop by spoonfuls onto a buttered cookie sheet. Bake at 375° for 15 min. or until golden brown. Remove from sheet at once.

Quickie-Cookies (for little children)

1 graham cracker for each child
1 marshmallow for each child
1 red cinnamon drop for each child
   (or 1 chocolate kiss)

Assemble as shown & place under the broiler for a minute, until marshmallow melts.

Turtles* (makes 24 little turtles)

2 squares baking chocolate	1 c. flour
1/3 c. margarine	1 t. vanilla
2 eggs, beaten	2 t. cream
3/4 c. sugar	chocolate icing

Melt chocolate & margarine. Mix together eggs, sugar, flour, vanilla, cream. Add chocolate mixture. Lightly oil waffle iron; heat iron until quite hot (steaming). Drop 4 individual T. of batter onto iron & bake 2-4 min. (thus making 4 turtles at 1 time). Chocolate icing (mix) may be prepared while turtles are being baked. Cooled turtles are frosted & 2 silver shot eyes may be added to each if you like.

*Name refers to crosshatch markings of cookie.

No-Bake Brownies (makes 36)

2 c. chocolate bits	1 c. chopped nuts (pecans)
1 c. evaporated milk	1 c. sifted confectioner's
3 c. finely crushed vanilla wafers	sugar
2 c. miniature marshmallows	1/2 t. salt
	2 t. evaporated milk

Stir chocolate bits & milk (1 c.) over low heat until melted. Remove from heat. In a large bowl mix vanilla wafer crumbs, marshmallows, nuts, sugar, salt. Save 1/2 c. of chocolate mixture for icing; stir remainder into crumb mixture. Mix well. Press firmly into a buttered 9 x 9 pan. Stir 2 t. evaporated milk into the reserved 1/2 c. chocolate mixture. Mix until smooth. Spread evenly over mixture in pan. Chill until icing is set. Cut into squares.

Coconut Bars (makes 36 bars)

1/2 c. butter	2 c. crushed graham crackers
1 egg slightly beaten	1/2 c. milk
1/2 lb. flaked coconut	1 t. vanilla
1 c. chopped nuts	1 c. pink butter icing
1/3 c. brown sugar	

Cook egg, butter, sugar over low heat for 1 minute. Stir in crackers, nuts, vanilla. Press into 9 x 9 pan. Mix coconut & milk thoroughly. Press on top of crumb mixture. Refrigerate until firm. Frost with pink butter icing. Cut into small squares.

Pink Butter Icing: Beat 1-1/2 T. butter. Gradually add 1 c. sifted confectioner's sugar. Blend until creamy. Add 1/8 t. salt, 1 t. vanilla, & a few drops red food coloring. Additional confectioner's sugar may be added if consistency of icing is too thin.

Miscellaneous Recipes:

Popcorn was introduced to the English colonists at the first Thanksgiving dinner on February 22, 1630, by Quadequina, brother of Massasoit. As his contribution to that dinner he brought a deerskin bag filled with several bushels of popped corn.

Popcorn Crackle

1 foil-wrapped pan of	2 T. margarine
ready-to-pop corn	1-1/4 c. granulated sugar
1/2 c. light molasses	candy thermometer
3/4 c. light corn syrup	

Pop corn according to directions on package. Pour into a bowl. Mix remaining ingredients in a large saucepan. Boil until 285° is registered on candy thermometer (stage at which liquid forms hard ball when dropped into cold water). Stir liquid into the corn. With oiled hands, spread over a 14" square cookie sheet. Cool. Break up. (Store in an air-tight container.) A.F.S.C.

Nut Log (makes 24)

1/2 gallon plastic-coated milk carton	2 c. Spanish peanuts
	2 c. chopped pecans
1/4 lb. margarine	1 c. raisins
1 c. semi-sweet chocolate morsels	3 c. popped popcorn
1 10-oz. pkg. miniature marshmallows	
1 8-oz. pkg. crisp rice cereal	

Open out the top of the milk carton. Wash & dry. Melt margarine, chocolate morsels & marshmallows together in the top of a double boiler. Mix remaining ingredients in a very large bowl. Pour melted chocolate sauce over dry ingredients in bowl. Mix *well.* * Spoon the mixture into the milk carton. Pack *tightly.* Refrigerate until hard, (1 hour). Peel back the carton & slice Nut Log. (I've made this often & its robust flavor always seems to please "the cooks.")

No-Bake Fruitcake (makes 3 lbs.)

2 c. miniature marshmallows	3/4 c. chopped raisins
2/3 c. evaporated milk	1/4 c. candied cherries
6 T. *undiluted* frozen orange juice	(chopped)
1 c. chopped pecans	1 t. cinnamon
1 c. mixed candied fruits	4 c. graham cracker crumbs
(chopped)	1 t. nutmeg
3/4 c. chopped dates	½ t. cloves

Put marshmallows, milk, orange juice in large pan. Stir over medium heat until marshmallows melt. Remove from heat. Stir in pecans & all fruit. Mix crumbs & spices & add to marshmallow mixture. Press firmly into a loaf pan lined with wax paper. Cover tightly. Chill 2 days.

Ice cream was first recorded in the first century A.D. when Nero Claudius Caesar, then Emperor of Rome, ordered snow to be

---

*"A wooden spoon is useless without an untiring arm to wield it": from *A Treasure House of Useful Knowledge.* a 19th c. "Ladies Home-Companion."

brought by fast runners from nearby mountains. Fruit juices & flavoring were added to the snow. It is believed that Marco Polo found recipes for water & milk ices in China & Japan in the thirteenth century, & he is thought to have brought them with him when he returned to Europe.

Homemade Ice Cream: crank style (makes 1 quart or more)

3" vanilla bean pod	3/4 c. sugar
(or 1 T. vanilla)	1/8 t. salt
1-1/2 c. milk	3-4 egg yolks
(1 T. cornstarch)	2 c. whipping cream

(Whenever possible, the mixture should be made the day before & refrigerated. This helps to increase the volume.) Split pod & scrape seed into milk; drop in pod, also. Scald milk. Dissolve sugar in milk over heat. Combine cornstarch, salt & slightly beaten eggs; mix well. Beat in a little of the scalded milk. Combine the two mixtures & cook over low heat, stirring constantly until mixture is thick & smooth. Chill. Stir in stiffly whipped cream & pour into freezer can (2/3-3/4 full). *Chill thoroughly.*

VARIATION:*No-Cook Recipe for Ice Cream (Chocolate):* Beat 5 eggs in large bowl of electric beater at medium speed. Mix in 2 (13 oz.) cans of evaporated milk, 2 c. sugar, 2 c. whole milk & 2 c. chocolate syrup. Stir until sugar dissolves. Pour into freezer can. Freeze according to following directions. (Makes 1 gal.)

VARIATION: *Vanilla Ice Cream:* Substitute 3 c. whole milk in place of 2 c. called for above, & 1 T. vanilla in place of chocolate syrup. Prepare as directed above.

CRANK PROCEDURE. Crush ice fine (in a burlap sack). Insert dasher into freezer can. Cover mouth of freezer can with wax paper. Put on freezer can lid securely. Fit can into freezer. Adjust frame & crank & tighten screws. Measure ice & salt: use 1/2 c. rock salt for each qt. of crushed ice. (To speed up freezing process, in which case ice cream must be used at once, allow 1 part of salt to 3 parts ice.) Tamp down the first quart of ice evenly in the freezer. Alternate salt & ice until freezer is full. (A two-qt. freezer takes 4 qts. of crushed ice & 2 cups [1 lb.] rock salt). Crank continuously until dasher becomes very difficult to turn: average time is 15 minutes. Drain off excess water. Unfasten the screws. Remove crank & frame. Remove top layer of ice. Carefully wipe top & side of freezer with a clean cloth; this is done to prevent salt from getting into the ice cream. Remove top of freezer can; slowly remove dasher. Ice cream may be eaten at once, although the flavor is *greatly* improved if the ice cream is allowed to mellow for 1-2 hours. This is done by covering mouth of freezer can with wax paper & replacing lid, plugging dasher hole with a cork. Ice & a double portion of salt are added until freezer is filled & can is covered. A blanket of burlap sacks & newspapers is placed over the freezer & it is allowed to stand for 1-2 hours.

Fresh Strawberry Ice Cream (an easier alternative)

1 pt. fresh strawberries, washed & hulled.
Place berries in a large bowl. Crush them
   with a toy potato masher.
Add 1c. sugar; let stand 10 minutes. Then
   add & stir with a spoon:

1 T. lemon juice
1/2 c. COLD coffee cream
1/2 c. milk

   Pour mixture into a refrigerator tray; let mixture freeze.
   Remove tray & put mixture in a large bowl. Whip with electric beater until mixture is stiff. Refreeze.

Recipes for Art Supplies

Carving Materials.

Girostone: 2 parts sand, 2 parts cement, 4 parts coarse Zonolite (available at building supply stores). Mix dry ingredients. Add water to make heavy paste mixture. Stir thoroughly. Pour into shoe boxes. Dry for several days. VARIATIONS: 2 parts cement, 3 parts coarse Zonolite; OR 4 parts fine Zonolite to 1 part cement; OR 4 parts fine Zonolite to 1 part cement & 1 part sand; OR 4 parts fine Zonolite, 2 parts plaster of Paris & 1 part sand.

Soapscraps. Collect soapscraps until there are 4 lbs. or more. Chop up fine. Add 5 gallons water. When soap is melted, add 3 lbs. wallpaper paste & enough finely sifted sawdust (NOT redwood sawdust) to achieve correct consistency. Pour into wax-lined milk cartons (or shoe boxes). Let stand overnight. Turn out of mold the next morning. This material is durable & easy to carve.

Pearlite Stone: In a plastic dishpan, mix 1 part casting plaster & 1 part to 2 parts Pearlite Insulation Material (both this & casting plaster are sold at building supply companies). Resulting mixture should be similar to wet commercial cement, but not soupy. Pour mixture immediately into 1-1/2 gallon milk cartons. Material hardens in 1 hour. When dry, remove from cartons & carve with beer can openers or butter knives. Carve figures out of material, rather than digging into it; i.e., don't dig out the features of the face.

Plaster of Paris: Mix plaster of Paris with silicate to desired consistency, OR mix 3 parts plaster of Paris, 5 parts Vermiculite, 1 part sand & 1/2 part wheat paste. Pour into molds. Let dry. Turn out of molds & carve.

Vermiculite: Mix 5 parts Vermiculite to 2 parts Portland White Cement. Add tempera or brewed coffee to color material. Pour into salt, oatmeal or milk cartons. Tap sides of cartons to settle material. This hardens in 24 hours, unless it is refrigerated, in which case it will harden in 36 hours. Carve while block is damp. Wrap in damp cloths if unfinished block is to be left out overnight. VARIATIONS: 4 parts Vermiculite & 1 part Portland White Cement. Add coloring. This produces a softer material than the former proportions. OR 1 part Portland White Cement, 2 parts plaster of Paris, 3 parts Vermiculite. Add sand for texture. Let stand for 25 minutes. Carve while still damp.

Used (broken) sand molds can often be obtained from foundries.

Modeling Materials.

Asbestos: Slowly add a small amount of water to dry asbestos. Knead until mixture holds its shape. Wheat paste may be added to mixture. (Quickly makes good finger-puppet heads.)

Baker's Clay (inedible dough): Combine 4 c. unsifted all-purpose flour, 1 c. salt, 1-1/2 c. water in a bowl. Mix thoroughly with hands; if too stiff, add a bit more water. Remove dough from bowl. *Knead dough for a full 5-10 minutes.** Shape into desired forms. Bake on cookie sheets in preheated 350° oven until dough has a golden brown color. You can check on your shapes from time to time to know when to remove them from oven. Baking takes from 15-45 minutes as a rule & depends on the thickness of the shapes. Remove shapes from pans. Allow to cool. Once cooled, shapes may be painted with acrylics which give a nice shine to dough, or with poster or water color paints & then lightly sprayed with Varathane.

VARIATIONS: *Vertical pieces* are possible by using chicken wire as armature. Remember that the finished piece must fit into

---

*This is imperative as kneading "lightens" dough's consistency, causing dough to rise while it is being baked.

the oven! *Large Vignettes* are modeled atop a board (23" x 20")
that is covered with blue foil paper & then with chicken wire.
When modeling the scene, many areas (for sky) are left open. Press
dough firmly into chicken wire beneath. Make use of stamped-in
textures. When dough is baked & cool, use sharp wire cutters to
remove chicken wire above sky areas. (This is not essential—but if
done, must be done carefully.) *Wooden Mold* is dusted with
cornstarch & dough is pressed firmly into it to reproduce design in
mold. *Slabs of dough* are cut into animal shapes. When dough is
baked & cooled, features are applied with vari-colored icings.
Stained glass effect is achieved by using thin ropes of dough,
twisted, for the "leading." Fill each space created by "leading"
with a crushed sourball or bright hard candy. As the dough bakes,
the candies melt, forming thin, transparent "stained glass." A bent
wire may be used as support by making it form the contour of
the dough (see illustration). *Colored dough* is obtained by kneading drops of food coloring into unbaked dough. *Detailed pieces:*
tiny details, i.e., curls, flower petals, eyes, feathers, can be rolled
out of small bits of dough & laid in place on basic shape with a
needle or toothpick. Blanched & unblanched almonds (for rays of
the sun or feathers of a bird) or decorative silver shot can be pressed into dough before baking. Lacy paper doilies or metallic paper
may be glued to under edge of baked dough as trim or for contrsat.
may be glued to under edge of baked dough as trim or for contrast. In Ecuador animals are sculpted of Baker's Clay & baked in
beehive ovens for All-Saints Day.

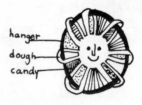

Cooked Salt: Mix 2 parts of salt to 1 part of cornstarch & 1
part of water. Cook over low heat, *stirring* vigorously, until
material is stiff. Ready to mold when cool. Dries in 36 hours if
small in size. 8 boxes of salt & proportionate amounts of
cornstarch & water make enough material for 32 small objects.
Crepe Clay: Cut 1 package of crepe paper into tiny squares;

place in bowl. Add water to cover & allow to soak until paper is soft. Drain off excess water. Mix 1 T. salt with 1 c. flour. Add flour enough to make a stiff dough. Knead mixture until flour is all blended into paper.

Magic Modeling Goop: Mix 2 c. salt with 2/3 c. water. Place in pan over low heat for 3-4 minutes (until mixture is well-heated), stirring constantly. Remove from heat & add 1 c. loose cornstarch that has been mixed with 1/2 cold water. Stir quickly. Mixture should be consistency of stiff dough. If mixture doesn't thicken, return to low heat & stir for 1 minute until a smooth, pliable mass is formed. (Food coloring may be added to portions of the dough.) Makes 1-3/4 lbs. Keeps indefinitely if wrapped in foil. Refrigeration unnecessary. Hardens in 36 hours if object is small. Large objects should be pierced with a pencil when moist in order to allow to dry out. May be painted when dry.

Papier Mâché Pulp: Soak toilet tissue overnight in water sufficient to cover generously; 3 rolls of tissue will provide an average class with pulp for 1 small item each. (To prevent mildewing, 1 t. of boric acid may be added for each pint of water.) Squeeze out excess water. To store, shape into loaves & dry. Then simply moisten & add 1 part flour to 2 parts pulp until dough is not sticky. (If boric acid was not added previously, now add salt or oil of cloves or wintergreen as a preservative.) Knead dough until it is of the desired smoothness. VARIATIONS: In water, soak torn pieces of newspaper until they are disintegrated. Drain. Squeeze pulp as dry as possible. Prepare a very thick & smooth wallpaper paste & mix 2 parts of pulp to 1 part of paste. Add 2 T. salt to prevent fermentation. Add whiting for whiteness. Mix thoroughly. Apply by handfuls directly on the model. OR soak torn-up newspaper in hot water. Beat soaked paper until soft. Make a thin paste of powdered wallpaper paste & water. Drain paper by squeezing in an old nylon stocking. Stir paste thoroughly into pulp. Remove excess moisture again. Shape into objects. OR add shredded asbestos & substitute casein glue in place of the wallpaper paste. This pulp is of superior tensile strength.

Play Clay: Mix 1 c. cornstarch & 2 c. baking soda. Add 1-1/4 c. cold water. Stir until smooth. Cook to boiling point over medium heat, stirring constantly. Boil 1 minute, until mixture reaches consistency of mashed potatoes. Turn out onto plate & cover with damp cloth until clay is cool. Knead. Roll out, & using cookie-cutters stamp out shapes, or model into desired shapes. Thin pieces dry overnight. When dry, paint & then coat with shellac or spray on clear plastic.

Play Dough: Mix 8 c. flour, 2 c. salt, 3 T. vegetable oil with water to make a soft dough. Add food coloring for color. Store in airtight container.

Sawdust & Paste: Use 2 measures of sawdust** to one measure of wallpaper paste. Add cold water—enough to obtain a pliable consistency. An eggbeater is helpful. Finished models are rough textured & can be sanded & painted when dry. VARIATIONS: Mix together 1-1/2 to 2 c. fine pine sawdust, 1 c. water & 1/4 to 1/2 c. wheat paste which is of thick custard consistency. Add 1 t. viscote adhesium OR 1/2 t. powdered casein glue. Makes 1 puppet head. OR mix 2 c. sawdust, 1 c. plaster of Paris, 1/2 c. wheat paste & 1-1/2 to 2 c. water. OR 4 parts sawdust to 1 part wheat paste. OR cook over low heat until clear, 1 c. cornstarch & 1 c. water. Add a few drops of oil of cloves as a preservative. Add sawdust until mixture reaches correct consistency.

Finger Paint: Prepare cornstarch according to directions on package. To each pint of starch add 1 T. glycerine (to obtain a good texture) & 1/2 t. oil of cloves (to prevent paint from souring). Food coloring may be added while mixture is still warm: good idea if paint is to be used by very young children. Or dry powder-type paint can be sprinkled on starch after it has been applied to surface of paper. VARIATIONS: Sift 1/2 c. flour into a cup of water. Make a smooth paste. Cook mixture until it bubbles. Stir continually to avoid lumps. Cool. Add 1 T. glycerine for smoothness. Add 1 t. sodium benzoate if paint is to be stored for more than 2-3 days. OR mix 1/2 box of cornstarch in cold water to make a paste. Add 3 qts. boiling water & cook until glossy. Stir while cooking to prevent sticking, lumping. Add 1/4 c. talc. Cool. Add 1-1/4 c. soap flakes; stir until flakes are evenly distributed. Put in jars. Add color if desired. Talc adds to smoothness but can be omitted. This is enough to supply 20 children.

Fixative: At least 3 weeks before needed, mix 1/2 pt. white shellac & 2 qts. denatured alcohol. Keep tightly covered. Shake well before using. Use as a spray to fix chalk or charcoal drawings. VARIATIONS: Substitute gum arabic (thinned in water to

---

*Found in the *Noe Valley Coop Nursery School Cookbook* & quoted in *The San Francisco Chronicle*, 3/72.

**WARNING: *Do not use plywood or redwood sawdust!*

the consistency of thin mucilage) in place of denatured alcohol OR mix 2 parts denatured alcohol & 1 part white shellac.

Glue (casein or "milk"): Pour a pint of skim milk into an enamel sauce pan & add 1 c. vinegar. Heat & stir until lumps are formed. Pour coagulated milk into a bowl. Cool. Discard excess water that forms, add 1/4 c. water & 1 t. baking soda. This type of glue was used by the Egyptians thousands of years ago. Objects on which this glue was used have been found in tombs today, & the glue is still holding. Furniture makers of the Middle Ages also used it.

Paste: Add 1 T. white alum & 1 c. sifted flour to water, making a thick paste. Keep adding the water until the mixture is like milk: approximately 1 c. water required. Cook over low heat, stirring constantly, until mixture becomes a translucent paste. Add 1/2 t. oil of cloves. Keeps indefinitely.

Art Aids

—For more vibrant colors, mix liquid starch with your tempera paints.
—Cut down plastic starch bottles & wedge them into the paintholder on each easel. Plastic paint containers are, you will find, preferable to all others, as they do not weaken with time.
—Using a funnel, pour mixed poster paints into large plastic bleach bottles. This will greatly simplify storage & will reduce time spent in weekly preparation of paints.
—Tie a pencil by heavy yarn to each easel so that the children will be reminded to sign their paintings.
—Keep a stack of magazines on hand for collage materials, lettering samples & reference work.
—Fill doll-size plastic baby bottles with diluted milk glue so that the children may have individual squeeze bottles to use at their desks.
—Try to keep a bottle of ink eradicator & a tube of "K-2r" in your desk for classroom emergencies.
—Baby oil helps when you're removing gum from a child's hair.
—An ice-cube applied to the fabric will aid in the removal of gum from clothing.

Hannah Adams (1775) 1st American woman to become a professional writer. A contemporary said of Hannah:" No woman can expect to be regarded as a lady after she's written a book."

And with that

An Afterword

I would be very happy to hear from you, to learn your impressions of "Teacher's Almanack," to hear your comments, suggestions, ideas.

I compiled this book, but not without help.

Thank you Gene, for going over the manuscript with me & for going through it all with me too.

A special thanks to my sister Dixie Anter, who has shared her teaching ideas with me for years. She is an unfailing source of those seldom-paired talents: creativity AND practicality.

My thanks to Dorothy Taugher for the hours of loving care & labor she gave typing the majority of the manuscript.

Thank you to David Kronen for the very helpful snake & reptile information, to Viola Bellemans for the instructions for the erupting volcano, to Beaulah Carswell for the magnet mimeo idea, Imogene Speiser & her original 'Alexander' puppet & to Robert Skiles who showed me how to make Giant Pilgrims & _much_ more, the 1st year I taught.

I do hope to hear from you. You may write me in care of the publisher.

Warmest regards,
Dana Newmann